TEXAS
BLOOD
FEUD

TEXAS
BLOOD
FEUD

DUSTY RICHARDS

PINNACLE BOOKS
Kensington Publishing Corp.
www.kensingtonbooks.com

PINNACLE BOOKS are published by

Kensington Publishing Corp.
119 West 40th Street
New York, NY 10018

All Kensington titles, imprints, and distributed lines are available at special quantity discounts for bulk purchases for sales promotions, premiums, fund-raising, educational, or institutional use. Special book excerpts or customized printings can also be created to fit specific needs. For details, write or phone the office of the Kensington special sales manager: Kensington Publishing Corp., 119 West 40th Street, New York, NY 10018, attn: Special Sales Department; phone 1-800-221-2647.

ISBN-13: 978-0-7860-3773-5
ISBN-10: 0-7860-3773-3

First printing: November 2009

10 9 8 7 6 5 4 3 2

Printed in the United States of America

I want to dedicate this book to the late "Doc" C.L. Sonnichsen, a great historian who took me under his wing when I was a rank novice writer at some of my first Western Writers of America Conventions, and told me story after story about the great Texas Feuds. They must have stayed with me for they are still vivid today. Doc was such a realist. He once told a writer friend of mine, John Duncklee, when John sold his first article back in his college days at the University of Arizona, that it was wonderful— "Just don't quit your day job."

"Doc" had an eye for Western fiction, too. He worried a lot about political correctness *interfering* with writers telling a good story. I moderated a panel at the Cowboy Symposium in Lubbock, Texas, with Elmer Kelton, and they asked Elmer about that. Mr. Kelton smiled and said in his best Texas drawl, "I sure don't think about that writing my books." Neither do I.

Dusty Richards
www.dustyrichards.com

Chapter 1

The acrid smoke from the blazing live oak fire swirled around his batwing chaps when Chet picked up the branding iron. He headed across the pen for the bawling calf stretched out on the ground by Chet's cousins, Reg and J.D. Bending over, Chet stuck the hot iron to the calf's side, and it let out an ear-shattering bawl. Chet left a smoking —𝒞 on its hide. It was a good enough job of marking the animal. The letters stamped on the dogie had the color of dark saddle leather. Chet nodded for the two boys in their teens to turn the critter loose.

"You made a swell earmark on that one's ear," Chet said to them, then went back to the fire and set the iron's face back in the red-hot coals,

Chet's thirty-year-old brother, Dale Allen, came dragging in another protesting calf to the fire with his reata around the dogie's hind legs. The entire Byrnes clan busied themselves working cattle. Catching the late calves they'd missed in the spring, cutting the bulls, ear-notching, and branding 'em. There'd be plenty of fried mountain oysters for supper. The old man, Rock, and Dale Allen's oldest boy,

Heck, held the herd on the flat. Good cool mid-October day to work them—and maybe the last screwworm flies had gone south for the winter. Not taking any chances, they painted all the surgical cuts with pine tar.

Chet made a note with a pencil in his logbook about the newest steer in the herd. "Steer—black, white spot on his neck right side—Summer 1872 crop." He kept the records on all the cattle in the herd. Shame someone else had had the "bar-B" brand in the Texas Brand Registry when his dad had sent off for it over thirty years earlier. *C* stood for Cooney, his grandfather's name on his mother's side. Grandpa Abe Cooney and Chet's father, Rock Byrnes, had brought their families out of Madison County, Arkansas, and settled in the Texas hill country on Yellow Hammer Creek twenty years before the war.

In those early years, the fierce Comanche made raids on them in the fall under every full moon. The Byrnes men farmed and worked cattle with loaded rifles and powder horns slung over their shoulders while they held plow handles or reins. Every night they slept lightly with their cap-and-ball pistols under their pillows. Womenfolks kept shotguns ready beside the front door, and the shutters on the windows at the rock house still bore the bullet holes and arrowheads embedded in them. Over the course of years in the long-running Comanche-Byrnes war, three of the Byrnes siblings were carried off by those red savages and never found or heard of again. Two boys and a girl. Keeping a life-long grudge, Chet's father, Rock, never saw an Indian, man or woman, he didn't stop and spit in their direction.

Chet checked the sun time and hollered at Dale Allen as

he brought another calf up to the fire. "Better break for dinner after that one."

His brother nodded to him as the boys took control of the calf, and coiled up his rope. "About a dozen left to work in this bunch."

"Leave them in this trap. We'll get them out after dinner," Chet said as he fetched the book and pencil out of his shirt pocket.

"Good. I've got to fix my girth anyway," Dale Allen said, and headed for the shade of some spreading live oaks.

"Go ahead. We'll work the rest of them this afternoon," Chet said over his shoulder.

"Red heifer—scar on right leg—summer 1872 crop," he wrote in the tally. The two boys flanked the calf and Reg, seventeen, the older of the pair, notched her left ear on the underside. His fifteen-year-old brother painted it. Then they stretched the bawling critter between them for the branding.

"We're ready for you," Reg said.

Chet went for an iron and walked back to apply it. He glanced up to see someone coming. The firebrand was stamped on the calf's right side and the bitter smoke from the singed hair filled Chet's nose. He looked again at the rider driving in hard.

"It's Susie," Reg said, standing beside him. "Wonder what in the hell's wrong now."

"Rustlers!" she said, out of breath, and skidded the lathered bay to a sliding stop on his hind legs.

Chet ran over to his twenty-year-old sister. "Rustling what?"

"They took all the horses in the north pasture and headed out with them."

"In broad daylight?" Chet asked her in disbelief. What fools would do that?

"Yes, two hours ago. I had to wait for May to get back to watch the children. You know Mother can't do that."

He gave her a grave nod. His mother, Theresa, hadn't been right in her mind since the Comanch' took little Cagle. Then when those reds got the twins, Phillip and Josephine, she'd lost it all.

"Who was it?" he asked.

"I don't know for sure, but I think one of them was a Reynolds—I recognized his paint horse."

"What in the hell's going on?" Dale Allen asked, coming over on his stout roping horse from where he had been working on his saddle over at the side.

"Rustlers took our cavy out of the north pasture a couple of hours ago," Chet said. "You boys put out that fire. Reg, you go get Pa and Heck up here. Branding's over for today."

"Is May back?" Dale Allen asked about his wife as he sat on his fretting horse that circled around under him.

Susie nodded. "I had to wait for her to get back to watch Ma and the kids."

"They've got a big head start," Chet said. "But they can't race that many horses."

"They can sure scatter them from hell to breakfast." Dale Allen shook his head in disgust.

"Aw, they must be nuts," Chet said, the consuming anger firing his veins. "They sure as hell know we'll run them down."

"We won't standing here."

Chet heard his impatient brother's comment and tried to ignore it. When he could see Reg and two others riding up from the cowherd, he went for his mount. "Paw's coming with Heck. You tell them what's happened."

Damn, what next? About the time the Comanche had been run off that part of Texas, white rustlers had taken their place. There were close to sixty broke horses in that pasture, and Chet intended to use them on their cattle drive in the spring. No small investment, and one he could ill afford to lose—he had every intention of sending Dale Allen as the ramrod on this year's push north. Chet had been up there several times, and possessed no big urge to sit on a horse that long again. Besides, it was his brother's turn. Chet needed to gather up another herd for the following year—something he was better at than anyone else in the family. Most of it involved dealing with Messikins on the border. Any more the cattle available for them to drive north besides their own had to be bought up from deep in Mexico—those were the last remaining ones aside from them from the small outfits' assignments.

He tightened the cinch on his blue roan and threw a leg over, reining him back to the others. Even in the distance he could see how red Pa's face was over the news of the theft. The old man hated rustlers—red or white.

Waving his finger at all of them, the old man shouted, "I want them sons a bitches hung by the neck till they're dead."

"We'll catch 'em, Pa. We're headed for the house to get some grub, bedrolls, and rifles. They won't get away."

"Well, by Gawd, they've got a good head start—"

"Easy, you'll have your ticker all upset," Chet said, concerned about the old man's anger flaring up his heart again.

Pa spit to the side and wiped his mouth on the back of his

hand. "If I was ten years younger, I'd go after them by myself."

Chet nodded. From his boyhood, he recalled how the old man and a posse went to look for the abducted Cagle. When they returned empty-handed, Pa was never the same. But it was his last desperate trip five years later, looking for the twins as he pursued the Comanche, that hurt his heart so deeply. He hadn't been heard from for three months. Nothing to eat, nothing to drink for days. He'd returned broken down and demented from his relentless pursuit and coming up empty-handed. For months on end afterward, he never said a word, simply sat on the front porch in a rocker and stared off at nothing.

That year, Chet turned eighteen and began running the ranch, and had ever since. His brother, Dale Allen, younger by a year, would always stand back and let him do it all, too. Then Dale Allen would complain if it wasn't just right. The thing Chet regretted the most was that he'd never had time to be a boy—to ride off and see some new country, raise some hell, stake out a place of his own, his own brand, his own house, and even find a woman of his own like his brother had.

"Susie, you take Reg's fresh horse and he can ride that hot one back. Go home and get some food ready for us to take along and we'll be coming."

"How much?" she asked, stepping down and exchanging reins with the lanky boy.

"Oh, enough for a couple of weeks."

"I'll get the bedrolls out." She looked at him with the question of how many as she slipped into the saddle and pushed down her dress to cover her exposed knees.

"Three. Reg and J.D. are going along."

"But they're boys." Dale Allen frowned in disapproval.

"I need you here to run things." Chet knew he sounded sharp, but sometimes his brother needed the truth spelled out. "Pa can't go and your oldest boy's too young. We'll find them and deal out the justice that's needed."

"What'll Aunt Louise say about you taking them two after rustlers?"

"Maw'll say good riddance." Freckle-faced Reg grinned big at him.

"Like hell—you better think about this, Chet Byrnes," Dale Allen shouted after him.

Chet was already trotting his horse and a hundred feet ahead of the rest. He had thought it over and that was his answer. Dale Allen didn't like it, he could go stick his head in a pail of water. Chet ran the ranch. He jabbed spurs to the blue roan. Already out of sight, Susie was heading for the ranch house.

There was lots to do.

Chapter 2

The two-story limestone house that Rock Byrnes first erected had grown into a fortress over the years. The huge wooden front gates had not been closed in a decade. A twelve-foot-high wall encircled the headquarters and inside the compound, the once-small two-story structure had festered into several connected residences, a bunkhouse, multiple corrals, pens, barns, a blacksmith shop, and a grain storage building. Two windmills filled the tank towers that provided water pressure to the faucets in the kitchen, the bathhouse, and the livestock tanks.

When Chet came in sight of the main house, Dale Allen's wife, May, stepped out on the porch wringing her hands in a tea towel. The short woman had lost most of her shine since the pudgy girl had married his brother a few years earlier as his second wife. Childbirth and having to oversee things with Susie had been a big chore for a town girl and banker's daughter who'd lived a sheltered life up until her marriage.

"What're you going to do?" May asked.

Everyone asked him that all the time. "Take two of the boys and go get them back."

"Boys?"

"Reg and J.D. We'll need to be ready to leave in twenty minutes. When they ride in, you wave them in to eat lunch." He gave a head toss. They were a quarter mile behind him. "I'll get a packhorse and then be back."

"Why not get the sheriff?"

"They'll be in Kansas, May, before I could even tell him."

"Guess you're right. I'll get the boys fed and the food ready for the trip. Good thing we've got plenty of jerky."

"Thanks." He turned Blue toward the corrals and at the horse pen, dismounted to hitch him. He took a lariat off a post and shook it loose while walking to the gate. In the lot, the dozen horses threw up their heads from eating hay off the ground, and he picked out a stout black he knew would lead good. The bunch broke hard around the pen, and he raced on foot to head them off. Overhanded, he tossed the rope, and it settled over the black's head. Chet sunk his boot heels in the dirt and put on the brakes when the noose jerked tight.

Snorting and acting the part of a walleyed fool, Black shied from Chet like he was ready to plunge off as Chet came up the rope hand over hand. "Whoa, stupid."

He fashioned a halter and led the horse out. Dale Allen's six- and eight-year-old sons by his first wife Nancy, who had died in birthing the youngest, a girl, Rachel, sat on the top rail, watching it all. They rushed over to walk beside him to the barn.

"He's pretty spooky, ain't he, Uncle Chet?" Ray asked, acting grown-up and making his younger brother Ty stay up with him so the horse didn't step on him.

"He's full of boogers," Chet said.

"I got boogers, too," Ty said.

Chet frowned at him, and the younger one put his finger up his nose and then showed him the results.

"You sure do." Chet jerked hard on the lead to settle Black down, then tied him high in a ring on the wall and went into the tack room for the packsaddle and pads.

"What's that smell in here?" Ty asked, sniffing the rich odors.

"Saddle soap and neat's-foot oil." Chet stepped around them with his arms full of a cross-buck saddle and pads. He put blankets on and talked the whole time to settle Black down. Then he looked around for the boys. "Stay there, fellas, he's still kinda wild."

"May says we're wild."

"Hush up, Ty. Uncle Chet don't need to know all that."

Chet paused and frowned at them. "Maybe I do. What's she been telling you boys?"

"Nothing."

Ty gave his older brother a two-handed shove. "She did, too."

"Aw, she was just in one of them crying moods. She never meant it, she told us later."

"Did so. Said she wished the Co-manches would get us—we was so wild."

Ray shook his head in disgust over his younger brother's disclosure. "May's got them two babies and that's lots. Paw said we got to be nicer to her."

"I'm glad you're trying to be nice to her," Chet said, untying the lead rope.

"Yeah, we don't want her to get like Grandma," Ray said.

"Yes," Chet said, a little heartsick at the words coming from an eight-year-old. "Let's go to the house."

"Can we ride him?"

"Boys, I'd love that but he's still pretty high. Might throw you."

"We understand. Maybe you can find us a pony we can ride."

"You wasn't supposed to ask him for that." Ty put his hands to his mouth over his older brother's transgression.

"We won't tell on him and I'll look for a good one." Chet hitched the black at the rack with the other horses in front of the yard gate. "We better get washed up. Looks like they're eating without us."

"Okay, Uncle Chet," Ty said, and they hurried for the washbasins on the porch.

He waited for them to wash up. Susie appeared in the doorway and set an armload of bedrolls on the stone floor. She clapped her hands together. "May's about got the food-stuff in the panniers."

"Thanks, hate to leave the place in so few hands—"

"We'll make it. I hope you can get the horses back."

He nodded. They had to.

After the meal, Chet first made a quick check of all they were taking along. Coffee, jerky, beans, salt pork, lard, flour, saleratus, sugar, raisins, and dried apples. A small Dutch oven, coffeepot, and skillet, plus big spoons, spatula, tin cups, plates, silverware, and a few towels. Matches, some candles—three extra shirts. And plenty of hemp rope. He and Reg carried the panniers out and hung them on the packsaddle. Dale Allen threw on the bedrolls, and then he put the canvas tarp over it all.

Susie brought out the three .44/40 Winchesters and two boxes of shells. J.D. put the rifles in the saddle scabbards on each horse and the cartridges in Chet's saddlebags.

"Tell Louise when she gets back from Mason, the boys've gone with me and we'll be back in a couple of days," Chet said to Susie. "Keep watch. No telling what'll happen next."

"Don't let them filthy savages get you boys," Theresa screeched from the doorway, and clawed the air like a cat with her arthritis-deformed hands. "They all should have been drowned as pups. My Gawd, I'd've held each one of them under the water myself."

"Now Mother, get hold of yourself." Susie guided her back inside. "They ain't going after Comanches, just rustlers."

"They took Cagle—they took my twins—"

Rock sat in the cane rocker and nodded his head. "If I was ten years younger—"

In the saddle, Chet looked down at Dale Allen. "Hold her together. We'll be back shortly."

"Watch out for them boys."

"I will—you go fishing with yours."

"Why?" Dale Allen blinked at him in astonishment.

"They need some fathering—since Nancy died you ain't been much of one, I'm afraid."

Dale Allen nodded in surrender. "They remind me too much of her, I guess. But I will."

"See you all," Chet said, and the three of them, leading the packhorse, rode out of the compound for the north pasture in a long trot.

"You ever go after rustlers before?" Reg asked Chet when they were beyond anyone hearing him.

"Several times."

"You always get them?"

"Most."

"Guess you hung them?"

Chet looked hard at the far ridge. "Yes, we hung 'em."

"If it's the Reynolds bunch, what'll you do?" J.D. asked, pushing his horse in closer.

"A horse thief is a horse thief."

"Even, like, if you know them?"

"Even then."

"Gosh, I hope Susie was wrong . . ."

"Maybe she was, J.D., maybe she was."

Over a fourth of the cavy was shod, so it wasn't hard to pick out their tracks from where rustlers drove them out the wire-and-stake woven gate and headed 'em northwest. Chet pointed at the hoof marks, and they short-loped for a ways down the dim road.

Late afternoon, Chet spotted some smoke, and led the way off the trail to a place up in a canyon. A white man in his underwear top and pants came out of the jacal. He looked them over, then combed his too long hair back with his fingers and gave it a toss back.

"Gents, can I help you?"

"J.D., you look over them horses in the pen," Chet said, and reined up the roan. "Evening, mister, we're tracking some rustlers."

"I sure ain't one." He made a frown like it was all a mistake.

Chet nodded, and looked for J.D. as the youth studied the stock. When the boy shook his head and started to ride back, Chet nodded again to the man. "Much obliged. Sorry to bother you."

"How many did they get?"

"Over sixty head. Any of them with the bar-C brand on them will bring a reward my brother will pay if I ain't back. I figure they'll lose a few in their haste."

"Thanks, I'll be watching for 'em."

"Sure," Chet said, and turned Roan to leave. The boys leading Black joined him, and when they reached the road, Reg looked back. At last, he turned forward and frowned at Chet. "What's he do for a living?"

"Eats our beef and lays up with that Mexican woman."

Reg turned up his lip in disbelief. "You figure so?"

"Yes, and some day I'll catch him red-handed at it."

"Be kinda easy to live like that. I sorta wish I could live like he does." Reg snickered. "I'd sure like to try that for a spell."

"What's that? Steal beef or rut with some old Mexican gal?" Chet grinned.

Red-faced, Reg pounded his saddle horn with his fist. "The latter, I guess."

J.D. shook his head as if disgusted. "I ain't having no part of either."

"We better lope a ways," Chet said, suppressing his smile and setting his spurs to Roan.

At sundown, they found a tank and set up camp. Horses hobbled, they made coffee and gnawed on May's jerky. Too late to cook much, and they were tired. Chet fell asleep to a coyote's yapping while wondering how far ahead the rustlers were that night.

Before dawn, he shook the boys awake in the morning's cool air. Leftover coffee was reheated and some more peppery jerky was gnawed on. They saddled, packed, and rode off when the gray light touched the eastern horizon.

"Sure is cold," J.D. complained, rubbing his arms. "I must have missed fall this year."

"I guess," Chet said, wishing for some rain on his winter oats. They were up, but wouldn't grow much without more moisture. He'd planted close to eighty acres in the creek bottoms. Large acreage and an expensive outlay. But he'd needed the feed for horses and the milk stock. They'd farmed that much corn the past summer and made a good crop. Some of the crop made forty bushels of ear corn to the acre. His heart wasn't into dirt farming, but he needed the output for the rest of his operation. Still, he recalled plowing with a fifteen-inch Oliver hand plow and hitting root snags that jerked the wooden handles out of a thirteen-year-old's hands.

These days, they used hired help, five mules, and a riding sulky plow that could really lay the ground over. Did more work than four hands with walking plows could in a day and lots easier. Still, farming was not his favorite game. But he and Pa planted many crops, broke many teams, and until his Comanche episode, no one could stack hay faster than the old man. Real sad how both of his parents had become so done in by the twins' abduction. But even death was better than that—with death you knew they were planted and nothing else you could do. But them red devils stealing those babies and never to know what became of them was a thing that had ruined his parents' minds and lives.

"Them horse apples we're seeing look fresher today." Reg broke into Chet's thoughts as the boy rode along and leaned over in the saddle to study the manure.

"I don't think they stopped last night—kept going." Chet stood in the stirrups, looking for signs of their dust on the northern horizon.

"You thinking that they ain't got a batching outfit?" J.D. asked.

Chet nodded. "It may have been a lark they went on."

"A lark?" Reg screwed up his face.

"I've done some dumb things being a little liquored up."

"You never stole no horses."

"No. but dumbest thing I ever did, I sang a song to a girl one time."

"You did what?" J.D. was about to bust into laughing.

"Aw, I had a crush on Kathren Combs before she married Luther Hines." Chet shook his head while looking hard at the long mesa ahead of them in the north—no sign of dust. "Well, one night, I got liquored up and took this Mexican fiddler along with me to play. Boy, was he drunk, and in the dark we went down to her folks' place, and I sang some ballad in Spanish outside the house."

"Were you any good?" Reg asked.

"Her father thought we were alley cats and shot at us with a shotgun. My, my, that damn Mexican sure outran me."

"He hit you with the shot?"

"No, he was laughing too hard."

"I sure hope I have some adventures when I grow up," J.D. said.

"How old are you, fifteen?"

"Be that this next spring."

"You will. Just don't get pie-eyed and go sing to some gal. Her pa won't like it."

"How serious were you about her?" Reg asked.

"I asked her to marry me a couple of years later."

"She turned you down?"

"Sure did." Chet rubbed his calloused fingers over his whisker-bristled mouth. "I guess I was drinking a lot in them days and she was kinda upset about that, I reckon."

"Then you decided to serenade her and win her back?" J.D. snickered out his nose.

"No that was a few years before that. Damn sure didn't work anyway and that Messican he said, 'Oh, *mi amigo*, it works every time.'"

"What did he say after you two got shot at?" Reg asked.

"*Madre de Dios!* That never happened before to me, hombre!"

At noontime, they reached a crossroads store, dropped out of the saddle, and tied the horses at the rack. Chet hitched up his canvas pants and led the way inside.

"Howdy, gents," a man in his forties with a bushy mustache said from behind the counter. "What's on your minds?"

"Food sure smells good in here," Chet said, sniffing the rich aroma.

"My wife Alisha has some great stewed chicken and dumplings. Lunch is ten cents today."

"We'll take thirty cents worth."

"I'll tell her that she has customers." He picked up the coins that Chet laid down and said, "My dear, three chicken dinners."

"Coming, Russel, dear," she said, as musically as he had. From the side room, she came with two dishes full of steaming chicken and homemade noodles. With her silver hair braided and piled on her head, she stood less than five feet tall. She handed them out and went back for more and a pan of fresh-made biscuits.

"Sure beats jerky," J.D. said as if in disbelief. He dug into the food on his tin plate as he stood at the counter.

Reg grinned at the big biscuit in his hand. "My, my, this is living."

"What brings you gents here?" the storekeeper asked.

"You seen anyone driving horses through here?" Chet asked.

"They went through here last night. Acted strange, bought some food and left—said they had to deliver their horses up in the Nation."

J.D. pointed a fork at him. "One of them redheaded and lots of freckles?"

"Yes, what did they do?"

"Stole those horses from our ranch," Chet said, and felt a knot in his throat. They finally knew for certain. He turned to his cousin. "I know, J.D. That sounds like Roy Reynolds. Sorry."

J.D. shook his head. "He's the one that's gonna be sorry."

"You know one of the rustlers?" the store man asked, looking shocked at them.

"All our lives," Reg said with a wary look, and bit down on another biscuit.

The rich tasty food had drawn the saliva into Chet's mouth, but somehow the realization that one of the rustlers was someone they knew made his tongue turn dry and the food become hard to swallow. This wasn't going to be a nice trip—no way. Nothing he could do about it either.

After they finished the meal, they left the store and rode on. At dark, they made camp at a windmill. Tracks showed the cavy had been driven past there, too.

Chapter 3

"They was here last night," the white-bearded man said to Chet and the boys, who were sitting on horseback. "Tried to sell me some of them horses. But I was wise to their game. Them horses in the herd had a bar-C brand on them. The horses they rode had 6Y and a lazy R on them. I knowed they wasn't working for the man owned the herd."

Chet nodded. "They stole those horses two days ago down on Yellow Hammer Crick."

"I had 'em pegged then?"

"6Y, who's is that?" Reg asked when they were back on the road and out of the old man's hearing.

J.D. shook his head. "You know that one, Chet?"

He did, but he shrugged it off. Might just be a horse that Luther Hines had sold someone.

"How many days are they ahead of us?" J.D. asked, sounding weary.

"We must have cut it down to a day—or less," Chet said.

"Let's lope then," J.D. said. "I want to get this over with—soon as we can."

Late afternoon, they discovered a limping horse from their cavy. A stout dun that was favoring his right front foot and moved aside when they trotted up.

"That's Sam Bass," Reg said, recognizing the gelding.

Chet agreed and shook out a rope. He rode in and tossed the loop over the horse's head, and made a wrap on the horn to shorten it up until he was beside the horse. J.D. pushed his mount in close and held Roan's reins while Chet dismounted to inspect the damage to Bass's foot. He lifted the hoof and cleaned it out with his jackknife. He pried a pea-size stone from the horse's frog and then let it down.

"That ought to help you," he said to the big cow pony, then clapped him on the neck and slipped the rope off him.

"What'll we do with him?" J.D. asked.

"Horses go home," Chet said, finished coiling the lariat and taking the reins back. "He should heal and be back at the home place in a week, if no one steals him again."

"I never thought about it, but they do."

"They do." Chet mounted and they set off again.

"We're getting closer," Reg said. "Them horse apples are about steaming."

"See that cloud bank?" Chet said, indicating the blue-black line that crossed the northwest sky. "It's going to be a norther."

"It's only October," Reg said.

"Never mind, it's a-coming in and fast. I've been watching it all day," Chet said.

"I'm getting cold just thinking about it. What are we going to do when it hits?"

"We may have to find someplace to den up." He was

disgusted not only about the threat of bad weather, but also about the time they'd lose as well.

"Any idea what they'll do?" J.D. asked with a frown, and reined his horse around to look at Chet.

"No telling. Let's push these ponies harder, maybe we can catch up."

Both boys agreed. The rolling grass country, occasionally dotted with mesquite, spread out before them. They were somewhere in north Texas—west of Fort Worth by Chet's calculation. The cold front moving at them out of the northwest had begun to show dark ragged edges when Chet spotted some buildings and pens.

"They might put us up," he shouted above the rising wind.

With over a half mile to cover, they put on their slickers as the temperature fell. Chet smiled as he buttoned his coat—a man could freeze to death in one of them, but they did shed rain. The three raced for the outfit. They reined up hard in front of the low sod-roofed cabin.

"Hello the house."

No one came to the door.

He looked around the place for a sign of someone. "Try the door," he said to Reg.

The youth bounded off his horse, pulled the string, and pushed on the door. It went open, and he shouted from inside, "Nobody's home."

"Good, we'll use it. Get the panniers and the saddles inside 'cause in less'n ten minutes it's going to be hailing here."

"How do you know that?" J.D. asked, jumping off and fumbling his latigos loose.

"See that green line under the clouds? That's hail." Chet

carried his saddle inside and set it down on the horn. Reg was undoing the diamond hitch. When it was off, Chet loosened the canvas, and then grabbed the first pannier with the wind whistling in his ears. He packed it in the doorway and hurried back, meeting Reg with his arms full of bedrolls.

Hard drops began to pelt on Chet's felt hat. "Is there a shed for the animals?"

"I think so, over there," J.D. said, looking anxiously at the worsening weather.

"Take 'em. We can get that packsaddle later."

The youth set out leading two horses, and Reg led the other two. Lightning struck close by. The air stank with the sulfurous smell and the crash came right behind it. Chet dodged inside, and watched from the open door for the boys' return as the rain began to turn to ice pellets.

It grew dark as night. Then, to his relief, they came for the house, making long strides and shouting over the hail's noisy rattle on the porch roof.

"Horses undercover?" he asked, closing the door.

"Whew," Reg said. "Yes, that was close to a wreck."

J.D nodded. "They're fine, even got some hay."

"Yes," Reg said. "They'll be all right."

"We should have a candle in the pannier," Chet said, unbuckling the straps to open the lid, then feeling around for a wax stick. He soon produced one and laid it on the table. He scratched a match and lit it to melt some wax into the cut-down tin-can holder so he could set the candle up to illuminate the room.

"What've we got?" he asked, looking around.

"There's cooking wood by the stove and I guess if we

had a bucket of rainwater, we could make some coffee," Reg said.

"You're in charge," Chet said, picking up a letter on the table. It was addressed to Nick Van Rooter, General Delivery, Max, Texas. The letter might tell him something about the absent owner. He took the letter out and carefully read the first page.

My name is Hilga. I am eighteen. I will be arriving in Fort Worth on November the 15th at twelve noon on the train. You and my father have corresponded about me coming to your large fine farm and becoming your wife. If I do not suit you at the train station, you must do as you promised and buy my ticket back to St Louis.
                        Yours Truly
                        Hilga

"This Dutchman who owns this place is in Fort Worth today, getting his mail-order bride," Chet said, and thunder drowned out his last words.

"Getting what?" J.D. asked with troubled look on his face.

"A mail-order bride."

"Sears and Roebuck has them, too?" J.D. blinked in his confusion.

"Yes, brother, and I want one of them I seen in last spring's copy wearing a corset." Then Reg dropped his head in wary disgust. "Hell, brother, they don't sell brides."

"They sell everything else."

"I think this has been arranged," Chet said. "She's

eighteen and if she doesn't suit him at the train station, he has to buy her a train ticket back home."

"Guess the bride market out here ain't holding up too good," Reg said as his brother took the letter to read. "Maybe we should bake her a cake before we leave."

"How about an apple-raisin pie?" Chet asked above the noisy storm. "For our use of this cabin."

"Way it's raging out there, I'm grateful enough to do about anything."

"We don't have any lard to make crust," J.D. said.

"We've got some, but all I had in mind was an apple-raisin crisp. Coffee's about done," Chet said, and rubbed his palms together to warm them. The temperature must have dropped forty degrees outside. The cookstove was heating them some and felt good.

"She's sure going to be disappointed." J.D. put the letter down after reading it. "This sure ain't no large fine farm. It's a patch of grass and mesquite in north Texas with some pear thrown in."

"Heavens, she'll think that's fruit," Reg said. "Prickly pear cactus beds."

"I wish I could be here." J.D. spread his arms out. "And she comes over the rise to the east in that buckboard and for the first time feasts her eyes on this dump. 'Otto, Otto.' She elbows him. 'Give me de train fare to go home.'"

Chet blew on his coffee and chuckled. Those two were more than funny at times. He could recall laughing in his own house growing up—but since he'd turned seventeen, there had not been much fun coming from that place. He'd be thirty-one in May. Had it been almost fourteen years already?

He scrubbed his bristled mouth on his palm. Time sure flew.

"You ever plan to marry?" J.D. asked.

"Oh, if I can find the right woman."

"You going to serenade her, too?"

"If it suits the occasion and I can find a drunk Mexican fiddler." They all three laughed.

The storm passed in the night, but the clear sky before dawn was cold as an iceberg. Everyone put on their second shirt over the first for warmth and wore a slicker to break the wind. The sweet-smelling apple-raisin crisp was cooked and cooling in the oven for the newlyweds, along with a note wishing them the best and a thanks for the shelter in the storm.

Late afternoon, they located the cavy spread out grazing across a wide basin. Sitting abreast on their horses atop a rise, Chet looked for campfire smoke, but the strong gusts they faced wouldn't let any traces stay long.

"Think they've abandoned them?" J.D. asked.

"Naw," Chet said, still searching around. "This cold's disheartened them is all. They're hunkered down somewhere near here, I'd bet, keeping warm."

"Disheartened me and I ain't stole nothing," Reg said.

"Freezing their asses off is the right thing." J.D. huddled in his raincoat.

"We better split up. Try to not let them see you if you do locate them. We'll all meet back here in the next hour." He checked the sun. That would leave them some daylight if they found the rustlers.

Reg went north, Chet rode west, and J.D. took the south side of the basin. Finding nothing but a few of the horses, Chet rode back in the long shadows and sun rays that glowed red over the tops of the mesquite and grass heads. He spotted Reg's horse standing hipshot and the boy squatted down out of the wind.

When he rode up to him, Reg shook his head. "Nothing. Sure wish J.D.'d get back."

Chet dismounted, and saw J.D. coming in a long trot standing in the stirrups. He could tell by the look on his face that the boy'd found something.

"They've got a dugout about mile or so up a side draw." J.D. pointed behind him. "I seen the paint hobbled up there. They're in that dugout sure enough."

"We waiting till morning?" Reg asked.

"I try not to put off the things I dread doing," Chet said with a grim set to his jaw. The next thirty minutes would be tough. Two boys would become men.

They mounted up, drew out their rifles, and loaded the breeches. Not a word was said. They rode close together. Hats pulled down. The sharp wind had stopped being a factor—capturing the rustlers was all Chet had on his mind.

J.D. pointed to the draw. Chet nodded and turned Roan that way. He could see the crude log end of the dugout and the board door—probably cut from some old wagon flooring. They dismounted, and the boys stuck their Winchesters in their scabbards and drew their six-guns. His Colt in his fist, he nodded in approval. This would be the test— he didn't want to think about what or who they'd find inside—he steeled himself, leading the way.

No sign of anyone, but he could smell the sharp smoke from the rusty stovepipe. It reminded him of being warm again. He put a finger to his lips for the boys to be quiet.

Both nodded, but he could see the tension in their eyes. They stole closer.

He reached the side of the door and eased the drawstring. He felt it lift the bar. Then he jerked it open on wobbling leather hinges and stuck the cocked revolver in first. "Hands up or die!"

"Huh?"

"What the hell?"

"Don't go for a thing," he said, looking down the barrel at the shocked face of the Reynolds boy in the candlelight. He couldn't see much more than silhouettes of the other two. This was the moment when things could become a mess. "Come out on your hands and knees and fast or I'm going to start shooting."

"We're coming," Hines growled.

When they went past him coming outside in the twilight, Chet saw Hines's hate-filled glare. He also recognized the third man, a drifter, Dab Stevens.

"How—how did you find us?" Roy Reynolds asked, holding his hands high, standing on his knees in the dirt.

"Your tracks, stupid," Reg said in disgust.

Soon, the rustlers were outside on their knees in the dying light, holding up their hands as the two boys disarmed them. Then the two brothers shoved them down one at a time and tied their hands behind their backs. Colt ready, Chet covered them until the tying process was over.

"Now, on your feet. There's some cottonwoods about a quarter mile north on that creek. J.D., you and Reg saddle their horses and bring them. Get that hemp rope, too."

"You ain't going to hang us?" Reynolds asked in a high-pitch voice.

"Hell, yes, they are," Hines said, scowling in disgust at the boy's whining.

"Aw, hell, I just came along—"

"Well, you gawdamn sure came along with the wrong ones," Reg said, and started with his brother for their horses.

"Can we cut a deal?" Hines asked over his shoulder as Chet marched them north in the fading light.

"Better make one with your Maker. I ain't cutting none."

"You and I've been crossways before, Byrnes."

"I can't recall it. Besides, this ain't about nothing from the past. See those horses scattered all over out there? Those are my horses—you boys stole them."

"Yeah, but we—" Reynolds sounded ready to cry.

"Aw, shit, buck up, kid. The sumbitch's got his mind made up. Talking and crying ain't going to change it," Stevens said.

"Yeah, but I ain't ready to—"

"Just shut up!"

Chet made them sit on the ground under the rustling cottonwoods while he waited for the horses. The wind hadn't cut down much, and the temperature was dropping in the twilight without the sun's warmth. When the two boys arrived with the mounts, he took the hemp rope from Reg and began to build a noose. J.D. guarded the prisoners. Reg watched how Chet built the noose and then he made one. Then in the faded light, Chet tied the last noose. His fingers were cold and close to trembling. The knot in his throat was hard to swallow.

Reg held the paint while Chet stood on the saddle and tied the nooses on the limb. The three loops were at last in place so the condemned rustlers' feet could not touch the ground when they dropped down. One by one, Chet and Reg placed the rustlers on their horses, which J.D. held by the bridles. The nooses were drawn up on their throats and the knots set beside their left ears for what Chet hoped would be a quick death by snapping their necks.

"You got anything to say?" he asked.

"I don't want to die," Reynolds wailed.

"Cut the crap and get it over," Stevens said.

"I'll see you in hell," Hines said.

"May God save your souls," Chet said, and waved J.D. away from the front of their horses.

"I'll take these two. You bust that one," he said to Reg. "Eeha!"

The three horses bolted away from under their riders. The ropes creaked. Two of their necks snapped like shots— Stevens gagged—dancing on his noose. His struggle was short-lived, but not before his bowels released and he fouled his pants.

"What now?" Reg asked, looking sick.

"Make camp—" Chet clapped the downcast J.D. on the shoulders. "It's a tough world. Tough solution, but they'd only've laughed at us for letting them off. You going to be all right?"

"I'll be fine."

"No, you'll never be the same. But in time you'll understand it better."

Reg gave a hard sigh. "I kept thinking. Kept waiting. Hines, he never mentioned his wife Kathren or their daughter Cady."

Chet agreed. "They must not have mattered to him."

"Yeah, I guess they didn't. What about their horses?"

"Horses'll go home. Let them go." Chet said, and started

them back for their own mounts. "Daylight comes, we better gather our bunch and get back."

"Yes, sir," they said.

They'd never said that to him before. In disbelief, he blinked after them. Turning in the saddle, he looked back, and could see the three dark silhouettes swinging in the wind. Damn, what a day.

Chapter 4

Four days of horse driving later, the weather had warmed. Chet was grateful. They were fast approaching the home place deep in the live-oak-and-cedar-clad hills. When they broke camp that morning, Chet told the boys that the less that they said about the ordeal, the better it would be for all of them. Word would filter down soon enough. The rustlers' saddle horses would wander back.

Along the way, they'd even found Sam Bass and he was sound again. Chet considered himself lucky—he had recovered every horse that had been stolen. When the last one went through the gate into the north pasture, they *wahooed* and fired their pistols in the air. Then, on the fly, they headed for the headquarters.

"I want a hot bath," J.D. said, running side by side with Chet. "What do you want?"

"A good drink or two of whiskey." Then Chet laughed.

"What about you?" J.D. asked Reg on the other side, ducking his head so he didn't lose his hat.

Tall in the saddle, Reg grinned and shouted, "Some of Susie's cooking."

"He thinks our cooking's bad," Chet said to J.D.

"Aw, hell, he's too hard to please."

Chet nodded, filled with excitement, drew his Colt, and fired two more shots.

"What's that for?" Reg asked as they pounded across the bottom between the rail fences and green oat field.

"To let them know we're coming in."

"You bet," Reg shouted, and went to whipping his horse for the final leg of the journey. It was a horse race, and Reg let go of the black's lead rope so he could concentrate on the last burst. Shoulder to shoulder, the three charged for the ranch gate, urging their mounts on. Roan began to gain on them. When they sped through the wide opening, he won by a nose. Sliding their mounts up to the hitch rack on their hindquarters in a cloud of dust, they faced a porch full of anxious onlookers.

"Well. You must've got them back," Susie said, standing with her arms folded on the porch.

"Every damn one of them," J.D. said, and went to brushing himself off.

"Better watch your language, Ma's here," Reg said under his breath.

"Oh." He slapped his hand over his mouth.

Chet saw her first. His Aunt Louise, the boys' mother, came storming out of the house. "Chet Byrnes, have you lost your mind taking my boys after those rustlers?"

He slipped out of the saddle and turned to Reg. "You two go get the black and unload him."

Louise stood with her buttoned-up shoes planted underneath the many layered lace petticoats. Her feet were set apart on the rock-floored porch. Her face was black in anger, her dark hair pulled back so tight her eyes looked like slits. Hands on her slender hips, his late uncle's wife looked mad enough to bite the head off a diamondback. Mark Byrnes had never come back from the war. Died or killed in Mississippi near the end. She never forgave him for not coming home either.

"You may run this ranch, but you are not ever again to haul my boys off on a vigilante ride. I suppose you hung them?"

He looked at her mildly. "Yes, Louise, we hung them."

In screaming fury, she came off the porch and tried to pound him with her fists. He caught her wrists. "Listen to me. Those men stole our horses. They stole our horses that will drive our cattle to Kansas. Stand still or I'll break your arms. Listen to me." He forced her down to her knees. "Those horses were yours, mine, your boys' and this whole family's livelihood. We hung those rustlers. They were people that lived around here. No one needs to know what we did—do you understand me? No one—"

She broke into sobs. "They're only boys. Only boys."

"No one on this ranch is to ever speak about it ever again, Louise. Do you understand?" He looked hard-eyed at the rest for their nods. Then he released her.

"I—I understand, but Chet, for God's sake, they're only boys."

He shook his head. "Not anymore. They're men."

With Louise on her knees, crying in her hands, he went on inside the house. Susie scowled at him. "You know how she is. Why do that to her?"

"Because this may be the most serious thing ever happened to all of us. I don't need her whining around about it all over. They'll find out soon enough."

"I was right about that paint horse then?" Susie's hands flew to cover her mouth.

"Hell, yes. He wasn't the only one in on it either."

"Who else?"

"It doesn't matter—no one is to talk about it ever again." He threw his hat across the living room. "They stole our damn horses. That makes them no better than anyone else that steals horses." He ran his fingers through his hair and shook his head. They had to understand him. This got out, it might be the worst thing that ever happened to the Byrnes clan. Rustlers or not, those thieves' families might take up the sword of revenge.

Distraught, her face wet with tears, Louise ran by him sobbing. "They were just boys. Why did they have to do it?"

He started to reach for her, then at the last moment, dropped his hand and let her go on. "Susie, go tell her so she understands. They aren't boys anymore. We all have to grow up in this harsh world. And how important her silence is."

Without a word, Susie nodded and ran after her aunt, who'd disappeared back in the dining room. He shook his head and fetched his hat. He had to think for too many people. Hat on his head, he stormed out the front door and headed for the barn. He wasn't ready to hear his demented father's repeated lectures or his poor mother's ranting.

He took a quick shower in the bathhouse. The water was icy cold, but it woke him some from the dullness that had invaded his brain. He put on clean underwear, a clean shirt, and canvas pants. He wished he could shave, but there was no heated water down there. The temperature had warmed the past few days, but he put on a jumper to cut the oncoming night's cold.

In a short while, he saddled a fresh horse and rode out the front gate to escape. It was Wednesday night—her husband'd be in town playing cards. Close to sundown, he sat the bay gelding called Jack on the cedar-clad hillside and looked over the corrals and small rock house. The buckboard was gone. Good. Chet booted Jack out of the brush and down the hill.

Marla Porter came to the door and holding the facing, she rested her forehead on the hewed wood not looking at him. She was tall, willowy, in a wash-worn blue dress that flared over layers of slips. On the top of her head the prematurely gray-streaked dark hair was braided and put up. Her lips at last broke into a knowing grin as if she was pleased he'd come by. He could see the glint in her blue eyes from the late afternoon light, and then she turned away to stare at the facing again.

"I thought maybe you were mad at me," she said, not looking at him.

He dismounted and hitched Jack at the rack. "I had some business to tend to."

She looked mildly at him and shrugged. "Who am I to ask? I'm Jake Porter's wife, huh?"

"I sure can't help that." He stopped at the stoop.

"Yes, you can," she said, and rushed out to hug and kiss him. In her fury, she knocked off his hat and her hungry lips and tongue consumed his. He squeezed her hard against his chest and savored her mouth.

"Come inside," she said, sweeping up his Stetson. She checked around warily and then steered him into the house.

"We better hurry," she said, unbuttoning her dress.

"He due home?"

"I never can tell. Undress," she said, impatient for him to move.

Twilight was long set and night had settled over the hill country when he checked the girth on his saddle and prepared to mount Jack and leave. She stood with her back against his horse and fussed with the silk kerchief tied around his neck. "Why do you come see me?"

"I guess 'cause we're both lonely."

"You could have a wife. Why, I know a dozen women would jump up if you asked them to marry you."

He rubbed his palms on the front of his canvas pants. "No. I've got a ranch and family to run. Why don't you leave Porter?"

"And do what? Become a dove? A thirty-year-old shady lady don't make the big money. They work on hog ranches."

"You could find another man and marry him."

She slapped him hard on the butt. "And then I wouldn't have you—part of the time."

He swung his leg over the horse and checked Jack. "You need anything?"

She put her hand on his leg and walked beside the horse. "For you to come back to visit me."

"I will."

"Don't stay away so long."

He nodded in the growing darkness and rode off into the night. He made a wide circle using the stars and his knowledge of the land to guide him. He wanted to be sure that everyone was asleep when he got home. There'd be lots to do in the morning—finish the branding. Check fence, check cattle, and turn back strays that wandered on the ranch, break some two-year-olds—his list was as long as his arm.

A coyote called to the stars. Another answered as he crossed the ford on Bowles Creek. Jack stamped his hooves to splash the water; Chet stopped him mid-stream and let him take a drink. He should do something about Marla, but what? She never acted like she'd really leave Porter for him—it was more like their illicit affair was the excitement in her life and she wanted to leave it like that. Jack finished slurping, raised his head, and water drizzled from his muzzle. Chet booted him on.

It was that time. He needed to start lining up the ranchers who wanted their cattle driven north with his herd. Nothing ever ended in his life; it just led to more complications. Times he felt trapped in his own small world like an animal dumped in a deep pit.

When he rode in, the home place was dark, save for a light in the kitchen. His boots hit the ground and his sea legs bent at the knees. Gradually, he regained his strength and undid the latigos, stripping off the saddle and pads that released the sour smell of horse sweat. Saddle on the rack, he led Jack into the corral and pulled off the bridle. The big horse went ten feet and dropped on his knees to roll.

Chet stopped and watched him wallow on his itching back in the dust. Grunting, Jack rose and shook dirt like water in all directions.

"Louise understands," Susie said in a soft voice.

He turned from holding the top rail and saw his sister's silhouette in starlight. "You still up?"

"Yes."

"Hell, girl, you ought to be in bed."

"I couldn't sleep. You know," she said, taking a place beside him and looking at the dark forms of the horses roused from their slumber by Jack's return to the pen. "All Louise really has are those two boys. I think she's afraid they'll grow up too fast and leave her."

"Maybe I was wrong taking them, but they've got to know the truth. Life ain't easy."

She nodded. "They're your men all right."

"At times this job about drowns me and I want to go off and be someone's drag rider."

She shook her head in despair. "I agree. Mom and Dad are no better. You know how that drags on me. May tries to help, but she's overwhelmed by the baby and little Rachel. And Louise lives in her own world."

"I'll hire you some help."

"Can we afford it?"

He nodded. "You have anyone in mind?"

"Maybe a couple Mexican girls."

"Hire them."

"Louise will be upset."

He looked over and blinked at her. "Why?"

"She said we don't need any *putas* around here corrupting our men."

"Oh, for crying out loud."

"It's been seven years, I know, she should be over mourning him. She's not."

He slapped the top rail with his palm. "It's a crutch she beats us all over the head with. You hire them or I will."

"I will. Thanks, Chet."

"Get back up there to bed."

"What about you?"

"I'll sleep a few hours."

"Good night." Susie departed, holding her skirts, and left him in the starlight.

He went to his own room in the bunkhouse, thinking about Marla and wishing they were off somewhere in the Rocky Mountains by themselves. In bed, he imagined he could smell the pungent pines and feel her silky skin. The morning bell ringing rolled him out of the blankets. He splashed water on his face, brushed down his hair while looking in a fading mirror. Then he headed for the house in the cool air, knifing in his shirttail with his flat hand.

"Chet?" Reg caught up with him on the porch. "How long before they find out what happened?"

"A few days or a week. They may know already. We just don't need to talk about it."

"I savvy that. I wanted to go see Molly Ash this Saturday at the schoolhouse dance."

"Should be no problem. Go with someone you trust and pack a gun even if it's in your saddlebags."

"I understand."

The crew was coming into the kitchen after they washed up. Chet could smell ham cooking and fresh-baked sourdough bread. He went inside and nodded to his brother, already seated. Reg, J.D., and Heck piled in; then their father made his way in with a cane. The younger boys took their place and Susie asked Chet to give the prayer.

"Dear Lord, thank you for our many blessings and safe return. Thank you for this wonderful food. Guide and protect us, Lord. In your name, amen."

May poured coffee all around and Susie served the platters of eggs and ham. Bowls of butter and plum jelly were out. A small crock of "lick" was on the table for sweetening and the hot bread.

Chet ate light—an egg and then a small piece of ham. He excused himself, then took his coffee and went back in the kitchen where Susie, May, and Louise were eating at a preparation table.

"You out of coffee?" May asked, ready to jump up.

He held out his hand to stop her, and went over to the large pot and refilled his own tin cup. Then he came back, put a boot on a chair, and blew on the steaming contents while looking at the three.

"We're hiring two girls to help you ladies."

"What for?" Louise demanded.

"We have two babies to look after." He glanced around to insure privacy. "The folks are a handful enough for one person. We need two girls to help straighten the house, make meals—"

"You have some Mexican darling to move in on us?"

"Louise, you aren't the only one here. I won't pick them. I told Susie to. You can be civil to them. They won't be slaves like you are used to. Now that's settled."

"If you ever—ever take my boys on another one of your vigilante rides, I'll kill you."

"Louise, you want the money to go home, I'll settle with you."

"Sure settle with me. What do I have left? A portion of a ranch depreciated by the war to nothing. You want to settle with me because my husband got himself killed in that damn war and left me with the potato peelings." She shook her head. "I am damn sure not taking your sorry settlement!"

She threw down her fork and stormed off.

He wanted to go drag her back by the arm and shake her until he loosened her teeth. It would do no good. Louise came from a better life on a Louisiana plantation. She was accustomed to slaves doing her bidding, not her being the scullery help. Her days on the ranch had never pleased her. Without Mark to complain to, she'd turned her wrath on the rest of them.

"Chet?" Susie said quietly. "May and I can do it without help."

"Hell, no, she doesn't run this ranch. Hire the help."

He stormed out into the dining room. "Saddle and get ready to ride. I want those last calves worked this morning and those oat field fences rode out and checked. Reg, get the irons, pine tar, and do we have fuel down there for a fire?"

"There's plenty down there," Dale Allen said, cradling a coffee cup in his hands.

"Good. Some of us want to go to the Saturday night dance at the schoolhouse. That means some of us will need to stay here." No one said a word when he paused for their answer. "I'll figure out who goes and who stays later."

He put on his hat and went outside. He was still upset over his confrontation with Louise, and his breath raged through his nostrils. In the pale light, the cool air swept his cheeks and he scrubbed at the beard stubble with his palm. He still needed to shave.

They better go as a crowd to the dance. No telling what would happen because of the deaths of the rustlers.

Chapter 5

By Saturday at noon, the women had loaded the food, utensils, cooking gear, bedrolls, and a tarp for a fly in the army ambulance that had been converted into a chuck wagon. The wooden barrels on each side of the wagon were full of fresh water. Hat cocked back on his head, Reg sat on the spring seat, the lines in his gloved hands, and he kicked off the brake. He clucked to the big team of black mares with feathered hocks, and they stomped out the gate in a high-stepping trot.

On the buckboard sat Louise and Susie, who was driving the team of matched bays. Dale Allen; May, who was holding the baby; and J.D. stood on the porch, holding back the two young boys. All waved of them at the group's departure. Heck and Chet rode out after the buckboard, waving good-bye to the people on the porch.

The Warner School House served as the social beacon for the countryside. Mason, the county seat, was thirty miles away. Besides serving as a church, the school also boasted a community cemetery. There wasn't enough water close by to suit the Baptists, so they rode clear over to the San Saba River for their submersion of sinners. That's why they named the branch that ran beside the school Methodist Creek.

The Byrnes set up in their usual place on the west side of the schoolyard. That gave them some cottonwoods to hang ropes between to make the fly work as a tent, or a shield against the north wind if it should it blow in. Reg had the chuck wagon wheels scotched and the backboard down for the women to prepare supper on. Susie was soon there to help him. Chet and Heck strung the ropes for the tarp. Heck held the bridle of Strawberry, a big red roan, and Chet stood on the saddle to get the ropes tied high enough on the tree trunks.

Louise came by on her way to go see Maude Mayes, another war widow. "I don't think it'll rain, but it'll be nice to have that up anyway."

"I'd hate installing it in a storm," Chet said, tying the side off, and Louise moved on.

Ten-year-old Heck grinned big. "So would I."

The last rope strung, Chet slid down easily into the saddle and off the roan. "Thanks, Heck. Now we have to haul up that tarp and stake it down."

"Lots of work making camp for women," Heck said.

"Oh, I've seen the time I'd've gave my soul for a tent to get out of the rain under one."

"When do you think they'll let me go up the trail, Uncle Chet?"

"Year, maybe two, why?"

"I want to go. I want to go with you and the others."

Reg was helping them unroll the large canvas. "There's still going to be drives when you're twelve."

"I'm just itching to go."

"So was I," Reg said. "Now I been there, I can take it or leave it."

"Yeah, but I ain't been there." He was pulling with Chet on the tarp slung across the ridge rope to start it over.

"Here, I'll get Strawberry and let him pull it." Chet ran for his horse and returned in the saddle. He soon had the rope dallied on the horn, and the gelding made short work of getting the tarp in place. Then Reg went to flipping it to spread it out overhead. He and Heck soon had it in place and the staking process began. In a short while, the shelter was up and secured.

Wade Morgan came by and squatted down on his boot heels to talk to Chet. "I guess you're going north come spring?"

"I'm counting on it. We've got several head promised besides our own. You got some?"

"Not many, maybe two hundred steers."

"I can take 'em."

"What'll it cost me?" Morgan was close to forty. Short, squat built man did some blacksmithing and had the shoulders for the job.

"About twelve bucks a head."

"That's higher than others've been quoting me."

"I've not missed delivering them. My losses so far have been low. The prices I get there are all the market will allow. The France boys sent their cattle up two years ago with a man cheaper than I was, and they never saw that fella again. Lost everything."

Morgan exhaled deep and nodded. "I know. I know. Five years ago, I send two hundred steers north with a fella named Sears and got the low price on fifty head. Said the others stampeded into a river and drowned."

"So we've discussed the bargain deals. I may lose all of them. But I've paid life insurance of four hundred dollars on every hand I've lost, if they had an heir, plus their wages for the whole trip."

"Hell, I know you've been fair, but I need all I can get out of 'em."

Chet clapped him on the shoulder. "So do I. And I can't guarantee I can come back with a dime, but it won't because I didn't try."

"Mark me down for two hundred."

Chet took the logbook out and on the page marked "Drive of 1873" he wrote down, "Wade Morgan 200 head." "We'll be road-branding them in early March. The grass breaks loose, we'll go north."

They shook hands on the deal.

Morgan left him, headed back toward the building. Chet noticed Marla Porter drive by seated beside her husband on the buckboard. Porter's fine team of matched horses were trotting along in step. Straight-backed, she sat head high, with a wide-brimmed hat and a tight-fitting jacket that emphasized her figure. Her posture drew a hidden grin from Chet. The sight of her also made his guts roil. She was like a bad habit that he needed to quit—but he couldn't—damn her anyway.

Louise came back looking stern-faced, and after looking around, talked to him from behind her hand. "The word is that Felton and Mitch Reynolds went north yesterday with a wagon for three bodies. One of them, they said, is Roy. The other was Luther Hines, Kathren's husband. And the third was a Dab Stevens, some cowboy worked around here."

"So?"

"Those were the men you hung?"

He looked around, then hustled her aside. "Shut your gawdamn mouth. Now, I told you this was going to get volatile. Those men were common thieves. What they got they deserved."

"But they were men you knew—my boys went to school with Roy."

"Louise—"

"Don't threaten me."

"All right, but your damn mouth is going to get your boys killed. That's not a threat, that's a promise."

Her brown eyes flew open and she put her hand to her lips in pale-faced shock. Teary-eyed, she pushed past him for the wagon. "Damn you, Chester Byrnes. Damn you."

Shaking mad, Chet went to the fire ring and poured himself a cup of fresh coffee. Susie came from the fly on the wagon, her hands white with flour. "What did you tell her?"

He looked off at the late afternoon sun shining through the high mare's-tail clouds. "That her mouth would get her boys killed if she didn't shut up."

"What set that off?"

"She came back babbling about them going up north after three bodies."

"Who?"

He blew on his coffee. "A couple of the Reynolds men."

"Who were they going after?"

"Roy, Dab Stevens, and Luther Hines."

"Oh, my Gawd. That's who was in on it?"

He nodded.

"I wonder how Kathren is taking it."

"I have no idea. I can say this. He never mentioned her

or the girl. It was like he'd turned his back on them. Even the boys wondered about that."

"Bad deal. You know Louise may want to go home tonight after your confrontation."

"Sis, she's been a thorn in my side for years. I didn't send Mark to Mississippi to fight. But we've all had to bow to her wishes ever since. I am tired of it."

She wiped her hands on her apron and made a disappointed shake of her head at him. "Why don't you go up to Mason and find you a nice plump little German girl who will raise you some kids and smile whenever you come home to her?"

"How's that going to help me?"

"I don't know, big brother. I don't know, but you do need a wife."

"I don't need one."

"All right, you say you don't. I'll have supper ready shortly. They'll start dancing soon."

"Stanton going to be here?"

She shrugged.

"Maybe you need a husband?" He wondered how serious Ryan Thomas Stanton was about her anyway.

"I have enough to say grace over now," she said.

"Try to have a good time."

"Why? Do you think it is our last chance to have any fun?" She frowned at him for an answer.

"No, but I know how hard you work. You need to relax for once."

"I'll get back to work then." Susie laughed at him and left for her cooking.

Reg and Heck came back to camp for supper. Heck looked pleased to be getting to tag along with an older boy.

He was busting to get off the place and see more of the world. Chet could read it in his eyes. The most inquisitive ten-year-old he'd ever seen. He wondered where he came by those footloose ways.

Susie asked Reg if he'd seen his girl, and he nodded. "I'm going to dance with her later. Those lessons you gave me should work."

Chet laughed. "They will. Sis is a great dancer."

She shook her head and began forking out the sour-dough biscuits from the Dutch oven. "Time to eat, men."

After the meal, Susie sent the rest on, refusing any help washing the dishes. Chet wandered across the schoolyard, which was full of excited children running and playing tag. Someone had built a bonfire for light and some heat as the cooler night set in.

"Any word on cattle prices?" Elmer Stokes asked Chet when he joined the ring of men.

He shook his head.

The older man nodded. "You hear they think Hines, a Reynolds boy, and some cowboy named Stevens were hung a week ago way up north in Palo Pinto or Parker County?"

"I heard that."

"I wonder what they were hung for."

Chet looked hard at the orange and blue flames consuming the wood sticks. "I imagine for rustling."

"Damn, I can't imagine them stealing stock."

"Gawdamn you, Byrnes. My son Roy wasn't rustling nothing. I can damn sure tell you that." Earl Reynolds went to elbowing people out of the way like an angry bear until he faced Chet.

"I suppose he was riding full out and accidentally got

his head in a noose. Folks up there must not take to rustling. I'm sorry for you over the loss of a boy, but you know the law."

"Law? That's murder."

"I guess those three men that ran out of a place to walk down on Calahan's place last spring were just unlucky, too."

"They were gawdamn horse thieves and caught red-handed."

"Maybe you answered that yourself, Earl."

"How do you know so much about this?"

"Word of mouth, Earl. I heard this morning you sent for their bodies."

Earl waved his threatening finger in Chet's face. "I'm going to find those killers and get every one of them."

"Better get on your horse and ride up there where it happened. Take plenty of ammo and your funeral suit." He'd had his fill of having the larger man in his face, but he didn't want a ruckus with all the women and children around.

"Funeral suit?"

"I imagine those folks aren't going to take your murdering them as a friendly act."

"They'll pay! Everyone that was there at that hanging of that poor boy will pay with their lives."

"Back off," Chet said. "There's young folks here don't need to hear this."

For a few seconds, he thought the larger man might take a swing at him. On the balls of his feet, he was ready to duck and drive a fist. But that moment came and passed when others in the circle began to solemnly agree with his comments. *Not the right place . . .*

Earl left, threatening everyone within hearing of his voice that his poor boy's death would not go unavenged. Many shook their heads warily, and the crackling of the fire was the only sounds, save for the music of a fiddle coming from inside the schoolhouse. The dance was about to begin.

Chet headed for the lighted doorway and climbed the stairs, deep in concern. They'd learn in time. Those Reynolds—

"Susie coming?" the lanky Ryan Thomas asked, standing on his boot toes, looking all around.

"She's coming. Finishing the dishes."

"I'll go see about her then." He smiled big at Chet and started off. "Thanks."

It would be nice to be twenty-some years old and innocently in love. He nodded to a few that he knew who were standing around watching the dancers, and found a peg on the wall for his gun belt and hat. Since the Comanche threat had eased so much, folks hung up their guns—made thing more peaceful.

"I want a dance later, cowboy," Nancy Brant said. The tall broad-shouldered wife of a neighbor always danced with him a time or two, since her husband Ralph seldom shuffled his feet. He agreed, and shook hands with Jim Crammer, a short, soft-spoken, man who ranched west of their place.

"I thought Earl was going to drag you into a fight earlier."

Chet nodded. "He's like a sore-toed bear. Shame about his son, but he knows the law."

"It's hard to accept things when they touch you."

"Yes, sir."

"He ain't going up there and shoot up anyone. Why, those folks won't stand for it."

"I wouldn't think so."

"A boy gets mixed up in bad company and that's what happens."

"I agree. I better dance with Nancy. They're playing a waltz."

"Always good to see you, Chet. Tell Rock hi."

"I will."

His movements around the room with the tall woman were easy flowing. She talked about her three children and a new colt. Lighthearted, she laughed about some wreck she'd had with a goat. As usual, it was a fun few minutes with a good dancer.

Next, he asked Marla to dance—the one time they would dare to make contact during the evening.

"Bad about the Reynolds boy."

His hand in the middle of her back, he could feel the familiar muscles under his palm as they went around. "Yes."

"How's Kathren Hines? I haven't seen her."

"I don't think she's here."

Marla shook her head. "Poor thing. Husband hung for rustling, I guess."

"I guess."

"When will you come back and see me?"

"Next week, I guess."

"He's going to San Antonio Monday. Be gone all week, he says."

"I'll see how things go."

"Two trips over wouldn't hurt."

"Thank you, ma'am," he said, politely returning her to her place along the wall. Damn, he felt cheated that that was as long as he got to hold her. If she was *his wife*, he wouldn't leave her home by herself to do all the chores. Then he kept the smile to himself and nodded to Neddy Coleman.

"Dance with me cowboy?" the straight-backed woman asked him.

The seventy-year-old rancher in her divided skirt and man's shirt still showed lots of the beauty her late husband Wye had seen in her years before. She was the picture of a west Texas take-charge-when-the-man-is-gone woman. Able to ride and rope with any male, she had the look of a lovely younger woman with her movements and still soft features.

"I see you haven't found a woman yet. Old bachelors are not that swell. Find you a woman." Her hand on his waist gave him a small squeeze. "Besides, a good woman can push you into better things."

"Neddy, I'd ask you in a minute to marry me."

She shook her head in disapproval. "I'd be about as much fun as a wind-broken, stifled horse. You know what I mean."

They both laughed. She damn sure got to the point in a hurry.

He saw Susie and her man dancing and talking to each other. What would Chet do without her? He might have to—cross that river when he got to it.

"I have a tough colt needs the edge took off him. He's out of good stock but—well, if you don't have time to mess with him—"

"Did you bring him along, Neddy?"

"Yes, I thought—"

"We'll take him home and curry him down some." The dance was over.

A smile spread over her handsome face as they stood on the floor. "Bend down."

He did and she kissed him on the cheek. "You're a darling, boy."

Drinking sweet lemonade, he watched Marla dancing the next set with a rancher from over east. Sometimes, being this close to her made him fidgety—even jealous. Why couldn't he find a woman of his own? Maybe he wasn't looking hard enough.

Early in the evening, he excused himself and went back to camp. It was empty when he flung out his bedroll. Clear sky full of stars, no need to sleep under the tarp, so he planned to sleep in the open beyond the buckboard. Seated on his butt, he took off his boots, unbuckled his gun belt, and wound it up so it be by his head, then crawled inside and looked at the stars. How much trouble would he have when Earl Reynolds discovered the truth? *Time would tell.*

Chapter 6

Monday morning, a light frost hung in the air; Neddy's big Roman-nosed bay was a stout three-year-old. Snubbed to the post in the center of the corral, he had a head-slinging fit. His nostrils flared open. He could have been breathing fire out of them. He was also too handy with his front feet, pawing and striking at Chet. But the hemp rope was looped around his flank, then between his front legs and through the ring on the halter, and every time he flew back, it was pinching down on his back and kidneys.

Hazing him with the saddle blanket was lesson number one.

"What does she call him?" Ray asked as he and his brother Ty sat on the fence to watch the operation.

"I call him Bugger."

"He's not very friendly."

"Don't worry, he'll get that way if we sack him down enough." Chet waved the blanket, and Bugger showed him the whites of his eyes and flew back again. This was not going to be a fast training process. But he agreed with Neddy on one thing. The big horse broke would be a helluva powerful roping horse and could drag off the world.

After an hour of messing with him, Chet left the gelding tied and gathered the boys. From there on, Bugger would get his water and feed when Chet led him to them. They went to the main house to see if Susie had any hot cinnamon rolls left lying around.

"Uncle Chet?" Ty asked. "There going to be bad trouble for us?"

"Who told you that?"

"Daddy told May there would be a war."

"I hope not, boys."

"Were you in the war?" Ray asked.

Chet shook his head. His father and mother both were too disturbed for him to leave them alone on the place. His Uncle Mark went, but Dale Allen was too young. They'd stayed home to fight Comanche and rustlers.

"What's war like?"

"Bad. People get killed."

"We don't want you killed."

"I don't either. Let's not talk about it anymore." He opened the back door and stuck his head in. "Any rolls today?"

"Oh, for loafers, no," Susie teased, coming to meet them.

"I've got two bronc busters with me. We've been taming Neddy's bad colt."

"Oh, well, I have rolls for bronc busters. Come in my kitchen."

"There we go," he said, and herded his boys into the kitchen's warmth.

"I may need to go to Mason and get some supplies this week," Susie said. "And the choice of material at the Maysville stores is so limited."

"Take Reg and J.C. along."

Helping the boys up on chairs, she turned and frowned. "Why?"

"I don't want anyone out by themselves from here on."

"Do they know?"

He shook his head for the boys' sake. He and Susie could talk later.

She agreed, and the four had a fun time eating cinnamon rolls. She fixed him some tea with honey, and he sipped it by the window as sunlight poured into the room. When the two little ones finished, they went out to play and to keep an eye on the Bugger for him.

"Don't go in the pen with him," he said as they went outside.

"We won't."

"Why should I take the boys along?" she asked, closing the door behind her back.

"They'll find out sooner or later about our remuda being stolen and us going after the rustlers."

"But they're boys."

He shook his head. "You grow up fast in this world we live in."

"Then you feel it will be more than Earl's blustering that he did at the dance that Ryan Thomas told me about."

"Lots more. Take the boys. You hire anyone to help?"

"I thought I'd find someone in Mason."

He nodded. Then, sipping on her sweet tea, he looked across the yard and watched the small puffs of dust the rising wind picked up. The wreck was coming. He only wondered when.

Late afternoon, he checked on his oat patches. The oats were a few inches tall and waving in the ruts. He might need to graze them if the warm weather held on. Once the plant grew past the first joint, a sharp freeze could kill it. Plenty of deer were coming in and eating the oats. Their hoofprints were all over. After checking his fields, he spotted a fat deer moving across a hillside, and slipped the .44/40 out of the scabbard. Taking aim, he downed it. The deer fell downhill and he rode up to it. Roan snorted at the blood, so he hitched him to a bush. Rifle in the scabbard again, he drew out his skinning knife and cut the deer's throat. The blood ran out and soaked into the grass and rocks. It was young, so he could lift it and strap it on behind his saddle. Then he mounted up and took in some more range, circling around until he was satisfied he had no one watching him. Then he carefully dropped off into Marla's country. From atop the ridge, he used his glasses. The team and buckboard were not in sight. Gone to San Anton. Good. A red-tail hawk screamed and circled on the wind looking for a meal. A smile crossed Chet's face as he dropped downhill.

The roan hitched behind the outhouse in the cedars, Chet eased his way to the back door. When he knocked, he heard her hurrying across the floor. She cracked the door, and a pleased look crossed her face as she opened it wide. "Well, you did come."

"I shot a fat deer coming here. We better gut and skin it. I guess he got gone, all right?"

"For five days." She threw open her arms and hugged him.

I figured you could always use the meat."

"Sure, thanks. I'll get a pan for the liver and things and some knives. We can hang him in the shed and do it there."

"Won't cause you any problems, will it?"

"I shoot deer when they get in my garden. What will be the difference?"

"I mean," he said, leading roan over there, "will he ask a lot of questions like how and why?"

"I'll shoot that old single-shot rifle off when we get to the house. He can smell the barrel when he gets home, and he knows I'm capable."

For the next thirty minutes, they worked shoulder to shoulder to eviscerate the strung-up deer. The air was filled with the copper smell of blood and guts as she worked right beside him. The blood dried on his fingers and stiffened them. They separated the heart, liver, and kidneys into her pan, along with the lacy fat. Then, working as a team, they pealed off the hide, and soon the deer was dressed and its red muscles shone in the light.

"He's fat enough."

"Been eating my oats."

She laughed as Chet tossed the heavy hide on a bench. "It's fine right there. I'll tan it later after I scrape the fat off the inside. Get an ax. I want his brains for that job."

This was the first time he'd ever worked beside her doing anything like this. Her efficiency and skill impressed him. When the deer was pulled up high enough and tied up so a varmint couldn't reach it, she nodded her approval. "Thanks, some fresh meat won't hurt me. Let's go wash up."

She brought hot water out on the back porch and poured some in the basin. They went to work side by side, washing their hands and forearms with lye soap. With a big grin, she bumped his hip with hers.

"You ain't half bad help. Jake Porter would have squatted

on his boot heels and let me do it all." After they rinsed, she flung out the water and handed him the flour-sack towel.

"Let's go inside. When you get out of that sun and you ain't working, it ain't real warm."

"I been thinking—" He came inside behind her and closed the door.

She looked up and blinked her eyes at him. "Yes?"

"Why don't you get a divorce and marry me?"

"Your conscience bothering you?'

He shook his head. "No, but I'd like to stop having to sneak around to see the woman in my life."

"You know there's a lot more attached to being the woman who divorced her husband than for a man who divorces his wife."

"You talking about them shunning you?"

"That and the rest."

She moved up against him, untying his kerchief and fussing about him. "I say we get in bed and then we can talk about it there."

He looked at the kitchen ceiling for help. He gathered her in his arms and shook his head. Their conversation was going nowhere. She wasn't going to leave Porter. No way on earth to ever convince her.

It was sundown when he rode off for home, taking a wide circuit. He rode in when twilight shut down, and Reg met him at the corral. "I led ole Bugger over to the water tank and feed him two measures of oats and tied him back up."

"Thanks. That's all he needs." Chet dropped heavily out of the saddle.

"He's a handful, isn't he?"

"I'd call him a double one. He strike at you?"

"Yeah, he did bringing him home, too."

"We'll get that out of him."

Reg made a face. "What in the hell was that old woman doing with him anyhow?"

Chet laughed. "She's broke tougher ones than him before."

"She must be wiry."

"She is. Good gal. Just don't get her mad."

"We've got two strange horses in the north end. They took up with the mares. Two saddle horses. One's got a blotched brand and the other a YT on his shoulder. They don't belong around here."

"Cut them out and we'll corral them. We can cut a notice and tell the brand inspector. Thirty days we can claim them."

"I just wondered why they showed up."

"We ain't missing any horses, are we?'

"Why's that?"

"Someone on the run may have traded us them for fresh ones of ours."

"I guess I never thought about it that way. All those mares were at one time broke to ride, but they ain't been rode since then. Wow, I bet they bucked."

They both laughed and washed up on the back porch. Susie had two heaping plates ready for them and placed the food on the table. "You two are getting around slow tonight."

Chet stopped astraddle his chair. "I've been checking oats and Reg's been checking mares."

"Sounds busy. Reg, we're going to Mason tomorrow to get some material. The boss says you and J.D. need to attend our trip."

Reg poised his fork and looked over at Chet. "How come?"

"We need to be prepared," Chet said.

With a shrug, Reg gave her a grin. "Sure. J.D. and I can watch you girls and watch the ladies over there as well."

Susie shook her head. "You men."

"On second thought—" Then Chet laughed at his sister's disapproval.

"You two want some pie?"

"Do we look like we want some pie?"

"Can I tell her about the apple crisp we made?" Reg asked.

"You two made?"

"We did. At a place we stopped at. We made it for Hilga." Reg told her the whole story while she served them slices of her dried apple-raisin pie.

"My, my, I bet she was shocked at what she found."

"Take me back. Take me back," Reg mimicked.

They all laughed about it.

After breakfast, Louise got on the spring seat with Susie driving the buckboard, and the boys rode along on horseback. Chet and the small ones went to give Bugger another lesson. May was left doing dishes, and Dale Allen was going to do some repairs on the hay wagons.

Bugger was a little less feisty, but he still had a ways to go. Chet hitched him back to the snubbing post, then looked up when he saw a rider coming.

He walked over to the fence. It was Jim Crammer.

"Get down, Jim. What can I do for you?"

"I don't have time. Got to get back. I've got a mare trying to foal. I need to save her colt. She's a daughter of Sam Houston and there aren't many left of that bloodline. I just came from Mayfield. I wanted you to know that Earl Reynold's saying you hung his boy."

"Boys, you go find you father and help him awhile." He waited until they were out of hearing.

"I never said I did or didn't," said Chet. "Rustlers are rustlers. It was no joke. They stole my entire remuda, and I caught up with them this side of the Red River, somewhere west of Fort Worth."

"You don't need to explain it to me, but you better watch your back is all I can say."

"I just wanted you to know how it happened."

Jim made a sharp nod. "Sorry, I understand, but it looks bad. I better get back and check on my mare."

Chet watched him ride out. Dale Allen joined him. "What did Jim want?"

"Reynolds knows who hung their boy."

"Son of a bitch."

It was only a matter of time until he knew anyhow. Hell, Chet had whipped the Comanche. How much worse could those loud-mouthed Georgia crackers be?

Chapter 7

The dust churned by the buckboard the next afternoon signaled his crew's return from Mason. He relaxed when he saw both women on the seat and another in the back. Good. Susie must have found some help. Reg and J.C. were loping ahead of them.

The boys dropped off their horses at the corral.

"Well," Reg said. "They're bringing their bodies back. We seen them in Mason with three pine boxes. Funeral's tomorrow. We going to go?"

"I guess we should pay our respects to the dead," Chet said.

"Hell, have we got to wear ties and coats?"

Chet nodded. "Won't kill us."

"One of you boys go help Susie unload," Dale Allen said to them.

Reg started to say something, then handed his reins to his brother and set out for the house. Why did Dale Allen order those boys around like that? It made Chet about half mad, too. Everyone pitched in and helped, but that surly way Dale Allen had of speaking to them got under Chet's hide, too.

"I guess we all could go help her," Chet said, and started that way as J.D. began to unsaddle.

"I got these, Chet," said J.D.

"Good."

"How was Mason?"' Chet asked Reg as they walked across the yard.

"Fine, but I saw something there." He looked around and then lowered his voice. "Jake Porter was up there. I seen his team in a lot. You'd recognize them a mile away."

"What was he doing?"

Reg shrugged and then grinned big. "He was staying there at some widow woman's house. It's a big fancy place. They called it Colonel Bridges House. Two-story and brick. He never came out while we were there."

"Hmmm," Chet said. "That's kind of open, isn't it?"

"I guess he had his reasons."

"Yeah," Reg said. "Like that fella up north has with that Mexican woman."

Dale Allen frowned at what they meant, but the rest laughed.

"Susie get someone to help?" Chet asked.

Reg nodded. "Her name's Astria."

"Good."

"Susie, how did it go?" Chet said as she came out and pushed a wave of brown hair back from her face with a smile.

"I found material, some items I couldn't get in May-field, and I hired Astria Valdez."

The men swept off their hats for the girl in her teens on the porch who looked very self-conscious biting her lip and nodding at them. Slender and maybe fourteen, she looked taken aback by all the people that Susie introduced. Then everyone took something inside.

Chet spoke to her in Spanish. "We are glad to have you here, Astria."

"I am grateful that the *señorita* hired me. This is a large hacienda and a pretty place to live. *Gracias*."

"You will be a family member here."

"I will try, *señor*."

"No, Susie is very fair. You will like her."

"Oh, I do already."

He nodded and took a load of purchases inside. He still did not understand what Jake Porter was doing in Mason at some widow's house when he'd told Marla he was going to San Antonio. Would that knowledge change Marla's mind about leaving him? Chet better not tell her. Telling gossip wasn't his game. She'd find out. Someone would slip and Chet would be there. The notion made him feel stronger about reaching some permanent arrangement with her.

On the living room rocker, May was nursing six-month-old Donna. She smiled at Chet as she hoisted the baby up for a better position.

"Well, your help's back," he said to her.

"Yes. I missed them." She shook her head like she was tired of being chief cook and bottle washer. Besides nursing her own, she had eighteen-month-old Rachel crawling around, getting into everything. "I'm glad Susie brought us some help."

The poor girl had come from being a pampered banker's daughter to becoming a mother of two—one was Rachel, whose birth cost Nancy her life, and the second one arrived nine months after the wedding. May still carried some baby fat. Not as pretty as Nancy, she still tried hard in Chet's book, and did not receive a lot of help or attention from his brother—her husband.

"Louise and I are making new shirts for the men," Susie announced, showing him the bolt of blue denim. "We have material for dresses for the spring and even for Mother."

Louise stood back silent and helped unpack staples like coffee and baking powder from the wooden crates. She'd not said one word to Chet since the schoolyard, and he could see behind her darting brown eyes that she wanted to rake him over the coals again.

"There's a new doctor in Mason," said Susie.

"Good. Always can use one to them," Chet said, making room to set his load on the table. "I understand the funeral is tomorrow. I think we should go and pay our respects."

"Isn't that hypocritical?" Louise asked.

"You don't have to go if you feel that way," Chet said.

"You're right, Chet Byrnes. I don't have to do one thing that you tell me to do. I have wired an attorney in Shreveport and asked him what my rights were."

"Does that mean you are leaving, Louise?"

"I want my sons to grow up in a more civilized place than this outpost in hell."

"You sure they want to leave here?"

"They are both under eighteen and they will do as I say."

"Fine, when you get that letter from that lawyer, show it to me. You have not seen Shreveport in a number of years. May I suggest you go there on a visit and see it first? I understand that much of the South is still so torn up from the war, it hardly is the same."

"You want rid of me, is that it?"

"No, ma'am, but you don't know what the South is like today. We may live in hell, but there are worse places."

"How would I get the means?"

"We can pay for it." He waited for her answer.

She turned on her heel to leave, would not look back at him, and tossed her words at him while leaving. "I will consider it."

Reg dried his palms on the front of his pants. "I damn sure ain't going along with her."

Chet shook his head to quiet him. A trip to Shreveport might settle her for a while. At least she would not be around to harass him; let her go see the slave-free South. All those once-rich people doing their own wash on boards in tubs. She might think the ranch wasn't so bad after all.

The taste and quality of the food picked up with Susie back, and so did everyone's appetite at the supper table. After the meal, he excused himself, slipped off, saddled a horse, and rode out in the twilight. The short days wouldn't be getting longer for months.

He rode up on the ridge under the stars, listened to the coyotes. Huddled in his jumper shell, he wished he'd worn more clothing. A new cold front had moved in and no rain. His thirsty ranch needed all the rain he could get for it.

This mess with the Reynolds clan might hurt his spring cattle drive. People might be challenged not to use his services. Those extra thousand head paid the expenses for the drive. There was still money going north with a herd of his own, but the extra insured a profit. Time would tell.

At the end of the ridge, he looked off across the pearl-lighted country. Better forget about seeing Marla for the night and head home. He short-loped the good horse for the house.

When the roan was put up, he realized that that late smoke was coming from the fireplace and a light was on in the living room. The notion of warming up at the hearth made him head for the main house's front door. He opened it quietly and in the rosy glow from the hearth, May was rocking the older girl in her lap.

"Baby sick?" he asked quietly. Pulling off his thin gloves, he held his hands out to the radiant heat.

"I am afraid Rachel's not the healthiest baby. I try. I make sure she gets food, but it upsets her stomach a lot and she must have had a bad dream tonight." May made the rocker go faster and hugged the child closer. "Do you think she will go?"

He turned and frowned at her.

"Louise—you said she could go on a visit to Louisiana. You'd pay her way."

He shrugged. Why did that sound so important to May? "Yes."

"Maybe when she's gone away, my husband will share our bed again."

Shocked, he stopped warming himself. Was she telling the truth? Why wouldn't she? Slowly, he nodded, "I'm sorry, May. You have a large cross to bear."

"I just want to be his wife."

He saw the tears in her eyes. Two days doing Susie's job and all the rest had worn her out—but his brother's spurning her had hurt her the worst.

"I will press her to go on that visit."

"Thank you," she said, and rocked harder.

All the way to the bunkhouse, he wondered what he should do next. Damn Dale Allen's worthless soul.

Chapter 8

The men rode horses. The rest were in the farm wagon that Reg drove behind the big black mares to the schoolhouse for the funeral. Louise, in the end, had decided to go along. May and Astria stayed home to watch the babies and old folks. The boys were dressed in suits and looked stiff-necked wearing ties. Chet wore his six-gun under his brown suit coat.

A crowd was gathered when they arrived, and lots of hard looks from the Reynolds clan came at Chet. He didn't expect anything less, but he felt the schoolhouse was public-held land and he had as much right as anyone to be there.

He herded the two women ahead, and had reached the three-step stoop when Earl Reynolds burst through the shocked onlookers and brandished a pistol in the doorway. "Gawdamn you, Byrnes! You hung my boy."

"Put that pistol away," Chet ordered. "There's women and children here."

"I don't give a damn. I'm going to kill you."

Chet was never certain who hit Earl in all the confusion

and women screaming, but whoever delivered the blow knocked the gun out of his hand and may have broken his forearm. Earl went to his knees screaming. A bystander swept up the revolver and promptly stripped the caps off the nipples.

Earl, on his knees, held his disabled arm and swore revenge.

"Stand aside," Chet ordered, and the man reached for him. A swift kick spilled Reynolds on his back and Chet jammed a boot on his chest. "This is a funeral, not a bar fight. Go to your seat and pray for that boy's delivery to God. They stole those horses and were nearly to the Red River before I caught them. That was no prank, it was thievery. He took on a man's part of that crime and got the same in punishment."

"I'll kill you—I'll kill you—"

Chet jerked him up by his collar, dragged him outside, and threw him down the steps. "Come back when you're civil."

"I'll get my damn rifle—"

"You people that are kin of his get him under control or you'll have another funeral."

Earl's wife and two daughters ran over to settle him. Chet nodded sharply and went back inside. *The fucking war was on.* A first blow had been struck, and there would be no peace in the future. Earl would never accept the truth. The "law of the range" fit everyone but him and his.

The Byrneses sat in a row of benches, midway to the front, and no one else joined them despite the overflow crowd. On the small stage in the front of the room, three fresh pine boxes rested on top of sawhorses. Was this being shunned, or were folks simply afraid to join them for fear they'd get a taste of Reynolds's wrath?

Reverend Meeks gave a long soul-saving sermon. He was trying to pry anyone not saved to come to the front, and only a few dared go. Those that did go forward had been saved before. The sobbing of women at times about drowned out his strong voice—but in the end he prevailed and led "The Old Rugged Cross" as a final hymn.

People filed outside talking in low voices and behind their hands to each other. Chet knew he was on trial by the jury of funeral attendees. But they had no right to judge him. The lynching was out of their jurisdiction. His main concern was how far would they carry it to him. They wouldn't face him. They'd back-shoot at him from cover, and no one branded as a Byrnes from the babies on would be spared.

He'd prayed in there. Prayed hard for his family's safety. Prayed hard that God would make the Reynolds clan see their errors in how they'd raised Roy to take up with hard cases with no regard to the consequences of his crime. Took a man's livelihood lightly when they rustled those horses—they weren't range horses. They were a remuda for his cattle drive.

He was so angry, he could hardly concentrate on anything. From the corner of his eye, he saw the serious face of Marla looking at him. Had he soured their affair? No telling. Jake Porter was due back any time. He'd better keep his wits about him. When Susie was loaded in the buckboard, he turned around to look for Louise. He discovered she was standing aside talking privately to Dale Allen.

"You load her," Chet said. "We best go home."

Dale Allen nodded and took Louise to the front wheel to assist her up into the box. Chet wanted his brother to know he knew and disapproved of his affair with Louise. How would he do that? Maybe just tell him. That should make for a good fistfight. It had been years since they'd had one of those. The last one was a dragged-out struggle that left them both out of commission for a couple of weeks.

He mounted Strawberry and rode up to the side wheel of the farm wagon to tell Reg, "Take the ridge road, it's easier to defend."

That meant an hour longer ride—he didn't care. It meant less exposure to potshots.

"J.C., you go ahead of them. See anything suspicious, ride back and warn them. Don't fight them by yourself."

The youth nodded.

"What are you going to do?" Susie asked, sitting on the spring seat with a rifle in her lap.

"I'm going to see if there are any war parties on the low road. They'd expect us to take it."

He heard Louise say to her, "Let him go. He wants to get killed anyway."

"Dale Allen, stay close to the women." He jerked the gelding up short to stop his impatient circling.

His brother frowned at him. "You know, you're a damn fool. They want you worse than anything."

"They ain't getting me. Take care of 'em." He tore out on Strawberry.

In a short distance, he busted him off a steep hillside, sliding him on his heels off the face of the slope. It was a dangerous route he'd chosen, but the big horse was sure-footed, and a smaller, weaker animal under his weight and the saddle might have gone end over end. Strawberry hit the flats on a hard run. They were on the Hammerhead Creek's lower reaches, and he felt if they tried to ambush the family, it would be at the ford a few miles north.

When he drew closer, he let the horse walk so as not to

let them know of his presence. The water ran over enough small rapids to muffle the sound of his approach. A quarter mile from him, he could see a horse standing hipshot in some cedars. How many more were there?

He left Strawberry hitched in a small grove, and moved like an Indian down the bottoms against the cliff side, staying in the brush. In no rush, for they wouldn't expect the wagon to arrive for at least another forty-five minutes, he moved with his redwood grips in his right fist. When he reached their horses, there were three of them in all.

Good. Three he might handle with an element of surprise in his favor. He crept closer, hearing their guarded talking. Outbursts of cuss words and what they planned to do to him and the others filled the air. He eased in behind where they lounged behind some large boulders. Their rifles were set aside and they smoked roll-your-owns. The tobacco smell came on the wind to him. None of them could get to a rifle if he got the drop on them. He only knew one. Kenny, a couple years older than Roy. The others might be Campbells.

"I want first shot at that damn Chet. I'll blow his ass out of the saddle and send him to hell," Kenny said.

"Stand tall and hands high!" Chet ordered, filled with a new fury over those words.

"Huh?"

"Make a move and you'll join Roy. Now, one-handed, drop those gun belts. My finger's itching to cause another funeral so be quick." They obeyed, looking at each other and wondering how bad off their situation might be at his hands. "Now sit on the ground and take off your boots."

"What?"

He brandished the revolver at them to punctuate

his orders. "You heard me." He collected the good Winchesters—brand-new, out of the box. "Now shed your pants, vest, and shirts."

They made faces of disbelief at his orders, but obeyed.

"Now the underwear."

"It's cold out here," one of the Campbells said, stripping off his long underwear.

"Not near as cold as you'll be."

"We ain't done nothing to you—"

"No, you just were going to shoot me in the back a few minutes ago."

"No, no, not me—"

"You boys get in the middle of the creek and start running south. You try to get out on the bank, I'm going shoot you."

"Hell, it's like ice!"

Chet nodded. "This is a lesson. I want you to remember it well. You try to ambush me again or hurt my family, you'll be dead instead of wading cold water."

He herded them in the water. They were already screaming in high-pitched voices in the knee-deep water. "Now run like hell right down this creek."

He fired a shot in the ground close to the oldest Campbell, who jumped back and fell in the water. Getting in, Reynolds went facedown and popped up shivering. The third one got his at the next falls, stumbling over a boulder and his feet shooting out from beneath him. Chet had switched to a rifle, shooting to the right and left of them to keep them in the creek. They soon were out of sight, yelling and screaming and cussing.

He gathered the rifles, clothes, and went back to the horses. Leading them westward, when he was satisfied the naked ambushers couldn't find them, he cut each cinch and let the saddles and pads fall on the ground. He took off their bridles and threw them on the saddles. Mounted on Strawberry with his three new rifles tied in a bundle, he drove the loose ponies south until he knew they'd find their way home long before the boys crawled in. Then he headed for home.

Reg was rumbling the wagon up the valley with his two outriders. Those big mares could cover ground and had lots of wind. They'd made good time.

"Any bushwhackers?" Reg asked, reining up.

"Three."

"What did you do to them?"

"I took their horses and sent them home naked."

Reg shook his head in amusement. "That should be a big lesson."

"Oh, they had to swim down the creek below the ford, too."

"It ain't that deep."

"No, but you couldn't stand up either and run it with a fella shooting at your heels."

"Whew, that would be cold," J.D. said. "Who were they?"

"Kenny and two of the Campbells."

"I guess they've got the whole clan after us?" Reg asked, propping a boot on the dash.

"Sounds like it." J.D shook his head as if it was too hard for him to fathom.

"If this celebration is over, take us to the house. I don't know who is the most childish, you or my boys," Louise said.

"Yes, ma'am." Reg kicked off the brake and clucked to the mares.

Ah, the spoiler had spoken. She couldn't leave for Louisiana fast enough for Chet's part. But if it was his idea, she'd never go—

He dismounted from Strawberry at the house, and he swept up Ty and Ray and put them in the saddle. They beamed as they rocked back and forth in their seat to the horse's swinging walk.

At the corral gate, he took them down. "Short ride this time."

He hooked the bridle on the horn, wrapped up the reins, and turned the horse into the pen. He might need him. Keeping him saddled wouldn't hurt him. He crossed to the Bugger horse, untied him, and led him to water. Then he took him over to the side door of the tack room. Ray had a measure of oats ready in a feedbag, and opened the door with his other hand.

"Thanks, I better hang it on him." Chet took it, and the horse bowed his head, knowing where his rewards came from, and let him put it over his once-tender ears.

"He's getting smarter, Uncle Chet."

"Yes, he is. Next week, I'll saddle him. Can you boys keep a big secret?"

Ray nodded and Ty joined him. "You can't tell anyone until after whoever goes to Kansas comes back. But we're going to find you boys a couple of small horses or ponies." He put his finger to his mouth. "That is our big secret."

"I hope they aren't wild as Bugger," Ty said, looking concerned.

"If they are, then we'll break them."

Susie met them on the back porch. "Go inside, boys,

after you wash up. There's some cookies in there on the table for you and some milk." When they were in the kitchen, out of hearing, she spoke to Chet. "It was a bad day today. We're back like the days when the Comanche made raids on us."

"I know and it'll get tougher." He hugged her. "Louise say any more about going home for a visit?"

"Not a word. I think she was simply threatening you."

"It might ease a situation around here if she went."

Susie stopped and blinked at him.

"Sis, you are my confidante. I tell you things that I don't tell anyone else." He sighed. "May says that Dale Allen is having an affair with her."

"No."

"May's been upset, tired, and worn out with those two little kids and the bigger ones. As well as what she tried to do to help you. But she didn't make that up. I saw it today between them. I just wasn't looking for it before."

"Oh, my God, Chet. What can you do?"

"Send her on a long trip back home and send him to Kansas with the herd."

"Have you talked to him about it at all?"

"I can't—he wouldn't listen. He counters my orders. Talks to those big boys like they were his slaves. Really piss—I mean, it makes them mad." He dried his hands. "And she's using him against me."

"You know I bite my tongue when she starts in to me about you. How if Mark was still here, this place would be run so much better."

"Mark never did anymore on this ranch than a hired hand would have around here. He left her nagging for the army. I would have gone in his place, but he told me no, he had to get away from her. I doubt he planned to ever come back here after the war. Sometimes, I think he may simply walk or ride in through that front gate like nothing ever happened."

Susie grew pale. "But it's been seven years."

"They said he was buried in that Mississippi mud. But mutilated bodies could be anyone—change identities and go on."

She shuddered and he hugged her. "I'm sorry, Susie. Mark is probably dead, but I don't think she believes it. Other men have come around and she avoided them like the pining widow."

"But why," she whispered, "Dale Allen?"

"To get to me is all I know. She would like to run this ranch and order everyone around like they did on her family farm."

"A war with the Reynolds clan and one of our own. You at least knew what a Comanche wanted when he came."

He agreed. "I think my boys are through. I'm going to split some stove wood and let them bring it up here. They like work. I sure don't want them to quit liking it."

At the woodpile, he let the boys work the bowed hand-saw to cut short blocks off the post oak logs he put up on the cross-bucks for them. "Be careful."

With those two busy, he began to bust the shot sticks into easy kindling wood on top of a large block cut out of an ancient oak. The double-bit ax raised high over his head and the kindling flew. The sound of someone pounding iron came on the wind. Dale Allen was working in the blacksmith shop, replacing or repairing some parts on the chuck wagon. He also was making extra single- and doubletrees out of some ash blocks they'd bought at the mill.

His brother was handy at blacksmithing. Never minded working alone, and did good craftsmanship. Suited Chet fine. He busted off some more kindling. Using the big ax gave him time to think, consider what the Reynolds clan would try next, and use his muscles. The pile began to grow, and the boys were cutting them faster than he could make them into kindling.

They began giggling over how far ahead of him they were.

"Oh, my gosh, you boys better take a break."

They agreed and sat down in the sawdust, hugging their knees to watch him work. At last he sunk the ax in the block. "We better carry some up to the house."

"We get a pony, I'll train him to pull a sled and we'll haul it up there." Ray said.

"Now that's thinking," Chet said, and loaded up his arms with the short wood.

"You boys haul some more up there on the porch after this. I need to go do something."

At the house, he stuck his head inside and told his sister he was going scouting and would be back later.

The boys agreed to pack more up there, and he paid them a nickel each. He walked to the pen and took the feedbag off Bugger and caught Strawberry. Porter'd come home, but maybe he'd be gone to town to play cards. When the horse was bridled and cinch tight, Chet swung up in the saddle and rode off.

Maybe talking to Marla would help—she could usually cheer him up.

Chapter 9

Twice, he stopped and listened. Was it wind or someone? Maybe he was just getting apprehensive about it all. Their plan to ambush the Byrnes family was worthless. Those boys probably couldn't hit a barn door. Their rifles he collected had not even ever been fired. What did Grandpa Cooney say? *Don't send a boy when you need a man.*

He reined up and sat on Strawberry with his own rifle across his lap in a pungent-smelling cedar thicket. Crows were calling loudly that something or someone had upset them. Nothing showed up out of the ordinary. He scoped the house twice with his field glasses. Maybe his nerves had got jangled by all that had happened. A snort of whiskey would go good at the moment. When had he had his last drink? Years ago, he'd fallen in love with the bottle, but he'd whipped that. No time to start back now.

When he set out again, he felt that someone was looking at him. Who and why, he had no idea. Could be them. But where were they watching him from? He diverted up a side canyon, and came out on top watching his back trail and the valley. Nothing. Still, his intuition had always worked when Comanche hunting.

He broke off the hillside and short-loped across the wide basin. Setting Strawberry down in some more cedars, he used the scope again. Nothing.

Satisfied, he went to her place, slipped in behind the outhouse when he was certain that Jake wasn't there. With Strawberry hitched, he went through the weighted self-closing gate, crossed the yard, and knocked softly on the back door.

"Coming," she said. "Well, how did it go after the funeral?"

"No problem."

"I was afraid he'd shoot you in the building."

"Bad deal. Earl had a fit, drew a gun to bar us from the schoolhouse, and someone broke his arm. Then three of the boys tried to jump us at the ford when we were going home."

She went for her coffeepot while indicating a chair at the table. "Tell me more."

"He's in town?"

She nodded, then set a tin cup down and poured the dark coffee in Chet's cup. "Tell me more," she said.

"I slipped up behind those ambushers and made them undress. Told them they had to run down that creek or I'd shoot them."

"Undressed?"

"I didn't want them to forget their foiled ambush."

"They walked home soaking wet?" She bowed over and kissed him on the mouth. "Porter got back yesterday. But I'd almost swear he has a woman stashed somewhere."

"Strange. Today, I thought someone might be following me. I doubled back twice and waited for twenty minutes each time for them to show." He shrugged it off. "Years ago, I was like that, always imagining Comanche were trailing me."

The coffee tasted all right, and simply being in her company brightened his outlook. He reached over and squeezed her hand. "I guess I'm in a safe haven for now."

She jumped up and came over to sit on his lap. "Safe as you can get it."

His mouth closed on hers and her arms surrounded his neck. He knew any minute they'd be swept up in a clothes-shedding whirlwind. Damn, that was what in the hell he came for. That and to forget the whole blasted damn day. Oh, God bless you, girl.

Coyotes were serenading the stars when he left her place. Strawberry picked his way in a jog trot up the canyon. He tried to use a different way each time in and out so his tracks weren't obvious. Some of her other horses stayed around that gate so some fresh piles there wouldn't be telltale. The home place was near dark when he came in the gate.

"That you, Chet?" Susie asked, coming out on the porch packing a rifle.

"Something wrong, sis?"

"They chased Reg and J.D. in the yard when they were coming back from checking the mares. Three of them pulled up out there and they fired some bullets at the wall. I wouldn't let the boys shot back at them."

"Recognize any of them?"

"They were cowboys is all I could tell. Had masks pulled up."

"Any fancy horses?"

"No, just bays."

"Next time don't stop the boys from shooting at them. They think we're weak, they'll get bolder."

"I know, but they probably were only boys."

"Boys can kill you."

"All right. I won't do that again. You see anything?"

"No. I sat waiting for them and they didn't show."

"You look better. More relaxed."

"Good, I must have rode it out. You better get some sleep. I'll sleep out here on the porch. They can't slip past the dogs and me."

She hugged him and went inside. Rifle in his hand, he went to put up Strawberry. Something of Marla still clung to him—her musk, slight perfume. Susie probably didn't miss it. He'd have to fest up with her about Marla before this was all over.

At morning's cool predawn, she brought him coffee on the porch. He threw the blanket cover back and sat up.

"No trouble?"

"Nothing."

"I better ride up and look at those mares today." He used the porch's post to lean on. Brazen bastards riding up out there and challenging them. They'd be dead if they ever tried it again. If Susie hadn't told them to hold their fire, those boys would have counted coup on that bunch.

After breakfast, Reg and Heck joined him for the trip. Rifles loaded in their scabbards, they left out on fresh horses. Two days into this deal and already the Reynolds clan was acting very open in their hostile moves toward them. They short-loped their way up into the north pasture beyond where they kept the remuda horses. Reg bailed off and opened the gate.

Chet searched the open country. Nothing.

"When we shut that gate last night, they busted down here on us from over there." Reg pointed to a cluster of cedars.

"I wanted to stop and shoot it out with them, but J.D. wanted to go home and get help. I agreed, but when we got home, Susie wouldn't let us shoot at them."

"I changed that—next time shoot to kill. That's self-defense."

They rode across two sections of hill country to what they called Hornet Springs. There were several big-bellied mares grazing. They raised their heads and studied the invaders. The ditch carried a good supply of water that spilled over the rock-lined pool built back before the war. Then the water source ran into Yellow Hammer Creek.

"What the hell?" Chet shouted, standing up in the stirrups. Two bloated bay mares were floating in the pond. He spurred Sam toward them, and then he reined him in a sliding stop.

"It's the Ranger mares." Two of his prize brood animals heavy in foal. He jerked loose his reata, whirled it over his head, and roped a hind foot, then dallied it on the horn and began to pull the mare out. "Reg, get a rope on another leg. It will be lots more pull when we get her over to the dam."

Soon, they had the two dead mares out on dry land and he dismounted, coiling his rope. Damn them. He bent over and saw where they'd stabbed the first one's jugular vein in the neck. They'd led the mares into the tank and then murdered them. He took his hat off and sat on the ground. Close to tears with a knot in his throat, he couldn't swallow. With the side of his fist, he beat the ground. *You'll pay. You'll pay.*

"What do we need to do?" Heck asked, tears streaking his face.

Reg was looking off at the way north and beating his leg with his hat. "I should have shot them *coyotes*."

"Nothing we can do here. The rest of the mares appear to be fine. Wait, walk around and look for anything they might have dropped."

"There's a brass whorehouse token," Reg said, bending over to pick it up. "Reckon one of them dropped it?" He tossed it to Chet.

"Marie's in Fort Worth. Worth five bucks."

"Got a big cock rooster on the back."

"Wait," Heck said. "There's a fancy knife in this pond. I just saw it." He sat down, shed his boots and socks, then slid in the pool and bent over to get the knife. "They must have lost it after they killed the mares and couldn't find it in the night. Says right here, 'Made for Kenny Reynolds.'"

"That son of a bitch," said Reg.

"I know we don't have a case in court," said Chet. "It would be our word against theirs. We know who lost the knife, but did we see their faces? No. So someone stole his knife and they were the ones killed our good mares."

"That's the way the law works?" Heck asked, looking confused.

"That's why so many rustlers get hung. The law isn't liable to prosecute very hard. Lawyers mess the witnesses up. Some friend of the accused is on the jury."

"I thought law was law."

"Heck, you'll learn lots before this is over."

"You mean if I killed your horses and lost my knife beside the dead horses, I could get off scot-free?"

Chet nodded.

"How are we going to even the score?" Reg asked.

"Old Man Reynolds has six young pure-blood Short-horn bulls. Cost him a fortune. I was in Mayfield when they delivered them in freight wagons from Austin last summer."

"What about them?"

"We can bait them away for the house place and castrate four of them. We'd trade two good mares and what would have been two great colts for them. We'd be close to even then."

"What about the knife?" Reg asked.

"I may use it on their bulls." He eased it in his saddle-bags.

"Suits me fine. When we doing it?"

"In a week. There will be enough moonlight by then. Don't say anything about it. We boil over about this, they're liable to do some more harm. Less they know about our reaction, the better it will be."

"My first reaction is to cut their damn hearts out," Reg said. "You had promised me one of the colts or a choice if they were horses."

"I forgot. We'll find you one."

"I don't want that ugly-headed Bugger's Roman-nosed bloodlines."

"You can laugh, but that horse is going to be a tough one."

"He's double ugly, too."

Chet shook his head. "In a while, you'll be begging Neddy to give you that horse."

"Not likely."

"You know," Heck said, looking over the group of brood mares around the water hole, "I think one of those horses they traded us out of is the snip mare. I ain't seen her in the past week."

Chet agreed. "I haven't seen the coon-tailed mare either."

Both boys agreed.

"Let's head back in. That damn Kenny Reynolds better not kill any more of our stock or I'll stick his knife up his ass."

"Worse than the damn Comanche, aren't they?" Reg asked.

"Every bit as bad and it ain't over yet."

Feuds could go on forever—generations even. This one wasn't over when they killed two good brood mares. That only fanned the flames of revenge. Chet didn't want to think about it. The anxiety that coursed through his veins during the Comanche days was back.

Susie came out on the porch when they rode in. "What did you find up there?"

"They murdered two of the best brood mares."

"Oh, no. Chet, what can we do?"

"I may ride up and see Sheriff Trent at the courthouse. He needs to know what's going on."

"Can he do anything?" she asked.

Chet shook his head. "He's only got a handful of part-time deputies."

She hugged her arms as if she was cold. "What can we do?"

"We'll work on it, sis."

"Give me your horse," Heck said. "I'll put him up."

Chet thanked him and gave him the leather reins. He climbed on the porch and went inside with her.

"Killed some brood mares?" his father demanded, rocking in his chair. "I was younger, I'd ride over there and clean them Reynolds out. We done that once with some Mexican horse thieves. We found then denned up on the Llano. Shot 'em all."

"Easy, Pa. We'll get them. Don't get your heart worked up." Rock went to mumbling to himself.

In the kitchen, Chet looked back. "We'll have to be calmer around him. Where's Louise?"

"In bed. Said she had no reason to get up today."

"Susie, I'm sorry. How is the new girl?"

"She tries hard and is learning a lot. Big help to me. But since I got her, Louise does nothing."

"Nothing?"

"Nothing."

"I reckon she's got us both buffaloed."

"Don't say anything." Then she looked around and lowered her voice. "You were right about her and Dale Allen."

He closed his eyes and shook his head. There was no end to his problems.

Chapter 10

Sheriff Bob Trent was a big man, Six-four, broad-shouldered, in his late thirties. His cold blue eyes looked hard at Chet as the younger man explained his plight. Trent slouched down in the barrel-back chair that creaked on its springs, and tapped the desk with a pencil.

"So we have three rustlers hung and they'd driven your remuda almost to the Red River. They damn sure weren't going to sober up and bring them back."

"No."

Chet went on to explain the rest. The schoolhouse incident, the planned ambush he broke up, which Trent laughed over, the chase to the ranch, and the death of the two mares. Even the shooting at the house.

"Damn, Byrnes, you've got a full-fledged feud going on down there."

"I don't want anyone killed, but I'm going to fight fire with fire."

"I understand. I'll ride down there day after tomorrow and find Earl. Maybe we can call a truce."

Chet nodded. "I hope you aren't wasting your time."

"I don't have any deputies to keep you apart. I'd appreciate you holding off on anything until I see what I can do."

"You have a deal."

They shook hands, and after picking up a few things Susie had forgotten, Chet headed for home. Roan had a good rocking stride and Chet crossed a few ridges to shorten his ride, rode down through the backcountry, and arrived home after sundown.

Susie came out with a candle lamp and joined him.

"What did he say?" Susie asked, walking with Chet to the corral.

"He's coming down and talking to Earl day after tomorrow and try to arrange a truce."

"Truce? We never started this war."

"We'll wait and see what he can arrange." Chet undid the girths and swung the saddle off. Lugging it and the pads for the tack room, he looked over at Bugger in the starlight.

"Heck's already fed and watered him," she said

"Good bunch of boys. Couldn't make it without them."

"Do you have any ideas about what we need to do?"

He shook his head. "It's like the Comanche threat, only these people live much closer. No telling what or how they'll strike again."

"What about the spring cattle drive?"

"They will pressure folks not to send cattle north with us. That would hurt, but nothing I can do about it but continue planning on the drive. We'll have a thousand head counting the ones I bought in Mexico. And on top of that I need to sign up a thousand more."

"Will that work if you don't get any more?"

"The additional thousand head would sure cover our expenses."

She led Roan over to turn him into the lot. Chet caught up with her, threw his arm over her shoulder, and they went to the house. What would he do without her? His one grown-up ally at the ranch.

His supper was warming in the oven, but his appetite wasn't ravishing. She brought him some coffee and then she sat down. "I wish Mother would get out of bed. She's so stubborn."

At the click of heels on the floor, they turned to the door of the dining room. Louise appeared. He nodded to her.

"I have decided to go to Shreveport. I don't believe all the things that you have said about it."

"You can take the mail buckboard from Mason to San Antonio and catch the train from there. How much money will you need?"

"Four hundred dollars."

It was way more then she needed, but he never flinched. "When will you go?"

"I can't talk any sense into my sons, so I'm going this time by myself. Since Susie has that girl to help her, I plan to leave next week."

"I wouldn't tell anyone, I mean anyone, my plans. We'll take you to Mason on the day before and you can catch that buckboard. I'll get the money out of the safe when you're ready to leave."

"I don't understand all this business. The Reynoldses surely aren't that stupid."

"They planned to gun us down going home from the funeral. Senselessly murdered two great brood mares, and chased those boys in the yard shooting at them to kill. I think their threat is very serious."

"Have you reported it to the law?"

"Sheriff Trent is going to try to arrange a truce."

"Texas law. A truce in a war we did not start?"

"I'm warning you. Don't tell a soul about your plans."

"Good night."

He and Susie waited to talk until the front door closed behind her.

"Why, she could go to Europe on that much money." Susie scowled at him.

He held up his hands. "I want her to go and see how bad it really is."

"I know. She's no help here anyway."

He reached over and patted her forearm. "We'll see."

She agreed.

Under the cold starlight, he walked to the bunkhouse. In his room he lighted a candle lamp and then stoked the small wood stove. A little heat wouldn't hurt. He struck a match, and soon his kindling was taking off. He added some split wood and closed the door. Jake Porter was probably at home this evening. Wednesday was when he went to town to play cards.

He'd go over the next day and see Marla. In this fracas, he needed the loyal ones. Since he couldn't have her, he'd have to share her with Jake. Damn, what a mess.

His sleep proved troubled. There were more ambushes and bushwhacking. Once during the night, he sat straight up in bed broken out in a cold sweat. Who had they killed this time? He couldn't see the victim's face. Short of breath like he'd been running a hard mile—he still didn't get there in time to stop them.

His bare feet on the gritty floor, he mopped his face in his calloused palms. So many things wrong and they all looked insurmountable. He dressed, then put on a felt vest and jumper against the night's chill. His hat on, he left the bunkhouse and went to catch a horse. Maybe he could ride away some of the things making his belly growl and churn. He caught Big Tomas. A horse, sixteen hands high. Chet loaded his kac on him and quietly rode out of the compound. A man without a purpose, he swung north to check on the brood mares. They were mostly standing asleep around the springs in the starlight. He could see little wrong with them. Then he wanted to go by Mayfield. He wanted two bottles of good whiskey. It wouldn't help anything but to get drunk at home. He wouldn't give a damn.

Fall back in the bottle again. The Comanche had come close to making a drunk out of him. The Reynolds clan really might. At six, he walked into Casey's Saloon. The big Irishman looked up and smiled from behind the bar.

"You can't sleep?"

"It's been a problem of late."

"Them Reynolds fellas sure have been talking tough about you."

"They shot at my boys, murdered two good brood mares, and tried to ambush us coming home from that funeral."

"I don't doubt it one bit. They've talked real bad in here about you all." Casey put a bottle and a glass on the bar for him. "I've seen the likes of this before. Dumb hillbillies out of the mountains of north Georgia."

"They'll all be in a common grave if they mess with me very much more."

"Ah, son, I've seen these feuds in Ireland, too. They can go on for years."

Chet sipped the whiskey and nodded. "It won't take me long to clean them out."

"Just be careful, son. They're back-shooters."

He agreed, and Casey ordered them both breakfast from the woman he lived with. Hard-looking, with an angular face, she smiled at Chet and went off to fix it in the back. The whiskey didn't help him feel any better, so he quit drinking it.

Her hot coffee was rich, the ham tasty, and the scrambled eggs good. He buttered some biscuits and enjoyed them. "Good food. I was beginning to need something."

"Aye, breakfast is an important meal of the day, laddie."

"You miss Ireland?"

"It was a green land. But two kinds of people lived there, rich and poor. And the poor, God bless them, were so far down the ladder, you couldn't reach them."

"I see what you mean."

"My lucky day was when I landed in Houston and started to build me a nest egg. Then I came up here and bought this place. It was hard at first, but now it is much easier. Her and I get along."

Casey refused to let him pay for his meal, and sold him two bottles of whiskey. "You'll figure a way out of this mess. I know you will."

"I'm damn sure going to try."

He rode Big Tomas down south to a small Mexican village and bought Louise a full-length black and white woven poncho. She might not wear it, but she'd need it traveling in this hot/cold weather. The woman wrapped it in brown paper and tied it with string. Polite and quiet, she said, "Your lady will like this. It is very fine craftsmanship."

He nodded. *His lady.* Not quite.

It was close to sundown when he came in the back way at Marla's. The buckboard was gone and so was the team.

He eased himself around the outhouse, crossed the yard, and rapped lightly on the back door—no answer. He went around front to see if she was outside tending stock. She might be feeding chickens. No sign of her. Then he discovered the front door was wide open. His hand went for his six-gun. No good reason for that—

Inside, he called for her and went inside the kitchen. Despite the darkness, he knew at once something was wrong. There'd been a struggle and several things had been turned over. He went to the bedroom door off the kitchen, and in the last rays of light coming in the window, saw her bloody naked body sprawled facedown on the bed.

NO—no—no. He fell on his knees beside the bed. But already, her flesh was cold to his touch. Some madman had carved her up. It was the cruelest thing he'd ever seen outside of Comanche handiwork. Then he rose and saw where she'd written a name in her own blood on the sheet. Kenny R—it was plain as day. That could only be one person. He buried his face in his hands and wept.

What should he do? Get stoned drunk. No, he needed to go and find Jake. After all, she was his wife. Then Bob Trent—there was a strong case here. Good enough to swing a man legally. He paced the floor wanting to cover her up, but yet not wanting to disturb the evidence.

He picked up a page of stationery stained with a bloody boot print from the floor under the edge of the bed.

Dear Jake,
*   You have soiled my reputation long enough. I want out and I want a divorce. Your open affair in Mason with Madam Leubow has come back to me from repeated sources. I will be packing to leave.*

Damn. He folded it up. She was finally going to leave him. She knew all along about his infidelity. But no doubt one of the Reynolds clan must have followed him here. Oh, damn, what next? The grisly murder scene made him go outside and puke. He braced his shoulder against the porch post for support, the sour vomit fumes burning the lining of his nose. No matter the pain he felt, he still had an obligation to her. He'd ride to Mayfield, find Porter, and then Justice of the Peace Gunner Barr.

It was past ten o'clock when he located Porter playing poker in the Red Horse Saloon. He waved him over to the bar. Peter came across and frowned at his interruption. "What's wrong?"

"Brace yourself. I've got some tough news."

"Go ahead. What is it?"

"Sometime after you left the ranch today someone murdered your wife. I was passing through and stopped. The front door was wide-open. I found her inside all cut up by some maniac."

"You see anyone?" Porter looked powerfully upset.

"I hated to be the one told you about this. No, they were long gone when I got there. But she left a name written in blood."

"Who?"

Chet shook his head. "We need to get Doc and Barr to go up there. I never disturbed a thing."

"Who was it, man?"

"You'll see. I'll go get Doc. You go get Barr."

"Give me a whiskey," Porter said to the bartender. "Someone has murdered my wife."

Doc and Barr rode in Doc's buggy. The word was out, and

a handful of locals accompanied them in the frosty starlight. It was two in the morning when they reached the ranch.

Barr asked Chet to describe how he'd found her.

"Front door wide-open made me suspicious. I knocked, no answer. I found there had been a struggle in the kitchen. You will see that. She's in the bedroom. But I must warn you—it made me puke."

"Where is the name of the killer you said she'd written in her own blood?"

"On the sheet by her right hand."

Jake Porter went in the bedroom with Doc and Barr, and came right out to collapse on the kitchen floor. Chet brought him a chair and helped him get up and seated on it. The man's face was blanched snow white.

"Oh, dear God, how could someone be that cruel?"

Chet wanted to know the exact same thing. He sent one of the men after a bottle of whiskey from his saddlebags.

Looking sick to his stomach, Barr came out shaking his head. "They raped her, too, Doc said."

"Judge, tell us who she named as her murderer," said Jake.

"Kenny R."

"That has to be Kenny Reynolds."

Barr never nodded to agree; instead, he pushed his way out the back door to puke off the back stoop. He vomited and vomited until he was racked by the dry heaves.

He came back in bleary-eyed. Wiping his mouth on a crumpled-up handkerchief. "I'll have the hearing day after tomorrow. I'll need you there, Byrnes, to testify. Then I want the rest of you to go read what she wrote on that sheet and testify as well. Doc has her covered up. You wouldn't want to see the poor woman anyway."

He took the half glass of whiskey and thanked Chet. "Times like this, I'd rather have a small-town law practice."

Numb, Chet started for home. Porter ran out and shouted for him to stop. "I'm sorry, Byrnes. I never had chance to thank you for all you did for me today. I'd found her like that, I'd'a been a screaming imbecile."

They shook hands and Chet rode on. He was one— a screaming imbecile. All his planning to sneak in there and they'd still seen him. Must have been obvious as all get out.

"What's wrong?" Susie asked, running out to meet him in the cold predawn. "I can tell by your look like something bad's happened last night."

He nodded woodenly. "They murdered Marla Porter."

"What?"

"I'll tell you more later."

"Heck will put up your horse. Come in and set down. You look like you've seen a ghost."

"I have."

"Who would murder her?"

"She wrote his name in blood on the sheet."

"Oh, my God. Who was it?"

"Kenny Reynolds."

"You found her?"

"Raped and murdered—Doc said."

"Why would anyone—"

"Revenge." He dropped his chin in defeat.

"Oh, I'm sorry. I never knew."

He handed her the partial note. "I found this, too."

After she read it, she collapsed on the sofa. "What will we do?"

He shook his head. "I have no answer."

Chapter 11

Chet was grateful that Susie was with him walking from the schoolhouse to the cemetery behind the pallbearers and Marla's people. A cold north wind blew out of Kansas and swept across the Indian Territory and north Texas to get to them. It tugged at their clothing and tried to tear folks' blanket wraps away from them. The kind of cold that penetrated like a wood bee bored in wood.

Jake was wet-eyed helping his frail seventy-year-old mother up the path. Chet felt grateful he'd never shown him the farewell letter that Marla had started to write. The mourners stood up on the open hill with their backs to the hard breath of winter. Chet couldn't believe any one was cruel enough to murder good horses, but to do what they did to Marla was monstrous.

The preacher's words sounded strained. "Dear God, we send you this lovely woman and wife, her life cut short at the hands of a killer . . ."

His words went on and on. But Chet expected it. Even the chilling force pressing them down was not enough for him to shorten his finale at the grave site. Chet had been there before in driving rain that half filled the grave before the preacher finished—but the preacher never shortened his call to save everyone. Maybe he got his saved souls from those that couldn't stand another ten minutes of his words.

After the service, Chet and Susie rode home in silence. The boys had gone on.

"It was a fine service," Susie said.

"I'm sure she would have felt that way. She always worried how she would be shunned if she divorced him. Said it was easier for a man than it was for a woman."

"I imagine she was right. She needed a connection with other women, and to be excluded might have been a severe thing for her."

"I came so close—those damn Reynolds—" He clucked to the team and sent them trotting off.

"Spoilers, I'd call them."

"Worse than that. I can hardly wait for the hearing in the morning."

"I'll go with you."

"Good, maybe I can keep my anger under control. Louise take the poncho I bought for her?"

"Certainly, it was nice of you to think of her. I guess a blanket would have done for me. She's fancier than that."

"No, she's fussier than you are."

They both laughed and dropped downhill to the ford. He recalled those boys waiting in hiding for his bunch to arrive that day—made him mad all over. But the crossing was uneventful, and soon the wheels were churning for the ranch.

On Saturday, the hearing was held in Mayfield's Red Horse Saloon. The only place large enough for such a crowd in the village. The Reynolds clan was there in force, except Chet didn't see Kenny in that crowd. No doubt word had got back to them that he was the chief suspect and a writ would be issued for his arrest. Kenny could be in Kansas or New Mexico by then. From time to time, Chet overheard Big Earl boasting they wasn't indicting his boy for this crime. Why, he was plumb in the other end of the county all that day and Earl had witnesses to prove it.

When Chet took the stand, he heard several boos. Judge Barr rapped the gavel. "Another outburst like that and I'll sentence you to thirty days in the county jail."

In the middle of Chet's testimony, Earl jumped up and said he was lying. "I've got six men here will swear where my boy was at that day."

"Mr. Reynolds, we will hear that testimony later."

"Your Honor, I can't stand that that no-account up there lying about my boy."

"Mr. Reynolds, you will have your turn to speak. You interrupt these proceedings one more time and I'll have you escorted from this room."

He sat down again.

Chet finished his testimony and stepped down off the stage. He joined Susie and the boys. "You did well." she said.

Doc came next, and showed the judge the bloody sheet and the name. He went through some fancy words, but it meant she'd been raped and then murdered sometime in the afternoon of the day she was found. Four others verified the sheet as the one found under her body and testified they'd read the words she'd written in her own blood.

Then two from the Reynolds clan and three Campbells swore that Kenny had been with them in the other end of the county all that day.

"Mr. Campbell, I have heard from five of you," Judge

Barr said to the last witness. "That you were all with this man on that day. However, no one but family members saw him by your account. No reputable storekeeper or saloon man saw him that day?"

"Hell, I don't know. He was damn sure with us."

"Name some other reliable witnesses that saw him."

"You calling me a liar?"

Barr shook his head. "I asked for a witness that was not a family member."

Earl bolted up and shouted, "By Gawd, I'll get some!"

"Sit down, Mr. Reynolds. I am issuing a warrant for Kenny Reynolds's arrest for the rape and murder of Marla Porter. When arrested, he will be bound over to the circuit court for his trial."

"He's not guilty!" Earl shouted.

"Mr. Reynolds, no one is guilty until a judge or jury says so. He will have his day in court."

"Those lying sons a bitches you had here need their tongues cut out."

"You lay a finger on any of them, even threaten one of them, I'll slap an obstruction of justice charge on you. Am I clear?"

"Yes, Your Honor."

"Mr. Reynolds, I suggest your son Kenny immediately surrender to Sheriff Trent. As a wanted person facing a felony trial, his life might be endangered if he doesn't."

"And you think he'll get a fair trial? No, I saw you today turn those witnesses around against him. I won't say nothing of the like to him."

"If you're concealing him, that could make you an accessory."

"I seen all your kinda law I want to see. They lied about

my other boy stealing their gawddamn horses; now they're lying about poor Kenny."

Barr rapped his gavel. "Court is dismissed. Reynolds, approach this bench."

He sauntered up there and stood feet apart and arms folded. "What now?"

"Marla Porter was raped and then murdered by an insane person. It was such a horrible scene that I vomited at the very sight of it. If a jury finds him guilty—he'll be hung."

"Not while I'm still alive he won't be."

"You better go find a good lawyer and surrender him."

"Fuck you."

Barr shook his head in disgust. "You may think you're greater than the law. You aren't."

"I'll show all you sons a bitches. All of you. You ain't hanging my boy for something he ain't never done."

Chet led Susie out of the saloon. "I'm sorry. He needs his filthy mouth washed out with soap."

"No one knows, do they?" she asked softly.

"No, and I won't tell them."

"I'm so sorry. You have the worst luck with women."

"I must work at it."

Susie nudged him. "It's Kathren Hines."

Her hair wrapped in a scarf, Kathren booted her horse in front of him to cut him off.

"Good day, Kathren." He removed his hat.

"Did you hang my husband?"

"Yes, I did." He wanted to tell her lots more, but she simply nodded at him. No emotion on her face, no accusation in her eyes.

"I just wanted to know." Then she turned the horse aside and rode off.

"I guess we can scratch her off the list," Susie said as he helped her on the seat of the buckboard. "I doubt you'll drive any of her stock to Kansas."

"She knew he'd closed the gates on ever coming back by stealing our horses."

"Didn't make her any happier."

"Susie, I don't make anyone happy anymore."

He clucked to the team and the boys came along on their mounts. There were lots of things that upset him, but that short moment facing Kathren brought back many memories and left a bad taste in his mouth. How could Luther Hines have made it any more of an open-and-shut case? No way. And one thing more. Earl Reynolds would hide his son until his last day on this earth.

Hiram Jenks came by the ranch that evening to visit. Susie made him up a plate of food since she felt he probably had not eaten.

"I've got a hundred steers to toss in your drive if you can get them in," he said.

"That's good, but you may be subject to the Reynoldses' terror tactics. Several folks I've talked to said they won't send cattle up there with me for fear of some kind of revenge on them."

"Earl don't worry me none. I made up my mind this morning in that courtroom. You've been a good drover for many of us. That bunch of windy Georgia crackers sooner or later is going to have the whole country siding against them."

"I can't promise anything, but I'll do my level best to get the cattle there."

"I don't worry a minute when I deliver them to you."

"We'll road-brand in late February."

"Good," Jenks said, and Chet let him eat.

Eleven hundred head looked better. There had to be others that wanted their cattle driven north. He still had time. If a few more of the regulars threw in their cattle, he'd be full. Next, he'd need to map out a route for Dale Allen.

"Well, I'll be heading home," said Hiram. "It was sure wonderful food, Miss Byrnes, and filled in a big hole inside of me. I sure didn't come to beg a meal."

"Any time you're in the area, door's open and the food's here," Susie said.

"You folks are family to me, and I can't help but think those vengeful folks are getting some of what they deserve. It may put a stop to them."

Chet shook his head. "It won't. They murdered two of my great brood mares. We found Kenny's knife in the pond where he killed them. I figured it would be my word against them like the liars they had in court."

"That was pathetic."

"But it's what you face charging them with anything."

"I understand. I better get home, wife'll think I went off on a spree."

Chet laughed with him as they went out the front door, and Jenks rode out in the night.

Things were quiet in the morning at breakfast. Like no one wanted to speak. Only a fork or knife's edge on metal plates broke the silence, or a spoon's clink on a cup edge to be sure all the sugar was in their steaming coffee. Louise, who seldom was up for breakfast, sat her straight-back, stoic self across from Chet.

"I plan to leave for Louisiana in the morning."

"Then I suggest the boys take you to Mason this afternoon and you spend the night. That buckboard leaves around nine in the morning."

"I need some metal bars. I'll take her this afternoon," Dale Allen said.

Chet saw his sister at the stove flinch, but there was nothing he could do but agree. Saved a big argument, but it no doubt would send May into a deeper depression. He mopped up the gravy on his plate with half of a soft biscuit—being everyone's keeper at times overwhelmed him.

"Reg, you and J.D. check the mares today. Watch your backsides. Don't make a stand if you can get away. No need to die. Heck and I will be down in the south end looking at cattle. I feel from what Reg and J.D. said, we are gaining cattle numbers on our land. I'll make a decision today how to handle them."

Everyone nodded.

"Ray, you and Ty count the chickens for me today. You boys can do that?"

"Yes, sir, Uncle Chet, we can sure count 'em. You thinking about branding them?"

"Not right now." He winked at the others and about choked on his own amusement.

"Ty and me, we'd sure help."

"Why, it would be a roundup deluxe, but you better stay with counting today."

"I hope that you keep my boys out of harm's way in my absence since they don't have the good sense to join me," Louise said.

"Louise, I do that all the time."

"That is a matter of opinion."

Chet nodded curtly to her. "Have a good trip." Then he slammed on his hat and jumper and left the dining room.

That woman could burn down a devoted Christian, much less *him*. He had two horses caught when Heck came running to join him. The ten-year-old was rawhide tough and never wanted to be left behind—restless as a sixteen-year-old with surging hormones—he was sure all boy. Avoided by his father, he was anxious to be part of the ranch either with the older ones or Chet.

"You ever ask your dad if he'd show you how to black-smith?" Stirrup across the seat, Chet fussed with the lati-gos and eventually cinched it up.

"Told me when I was old enough he'd do that." Heck shrugged. "I tried to work the bellows, but I sure didn't please him so I quit that."

Chet jerked down the stirrup. "I would have, too." Hell, what was wrong with Dale Allen? He ignored those three boys. Ignored his wife and the babies. Maybe Chet needed to have a good down-and-out fuss with him—he'd hoped his sharp comments to him before they went after the rustlers would have been enough. Dale Allen had never changed one drop toward any of them.

Chet rigged up Heck's saddle for him and they led their horses out of the pen. The ten-year-old could climb in a saddle like monkey going up a circus pole, and he reined Dobie around with the confidence of a much older rider.

They trotted the horses and the sun began to melt the morning. When they crossed Batterman's Flat, Chet dropped down to a walk.

"What was my mom like?" Heck asked. "I just recall a few things about her."

"Nancy was a good mother. She made you nice clothes. I guess the firstborn is always the most pampered."

"You're firstborn. Did your mom pamper you?"

"I guess some. I was born in worse times than you were. We lived out here because of the fort that Grandpa and the others built so we could defend things. Most of our neighbors pulled out, went back to San Antonio. Others were killed. It was never easy. And they still kidnapped three of my brothers and my sister."

"Will they ever come back?"

"I don't think so."

"What do you mean?"

"I think for a young child to have survived the Comanche way of life would have been a miracle."

"I could have."

He looked over at his nephew and nodded. "You'd fit right in."

They both laughed.

They found no shortage of other folks' cattle on his grass. He'd need to separate them out and drive them off the place. Either folks were pushing cattle on the Byrnes land, or no one was riding herd on them. There were some jacales and some ruins above the Rosa Springs. A large tank made of stone built by Hispanics years before the first gringos came to this land made it a nice place to check on the cattle coming to drink. Considerable water poured over the spillway to feed Rosa Branch, which ran three miles southwest into Yellow Hammer.

If he ever found a woman of his own—maybe he'd build her a house down there and leave that smothering hacienda for the rest of them to argue over. No—he couldn't do that to Susie.

"You see that flash?" Heck asked, looking around.

"Flash?" He'd missed it.

"Yeah, a flash off a mirror—"

"Ride like hell for them jacales. That could be a scope on a rifle pointed at us."

They charged for the buildings, Chet's back twitching the whole time, expecting hot lead in the muscles. Sliding in a hindquarter stop, they dismounted and quickly led their horses inside the first jacal to take cover.

A high-powered bullet struck the soft adobe and exploded into a cloud of dust. The whine of the long-range rifle rang across the countryside.

"We did some good thinking getting here," Chet said, realizing how close they'd come to becoming victims.

"What should we do now?"

"Keep your head down. They're a long ways away. That shot came from way over east on the hillside, I imagine."

"Holy shit! That far?"

"Watch your language. Being bushwhacked is no call for cussing."

"I've heard my dad say—"

"I don't care—ten-year-old boys aren't supposed to cuss around grown-ups."

"Who can I cuss around?"

"The dog, but better be sure no grown-up hears you."

What was he doing anway? Dodging bullets with a ten-year-old freckle-faced boy. Heck was not a grown-up, though at times Chet expected that from him. This Reynolds feud had become more than out of hand. It had reached a serious enough point where he needed to put a stop to it all.

"We going to wait him out?" Heck asked as they squatted inside the roofless jacal.

"Let them take a chance. Sometimes, ambushers get careless when you don't fight back. They think they've won and then swagger into range to see all the damage so they can brag on it."

"You think they'll do that?"

"That or slip away. We ain't on any job needs taken care of so bad we can't wait a little and see."

Heck agreed with a confident grin. "You ever been in a feud before?"

"Not unless you call the Comanche years a feud."

"They were bad, weren't they?"

"They took a toll and this will, too, if we don't stop it."

"Reg says we'll have to kill all of them to ever stop it."

"I sure hope not."

"Why won't they quit?"

"They can't. They lost a son in the horse-rustling deal. Now the law's after Kenny for Marla Porter's death and they blame that all on us."

Heck wrinkled the corner of his nose. "It's hard for me to figure."

"Heck, I'm three times older than you are and it don't make sense to me."

The shooter blasted the wall of another nearby adobe jacal. The shot reverberated off in a long echo.

"What would you do if I wasn't here, Uncle Chet?"

"Oh, something foolish like creep out of here and try to get around behind him or get a shot at him."

"Why can't we do that?"

"'Cause I'm responsible for you."

"I can take care of myself."

Chet shook his head. "Too dangerous."

"I can tell that it's eating you up with us being pinned down."

Chet leaned into his sore back. "That's beside the point."

Another bullet struck the adobe wall.

"He ain't shooting at us, he's shooting so we stay put," Chet said out loud. "I'd say he's sent for more help."

"Can I go get some?" The eagerness was written on his face as he waited for the answer.

Chet rose and looked things over. They could lead a horse out the backside and not lose the cover of the front wall. Then drop off the hill into the creek, which would be below the shooter's view.

"All right. You lead Dobie out of here down to the creek. Mount him down there and keep to this side of the creek until you get to the ford, then ride like hell for the ranch."

"I can do that."

"Good, keep your head down and they shoot Dobie out from under you, scramble for cover. Tell your dad where the shooter is at so they can circle him."

"I can. I will."

Chet clapped him on the shoulder. The bone and socket felt too small for Chet to be sending him on such a mission. Nothing would do but to get it done.

With a pounding heart, he watched the boy drop off the hill leading the big horse, and soon heard the hooves on the gravel along the creek. If he made the shallow ford, he should be safe. Some crows cawed over the wind, and he recalled some close scrapes of his own with Comanche. Not much older than Heck when he had tangled with them either, but that was him, not his brother's ten-year-old son. Damn.

He drew out his .44/40 from the scabbard and checked the receiver. It was loaded to the hilt. Staying low, he moved back and dropped under the brink of the hill. Then using a bushy cedar for cover, he came back on his hands and knees under it, trying to see the shooter's location on the hillside. The wind was picking up and the whoosh through the boughs sent needles falling on him. With a strong smell of pitch in his nose, he worked the rifle in place until he had himself braced, and then set the sight for the height he'd need to ever reach the slope where he felt the shooter was nested.

A shot came from the hillside, and he saw a flash of a red shirt and then the round ball of black smoke. It took forever for the shot's ring to sound out. Dust exploded on a jacal wall.

He replied, rapid-firing the Winchester at the source, knowing the range was great and the wind wouldn't help. But a horse screamed and broke loose. Good. He knew he'd gotten close enough to put some fear in the shooter or his mount anyway. From the corner of his eye while reloading, he caught a fleeting sight of someone on the move in the brush after the horse. Raising the rifle, he had three shots to put in that direction. He laid them down and then retreated backward, expecting the next return bullets from the Sharps to be made at his location.

"I'm hit," someone wailed. He could barely hear the cry over the wind. "Somebody help me."

He'd help him all right—help him go to hell. More desperate calls, and no one moved in that area. It had to be a trap trying to decoy him out in the open for the shooter. He went back and found his horse, rode down on the creek, and circled around until he was behind the hill. Then he hitched him to a snag and scrambled up the steep bluff, making testing steps of exposure, then moving in that direction again. Nothing but crows and an occasional distant cow bawling for a calf.

Making Indian-like moves so he didn't stumble on the wounded man or into his trap, at last he spotted the horse. It stood hipshot downhill, and all he could see through the cedars were its legs.

Where was the shooter? Easing his steps, he worked his way closer, six-gun in his fist. Then he heard a moan and slipped around the skirts of a cedar. He found him lying on his back, hardly more than a boy. Scotty Campbell wasn't much older than sixteen.

"Don't reach for a gun," Chet warned him.

"Huh?" Scotty blinked in disbelief and moved around some to see him.

"Where you shot?"

"My leg."

"Who went for help?"

"Huh?"

"I asked you who went for help?"

"Kenny."

"Left you here to pin us down, huh?"

"Yeah. My leg hurts a lot."

"Aw, Doc can saw it off. It won't hurt much when he throws it away."

"Aw, don't tell me that." He looked paler at the notion.

"Where did he go for help?"

"I don't know. He said we had you pinned down and for me to keep you there by shooting every once in a while so you'd be there when he got back with help."

"Where's the Sharps?"

"I dropped it."

"Never mind." He'd get it later. "How did this all start out?"

"Kenny come by and got me early this morning. He said we'd go see what you all were doing and mess it up."

"Where's he been staying?"

"I don't know, mister. I swear I don't."

"You know he's wanted for murder?"

"He said he never done it. It was all lies that you people swore to."

"You see her naked body all hacked up?"

"No." The boy wouldn't look at him.

"It would have made you sick. Now as for Kenny, you tell him if the law don't get him, I will. He comes messing with me, I'll show him pain—the same kind he gave poor Marla."

"He said you were sweet on her."

"What else did he say?"

"Not much. He's real mad about you lynching his brother."

"I'm mad about him killing Marla. So we're almost even."

"Almost?"

"Yeah, when he's dead, we'll be even."

"Mister, my leg's bad." He made a pained look and squeezed his upper thigh.

"I know, but if it was me in your place, you'd laugh at me."

"I swear I wouldn't—I swear I—"

Chet squatted down on his haunches. "You go with him when he raped her?"

The boy's eyes bulged and his face looked ashen. "No."

"You were there, weren't you?"

"No—"

"Who else was there?"

"Mister, I had no part of nothing."

"I guess I could let you bleed to death, or you could tell me the whole thing and then I could get you some help."

"All right, all right, Kenny said she was your girlfriend, or anyway you and her were having an affair. Said he'd caught sight of you going there twice when her old man was gone. We was only going over there to scare her a little, Kenny said."

"Scare her how?"

"Kenny said we'd tell her we knew all about you and her and would tell her old man."

"What happened next?"

"Then she got mad, her and Kenny fought. I didn't want to watch. He made me stay. Mister, my damn leg hurts bad."

"You rape her, too."

"No, I couldn't—I was too afraid."

"Who else was there?" There was something in the boy's hesitation that told him the boy wasn't telling it all.

"Just me and him."

"No, there were others."

"Mitch—" he admitted.

"He rape her, too?"

No answer. "Did he?"

"Ah-huh."

"He did, didn't he?"

"I said so."

"Felton there?"

"No, he had a bad toothache."

"Three, four of you?"

"Three of us. Where're you going?"

"Take the bridle off your horse and send him home, so they can come back and find you."

"You—you ain't—"

"Listen, you're damn lucky to even be alive." Chet jerked the bridle off Scotty's horse and talked through his teeth. "I don't know why I ain't already shot the hell out you for being there when they killed her. It's been tempting to me. But you can tell all of them, the Reynoldses and the Campbells, you're the last one I'm ever leaving alive that bothers me or my people."

"They may not find me—"

"Ain't my problem. Built a big fire." He slapped the horse on the butt hard enough that he went charging off the hillside and hit the bottom running.

Then Chet walked back to look for the Sharps rifle. Finding it and the boy's handgun, he jammed the handgun in his belt, carried the long gun, and went for his horse. Ignoring Scotty, who was calling out that he'd die, Chet caught up his own horse and headed for the house.

A few miles north, he met his own "family posse" coming toward him. He reined up and waved them down.

"What happened?" Dale Allen asked, joined by Reg, J.D., and Heck.

"Scotty Campell's shot in the leg back there. Just a boy." He shook his head grimly. "I sent his horse home for help."

"What else?"

"There was Kenny, Mitch, and Scotty Campbell at Marla's house the day they killed her."

"Aw, gawdamn them. Heck said there was a rider got away?"

"Kenny. He went for help, too." Chet shrugged. "I don't

want any more shooting today. The law can handle Kenny. They come back and find Scotty shot, they may back off. I could have killed him. He knows that. He's in as much trouble as his cousin is when the word gets out."

"What're you going to do with that Sharps?" Dale Allen indicated the rifle across his lap.

"Shoot back at them with it if they don't quit."

Dale Allen nodded and they rode for home. No one asked any more questions. Chet was grateful. He'd had all the warring for one day he wanted, and yet he knew it was not over. Not settled, and everyone in his posse knew it, too. They were a solemn bunch riding into the ranch.

Chapter 12

Chet planned to drive into Mayfield and pick up some salt. Susie wanted to go along to look for some more material. He hitched up the buckboard before breakfast. Told the boys to stay close, split wood, and fix saddles. He even asked Louise if she needed anything for her trip, which she'd postponed to see how things turned out.

Of course she declined his offer to get her anything, but at least she was wearing the poncho on the cool mornings over to the house for her appearances there. He wasn't sure she knew that the cape was his idea and not Susie's. If she did, maybe she wouldn't have worn it. His .44/40 Winchester was packed in the buckboard as well, just in case. He and Susie set out about eight. There was still silver frost in the low places on the wiry dry grass, and he huddled under a flannel-lined canvas jacket. She dressed warm and wrapped herself in a gray blanket. They crossed Yellow Hammer Creek at the ford and headed into the small village. Smoke from stovepipes streaked the sky when they drove into view of the cluster of buildings.

Inside Grosman's Store, Chet pulled off his kidskin

gloves and held his hands out to the radiating stove while nodding to the loafers sitting around on crates. Then he undid his jacket and let the heat seek his body while making small talk to the men.

"Sheriff Trent spent the evening here last night. Said he wanted to see you," Wylie Cook said, and then he spit in the ash pan.

"Where did he stay?" Chet looked around. Susie and Mrs. Grosman were busy talking at the counter.

"I ain't sure, but he should be showing up."

"Bad deal on Mrs. Porter," another added.

Chet nodded. They had no idea how bad it really was for him.

"Sheriff's been looking for that Reynolds boy. I think he's ran plumb off."

"If he was smart, he did." The conversation went on and Chet was barely part of it.

"One of them Campbell boys got hisself shot yesterday."

"How's he doing?"

"I ain't heard." The snowy-headed man leaned forward. "Anyone hear how he's doing?"

"He's over at Doc's. They said he was alive last night."

"You know anything about that, Chet?"

He nodded. "I shot him, and I will again if he ain't learned. He shot about six times at me and my ten-year-old nephew with a Sharps yesterday on my place."

"Was he b'ar hunting?" An older man got all choked up laughing about his joke.

"He'll think he's b'ar hunting. Next time I'm bringing them in feet first. Being shot at on your own land isn't funny. But I can fight fire with fire."

"Henry was just kidding."

"I know, but when they shoot at a ten-year-old boy with me, it ain't funny or a joke."

Solemn faces around the stove nodded.

"They'll get over it."

"No, Chuck, they won't. That's what worries me. Earl blamed me for his boy stealing my horses. Then he blamed me in court for Kenny murdering Marla Porter."

"I agree they ain't very smart."

Chet looked them over with a hard glare. "They'll get smarter or deader."

He left the stove and went over to tell Susie he was going looking for Sheriff Trent. His sister and Mrs Grosman were inspecting some checkered material off a bolt, and she looked up with smile at his words. "Be careful."

The cool air struck his face when he stepped out on the porch; instead of buttoning his coat, he started across the street for the café. With a glare of the low winter sun in his eyes, he could hardly see the man who challenged him with, "Byrnes, you no-good sumbitch."

The man was standing in the wagon in front of the spring seat and reached for a rifle. He even levered a cartridge in the chamber while raising it up. But despite his obvious thinking that he was fast, he wasn't fast enough. The Colt in Chet's hand barked twice and acid black smoke burned his eyes.

The man was struck hard. The rifle fell out of his hands, clattered off the iron rim, and he pitched headfirst in a dive that ended on his back in the street.

Chet's heart beat so hard when he swung around that it threatened to come up his throat as he searched the empty street for more of them. Cold chills ran up the sides of his face. Shaken, he poked twice, trying to find the holster under the coat to put away his revolver.

"Hold your fire!" It was the sheriff coming out of the café. His hands high, he looked all around. "Everyone put their firearms up."

Chet went over and squatted by the wounded man— Sycamore Campbell. He'd never had a cross word with the man before that moment.

"Gaw—damn—you—" the words came as the older man struggled to live. He had a heavy gray-streaked beard and hate-filled dark eyes. He coughed deep in his chest, and fresh blood came out on his plaid coat as he lay dying in the street.

"Someone get the doc." Sheriff Trent looked around for him.

"Why did you try to shoot me?" Chet asked.

"Ya hung the poor boy and then ya blamed innocent Kenny fur her murder," Sycamore managed.

Chet dropped on his knees and grabbed him by the coat. "Listen to me. You're going to hell knowing who killed Marla Porter. Kenny and Scotty and Mitch raped and killed her. Scotty admitted it yesterday. They did that to her!"

Sheriff Trent's hand fell on his shoulder. "Ain't no use. He's dead."

Slowly, Chet's hand unfolded to released his grasp on the wool coat and let the man fall back on the ground. His fingers were wet with the man's blood. They began to dry and grow stiff. He rose to his feet and nodded. "I hope the sumbitch heard me."

"You have proof of your accusations?"

"Go talk to Scotty Campbell. He tried to bushwhack me and Dale Allen's boy Heck yesterday on my land."

"He said a gun accident did that."

"He lied to you. I shot him. He told me yesterday that him and Mitch Reynolds were there with Kenny when they raped and murdered Marla Porter."

The lawman dropped his face in anger and defeat. "I was coming to look for you today. I of course haven't done any good with my truce. Looking at him over there, I'd say that it's escalated even some more."

"He challenged me and went for that rifle. I was looking for you."

"I heard it all in the café. Pretty damn foolish of him, I'd say."

Chet gave a loud exhale. "And I almost buttoned up my coat. This is my sister Susie, Sheriff Trent."

"You all right?" she asked Chet, then turned to Trent. "Nice to meet you, Sheriff."

He removed his hat and smiled big for her. "Under any other circumstances, Miss Byrnes, I would certainly enjoy this moment meeting you."

"Yes, it is a shame when you can't come to town to shop and not be threatened."

"Exactly."

"Drop by our ranch sometime. We'll treat you much more civil."

"I'll do that."

"I'm going back shopping. Don't get in any more scrapes, please." She left them.

"Ain't much we can do about him," Doc said, putting up his stethoscope and rising from beside the dead man.

"Doc, do an autopsy on him. We need to have a justice

of the peace hold a hearing, I guess in the morning. Chet, you'll need to be there."

"No problem."

"I'm sending for a dozen men I can deputize. I'm afraid this thing will boil over into a an open war."

Chet agreed. The Reynolds clan would be madder than ever. His life wasn't getting any easier. Sheriff Trent excused himself and went with Doc upstairs to talk to Scotty. The boy was staying up there after Doc dug the bullet out of him.

In a short while, Trent joined Chet in the Red Horse Saloon. Chet was standing at the bar, sipping on his first beer and still in shock over the first killing of the day.

The lawman gave him a grim nod. "That boy told me the same thing I guess he told you about the killing. Then I asked him why in the hell he tried to ambush you."

"What did he say?"

"Earl and Kenny told him to."

"What're you going to do?"

"I'm bringing Scotty before the justice of the peace tomorrow and charge him with assault and Marla Porter's murder, then take him up to Mason to sit in jail till the circuit judge gets here."

"You better have lots of backup to take him out of here."

"I will. I've sent for a dozen men."

"I hope it's enough."

"It will be." Trent wiped his mustache with a handkerchief after he sampled his beer.

"I've never been in a feud before with white folks," Chet said. "I fought the Comanche from age eleven on. But I think these people are insane."

Trent gave a nod.

"I better go find Susie and get back to the ranch. I'll be here for the hearing." Chet finished his beer and set the mug down. "When's your help coming?"

"Couple of hours."

"You want me to stay until then?"

Trent shook his head. "I'll be all right."

Chet wasn't certain about that, but he left the lawman and walked back to Grosman's. He needed to hire some men. But who wanted to be in the cross fire between them and the Reynolds people? It wouldn't be an ordinary job punching cows; he'd have to pay hazard wages, too. Damned if life didn't take some hard twists. He should by this time be married to a good woman and raising a family, building a ranch big enough for his own heirs—if he ever had any.

In the store, he found Susie, and loaded up her things in the buckboard. A young man put the salt blocks in the rig. They drove in the warming morning with the meadowlarks and scurrying roadrunners accompanying them back to the ranch.

"Any trouble?" Dale Allen asked, coming out of the house and picking his teeth over lunch.

"Sycamore Campbell went for his rifle and I shot him."

Dale Allen frowned hard at him. "That old man ran the sawmill?"

Chet nodded. "He's dead. They are having an inquest tomorrow morning on his death and charging Scotty with Marla's murder then too."

"You're thinning them out."

"Oh, brother, I'm so damn tired of all this."

Heck was on the seat ready to drive the horses to the corrals. "I'll unload the salt."

"Good enough." Chet waved him on, seeing Susie's things were out of the rig.

"There's no end in sight, brother," Dale Allen said, looking weary. "Louise wanted to leave in the morning. I'll tell her to put it off a day."

"That would be a good idea. I may go up to San Antonio myself next week and hire some hands."

"And turn this place into an armed camp?"

"It is now." He went on by his brother and washed his hands in the basin. Dale Allen went off toward the shop in his typical fashion to bury his head in the sand. *Armed camp*. They'd been living in one since the horse theft. And it wouldn't get any better. When those three boys were tried for her murder, things would only get worse—Reynolds and their kin would blame him.

His hands dried on the stiff flour-sack towel, he went inside, and the heat from the hearth felt good.

"Señor," Astria called to him from the kitchen with a heaping plate in her hands. "Do you wish to eat in there?"

He shook his head and moved toward her. "I'll eat in the dining room. Enchiladas?"

She nodded as if pleased.

"Muy bueno, gracias." He nodded to the girl. "How is the job going?"

"Well, I like it here. The boys tease me but in fun, and I love your sister."

He straddled a chair and set the plate on the table, then put his weathered hat down on another chair. "Perhaps you have a relative needs work."

"My cousin, Maria, who lives in San Lupe would like to have work."

"How can we send her word?" He used the side of his

fork to cut the rich-looking food layers oozing cheese and red sauce.

"I could send a letter along with you telling how nice you are to work for."

"When I get things straight, I will go and get her. Write the letter."

The girl looked excited. "*Sí,* I would love to have her here with me."

"I bet. These boys and I talk crude Spanish."

"Oh, *señor,* they aren't so bad."

"I'll put her on my list." Louise would be gone in two days. When she got back, she couldn't bitch about hiring more help since she did little anymore. Another girl might ease some of the load on Susie, too.

He'd need to go back to town in the morning. They'd need to check on their own cattle and be sure they hadn't wandered too far. Besides gathering his own, he wanted to shift all the grazers that they could cut out off the place and drive them beyond the boundaries. This feud wasn't leaving much time for anything that needed doing. Besides, he couldn't send the boys out in different directions under the threat that they'd be attacked. They'd have to sectionalize their jobs and work as a team.

Maybe take the three boys, a packhorse, and work one area. It had been pretty cold at night for camping of late. Those boys didn't give a hoot, but for himself, he sure wasn't all that fired up about sleeping on the cold ground.

After thanking Astria for the food, he walked down to the corral. He found Reg riding Bugger and plow-reining him around.

"We figured you wanted him broke," J.D. said, leaning on the corral.

"That's fine—he buck much?"

"Naw, but we've had his hind foot tied up and been getting on and off him quite a bit before we tried to ride him."

"Stout, ain't he?" Chet asked Reg.

"I think he may be the most powerful horse I ever rode aside from our work horses. Easy, Bugger, easy."

"He looks pretty light on his feet for a big horse."

"I'm surprised about that, too. How did he spook her out?"

"I think Neddy simply knew he was too much for her and sent him to us."

Reg patted his neck and made him walk around in the corral. "He ain't pretty, but he's a huge horse. I think he's smart, too."

"You boys don't get too much in love with him. I think she wants him back."

They laughed.

He went to his room and put some water on the small stove to clean his pistol. The new cartridge models were easier to clean than the powder-ball models he grew up with, and he sure liked the new ones better. Much easier to reload on the run.

With the revolver disassembled and spread on the small table, he used a brush to clean the two chambers in the cylinder and the barrel. A good gun was only as good as you kept it. Then he ran a rag through the Sharps rifle. From the soiled look of the rag at the receiver end, it sure needed cleaning. The rifle's actions were about gritty from not being cleaned in some time, too.

He purged the barrel and the cylinder with boiling water, using a swab until the rag he used came clean. Then he dried them and lightly oiled everything. With the .44 reloaded and on his hip again, he stood up at a knock on the door as he finished oiling the Sharps' bore.

"Yes?"

May looked both ways, then stepped in the room holding the small one. "I didn't come to bother you. I think that the doctor should see Rachel. She doesn't eat good. I think she's lost weight. Dale Allen tells me it is my imagination. That I worry too much."

Chet nodded. "I'll see Doc tomorrow and have him come by."

"Don't tell my husband I said anything."

"I won't. Where's Ray and Ty today?"

She shook her head. "I haven't seen them since breakfast."

"I better go see about them. They didn't come in for lunch?"

"No, but sometimes they get busy—"

"I know, but it's getting late. I'll see Doc tomorrow."

"Thanks, Chet."

He took the water off the stove and went to find Reg and J.D. He stuck his head in the door and found them reading *Police Gazettes* in the large bunk. "Those young boys didn't come in for lunch. You two know where they went?"

"No, sir."

"We better get up and find 'em."

No telling where they'd gone off to. But it made his guts churn. If anything had happened to those two—

Chapter 13

Coyotes were yapping at the moon. Chet pushed the horse up the canyon choked with towering live oak and cedar. With starlight engulfing the landscape and the temperature dropping off fast, the plodding of his mount made the only sounds. His concern had deepened for the two boys. Where and how had they gone? Reg and J.D. couldn't even recall them leaving that morning. They'd gone to mess with Bugger after breakfast, and hadn't seen the boys since that meal. Heck had heard them say something about Comanches—he couldn't recall.

Since Chet's late afternoon alarm, everyone had set out to find the two. Chet took the rough country west of the ranch headquarters. Without any idea in mind where they might be, he'd ridden up many blind canyons, calling out their names and wondering what they'd had in mind. An eight- and a six-year-old boy who lived in a world of their own without a horse couldn't go too far in a day.

Or could they? "Ray? Ty?"

His voice sounded lost in the deep night. They lived in a world all their own. Not that Susie, May, and the others didn't pay them any attention. There was a bonding between the two that he recognized as stronger than blood even.

Where could they be? It was long past supper. There wasn't much out there in the brush to eat, and they couldn't have taken much along in the way of food or Astria would have noticed.

She'd shaken her head and turned up her small hands about where they went. "They ate breakfast and were gone."

Susie and Chet had left for town at that time, too, so in the confusion, the pair had slipped away. Frustrated over his lack of success, Chet turned the horse toward the house. What had he told his brother about those two boys before they went after the horse rustlers? Find some time for those two boys.

He couldn't believe they'd run off. Just little boys. He closed his eyes and let his horse go home. At the house, he dropped heavily from the saddle and stripped out the latigos.

"No success?" Susie asked him.

"Nothing."

"No one else found a sign of them either."

"I need to be at that hearing in the morning." He lifted the kac off the horse and slung it over the fence for the night.

"We'll find them tomorrow," she assured him.

He wasn't convinced. When he went into the living room, Dale Allen was stomping the floor walking back and forth. "No sign of them?"

"None."

"I find them, I'll beat their butts."

"Dale Allen, listen. That's not the answer. That's probably why they left. None of us cared."

"Cared?"

"Cared. Those boys had no one to really care for them. So they left."

"Ah, hell, they're just kids."

"How the hell would you know? You talked to them lately?"

Dale Allen never answered him.

Susie came in the room and looked close to tears. "What can we do?"

"Look some more in the morning."

"I have some supper for you," she said to Chet.

"Thanks," he said, and followed her into the kitchen.

"Where's Rock and Mother?"

"Mother's in bed where she stays anymore. He went to bed a half hour ago."

"Sorry—I just had not seen them." Taking a chair, he dropped in place at the table.

"You can't do it all by yourself, Chet. I hope those boys are all right."

"So do I, sis," he said, taking his fork and without much appetite beginning to eat.

The little sleep he had that night was wrought with dreams of Indian massacres. Dawn, still no boys, and he saddled Roan. He'd shaved and taken a sponge bath. Dressed in a starched shirt and his suit—he wanted to make his best impression.

The crew was silent at breakfast, and he left them orders at daylight to look for any tracks they could find. Use the stock dogs, too. The dogs loved the boys—strange the boys left without one. Around the table they talked about nearby places the boys could have gone to. Half sick with worry, he rode for town after the morning meal. There had to be an answer—he considered getting drunk and trying to forget the whole thing. They needed to find those errant boys.

Deputies armed with rifles were posted on the saloon porch when he rode into Mayfield. The town bristled with people, horses, buggies, and rigs. No one was going to miss a thing. Since the Red Horse Saloon was secured for the hearing, Casey's was doing all the business. He went by Doc's office first and told him about May's concerns over Rachel's health. The physician promised to come by and check on her.

Inside the crowded saloon, he saw Wade Morgan, and the man waved him over to a group of ranchers drinking beer at the end of the bar.

"They're really hounding you," Morgan said with a concerned frown.

The others agreed with a nod. "We heard that the Campbell boy admitted they killed Marla Porter," Morgan said under his breath.

"He told me that he was there when they killed her."

"Those Reynolds boys have gone beserk. What's Sheriff Trent going to do?"

"They are having a hearing over the shooting yesterday of Sycamore Campbell." His answer drew some frowns of disapproval.

"That was self-defense?"

"I hope so."

"They're bringing the Campbell boy down and charging him for shooting at you," one of the others said.

Chet shook his head. "Must be for her murder. I didn't swear out a warrant for him ambushing me."

"Trent's damn sure got enough rifle toters in town."

"I think he expects trouble. He talked to Earl about a truce and said he got nowhere. That was his idea, to put this feud down, and I appreciated his effort. But nothing's going to stop 'em."

"There'll be four of them counting Kenny in jail or dead when this day is over."

"Make it five. Yesterday that boy said Mitch was with them at her place, too."

"Ah, hell. I can't believe anyone is that damn cruel and mean."

Chet agreed and refused the offer of a beer. "I better go over there."

"We're going with you," Morgan said.

"Boys, I can fight my own war."

"No, we want to show them that folks ain't taking to this bullying business."

"I appreciate it, but I don't want a showdown. I thank you all."

"You sure?"

"Sure as rain."

Several laughed. "That's sure."

He left the saloon and started across the busy street, shaking hands, speaking to folks, and went inside the Red Horse with a sharp nod to the armed men with rifles at the door. He took a seat, and several acknowledged him. It was quiet in the saloon, which was set up with rows of benches and chairs. Folks began filing in, talking in soft voices.

Gunner Barr soon called the session to order by the power invested in him by the great state of Texas. He rapped a few times on the table. "No outburst from the audience. If you wish to testify, see my clerk. But it must to relevant to the case at hand."

"Chester Byrnes, come forward." Barr rose. "You want to state your case?"

"I do, Your Honor."

"Raise your right hand and put your left hand on the Bible. Do you swear to tell the whole truth so help you God?"

"I do."

"Have a seat."

"Tell us your side of this unfortunate mishap."

"I left Groseman's Store—"

"Time and place?"

"It was about ten in the morning, yesterday. I started from the store to have a beer. My sister Susie was still shopping. Sycamore Campbell had parked a load of lumber out front here. I think he'd just arrived in town. He saw me and shouted something obscene. Then he went for his rifle in the wagon. He levered a shell in it and I drew and shot him."

"He went for his rifle?"

"Yes. He was not going for it to get down from the wagon. He was going to use it."

"Did he say anything else?"

"No, sir. When I shot him, he dropped the rifle and fell headfirst out of the wagon. He was dead before Doc could get to him."

"Was there a reason for his anger toward you?"

"Before he died, he said he was mad because the court had charged Kenny with Marla Porter's murder and it was all my fault."

"There any more witnesses?" Barr looked around, then announced, "Since both parties were armed, I am saying it was justifiable homicide. Case dismissed."

"Thank you."

"You're excused. Bring that Campbell boy in next."

A hush fell over the crowd. In a short while, they brought Campbell in on a stretcher and put the corners on some chairs. His condition had gone downhill and he looked pale as a ghost. Barr swore him in and began questioning him.

He gave his name and said who he was. Then he said that he had been shot by Chet Byrnes during an altercation the day before.

"Were you shooting at Mr. Byrnes and his nephew on his own ranch?"

"I was, sir."

"Were you also at the scene when the parties murdered Marla Porter?"

Long silence. "Speak up."

"I was, but I never laid a hand on her. I swear to God."

"Who else was there?"

"Kenny and Mitch Reynolds."

"Did they murder and rape her?"

"Yes—sir."

"Why didn't you come tell the law then?"

"I was 'fraid."

"'Fraid of what."

"They'd kill me, too."

"What made them go there to do that?"

"They said that she was having an affair with Chet Byrnes."

An audible gasping went across the room, and then

silence. Chet could have gone all day and not heard that for her sake.

"So?" Barr insisted.

"They said it was to get even with him for hanging their brother."

"You know that being there was as bad as doing it and you not trying to stop them."

"I would have if I could have, sir."

"Scotty Campbell, I am turning you over to the sheriff to stand trial for Mrs. Porter's murder. I am issuing a murder warrant for Mitch Reynolds as well." Barr rapped the desk hard. "Court adjourned."

The Reynolds clan had not even shown up. They must have known that the Campbell boy was going to testify against Mitch as well. But they weren't through fighting— it had only begun. Two dead, a third in bad shape, and two more wanted for murder. It would be slim pickings around their outfits. But as he rose off his chair, he knew the feud wasn't over.

He wished, nodding to folks as he left, they'd never heard about his affair with Marla from that boy for Marla's reputation's sake. But if it brought her killers to justice, then he had a tough enough hide to deal with the rest. The two missing boys were on his mind when he rode out of town. Short-loping the big roan, he made a record trip back home.

Heck ran out and took his horse. "They're all right. Scared 'em good. They were down on Yellow Hammer last night and got lost, so they denned up."

"Thank God."

"How did things go today?"

"They indicted Mitch today for her murder and took

Scotty off to Mason to stand trial for it, too. He don't look good. He might not survive that wound."

"What about your case?"

"Justified." He nodded and thanked the boy.

Susie ran out and hugged him. "They're fine. Reg found them right after you left."

"Good, I worried all day. The Campbell boy let the cat out of the bag. Said they got after her to hurt me. I sure could have left that unsaid. But they did swear out a warrant for Mitch, and sent Scotty to Mason to stand trial for her murder."

She nodded. "That's important."

"What's for supper?" He slung his arm over her shoulder.

"Oh, some beef roast, potatoes, and cold biscuits."

"Sounds good. Reynolds people weren't there in court." He looked around at the end of the winter-shortened day. There would be plenty to do and he needed it lined up.

The little ones had been headed off toward bed earlier, so he didn't get a chance to speak to them. He'd do that some other time. Astria was washing dishes, and smiled at him.

He talked to Susie and ate his food slowly. Blasted feud had him off course; he felt like a derailed railroad train scattered out all over the country. In the morning, he was sending Dale Allen and the three boys to get some of those drifting stock off their grass. It would take some hard riding and lots of time, but if the drifters ate up all his feed before spring break, he'd be in trouble.

Someday, there would be fences—he dreaded them. He had enough fences as it was, but someday, they'd have to fence all their range and who'd need a cowboy?

"You talk to anyone?" she asked.

"Morgan and few others. They don't understand this Reynolds-Campbell deal either, and it keeps getting worse."

She clapped his arm. "Do you miss her?"

He nodded between bites. Then he looked around to be certain they were alone and lowered his voice. "She was going to leave him and get a divorce." There, it was out, and he damn sure couldn't swallow.

Chapter 14

The next day, he sent his hands under Dale Allen south to sort cattle out—except for Reg, who he left to guard the place. Then he and Susie drove Louise to Mason so she could catch the mail wagon the next day. Her trunk in the back, she sat on it in her new poncho, which she wore against the chilly wind. She also wore one of her late husband's felt hats with a chin string against the wind. Straight-backed, she endured the ride, obviously anxious to see her long-separated kin and the old South that she remembered.

The four-hour drive ended with her taking a room for the night at the Sutter House. Then they had lunch with her at a small German café, and made ready to leave for home.

"Have a nice trip," Chet said as Susie and Louise hugged.

"Oh, I will. I am sure that to be back in civilization shall be a large treat. You two be careful going home. I will inform you of my future plans after I look over the opportunities in Shreveport."

"That would be fine," Chet said, grateful for a calm separation.

They went out and climbed on the buckboard and headed for the ranch.

"You think she'll be shocked at what she finds?" Susie asked.

"Yes. Her image of the South with slavery is very different than it is there today."

"What about our brother and her?"

He closed his eyes as the thin wheels sliced through a shallow ford, spraying water. The yellow cottonwood leaves still clung in places to the limbs and spun in the wind. What could he say?

"I'm not certain about anything. When he lost Nancy, I think he lost a lot inside. He rushed out and courted, then quickly married May, and somehow she didn't fill that void. His boys remind him so much of Nancy that he ignores them."

"Will it ever get any better?"

"Dale Allen will have to find himself."

"May won't divorce him. She can't go home. She told me that it would kill her to fail as a wife."

He clucked to the team, which started up the long hill. "What if Uncle Mark came home one day?"

"Oh, you don't think he's dead?" She frowned hard at him.

"I'm not certain of anything. Just don't be surprised at anything that happens."

"I won't."

"I'm hiring some more hands. Leaving Reg there in charge worries me. He's a good boy, but he's never shot a man. That's not easy. Knowing when to pull the trigger is a problem, too."

She put a hand on top of her flat-crown Western hat and tightened the string under her chin against the wind. "You think we'll have to kill more of them?"

"What I think doesn't matter, sis. They aren't through feuding. They could be watching for us to leave, too."

"I can tell you're concerned to get back today."

He nodded.

"You had that talk with Kathren Hines yet?"

He shook his head and forced a grin. "I think she found out all she wanted to know that day she asked me if I'd hung her husband."

"Oh, she'll have cattle to send to market, I'm certain. With him gone, she might even need some help in that matter."

He glanced over at her. "You know it roils my guts just being around her to this day. And I have never bothered her in the same way."

"You don't know."

"You can tell in minutes if you're connecting with someone. What about your fella?"

"He's nice. He's polite. He knows about my job at the ranch and respects it. I think he's more there to have a dance partner than a real partner. He's bashful and this way, he doesn't have to ask other girls to dance who might decline him."

Chet laughed aloud. "I thought the war would be over and I could go ride over the hill. Then the Comanche got worse. I wanted to ride to where the sunset goes and see the ocean, but I couldn't leave. I've never been a damn boy. Oh, I've been a fool all right several times, but I lack something in my life—I'd hoped once that Marla might fill in that gap and make me feel more satisfied with my place."

"Oh, you'll find someone."

Stopped on the high point to let the horses catch their

breath, he looked over the pale winter hills. He didn't in any way feel certain about that notion—*find someone.*

"Let me down," she said.

He helped her off and she disappeared behind a cedar. It bothered her some, he knew, that Ryan Thomas Stanton was almost two years younger than she was. Not unusual on the frontier. Age wasn't much of a factor in matching people, and Ryan acted mature. But Chet felt that either she couldn't leave her job as caretaker of their folks, or Ryan just wasn't the right one for her.

Squatted in the warming afternoon sun beside the wagon, he nodded when she came swinging back through the waving brown grass in her pretty blue dress. A man could do a lot worse than marry his sister. He wouldn't know what to do without her—they better hurry back. Maybe Doc had come by to check on Rachel. He hoped the physician had some answers that would settle May's concern and improve the child's health.

The dogs barked at their approach, and that made Chet feel better. Dogs barking meant there hadn't been much to upset them. They were in their place. He reined up and Heck came running out.

"Get her off okay? I'll put them up, Uncle Chet."

"Yes, she'll be on her way in the morning. Thanks. Any trouble?"

"Naw. We cut out several head today and sent them south."

"Good."

Astria had supper about ready. May smiled at them, then checked on her oven with the little one on her other arm. Susie took over for her and Chet poured himself some coffee.

"Doc came by and checked Rachel today," May said.

"He know anything about what was wrong?" Chet asked.

May shrugged. "He said to keep getting her to eat. He said sometimes children had some problems that he couldn't find. Like they didn't digest food or had an infection he couldn't find or treat."

"He leave you any medicine?"

"Yes. It's an elixir supposed to help her appetite and thicken her blood."

"Where is she now?"

"Worn out and asleep." May shrugged. "She tires very easy."

"Your stepsons now know they aren't supposed to get that far away?"

May nodded and took a seat at the table to feed her baby. "They were scared when they got back. I think they know now. Dale Allen is going to buy them a pony."

"He needs to do that."

"What are you going to do next?" Susie asked, refilling his coffee.

"I guess I'll ride over tomorrow and see Kathren Hines and see if she wants me to take her cattle north."

"I think that would be the thing to do."

"I'm also going to hire some help."

The next morning, a cold bitter wind followed him. He wore his fleece-lined canvas jacket, collar turned up, and huddled in the saddle on Strawberry. Crisp leaves danced around Strawberry's hooves, and even the crows fought to stay in the air. At mid-morning, he rode up to Kathren's frame house. Wood smoke from her fireplace churned by the wind filled his nose when he dropped from the saddle and hitched the gelding.

Nothing looked out of place when he stepped on the porch, and a friendly stock dog caught up with him. He knocked, wondering if she was home. Then he petted the dog and waited.

Kathren cracked the door. "Yes?"

"I dropped over to talk if you have the time."

"I think we've said all we needed to."

"I didn't come over here to ask to be forgiven. I came over here on business."

She looked undecided, and then relented and said, "Come in."

With her arms folded, blocking his advance any further, she stood looking at her shoe toes peeking out from under the petticoats and skirt. He didn't unbutton his jacket.

"I came to ask if you wanted to ship any cattle with us this year."

"I'd thought I might look around and find another drover."

"That's fine. I wondered since we'd done business in the past that you might need some help gathering or whatever." He felt too hot in the buttoned coat.

She chewed on her lower lip and then shook her head. "I'm sorry about Marla."

"I'm more sorry they ruined her name."

"Oh, take off your coat. My manners are horrible—" She turned away and sniffed. "I'm sorry I wanted you to pay—but I had no call—"

He undid the thick buttons. "You had every right."

She held out her hands and took the heavy jacket and

hung it on the wall peg. Then he gave her his hat and combed his too long hair back with his fingers.

"We can talk at the dining room table."

He held out a chair for her and she acted embarrassed. "I'm sorry, I forgot what real men do."

"I don't know anything about that."

"How is your sister?"

"Susie is fine. She sent her regards."

"She runs the household, doesn't she?" Acting nervous, she clasped her fingers together on top of the table.

"The folks are in bad shape. Dad does a little, but he isn't there mentally all the time. Mother stays in bed. They live in the past."

"Sorry. I told Cassidy I'd send my cattle with him this year."

"I understand." While the man wasn't his choice, he'd not argue with her.

"Do you really understand?" Her blue eyes looked hard at him.

"I knew Hines'd cut his ties with you when he drove those horses out of our north pasture gate."

She closed her eyes and shook her head with a pain-filled expression. "That's hard to realize. You marry a man for his strength and you're married for over a decade. But you don't know him. I never knew what he thought."

"I didn't come to bring you bad news. I came to offer some help gathering your cattle if you need help no matter who you ship with."

"Thanks, I'll manage."

"You change your mind or need help, let me know."

"Thank you. I know coming here was a hard thing for

you to do. A lesser man would not have bothered. But I really wouldn't have felt you'd've done any different."

"Excuse me then. My offer stands even if you ship with him."

She wet her lips. "Maybe someday I can face this better."

"Don't worry on my part. You need help, call on me."

He rose and took his coat down. There was so much unsaid between them, but it wasn't the time or the atmosphere for them to talk.

"How is your daughter?" he asked.

"Fine, she's visiting at her friend's house today."

He nodded. She must be six or seven, maybe older than that. He buttoned his coat and put on his thin goatskin gloves. His hat was in her hands, and he nodded to her while taking it. She was pretty as always; she still made his guts roil. Afraid he might be tempted to sweep her up and kiss her, he made a grim face and left her.

The first blast of cold swept his cheeks, and he realized he had not gotten over her and probably never would. He put a boot in the stirrup and swung in the saddle. Why didn't she go inside? She was standing on the porch, hugging her arms in the cold like it was her obligation to see him off.

"Get inside," he said, shaking his head. "You'll freeze."

She nodded, but did not move to obey him.

For a long moment, he considered getting down and putting her inside the cozy comfort of her house. Not his job. Better that he rode on. He reined Strawberry around and with a nod, sent him moving out. But when he reached the high point and looked back, she was still on the porch. Damn, she'd freeze to death.

All the way home, the thought of her bothered him. Like

he'd left something on the table with her—what was it? Damn, if he knew more about women—

It was after supper, the folks in bed. The boys gone to the bunkhouse. He and Susie sat at the kitchen table, sipping some fresh hot coffee she'd made for them.

He went over his tale of the meeting earlier, and ended with him telling her about Kathren standing in the cold until he was out of sight.

"You must have touched her." Susie reached over and squeezed his forearm.

"What would make her do that?"

"I don't know, except your visit took her back enough to shake her."

"I guess I'll never know what she thought."

"Oh, Chet, she has had a tough time. She said she did not know his thinking even after being married to him for so long."

He nodded in agreement. "You know being close to her still bothers me."

"I know. But you did the right thing."

"Good." He finished his coffee. "I won't bother you any more."

She smiled, stood up, and kissed his cheek. "We still have each other."

"Yes. And we're going to the dance Saturday night at the schoolhouse, too."

She frowned at him with concern. "Do we dare?"

"They aren't scaring me out of living."

She agreed and he left for his room. He was still thinking about the figure of Kathren standing on the porch watching him ride away. Damn.

Chapter 15

He drove up to the ranch that morning in a cart with a snowy-muzzled old mule powering it. His face hidden behind a full reddish beard, he sat on the cracked leather seat and nodded at Chet.

"My name's Matt Green. I heard you were headed for Kansas and might need a cook."

"What can I do for you?"

"I was looking for that job."

The man was in his forties. Appeared to be no stranger to work, and when he climbed down and swung his left leg, Chet could tell he was a cripple.

"I can't run a footrace, but I can cook, set broken bones, and make a team of mules head out."

"Who've you been north with?"

"Staver boys, Circle T. I went north with Howard Carr last year."

"He not going this year?"

"No, he got killed in Abilene last year."

Chet frowned at the man. "I saw him up there alive before I left for home."

"So did I, but some gambler named Riggins shot him. His widow's got her a new man and I didn't cotton to him."

"What's his name?"

"Yarnell."

"Logan Yarnell?" That worthless loudmouth wouldn't suit him to work for either.

"That's him."

"I reckon I can use you. We've had some trouble with some folks and it might get kinda tight around here."

"Tight?"

"Earl Reynolds and the Campbell clan have made it a feud."

"I ride for the brand."

"Get your gear."

"I got it here." He spread his hand over the cart.

"Come on and meet my sis Susie. The folks are little vexed, so don't mind them. My brother Dale Allen and the boys will be in tonight. They've been sorting cattle off our land."

"What shape's the chuck wagon in?"

"My brother's spent hours working on the hardware. Painting it. I'd say it was good as any ever rolled north, but you inspect it. He keeps it under cover when we're home. Down in the last barn. Come in now and meet Susie."

They drank fresh coffee and Susie laughed with them. Matt Green satisfied Chet that he'd fit in. Rock came by and shook his head. The old man hadn't been able to ride with the boys for several years. "You ain't smart joining this outfit."

Then Rock ambled off and Matt said after him, "Sounds like an outfit needs me, Mr. Byrnes."

Rock never answered him.

"You have any good dessert recipes that you'd share?" Susie asked, refilling their cups.

"I can take oatmeal and make a mean pecan pie."

"I want to learn that one," Susie said, and smiled.

"We'll get together and make some."

Chet was wondering who else he could hire. "Know any good boys that won't work for your ex-boss worth a hoot?"

"Berry, Pinky, and Stovepipe were sure getting restless listening to that damn loudmouth telling them what to do. They ain't point riders, but they're sure enough hands in a storm or stampede."

"How would you get word to them?"

"I'd go over there and tell them they can find work here."

"Hold that off till next week. Some of us plan to go to the dance Saturday night and I'd like you to stick around here and guard things."

"Makes me no difference. I ain't much on dancing with this stiff leg anyway." Matt laughed aloud. "I'm here for the ride with you."

"I'll show you the bunkhouse and you can put your things up. These girls ring the bell for meals."

"Maybe I could help them?"

"Lord knows, they won't turn down help."

He showed the bunkhouse to the new trail drive cook. It was early to have him on the payroll, but he needed the extra guard as well. After lunch, Chet shod Strawberry and Sam Bass. Most horses in the cavy didn't need to be shod because they weren't ridden enough. But the horses he grained he kept shod since they got the most usage. His back complained afterward, but he felt satisfied he'd done something that day—hired Matt and fixed two horses.

The cowboys and Dale rode in before Susie rang the supper bell and dismounted heavily. Dale began stripping out the latigos. "We moved several head today. There's lots of 'em out there eating our grass."

"We'll just work on it. You know we can't leave with the herd and have all this feud going on."

"I've been wondering about that."

Time to break the news to his brother. "I want you to take the herd north this time."

Dale Allen shrugged, "Guess I can find my way."

"I'm not worried about you finding it. I'm more worried if them boys'll work for you."

"Huh?"

"Being a cattle drive boss ain't the same as ordering slaves around. Don't tell them to do something you can do. You'll in time earn their confidence, and then they'll do those things for you without being asked."

"I've got to hold my temper is what you're getting at?"

"Part of it, and you can't go hide in the shop when things close in on you up there." He tossed his head toward the house.

Susie's bell was ringing for supper.

"I guess you made it plain enough for me," said Dale Allen.

"I just want you to make it. You know how important these drives are to everyone. Making a profit is only part of it."

Dale Allen looked around and, satisfied the boys had gone on, said, "Thanks for giving Louise the money to go home. She needed to go see it for herself."

Chet bit his tongue and saved his answer for another day. *You need to stop your damn affair with her.* He nodded and went on. "Oh, I hired a cook today. A fella named Matt Green who knows the way."

"Good. I may need lots of help getting up there."

Chet shook his head. "Follow that old North Star. Kansas ain't that far."

They went on to supper. The meal was topped off with Matt's oatmeal pie, and the boys all agreed it was larruping good. Dale Allen even agreed.

Chet held everyone up when they finished. "Dale Allen and I have talked it over. Due to this feud and all its implications, he's going to take the herd north for the ranch this spring. I want everyone to pitch in and make it a big success."

The reassuring head bobs around the room made him feel better. He'd see as time went on how successful it looked. A good crew had to be a well-knit outfit, and it started with the trail boss down through the cook's helper.

"This Saturday we're going to the schoolhouse dance. I expect trouble, but they aren't going to bully us out of living our lives."

"Will they be there?" Reg asked.

"It's a free country."

Reg nodded that he understood.

"Matt's staying here. Any others?"

"I'll stay," Dale Allen said.

"You two should handle it." The others faded out of the room, and soon only Astria and Susie were left washing dishes. Chet sipped on his coffee.

"Dale Allen act satisfied about getting the trail boss job?" Susie asked.

"I think he wanted a chance to show his leadership."

"He should do all right."

"He's been getting on better with the boys, sorting out the strays."

"You certain it's safe for us to go to the dance?"

"Safe? Are our lives ever going to be safe?"

Susie frowned at him. "Is this a curse that goes on and on?"

Chet slowly nodded. "I believe it is."

The next morning, they rushed around loading the wagon, currying down the big mares, and the whole place was in action. The buckboard team was brushed down and harnessed, too.

"Those are some big mares," Matt said, admiring them.

"They're bred to a mammoth jack. They've been raising our mules we use on the drive to haul the chuck wagon and to farm with. We keep over a dozen of them."

"I wondered what you drove up there."

"Two teams of mules. They're ten times tougher than horses on a long haul. But those big sisters like to pull, so we use them in the off season."

"That chuck wagon does look new. He's done everything to it I can see."

"Dale Allen's a good mechanic. He keeps up our farm machinery. Those two mowers in there are his pride and joy. I bet when I start haying, I'll have fits with them and him not here."

Matt laughed. "Better find you a real mechanic."

"I'll start looking." Chet went to see how Susie was coming along.

By mid-morning they were under way. Reg handled the mares. Susie drove the buckboard and the rest rode horses. The Warner School House was on everyone's mind. The trip proved uneventful. Several others were already there when they pulled up in the schoolyard and Heck scotched the wheels with blocks. Tarps were strung despite the warm sunny day, and Susie served a light lunch of cold meat and biscuits made earlier. Things fit quickly into shape. A mesquite-oak chunk fire in the ring soon roared under the coffeepot, which was full of fresh water from the barrel.

Reg had gone off to find Molly and her bunch. J.D. and Heck went to trade pocketknives with some boys their age.

Ryan Thomas came by looking like a fox ready to steal a chicken. All dressed up in a suit and tie. His hair was obviously fresh cut when he swept off his hat for Susie. Chet could see the pleasure in his sister's averted eyes. Good, maybe she'd have some fun.

Neddy came by, and they talked about Bugger.

"Them boys about got him broke, Neddy."

"Aw, you keep him and ride him like he's your own. He's more horse than I need right now."

"Want to sell him?"

She wrinkled her nose. Then she shook his arm to make her point. "You use him. I ever need him, I'll let you know."

"He'd dang sure pull a cow out of a bog."

"Might break a rope, too." She laughed, then lowered her voice. "Them Reynolds boys done any more to your bunch?"

"Two are dead. One's in jail, and two more are wanted for Marla Porter's murder."

"I heard all about that. Sorry about your loss."

He felt uncertain about what to say.

"Porter never treated her right." She hugged his arm and hauled him a short distance from the camp, then made certain she wouldn't be heard. "Must have broken your heart to find her like that."

"I hated they ruined her reputation as bad as they did."

"She was a proud woman. You know that can get in your way, too."

He looked off at the bare hillside. "I guess it did."

"I'd've been proud if you'd've come and courted me on the sly." Then she gave him a small shove. "You were supposed to laugh at that."

And he did as he hugged her.

"Don't let old Bugger throw you," she said. "I've got to catch Susie and tell her about Maudie Slavin."

"What about her?"

"She's going to have a baby."

"Ain't she a little old?" He guessed the woman past fifty and most of her family grown.

"Ain't nothing like an old fool. Thinks she was twenty-five." Neddy laughed, and went up the rise to the wagon to find Susie.

He knew the young man with his back to a big oak was waiting his turn to talk to him. When Neddy left, he came sauntering over. The youth in his twenties stopped and folded his arms. "My name's Sammy Martin, Mr. Byrnes."

"My name's Chet. Mr. Byrnes didn't come along this time."

"Chet, you know who I am?"

"Not really. My boys may."

"I'm a swing rider. I'm a damn good one."

Chet nodded.

"My brother Marco's married to Earl's middle girl, Talley. I ain't married to no one."

"Put you on the opposite side of the fence from your kin." He studied the suntanned face for an expression.

Sammy shook his head. "I sure didn't fall in love with her. I'm looking for a job as a swing rider."

"Going to make it hard for you at home?"

"If you hire me, I'll go get my gear, tell my folks good-bye, and that will be it." The cold set of his blue eyes looked hard enough that Chet believed him.

"How many times you been north?"

"Three times. Once as a swing rider—one and a half. We were well up in the Indian Nation with Carp Belton. Johnny McCormack drowned in some flooded creek. I went the rest of the way as the right swing. Went back last year with Belton, but after that drive he took off with some dance hall gal and went to Cheyenne, I guess, and blowed them folks' cattle money."

"Left his wife and three kids destitute and took money that wasn't his with him." Chet shook his head. Belton wasn't the first, and wouldn't be the last to abscond with others' proceeds and then leave a wife and kids for a high old time.

Sammy nodded. "You need a swing rider?"

Chet nodded. "But I'm not going north this year."

"Huh? I heard you had several small herds lined up—"

Chet put his finger to his lips. "No one needs to know. My brother is taking it up there. I can't leave because of the feud."

"Your secret. I won't tell anyone."

With his hand stuck out, they shook. "Get your gear and come on to the ranch. We've got gathering and road-branding to do this winter. As well as driving strays off our grass. You'll earn your pay. But I have to warn you. They may shoot at you as quick as they'd shoot at me."

A smile crossed his handsome face. "They'll just have to try. Thanks for the job."

"You ain't even had a taste of it yet. You may cuss me before this is over. We'll eat supper about six tonight. Come by and get a plate."

"That ain't mooching, is it?"

"No, Sammy, you're part of the crew right now unless you change your mind."

"Thank you. Mister—I mean Chet."

Chet went on to look for his cronies. How old was that boy? Early twenties. Ryan Thomas might have some competition for his sister Susie. No telling.

He noticed the towering cloud coming in off the gulf. Warm as it was for that time of year, they might have a storm building. Time would tell. He saw Wade Morgan and some of the other cattlemen squatted down on their heels. The talk was all about a yearling buckskin colt a boy held by the lead.

"Get in here," Morgan said. "Brooks's got a dandy colt he says he wants to sell. Show him how light on his feet he is." He motioned for the boy to lead him off.

Chet pushed his hat back and studied the high stride of the young horse. He looked like he was walking on air. Head high, his thin black mane unfurled in the wind, he made a stride like an artist had captured in painting he once saw in a San Antonio bar.

"What's he asking for him?"

Jim Brooks, a bearded man, nodded from across the circle. "Two-fifty."

"What's the best offer you got so far on him?"

With a shake of his shaggy face to dismiss that notion, Brooks said, "I'm asking two-fifty."

"He should make a fine stud." Morgan said, and heads bobbed in agreement.

"Raising a stud is lots of work, boys. You can't turn him out; he'll get in a fight or get eat up by wire. The saddle horses'll pick on him and kick him. So you raise him in a stall, and then he ain't fit to ride two hundred miles 'cause he don't know how to rustle a living away from a feed box and hay manger."

"You've kept some before."

Chet agreed. "Now I'd rather pay the stud fee and let someone else mess with them feisty stallions."

"You ever see a better prospect? His mother can run."

"Who's his sire?"

"A Barbarossa stallion."

Chet knew that line of horses and how few outside horses were ever bred to one of their studs on the haciendas in Mexico. "How did you do that?"

"His dam beat a hacienda horse in a race. If I won, I got her bred to one of their best stallions. He was a claybank that they called Golden King in Spanish."

Rey de Oro. Chet had seen that horse once at a race meet. That was also the horse in the painting, too.

"A hundred now and a hundred when the cattle drive money comes back," he said, causing grins of discovery around the circle.

"I have had many expenses getting him to here. Two-fifty."

"I don't have that much money on me. Bring him to the ranch Sunday or Monday and I'll pay you."

Brooks rose stiffly and shook his hand. "Thanks, you will have a great horse."

"I'll hope so paying that much."

Chet wasn't certain, but he thought the boy was about to cry over the sale as he led the colt off. On his toes, the frisky buckskin was a handful. Brooks trailed him shooing the colt when he hesitated.

Chet hoped the family liked him as much as he did. Whew. Lots of money for a young horse. In the distance, he could hear Nancy Brant's laughter—he'd have someone to dance with anyway. No sign of the Reynolds clan so far.

Chapter 16

"He's a Barbarossa Colt?" Reg asked, sounding impressed as they ate supper.

"Yes. I think he's a dandy. They're bringing him to the ranch next week."

Sammy had joined them, and spent some time introducing himself to Susie like Chet expected. Introductions went around the campfire as Sammy took his place in the ring and J.D. elbowed Chet.

"Ain't his brother married to a Reynolds?"

"Yes, but he told me that he wasn't married to them."

"Good." J. D. went back to eating.

Chet shared a private smile with Sammy, who'd obviously heard their conversation. He acted at ease.

In a short while, Chet was dancing with Nancy Brant and she was telling him all about a new colt. They waltzed across the floor that was lubricated with cornmeal, and the notion struck him that he wouldn't ever get to dance with Marla Porter again. It had been his chance to hold her in public and they could talk about anything. More than likely, though, she would ask when would he come by to see her. Damn, that made him nauseated. Even as he danced with the tall carefree woman, it saddened him—a lot.

"You feeling bad?" she asked.

"I've got a lot on my mind."

"I bet you do. There's two of them dead. One in jail. Two on the loose."

"It's real serious business. They'll shoot at anyone, even a ten-year-old boy."

She nodded and then looked seriously at him. "You miss her?"

"I guess she wasn't mine to miss."

"No, Chet, she was yours."

"I doubt that."

"Nooo. I saw it when you two danced together. You couldn't hide the pride."

"Hmm. I thought it was a good secret."

She winked and wrinkled her nose at him. "A woman knows. A woman knows before a man can even think about it."

He thanked her and they parted.

The walls closed in on him. He sought some fresh air. Taking his gun and holster down, he strapped it around his waist. Out on the porch, the fresh air off the storm slammed him in the face and threatened his hat. Several women, hearing the thunder, hurried outside to run off to protect or cover something in their camps. The storm was fast approaching. He crossed the schoolyard for their camp to be certain it was staked down good. He saw a corner of the tarp fly loose, and began to run.

No way that could come loose. His hand went to his six-gun butt when he saw someone bent over the next one.

"Get the hell away from there!" he ordered.

"Go to hell!" Another part of the tarp flew up in the wind, and the figure with his knife drawn was headed for the next one.

Chet stopped, aimed, and fired. The tent attacker screamed he was hit. A rider leading another horse bolted out in the opening to get the wounded one. Chet aimed at him and the pistol cracked and he fell off his horse.

"Don't shoot! Don't shoot!"

"Who in the hell are you?" He jerked the first one up by the collar. A damn kid. Then he saw the flames behind the canvas. He dropped him and hurried inside to see what he could do about the fire.

He grabbed a blanket and began beating out the fire. Joined by others, he soon had it down to smoldering.

"There's two kids shot out here?" someone asked.

"They were cutting the tarp loose and had set the damn fire inside," Chet said. "Who in the hell are they?"

"Billy and Sally Campbell."

The rain began in cold hard drops.

"Get them inside," Chet ordered as his own boys fought the tent down by making a cut, inserting a rope, and retying it. More thunder.

"How bad are they shot?" Susie asked Chet. Ryan Thomas was with her.

"I have no idea. They had set a damn fire and were cutting the tent loose when I got here in the dark. I told them to quit. They told me to go to hell and I shot 'em."

"She's just got a bad scratch. But he's got a bullet in him."

Chet moved into the candle lamplight. The smoke still coming off the things they had set on fire burned his eyes.

"Who sent you?" he demanded.

"My Uncle Earl."

"Good, he can answer for this. Rains stops, I'm taking them to Mason to the sheriff and he can swear out a warrant for Earl."

"That boy needs a doctor," a young man said, sounding concerned.

"He'll get one in Mason."

"If he lives that long."

"I'm not concerned. He took on an arson job. He didn't care who he hurt or damaged."

"Hell, he's just a boy."

"So was my nephew Heck, and they shot at him, too. With a damn Sharps rifle. It's pretty damn sorry when you send kids out to do your dirty work, ain't it?"

"Let someone take the boy to Mayfield," Susie said.

Chet looked around. "Anyone here willing? I've got to warn you, if he dies, Earl will damn sure blame you."

"We'll take him and he gets well enough to travel, take him to Mason." It was the young man who'd spoken out before about his concerns for the two kids.

"What's your name?"

"T.R. Hornby. My wife's named Scrotter."

Chet nodded to them over the sound of the hard rain on the tarp. "You better wait till it lets up some or he may drown in your wagon."

The womenfolks had bound up the girl's arm. Dejected-looking, she sat on a folding chair wearing a sling. Maybe sixteen, but older than the boy. The whole thing turned Chet's stomach sour. He was down to shooting kids—but he couldn't tell who it was in the dark and they wouldn't quit.

"What did they burn up?" he asked Susie.

"Not much, some wooden spoons, a few paper pokes. It damaged my dry sink pretty bad."

"Lord, I went in here to fight it, I thought all we owned was on fire."

"Are you really going to take that poor girl to the sheriff?"

"Hell, I'll make her go with them and Doc can look at her, too."

Susie nodded in approval.

"Take her with you," he said to Scrotter, whose husband had already left for their wagon.

"*Ja,*" she said with her strong accent.

"Here's twenty dollars for your troubles." He gave her a gold double eagle.

"No. I can't take dat." Her eyes bugged out at the sight of the coin in her palm.

"Yes, you can take it."

"Vell, all right, but if dere is change, I give it to you next time."

"Fine," he said. Was that the kind of woman that Susie wanted him to marry? No, thanks. She'd be like a tobacco shop wooden Indian as a wife.

The wounded ones were loaded in the wagon and sent off for Mayfield, and the musicians went back and began to play. But somehow, the spirit and fun had been dampened by the incident. Chet sat on a canvas chair. Now they had to even guard the tent at the dance. It wasn't worth it. Shooting kids niggled at his conscience—why didn't they stop? No telling.

Susie brought him coffee. "Kinda ruined the evening, didn't it?"

"I'm sorry. Where did your fella go?"

"I sent him back to the dance. Told him I had things to do."

"You shouldn't have done that."

She shrugged. "I was out of the mood."

"Hell, it wasn't hard to get that way." He put his face in his hands and shook his head.

"Is this going to be our life from now on?" she asked.

"I don't know. Tell me something. Did it show to you when I danced with Marla up here that we were having an affair?"

Susie blinked and frowned at him. "Whoever told you that?"

"Nancy Brant did. You know she's my dance partner. I like Nancy. Her husband won't dance with her. Said she could see it."

Susie smiled at him. "A person can always see things better after they learn the truth. No, I never saw it."

"Just wondered." He went to the edge of the tent and watched the streaks of lightning dance across the Texas night sky. Kinda like their lives—fireworks going off everywhere.

Chapter 17

"You boys seen the mules down south?" Chet asked them at the breakfast table Monday morning. They hung around an old mousy-colored mustang mare and she seldom went far, but he hadn't seen them in some time. The notion struck him earlier that he'd have to pick two teams for the chuck wagon and he'd need some more teams for the corn planting in the spring. A job he dreaded overseeing, but it fell to him, too, since he was sending Dale Allen north.

"It's been a spell," Reg said.

"Well, after breakfast we'll go mule hunting." He sure hoped that no one had stolen them. The mules had never before left the country, but with this feud and all going on, there was no telling. Time to find the jackasses.

"Well, we never seen 'em down south sorting out those strays," Dale Allen said.

"Good, that eliminates that part of the ranch." Chet cradled the warm tin cup in his hand. "Split up. Take the west side today. I'm taking a buckboard down to San Lupe and get Astria's friend Maria to help Susie and May."

"You might speak to Don Miguel when you're down there," Dale Allen said, "You can tell him to line up the families that usually come up to plow, plant, and cultivate the corn as well as put up in the oat hay. You'll need as many as we had last year."

"I've been thinking farming. Thanks. Susie, you better go along with me. Matt can watch the place today and fix supper if Astria needs anything."

The bearded man nodded his approval.

Why hadn't Chet worried about the damn mules before? Too much going on. Dale Allen should have thought about them. Chet had to do everything around that ranch—by himself.

After breakfast, they left in the buckboard. The team set in a good trot. They went south, and the cool November morning made him turn up his collar. Susie was wrapped in a blanket over her wool coat. Frost shone on the grass and short plants in the low places. Maybe the past rain would help his oats.

There were soft places in the road where the buckboard wheels sliced into the mud. Better than dust anyway. They crossed some low hills clad in cedar and live oak, and he stopped on top of the third crest to let the horses catch their breath and set Susie down. The sun had warmed enough so when she returned, she folded the blanket.

"Going to be a nice day," she said.

"Not bad."

"You think they'll find the mules?"

"We're going to have to."

"You think the Reynolds clan is behind them being missing?"

His jacket unbuttoned, he helped her up on the spring seat.

"I have no damned idea. Since the Comanche war let up, I've not worried much about stock stealing, but hell, those three took the cavy in broad daylight. No telling about our mules."

"That will cost you to replace them."

"Yes. Good mules are high priced."

She buried her face on his shoulder. "It never ends, does it?"

He clucked to the team. "Never."

Late morning, they arrived in the village of jacales clustered around the small chapel. A large spring fed some ditches that watered small farm plots. This village had been established back when Texas was under Spanish rule, and these people had lived at San Lupe for over a century.

"I see Don Miguel," Chet said, and nodded toward the man coming from the cantina's batwing doors.

Chet reined up the team, and the broad-shouldered man smiled brightly at them and removed his sombrero for Susie. "*Mis amigos,* what brings you to our humble village?"

"A young woman named Astria who works for us said she had a friend here who would like to work up there, too."

"Ah, Astria. A beautiful girl. Her friend Maria asked me if you needed more help, *señor*?"

"My sister Susie says that she does. How can I find her?"

"Come inside the cantina and I will send for her. *Señorita,* you may come too as nothing bad is going on in there."

Susie shook her head, amused at his flirting ways. "I would not be afraid."

"No one would do a bad thing in the presence of such a lovely woman." He took her arm in his and led the way.

Smiling after them, Chet tied the team to the rack and followed them into the cantina. They had taken seats where the heat radiated from the beehive fireplace. Don Miguel had ordered her some wine and him some mescal.

"Will you need the usual families to work this spring?" Miguel asked.

"Yes, my brother is going Kansas with the cattle this time. I will be the farm boss."

"You will plant lots of corn?"

"Yes. Oat hay, corn, and Susie's big garden. I'll need six good men."

"When should they be there?"

"After Christmas. Oh, second week in January. We can begin plowing the corn ground."

"You are a good employer and do good by these families. There will be six hardworking men at your hacienda on January fifteenth."

"I'll look for them."

"How is your *padre*?"

Chet shook his head. "He has a few good days."

"I was a boy and I worked with him on building those walls."

"Yes, I recall him telling me about that."

They sipped their drinks, and soon a sniffling woman and a girl in her teens came in with the girl's things in a bundle.

"Ah, this is Reya and her daughter Maria," Miguel said, standing up and waving them over.

"*Señora,* this is my sister Susie," Chet said. "Astria is very excited about your daughter coming to the ranch and helping her."

"He is the *jefe* at the ranch where Maria is going," Miguel said to the woman.

"*Señor,* look after my girl. I will be sad when she is not with me." The woman sniffed into a rag.

"She will be part of my family while she is up there," Chet said.

The woman nodded and hugged her daughter. "I must go now. I can't stand to see her go away."

She made the sign of the cross and left, shaking her head and crying.

Maria was a short girl in her mid-teens. Her large brown eyes dominated her slender face. She nodded and swallowed. Susie took her aside and they talked in soft tones as the men finished their drinks.

Don Miguel ordered lunch and they ate bean burritos with fiery red sauce. Maria looked ready for her next adventure after Chet paid the bartender for the food and drink and tipped Miguel two dollars for his assistance.

"Your help will be ready when you need them," Miguel promised, and they drove back to the ranch.

They arrived home at sundown and the crew formed two lines. The showoffs all swept off their hats and bowed for Maria to go to the house between them. Astria was laughing so hard, she had to cut it off with her hands before she hugged her friend.

She introduced everyone like a whirlwind and they went inside.

"Find the mules?" Chet asked Dale Allen on the porch, where they waited to wash their hands after the rest.

"Four of them."

"That mousy mare with them?"

"No, she and the rest aren't around. After all the ground we covered today, I think someone stole the rest."

Chet scowled. "It's damn strange they didn't get all of them."

"These that we brought in are the youngest and wildest ones. They aren't even broke to work. I figure they got away."

"You know people remember mules. Whoever took them left a trail, and I'd bet they also took that mousy mare."

Dale Allen shrugged. "They could be clear to California by now."

"I'm going find them."

"Sure, go ahead and do that while we're in a bloody feud. Trying to get ready to make a drive and you're going looking for mules."

"I'm going looking for a thousand dollars. Besides, I hate a thief."

"Do whatever you have to—" Dale Allen washed his hands and went inside.

I will. He followed them into the house without any appetite. There was lots of excitement over the new girl during the meal, and she blushed often as she helped to serve and refill cups with coffee. But Chet saw she also enjoyed the attention despite her discomfort.

After supper, the crew drifted away. Chet went in the kitchen and had a last cup of coffee. The two hired girls were busy washing dishes and jabbering like crows in Spanish. Susie tidied up things.

"Well, you must have something on your mind," she said, slipping into the chair opposite him.

"Mules." He shook his head in disgust. "I'm going to have to go search for them."

"Taking anyone with you?"

"Much work as there is here, I better not."

Her blue eyes stared a hole in him. "I guess if they shoot you, they would bury you someplace."

"Thanks for thinking about me."

She laughed and then reached over to tousle his hair. "You be damned careful."

"I will. I'll need a batching kit in the morning."

"I think we can do that. Can't we, girls?"

They both turned from the dishes, smiled, and agreed.

He went on to the bunkhouse, making plans. When he lit the lamp in his room, he heard someone coming down the hall.

"Did you decide to go look for them jackasses in the morning?" Matt asked, scratching the whiskers on his jaw with the ball of his thumb.

"Plan to. You want to go?"

"I thought I'd offer. I ain't doing much for my pay here."

"Be lots of riding."

"I think I can stand it."

"I'd appreciate it."

"I'll be ready. Pick me an easy horse. I ain't much on buckers with this leg."

"I savvy that. See you in the morning."

Dawn came early, and Chet caught Reg and J. D. before they left for breakfast. "Saddle Strawberry for me. Put a packsaddle on that black we used. He leads good. And catch Dobie for Matt."

"I've got my own saddle and pads," Matt said, lugging it along with his limp.

"Get it from him, J.D.," Reg said. "We'll bring them up to the house."

Chet tossed him his bedroll with his heavy coat wrapped in it, and nodded. "Thanks."

"You own a thick coat?" he asked Matt as they were going to the house.

"I got one."

"Better get it. It may be cold or hot where we're going."

"Sure."

"We've got rifles."

"Good. I got this cap-buster." He clapped the revolver on his hip as he walked stiff-legged toward the house.

"I may take that Sharps as well. We need any long-range shots, that might do them for us."

"I shot some buffaloes with 'em. They're amazing rifles."

Chet paused at the porch. The chill in the morning air snuck under his woolen shirt as he looked out the open front gate at the brown hill country. He hoped that all of this place was still there in one piece when he got back. *Lord help them.*

Inside, he stopped behind Dale Allen's chair. "I traded for a stud colt from Jim Brooks. He's supposed to bring it by this week. I expected him yesterday. The price is two-fifty. Susie can get you the money out of the safe."

"Kinda high-priced, ain't he?"

"Wait till you see him. He's out of that Mexican Gold stock. He should throw some great colts."

"What color is he?" Reg asked, passing the platter of fried eggs and meat.

"Buckskin. Dark points. Striped hooves."

A nod of approval went around the table.

"I'll handle it," Dale Allen said.

If his brother ever got enthused about something, he might enjoy living more. He was a wet blanket at a roaring fire. Oh, well. Chet pulled out his chair and took his seat.

"Where you going to start looking?" Reg asked.

"West by southwest."

Reg nodded at his reply and took up a flour tortilla to load with eggs and meat.

"Maria made those," Susie whispered, going past.

"They're real good," Reg said extra loud, holding his wrap up. "You figure they went that way?"

"Just a hunch. You boys work east and do some looking. I think we'd've heard if they were taken that way."

Reg nodded with his mouth full.

Chet hoped he was right. There was lots of country to cover.

The two rode out after breakfast. The black horse was in tow, with their bedding and a batching outfit, plus the Sharps rifle wrapped in a flannel blanket under the canvas and diamond hitch. Dobie was a dun horse with a little age and better natured than a dozen others, big enough to bear Matt in a long trot beside Chet and Strawberry. Fresh shod, the red roan would do to take to hell and back. It was noon when they watered them at a cypress box buried in a dry creek. The box was set down in the sand and captured the under-surface flow. The ranch had hundreds of them. Most of them Chet had planted in his youth. Each one took about two days to dig, set up, and be sure that they worked.

The cattle in the area were mostly steers and they looked edgy. Moved aside at the sight of the riders and then took to the brush. Some even threw their tails over their backs and ran off like a haint was after them.

A half-eaten salt block was close by. He'd remind the boys to scatter them farther out. Made the cattle range more.

In the saddle they rode on. Chewing jerky for lunch, they reached a small settlement west of the —*Ꮳ* boundary. A few jacales, some burros, a couple of skinny dogs, naked brown children, chickens, and goats populated the ranchero. Some women came outside and used their hands to shade them from the glare.

"Buenas tardes," he said, removing his hat for the gray-headed woman who looked in charge.

She returned the greeting in Spanish.

"In the past month did anyone come through here with several big mules?" He hoped his Spanish was good enough that she could understand him.

"Big mules?"

"Yes, big mules."

"Sí. They had maybe a dozen?"

He nodded to encourage her. "Did you know these men?"

"Bandidos. They demanded we butcher a goat for them and cook it for them."

"Did you know them?"

She shook her head.

"Did you hear their names?"

"Sí, Gill was the boss. Toledo was a Mexican. Napoleon was the other gringo."

"You know them?" Chet asked Matt.

"I bet his name is Gilford. Amos Gilford. Worthless outlaw. I don't know any Toledo. But I bet that Napolean is Napolean Thames. He's a remittance man."

"Ain't that a second son of some rich family in Europe living on a pension? What in the hell is he stealing mules for?" Chet shook his head and checked the sun. The warm winter day wasn't far from being over. "I would like to buy a fat goat and hire you to cook it," he said to the woman.

She blushed like a virgin bride. "I will choose a fat one for you, *señor,* and your amigo. *Gracias.*"

Matt dropped out of the saddle and stretched. "Sure beats me cooking it."

"I wanted to repay her for the information."

Matt lowered his voice. "I bet them rustlers did more than demand a goat from these women with their men gone."

"I thought the same thing." He waited until the woman gave the other three her orders. "Where are your husbands?"

"Down in Mexico working in the mines. We have no work up here, so they go down there and work for several months at a time."

Chet nodded. "Those *bandidos* say where they were going with the mules?"

"I heard them talk of El Negro once," the woman, whose name was Nina, said.

Chet frowned at Matt. "You ever been there?"

He shook his head. "It's a real hellhole on the Rio Grande. Outlaws and the scum of the earth gather there. Bad place."

"Bad place for my mules." Chet shook his head.

"We have some pulque," she said, squatted with them on the ground while the others dispatched the bleating young goat and began to butcher him.

"Oh, we could not drink her pulque, could we, Matt?" He glanced over at his partner, seated with his back against the jacal, his stiff leg out in front on the ground.

"Oh, I could use a little of it."

Chet shrugged. "Bring me some, too."

Nina was in her thirties and acted as the hostess. The other three women were in their mid-twenty or late teens. The youngest, Cherie, brought out a guitar. She sat on the ground and tuned it. The pregnant one, Louise, watched over the *cabrito* they'd put on the spit. And Deloris, the shortest and best-looking one, brought them the pulque in mugs.

Soon, Cherie was strumming a song about an outlaw horse. Her voice was soft, but it carried. Deloris began to shuffle-dance, her lace petticoats twisting under her denim skirt. Her actions made Chet forget about the mules and a place called El Negro.

Their pulque, a mild beer made from corn and sugar, took the edge off the approaching night. A warm fire reflected heat in their faces and made light. The women wanted to dance, and Chet obliged since his partner's stiff leg hobbled him. So he danced with them and they drank more pulque.

Their mesquite-roasted goat proved to be succulent, and mixed with tortillas, frijoles, and peppers, more pulque, and slow dancing, the night went by to the quiet strum of the guitar.

His head hurt when he sat up the next morning. Chilly air had awakened him. A hint of a woman's musk was in his nose. The sun still wasn't up. He dressed quickly and pulled on his boots. There was a fire blazing in the pit, and he put a blanket over his shoulder and went over there to absorb some of the heat.

The women and several small children squatted there and used the warmth of the blaze, too.

"You are hungry, *señor*?" Nina asked.

He shook his head. The saliva in his mouth waiting for a cup of real coffee about floated his teeth out.

"Señor Matt gave us some coffee. You want some?"

"Sí, gracias." Had she read that on his face? Whew. Coffee was a high-priced luxury for these people, and he'd expected some scorched barley water as a substitute. Good thinking by Matt.

The steaming brew delivered in his cup tasted very sweet when he sipped it. More of Matt's generosity. These people drank sugar with coffee added when they had the chance. His partner hobbled on the scene and nodded good morning.

"These lovely ladies sure know how to entertain us, don't they?" Matt asked, lowering himself to the ground.

Chet shook his sore head in defeat, and then he snickered. "They damn sure do."

"Maybe you will come by this way again?" Nina asked.

"If we don't, we'd be damn fools," Chet said, and laughed.

Nina smiled, pleased, and spoke to the other women about it. They gave their approval with nods.

When the sun was up, his head was still almost too big for his hat. They left waving at the women and children. Black horse in tow, they rode southwest. For a place he'd never been before. A place called El Negro.

Chapter 18

The land around Chet and Matt proved drier than the hill country. Even the pear cactus slabs were black on the edges and curled from the drought. Any grass left was long dry and blanched by the sun. Many lifeless mesquite trunks stood black and twisted. Dead cow carcasses littered the way, still covered with paper-thin skin with patches of hair. Like they'd died and cured out all at the same time.

Horse skulls with pinching teeth exposed were among the dead. It was not a country Chet wanted to dally in for very long.

"Campo Muerto," Matt said in disgust.

"That what they call it?" Chet asked.

"Hell, I don't know. I never been here before and I ain't coming back very soon." Matt twisted in the saddle like he didn't trust the place.

"It ain't a place where you'd wake up smiling," Chet said.

They found a small *rancheria* in the late afternoon. Hardly more than a ramada, covered with palms fronds, and a corral with a well. A shy woman with a baby wrapped in the scarf that went around her neck stood under the straw shade and watched them ride up.

Two vaqueros in leather clothing and high-crown straw sombreros showed up next. They sauntered around the corner of the jacal with a hard look at the two visitors.

"Buenas tardes," Chet said, shoving his hat back with his thumb. "Is there enough water here for our horses?"

"Ah, sí, señor," the shorter one said. "You will have to draw it. We have no windmill."

"That's fine. My name's Byrnes, his name is Green."

"Gracias, señores. My name is Toledo and my cousin is Vargas." He swept off his sombrero and indicated the well at the side of the corral.

Chet shared a private look with Matt. Had they found one of the rustlers? Or was it a coincidence? Better not mention the mules till they knew for certain.

"What brings rich men like you to this poor land?" Toledo asked them as they loosened their cinches at the wooden trough.

"Looking over the country," Chet said as casually as he could, rolling up his sleeves to draw water up with the windlass.

"You like it here?" Toledo asked.

"Dry, ain't it?"

"Always dry, *señor.*"

Chet nodded, taking notice that Vargas had slipped away. This was not the same atmosphere as the friendly village of the night before. This was a place to get your throat cut. Such people swooped down on travelers like buzzards and cut their throats while they slept. He and Matt could have some real concerns at this place.

Chet worked the reel and Matt dumped the water he brought up. Toledo excused himself, and Matt stepped closer.

"Where did that other snake go?" Matt asked.

"I think he went for help."

Matt frowned.

"They didn't think they could take us alone."

With a hard look toward the ramada, Matt nodded. "I think that's exactly what these sons a bitches have in mind."

"I agree. We get our horses watered, then we'll ride on. I have no intention of camping here tonight."

"Good." Matt shook his head as if upset. "This is sure a tough country, and even tougher people."

When the horses were full, Slocum rode over and thanked Toledo, who'd come back and was lounging in the doorway. "Do I owe you any money?"

"No. God gave us the water and you hauled it up."

"*Gracias.* Your cousin sick? He sure disappeared once we got here."

"No. He went to see a woman." Toledo was lying, and not doing a good job of it.

"We'll be moving on. Thanks again."

"No problem. Stop any time, *mi amigo.*"

He would, when Toledo was planted under a cross. He started to rein Strawberry around.

"Sell me that great horse," Toledo said, tossing his head at Strawberry.

Chet shook his head. "Not for sale." Then he booted the animal after Matt, who'd already started off with the black packhorse in tow.

They'd made some good distance from the *rancheria* by

dark. The land was flat, covered with short greasewood, and a small rise to the west hid the dying sun. It looked defensible enough to Chet. Besides, he felt bone tired when he dropped from the saddle.

"Jerky all right?" Matt asked, starting to take off the hitch.

"Jerky's fine. After we get what we need out, let's re-hitch that pack and leave our horses saddled. Hobble them and then take two-hour shifts at sleeping."

"You sleep the first two."

Chet wouldn't disagree. He only used one blanket to wrap in. His six-gun resting beside his head, he went to sleep on the ground—he could eat later. Somewhere, a coyote serenaded the moon, the last thing he heard before he fell sound asleep.

Matt woke him up. "We've got company."

"How many?" Chet came full awake. "How long I have I been sleeping?"

"Four hours."

"Why didn't you wake me?"

"You needed the rest. I think there's four of them."

"Where are they?"

"A couple are west of us and more east. I've heard horses snort both places in the last fifteen minutes."

"They coming in?"

Matt nodded in the starlight. "Working up their nerve."

"Makes sense."

Both men were on their hands and knees. Chet eased his Winchester half open, turned it to the dim starlight, noted the cartridge, and closed the chamber. "We better spread out and give them a real welcome."

"My idea, too."

"You stay here. I'll go south about fifty feet. Are their horses close? We sure can't afford to lose ours."

"I staked them a while ago. They should hold."

"You're thinking now. Thanks."

"I wonder if they'll move in before dawn," Matt said in a soft whisper.

"No telling. You stay close to the horses. They want them."

"I can do that."

"Good. I'll move a ways south and try to locate them."

"Keep your head down," Matt said after him.

In little more than a crawl to use the greasewood for his cover, Chet moved away from his warm nest. Grateful it wasn't freezing cold, he turned his ear to the night. A horse snorted softy at a distance from him. That one must belong to the raiders on the west side of camp.

He removed his hat and raised up in the pearly light to try to see their silhouettes. Nothing. They must be coming in low, too. It had become a waiting game for them. He hated waiting—sitting around. Fighting Comanche, he'd learned how, but it always made his skin crawl and he felt uneasy in his gut.

At fifteen years old, he got caught out away from the ranch. Him and three bucks played cat and mouse all night in a canyon. He had a Spencer repeater and a five-shot Paterson like the Rangers once carried. The revolver was only a thirty-caliber, so it was limited to close range, and the .50-caliber Spencer used a rimfire cartridge and its range was short, too, but it would fire rapidly enough to stop most chargers.

All night he eased up the canyon, wanting to keep the sun over his shoulder when they charged him. Indians could be quiet, but not that quiet. He could hear them brush bushes or step on something dry and make it snap before they got off it.

When dawn came that day, the Comanche charged him—sun in their faces. But they were mad that a fifteen-year-old boy had been outwitting them. He made good shots, and cut down two of them with his Spencer. No breeze. He became engulfed in a cloud of black gun smoke, and the rifle clicked on empty when the third Comanche came with an ax screaming enough to stop his blood flow.

He drew the Paterson out of his waistband and jammed it in the redman's belly. His left hand caught the hand with ax as he fired. Snap—a dud.

Somehow, one-handed, he managed to recock it, and the pistol went off, blowing a hole in the buck's gut. The warrior slumped to his knees, still trying to use his ax on him. He recocked the hammer again with his right hand and shot him point-blank in the face. The buck fell on his back.

He'd sat there a long time, thanking God, weak from the exertion and the fear that he'd felt all night. On his butt, he reloaded the revolver, and noticed the cap had fallen off the cylinder that wouldn't fire. At long last, he put a new tube in the Spencer and sought the other two warriors. To be sure they were dead, he executed them by shooting each one in the back of the head with the rifle.

Their horses gathered, he rode back to the ranch leading them. His mother ran out to learn what had happened to him and why he hadn't come in the night before.

He got sick telling her about it.

This was no different than that night except, so far, he'd never heard these ambushers. He worked his way west.

Maybe he could find them before they struck. With the strong creosote in his nose, he made snakelike moves. Go a few yards and listen. Then he discovered a dry wash, and could hear horses snoring. Where were the ones they'd brought? He eased himself down in the draw and found the two horses. No sign of the men. They must be up on top and close to Matt by this time. The cinches were tight. He mounted one and turned him away. Leading the other, he went down the wash and up on top.

"Hold your fire, Matt" he shouted, and drove his spurs in the mustang. "I'm coming in."

The pony responded in a big leap. He rode him low, hoping to draw some fire. He did. From the left and right, pistols went off in the night. Bullets whizzed in the air, but by then, he was dismounted and holding the reins. They'd be foolish to shoot their own horses.

"Where did you get them?" Matt asked, standing with his Winchester ready.

"Down the way. I wanted them on foot. They won't be so damn tough and sure of themselves without a horse to escape on."

He used the reatas off the saddles and staked the horses. The shooters faded and made no more moves he and Matt could detect, though both stayed awake. Matt told him he thought he'd heard them leaving, but it was dawn before they knew for certain they had gone. Searching on horseback, Chet found where the other two horses had been. "You were right. They left last night, I'd say. You want some sleep?"

"Naw, I'm awake. Never expected you to bring in two of their horses." Matt shook his head and laughed.

"I am, too. I'd like to track them down." Chet dismounted

and checked the hoofprints in the dust. They'd gone south. Obviously, they rode double from the deep tracks of the barefoot ponies. Chet took two tries to remount, then swung aboard.

"That's not a cheap saddle on that bay."

"No, it ain't. That damn Vargas went and found their partners and they came after us."

"That's what I figure."

"We should find them ahead someplace."

Mid-morning, they crossed a ridge and spotted a flag flapping in the distance at some low buildings. Chet got out his field glasses and scoped the place.

"There's two horses standing hipshot at the rack. The flag looks like a British one. I'm not sure. Let's put our horses in that dry wash and bring that Sharps up with some cartridges—we may do a little hunting."

"I'll get a blanket, too," Matt said, leading off all the horses.

In a few minutes, he was back and joined Chet. He began unfurling a blanket for them to use. "See anything?"

"Not really. A woman threw a pail of waste water out the front door."

"Real interesting," Matt said, taking a position on his belly beside him. "We're two horses up on them."

"There are a few more horses in the pen. I can't tell much except they aren't my mules."

"They sold them a month ago, I'd bet."

"That's why they stole 'em. I savvy that, but I'll go find them if we can make them talk." He took up the glasses at some movement. "Here. Who's that?"

"Must be Amos Gilford. The big man with black beard Nina told us about. I've seen that remittance man a time or two. It ain't him. He's kind of a cleaned-up-looking ladies' man."

"You know, I ought to pop Gilford with this Sharps right now. I could do it to a Comanche, but somehow to a white man, it don't seem right."

"I know the law of being fair. Sumbitch would kill you any way he could, but you have these gentleman's rules."

"Yeah, like shooting those two kids at the dance. I've hated that ever since it happened. Damn them anyway."

"You play with fire, you can get burned. That wasn't a prank. That was pure meanness setting the tent on fire."

Chet shook his head. "Still wasn't supposed to happen. Let's leave their horses and Black here hid out and ride in."

"That should be a big surprise."

"Oh, they want their horses back and our packhorse as part of the deal. Since we won't have them, they might ease off their trigger fingers a little."

"Ah, yes, the order of gentlemen."

They rode abreast a dozen feet apart, advancing on the outpost—rifles across their laps. The sun was warming the air. Chet expected one of the mule thieves to try to get in a place to shoot at them—maybe on a roof or at the side of a building.

Three of them came out the open door and stood spaced apart. Black-bearded Gilmore, the slit-eyed Toledo, and a fancy-dressed dude in a ruffled white shirt—all packing irons.

Where was Vargas?

"Watch for the fourth one," Chet said under his breath, and his partner nodded.

"Ah, amigos, what brings you here?" Gilmore said.

"You tell that damn Vargas to get out here in the open."

Chet set Strawberry down. "I know he's trying to get us in his sights."

"Vargas, he rode to El Negro this morning."

"Listen, he don't show up right now, we're shooting all three of you."

"No need for guns, *señor*—"

Someone shouted with a crash. Women inside screamed bloody murder. Obviously, someone had fallen through the roof. It distracted the outlaws. They went for their irons.

Chet's rifle nailed the shocked-faced Gilmore to the wall. Toldeo crumbled face-forward from Matt's shots. Thames, with his hands in the air, was screaming, "Don't shoot! Don't shoot!"

"Take care of him," Chet said, the acrid smell of spent gunpowder burning his nose. "I'll get the one inside."

His rifle slapped in the scabbard, every muscle tense, Chet swung down. The six-gun filled his fist. He ran to the open door. In the dark room, he found Vargas lying on the floor being tended to by two young women. He pushed them aside, took the man by the collar, and physically dragged the moaning outlaw outside and dumped him on the ground.

"Where are my mules?" he shouted at Thames.

"Mules—"

Chet holstered his Colt, grabbed the shorter man by the shirt, and drove his fist in Thames's gut. "My mules that you stole."

"Don't hit me. Don't hit me. We sold them."

"To who?"

Thames swallowed hard. "El Paso Freighting."

"They got a place around here?" He kept Thames's shirt

in his fist and held him so close to his face, he could smell the man's perfume.

"They've got a wagon yard at Coyote Springs."

"Where's that, Matt?"

"South of here."

"I lost ten mules worth a hundred dollars apiece. That's one thousand dollars. You can pay me that or I'm going to hang you."

"A thousand dollars—"

"You get to thinking. I'm hanging you and them three, too. Alive or dead. If I don't get my money out of them mules."

"Gilmore has some money—"

"Get it and count it, Matt."

Chet shoved Thames toward the door. "Now you get me all the money you got in there. I'm getting my money or satisfaction."

Like a whimpering pup, Thames went to a large safe and dropped to his knees. His fingers trembled as he twisted the knob. When he raised up to unlatch the door, Chet jerked him back, fearing a holdout gun inside.

Satisfied, he nodded for the man to go ahead.

"I found about two hundred on Gilmore," Matt said from the door.

"Check them other two."

Thames handed Chet a sack of coins and then a stack of loose bills.

"There a thousand here?" Chet demanded, holding the canvas bag in his face. "There ain't that much, you and your friends will hang in two minutes."

"Wait, wait. I've got some bonds—I can sign them over to you."

His head drawn back, Chet considered taking paper. It could be worthless. They needed to count what they had. Matt had his take on a table, stacking it.

"Fix us some food," Chet said to the cowering women. "Make it good it. This may be his last meal."

Doe-eyed, they slipped away, nodding that they'd do so.

Matt jumped up and ran outside. Chet wondered, then heard his horse bucking and snorting—two shots, and Matt stuck his head back in. "Vargas got well enough to get on Strawberry. He went to bucking and I shot Vargas off him."

"Good. Let's count this money. Thames ain't got long to live either."

"Don't say that! I'll find the money—I swear to God I will."

They finally counted out 863 dollars. The bonds were valued at five hundred dollars.

"Find forty more dollars," said Chet.

Thames swallowed. "I swear to God I don't have any more. Those Grand Bank of London bonds are worth near a thousand."

"Maybe there, but in Texas they may be toilet paper, too."

"Wait. Wait." Thames rushed over and went under the bar, then set a jar of money on top. "Here is all the money I have."

"Is it forty dollars?" Chet asked, hefting the jar full of coins.

"Want me to count it?" Matt asked.

"No. Sack it all up and we'll call us even."

Thames collapsed on the floor with a sigh.

Chet stood over him and drew out his pistol. "See this gun muzzle?"

"Yes." Thames swallowed hard.

"You ever steal as much as a fence post from me again, I'll shoot your damn head off with this gun. Am I clear?"

Thames nodded hard.

Chet went and sat down at the table. He had the money for new mules anyway. At least he could go buy some more—what worthless trash these men were. That freight company wouldn't still have his mules at their outpost. They'd deny buying them anyway. He'd have to prove it.

Him and Matt had done well.

The women brought the food and it tasted delicious. Thames was still shaking, and refused their offer to eat with them. In the late afternoon, they left. Gilmore was dead. Toledo looked close to death, and the remittance man still acted shaken.

They took all four horses and saddles with them.

"I'm ready to camp somewhere and sleep for a couple of days," Matt said.

"I was thinking if we slept a short while," Chet said, "with that money I paid Nina, she's probably bought some corn and sugar and has a new batch of pulque ran off, and we need to get back there and share it."

"Hell, yes. Two-three hours, I'll be ready to ride."

Chet nodded. "You're a great hand, Matt. I'd ride to hell and cross any river with you."

"Thanks. But I'd never dreamed you'd get your money back or anything but some mule apples they'd left behind. Amazing, but it worked."

"Yeah, mule buyer, now you need to find the replacements."

They both laughed as they rode on. What was the name of that pretty girl at Nina's?

Chapter 19

The pulque was flowing. Cherie strummed her guitar and sang a song about the wild vaquero from the ranchero. Oh, Chet was dancing, his boots shuffling dirt as he and Deloris danced apart in the firelight, twisting and turning as the song went on. Her hips and skirt like a weeping willow in a strong wind. Then, with her skirt and many petticoats in her hands, she raised them to free her brown knees and her shapely legs to kick to the music.

Oh, what a wonderful night.

Deloris shook his shoulder the next morning to wake him. He half rose, looked around out of bleary eyes, and told her he wanted to sleep all day. That was it. She let him.

At sundown, he got up, washed his face in a water bucket, and wished he'd not drunk a single drop of the pulque the night before. But shortly, Deloris came for him, dragging him to the large fire cooking where a fat young pig roasted on a spit.

"That is your three-dollar pig you ordered last night."

He poked his chest. "I ordered?"

"*Sí,* you said, 'Cook me a fat weaning pig tomorrow,' and gave me the money last night."

"Hell." He reached over and drew her tight to him, then kissed her hard. At last, they stopped to catch their breath. "I must have. He'll be *muy bueno* anyway."

"Sí," she said, and they kissed again like it would be for the last time in their lives.

They danced and drank and partied most of that night.

Damn shame that she was married. He woke up before she did in the predawn, and he covered her good when he climbed out of her pallet—so she didn't freeze—her being naked and all. He found Matt drinking coffee, seated on the ground by the growing fire. Nina poured Chet some.

"Today we better get home, Matt. No telling what they've got into at the ranch."

"We better," Matt agreed. "It's been fun and thanks to these ladies here, we were able to locate those thieves and you recovered enough money to buy new mules."

Chet agreed with an open-mouth yawn. "Get our asses home."

"Food will be cooked in a short while," Nina said. "You two better stay and eat."

"We will. We'll go saddle our horses if we even have any."

"They are fine," Nina assured him with a laugh. "We have watered and fed them well."

"Them mule thieves won't ever bother you again," Chet said. "And I bet that remittance man don't either."

She nodded in approval. "Matt told me what happened."

"They got what they deserved."

Their ride home was long and torturous. A dozen times, Chet considered getting off his horse, laying down some-place out of the wind and the sun, and sleeping a couple of hours. He didn't, and late afternoon in a blustery wind, they rode through the gates and were met by a hard-eyed Susie.

"Rachel died." She hugged him. Sobbing, she looked up, swallowing hard. "May did all she could for her."

Chet felt a great knot in his chest. "Sorry I wasn't here."

"You couldn't have saved her. I just count on you." She looked around. "You didn't find the mules?"

"No, but Matt and I damn sure got the money for 'em."

He could see by the bewilderment written on his sister's face that she didn't understand. "I'll explain. Did you have the funeral?"

"We were waiting a day longer for you to get back, but it's tomorrow."

Chet nodded. "How is Dale Allen?"

"Stone-faced. He keeps it inside."

"We haven't ate since before sunup."

Susie turned to Matt. "Matt, I'm glad you're back. Come on, I'll find you both some food."

"Music to an old cook's ear." Matt laughed aloud, and then sobered. "I'm sure sorry about the little girl."

Susie nodded and holding her dress hem out of the dust, led them inside the warm house.

"Oh, yes, your new stud horse arrived, too, while you were gone," Susie said to Chet, and some excitement danced in her blue eyes "He is light as feather on his feet."

"Good." Chet nodded to Matt in approval, and then they followed her into the living room.

"You get them mules?" Chet's father asked, rocking in his chair by the hearth.

"As good as. I got paid for them."

"Who paid you?"

"One of the fellas who stole them."

"Who were they?" Rock asked his voice cracking.

"Some old outlaws."

"Them no-account sons a bitches," the old man swore, and retreated into his own world.

The next day, Rachel June Byrnes, two years old, was laid to rest at the Warner School House Cemetery beside her mother. Lots of food was brought in and set up inside by the neighbors, as was the tradition in the land. Folks from all over came. It threatened to rain, but only misted for a little before the graveside service. After Reverend Meeks's last amen, folks gathered quietly in the schoolhouse for the meal.

Reg and Sammy stayed home to watch the ranch. The rest all came. Dale Allen hadn't said much to Chet since he came home with the mule money. That was fine with Chet, but he wanted in some way to comfort his brother over his loss. Nancy had died giving birth to Rachel not that long before. Another knife stuck in Dale Allen's heart.

Chet felt sorrier for May, who'd taken the loss so hard. She'd done her share, and Dale Allen looked like he was no support for her. The day went on.

He learned Scotty Campbell still lingered from his bullet wound in the Mason jail, and the boy that he'd shot at the dance was doing all right. The two older Reynolds boys were still on the loose, but Sheriff Trent had made some surprise raids looking for them.

"You know Earl threatened Jenks?" Morgan asked Chet.

He shook his head, blowing the steam off his fresh cup of coffee. "No, I was down on the border chasing mules rustlers all week."

"On the road one day this week, Earl told him it wouldn't be healthy for him to send cattle to Kansas with you."

"That son of a—did he threaten you?"

"No, but Jenks' wife is really upset. She's deathly afraid they'll ambush him or the boys."

Chet shook his head in disgust. "Someone is going to permanently shut Earl up someday. And it might be me. I'll go by and see them. Damn. Thanks, Wade."

Where was Dale Allen? Chet looked around at the crowd in the building; he hadn't seen him since the funeral was over. Not inside. He went out, and decided to go up on the rise to see if his brother was still up there. He found him on his hands and knees, crying at the grave.

"Hey, can I do anything?"

Wet-faced, Dale Allen looked up blankly. "It ain't your fault. First he took Nancy—dear God—I miss her. Maybe I'll miss her all my life. Now he went and took her image."

Chet helped him up. The mist on the wind grew stronger. "You're going to get a death of a cold if we don't get you under cover or under a slicker."

Dale Allen looked over at him. "Why, hell, you're getting all wet, too."

I don't count. Not today. You're the one that counts.

Chapter 20

"I'll read everyone's Louise's letter," Susie announced at breakfast. "It came yesterday and they brought it to me at the schoolhouse. We all got in so late last night, I've held it until now.

"'Dear Family, I arrived in Shreveport in good condition. Train rides are not fun despite the amenities they now have. I found my father ailing and my mother teaches piano lessons to support themselves. They lost the family plantation to taxes and now live in a small apartment.

"'Chet, you warned me. But I was not willing to accept the fact that this is not the thriving city I knew as a girl growing up. Now I know. It is not anything. I shall return to the bar-C when I am satisfied my parents are to be well enough cared for. I can't wait to get home to Texas and see all of you. Tell my sons hi. I love and miss you all so much. Signed Louise.'"

"Let me see that," Chet said, and she handed it to him. With a quick glance, he passed it back. "Yes sirree, it's her handwriting all right."

Susie swished him with the letter and shook her head in disapproval at him.

He held out his palms. "I couldn't believe she wrote that."

Several chuckled around the long table, but they made sure Susie wasn't close.

"Matt's going to San Antonio and look for some mules for us," said Chet. "Reg, you or J.D. want to go along and add your two cents to this deal?"

Reg shrugged. "Don't matter. Either one of us can go."

"J.D., you go this time. You can learn a lot getting in on this."

"And J.D., if he don't like the mules we bring back, I'll say you picked those out." Matt snickered and everyone else laughed.

"Damned if I do. Damned if I don't."

"That's it." Chet winked at him. "You boys getting other cattle ran off?"

"We've been working at it," Reg said with a wary smirk.

"I think someone is piling them in on us." Sammy said "I've seen the same roan cow with a down-turned horn three times this week. She's got a YT4 on her hip. She's no coincidence."

"She's way off her range. That's the Rasmussen brothers' brand. They're south of the Llano River."

"We need to stop the pushers," Sammy said. "They ain't drifting on us, they're being driven."

"I'll see what I can do about that. You see any hooves in their prints?"

"We've drove them up through Comanche Pass and way down on Bressler's Creek so many times, it's hard to tell."

"Yeah," Reg said. "They about beat us back."

"Keep doing it. I catch anyone driving cattle in on us, they can answer to me."

"Uncle Chet, they must be doing it with dogs and at night."

"We can stop them. Let me scout some first. Maybe I can get a lead on 'em. We may have to fight fire with fire."

After breakfast, the three rode off, Heck, Reg, and Sammy, with three of their best stock dogs. A good working dog could replace two or three average hands on horseback. So they had the force. Each carried a rifle and a pistol. Chet was taking no chances.

Then he sent J.D. and Matt to San Antonio to buy some mules. Matt took a rifle in a scabbard on the buckboard dash. With his crew gone, Chet saddled a big bay horse called Jeepers.

May came down to the corral and stood by the fence. He nodded to her. They had hardly spoken since the funeral. She looked tired.

"How are you doing?" he asked.

"I know you've tried to do your best for me and I wanted to thank you. I guess I must face that my husband doesn't want me." She bit her lip and turned away so he couldn't see her cry. "I know you tried, Chet—but what am I to do?"

He went around and hugged her. "We can only hope he sees the errors of his ways."

"He has. It's me."

"No, May, you've done your part. Dale Allen has to find himself."

"I thought after she left—"

"May, be patient. It is all I can say."

"I'm sorry. Maybe after the cattle drive, he'll have some time to think about it and make a good decision. Or he may never come back."

Chet closed his eyes. "May, you know I'll do all I can do for you."

She sniffed. "Chet, you've tried so hard. I just don't know where to turn."

He agreed and jerked down the stirrup. "Maybe I can find an answer."

Downcast, he nodded to her and rode off. What else could he do? He felt boxed in between the two, and he didn't choose either of them. After his wife died, Dale Allen rushed out to get someone to care for Baby Rachel. He didn't pick a wife—in Chet's eyes, he married a nanny.

A few hours later, Chet bellied down under some cedars and used his field glasses focused on the Reynolds family headquarters. A few low log buildings, cedar-shingle roofs, pole corrals, and there were several horses standing hipshot at the racks. They'd been there for a while. The fresh piles of horse apples were all around them, like they'd been ridden hard the night before and left hitched.

A few of the men finally staggered outside and stretched like they'd only woken up a few minutes earlier. Tired from the night's work herding cattle on Byrnes land, no doubt. Even Kenny was there—the sheriff had recently gone by there on a good piece of gossip. Shame he'd missed him.

Maybe Chet needed to hire a bounty hunter? He'd never asked anyone to fight for him before. He wasn't starting now. Where was Mitch? Probably not far away.

Chet remained out of sight, observing them until they checked their cinches and rode off loudly laughing. Obviously, they were laughing about shifting more stock onto the ranch. Must be easy to gather them; they sure never did anything for their horses. Left them standing saddled all night, didn't water them, and set out again to work cattle with them. He hated people who didn't care for their stock.

He let them ride off to the east, and then he slipped back to his own mount. Tightening the cinch, he stepped aboard. Then he rode north in a large swing; he wanted to see for himself this cattle gathering and how they shoved the animals onto his place.

He found the Reynolds bunch an hour later, gathering cattle and driving groups of them north. In a short while, they had several head assembled, and were joined by some of the Campbells that he recognized in the glasses. They also brought cattle into basin from the east. Cattle the boys had more than likely been turning back. Several hundred head of cattle boiled up dust, close to a dozen rope-swinging riders shouting at them to urge them north onto —$\mathcal{C}$ land.

The short winter day was fast fading, and the Reynolds riders were making good time up the wide-open swale, and the number of stock kept growing as they picked up more. He followed them at a distance. They crossed the south boundary of the ranch, and these cattle were moving hard enough, they'd not stop for quite a ways.

His blood about to boil, he whacked the top of his saddle horn with his palm. That bunch would get their comeuppance. If it was the last thing he did on this earth, they'd damn sure rue the day they pushed those cattle onto his ranch. Still angry, he knew what he'd do. Reynolds had several pigs they were feeding out. Like most hill folks, they ran hogs on the range and when they got big enough, they trapped them and put them in a feedlot for finishing. Raised in the wild, even after feeding them, they were still spooky enough to easily run off if shown an opening.

Pushing Jeepers in a hard lope, he headed right for the

Reynolds' spread. Circling around, he knew he had beaten them home. The strong odor of pig shit assailed his nose. With a quick check to be certain in the twilight there was no one around, he rode out of the brush from the backside, hearing the pigs fighting each other over some scraps in the confines of the rail-walled pen. He tossed his reata around a post and dallied the lariat around the horn. He turned the gelding off, and it set his muscles to pulling on the post. The post broke off at the ground with a snap, and an entire section of the rail fence collapsed.

Those pigs needed no encouragement to flee captivity. They tore out like they were on fire. Whuffing away, they went straight for the darkening cedars, and weren't hesitating.

Chet shook his reata loose of the post, and grinned at the shouting he heard coming from the house.

"Them gawdamn hawgs jest got out, Maw!"

"Aw. Hell, Paw will be mad as a hornet! How'd they do it?"

He didn't hear anymore. It was time to leave. He put steel to the big horse. Jeepers cat-hopped up the steep hillside and reached the top. Chet reined up to listen. Those loose hogs were still squealing, "We're free!"

And going in four directions as hard as they could run. They'd be days trying to get them back, and all the grain fat would be run off by then.

He headed back for the ranch in a short lope. Those damn Reynolds riders had not seen the full force of his ability to fight fire with fire. This old crap they dished out had grown past turn-the-other-cheek for him. Next, he'd ambush those evening cattle drives and send those cattle right through the Reynolds house. When he was through with them, they'd want this damn war over with and done.

Susie came out when he dismounted in the dark at the house, and accompanied him to the corral. "You have any supper?"

"No, but I'm fine."

She shook her head in disapproval as they walked in the starlight. "I have food in the oven, but you knew that."

"How did the day go?"

"All right. They came in about four and had sorted out lots of cattle, they said, and pushed them east."

"They drove in a hundred, maybe two, tonight in the south." He stripped out the latigos and looked over at her with a head shake.

"What are they doing this for?"

"To make life miserable for us. I did some getting even this evening. I pulled down their hog pen and send maybe forty head of them wild devils loose. They'll be damn busy for a while gathering those crazy pigs."

She chuckled. Her fist to her mouth to suppress her hilarity, she finally managed to ask, "How?"

"I roped a fence post and Jeepers here broke it off. Those pigs heard it pop, and they ran out of that pen like the devil was on their heels, and were still running last I heard of them."

"Some of those hogs they'll never get rounded up again."

"Good. Maybe that will teach them something." Jeepers was in the lot and rolling in the dust. Chet closed the gate. "Let's go see about that food."

"I got another letter from Louise today," Susie said, holding her hem out of the dust and matching his steps.

"What did she say?"

"Not much, except in three weeks she's coming back."

"Oh, that's good news. Poor May is about beside herself about her husband, and now Louise is coming back. I'd hoped she'd stay down there until the herd was headed north."

"And he'd be gone with it."

"Yes." He stopped and washed his hands on the porch. Wetting his face down with handfuls of water, he dried it on the proffered flour-sack towel and thanked her.

The house was quiet. The others were all in bed. Chet and Susie went in the kitchen, and she turned the lamp up on her way to the range. She served him a plate of potatoes and thin-sliced roast beef. A few biscuits, and she brought the butter in a small tub.

"Mother is failing—"

He looked across the table and studied his sister's serious face. "I guess we all knew it was coming. We just aren't ready for it to happen now."

"She's stopped eating. You know, I fought to make her get out of bed. I guess I didn't fight her hard enough."

"Susie, that's not your fault. Don't take on those burdens, too. She made those choices. I think a person wants out of this world, we ought to let them go."

"But what has her life been like over the years?" Susie shook her head, close to tears. "Three children kidnapped and never heard from again. That has eaten her heart out."

He agreed, and the beef wadded in his mouth. No way he could swallow it, but he did not want to upset her and kept chewing. Somehow, he needed to get this down his constricted throat. The fork set aside, he worked harder on the meat.

"Oh, Chet, I have tried."

His hand shot across the table and he clasped her wrist. "Don't you take on the guilt for this. There was no more any of us could do."

The load behind his teeth began to ease. Her wet lashes blinked and she chewed on her lower lip. "If only—"

"There is none of that. Mother wishes to leave us, then we must make it comfortable as we can for her."

She nodded. "We shall, brother. We shall."

"Thanks. I've had enough." He pushed the plate away and gave her a grim nod. "You need anything, ask me."

"I will, and thank you," she said behind him as he put on his hat.

Somehow, he was dragged into everything that happened on the ranch. Hell, he had big shoulders. What else did he need?

He waved to her and headed out into the silent night. The frost had silenced the bugs and croakers—be nice when spring came. He closed his eyes for a second. No way he'd escape all this simply with a change of the seasons. No way in the world.

Chapter 21

Chet drove the big black mares to Maysville for a barrel of flour and to have some cornmeal ground. Both of the mares were bred to a mammoth jack, and he expected some more good mules from them in the spring. The four mules stolen were from the big team. Matt and J.D would not find that good a grade of mules in San Antonio. He reined up at Grosman's Store, set the brake, and tied off the reins. When his boot soles hit the ground, they came from all corners.

There were four of them. Earl came in the lead. Red-faced, his wrinkled shirt half out of his pants. Unshaven and red-eyed, he looked like he'd just crawled out of a whiskey barrel. No way Chet could gun them down. They were too scattered, and they either carried sticks or rifles. He'd badly misjudged 'em. They'd set this trap for him, knowing sooner or later they could separate him from the rest.

Maybe it was by pure bad luck, but they had him between a rock and hard place.

"Earl! I can get one shot off and I sure aim to gut-shoot you." He held his left palm up to stop them. "They may get me, but you're going die an agonizing death."

They froze. Then the others looked at Earl for the word on what to do next. He repeatedly smashed a four-feet-long club in his palm, and the hatred danced in his dark eyes His breath roared in and out of his nose like a hard-run horse. "You sumbitch—"

Chet drew his Colt and blasted the hard dirt inches from his left boot. Dust and grit flew up. Earl threw up his arm to protect his face and eyes.

"Next one's in your gut. You call for it."

"You killed my boy—"

"He stole my remuda along with his friends."

"He was just a damn boy."

"He took on a man's job as a rustler and took his chances."

"He was—"

"Earl, if he'd made it to the Nation and sold those horses, you'd've laughed at me and said go get 'em back."

"He was my youngest." Earl looked close to tears.

"He was old enough to know better. Now, you ready to die in this street or not? I've got business to take care of."

"Come on, boys." Earl gave a toss of his head like he'd thought better about the deal.

"Earl?"

"What?"

"Stop driving cattle on the bar-C. I won't stand for it."

"What're you talking about?"

"Don't lie to me. I watched 'em night before last. They were your boys and the Campbells. I'll make buzzard meat out of them next time they drive cattle on my place."

"You got to prove that."

"You want more dead kinfolks and boys, send them back. I'll be waiting with a big gun." He knew which one, too.

"Come on," Earl said to the others. "I'll get that sumbitching Byrnes one day."

Chet took aim with his pistol and shot Earl's right boot heel off. He staggered and went down on his knee. "Why you—"

"You watch who you call that. Next time, I'll aim higher and shut your mouth."

They helped Earl up and looked back hard at Chet, but they'd also seen his marksmanship as the thick-set Reynolds hobbled on his heel-less boot, cussing all the way. They must have hitched their horses in the alley behind the saloon. Chet kept his eye on them as he poked out the empty casings and reloaded the cylinders with cartridges from his belt.

When he stepped inside the store's shady interior, he saw Old Man Grosman heading for the counter carrying a sawed-off shotgun. Behind the counter again, he stowed it underneath and then straightened up before he spoke. "I was watching them bullies."

"Thanks. Helluva a reception I got today. I've got a list Susie sent me to fill and while you fill it, I'll drive down and get my meal ground. His old steam boiler running?"

"It was yesterday." Grosman let out a breath and shook his head. "Them Reynolds folks better smarten up. Two of his boys are facing murder trials. He's going to lose 'em all."

"Revenge is all he can see. I'll be back in a few hours."

"Watch your back," Grosman said, holding Susie's list up to the lamplight to read it.

Chet could hear the huff of the steam engine over the rattle of the wagon when he drove the mares down in the bottoms. Buddy Lee ran the mill machinery that ground corn as well as sawed lumber with the same power source.

Buddy Lee was not the picture of industry—he'd rather drink or talk than work. But if one was lucky and found the boiler fueled and the engine running, one had a chance to get what he needed. This day Chet hoped it would be ground corn.

"Chet Byrnes, you old rascal." Buddy Lee stood up and adjusted his overall suspenders.

"What'cha need?" he asked over the whirr of the red belt driving the steel grinder that was shattering the corn falling out of a hopper into the mill.

"Two hundred pounds of cornmeal."

Buddy Lee looked at the sun. "I guess I've got time to grind it."

"Good. How much more of that you got to run?"

"Aw, he ain't coming fur this till Friday. I can start in on yours shortly. Throw some chunks of that wood in the firebox. I'll sack this last and we can do yours next."

"Thanks." One thing had gone right.

In no time, his corn was cracking through and Buddy Lee showed him a handful of the product. "That good enough?"

Chet agreed,

"You and them Reynolds folks still at war?"

Chet told him about the incident earlier, and the miller shook his head. "They're crazy."

"But they're crazy enough to hurt my family. No one is safe after they murdered Jake Porter's wife."

"That was the mean damn part. I liked her."

"Everyone did. She was a fine lady."

Buddy Lee hoisted the half-full sack of whole corn over his head and poured more corn in the hopper. "She was no part of that war," he said.

Chet agreed, feeling a gnawing in his gut. He didn't have her anymore either.

Late in the afternoon, he drove home with his six-gun in his lap. Nothing happened, and everyone rolled out when he drove in. They unloaded the wagon, and Reg took charge of the team to put them up.

"Have any trouble today?" Sammy asked as he climbed on to help him.

"Earl and three Campbells tried to jump me when I got to town. I about shot Earl in the foot and they backed off. Then, walking away, he called me a son of bitch and I shot his boot heel off."

Reg shook his head in dismay from the seat. "They're crazy."

"After you put those horses up, don't dally around, supper's ready," Susie said to them.

"Yes, ma'am."

"Shot off his boot heel?" she asked.

Chet took off his hat and hung it on a peg to wash up. "Yeah. He needed his filthy mouth washed with lye soap."

"You better not go anywhere alone either," she said, and with a swish of her skirts went inside.

He agreed to himself with a nod, and hand-washed his face. She probably was right. At last he dried his face as Dale Allen joined him to wash up.

"Boys said you shot Earl's boot heel off today."

"Anyone calls me a son of a bitch better think about it."

Dale Allen shook his head. "I'll be glad to be headed for Kansas. You have a solution for them pushing cattle on us? We're riding good horses into the ground sending them back. Not counting the work we haven't gotten done."

"I told Earl if he didn't stop, I'd shoot the next drivers."

"What did he say to that?"

"He left cussing mad on one boot heel."

"We're in a no-win situation, aren't we?"

"Outside of killing them all, yes, we are."

"I'll help you stop these damn fellas driving those cattle on us."

About to replace his hat, Chet stopped in the doorway and blinked at his brother. "Thanks. I'll sure call on you when the time comes."

"Good enough. I been watching the mare's-tail clouds all day. It may rain again."

"We could use it on the oats." Chet went inside and hung his hat on the rack. Dale Allen hadn't ever offered him a hand to do anything. But even he was tired of this foolishness. Maybe that would be how they'd solve it. Shoot a few more. That wasn't as easy as it sounded either, simply killing folks.

"We're fattening three turkeys for Thanksgiving," Susie announced to him, busy putting out bowls of steaming food.

"Sounds fine." He went and took Baby Donna for May. Holding her up, he talked to the infant and she made bubbles for him. A quiet small baby, she liked him to gently shake her, and smiled in return.

"You'll be walking soon," he told her and took his seat.

"Any Comanches about?" Rock asked from the other end of the table.

"No, Paw, there aren't any signs of them," he said in a nonchallenging response.

May came and took the baby. "About her bedtime."

"Night, Donna."

"You better keep that baby close. Them red niggers will get her."

"The baby will be fine, Paw."

"No one's ever fine living in Comanche country. We all should have stayed in Arkansas." Rock shook his head.

"Too late. We're all Texans now."

"Ain't too late to go back. Abe Cooney brung us here. He was restless, always looking for new land. Mark and me, we came. My brother Mark, he left for a while and went back to Louisiana. He brought Louise back. I ain't seen him in years."

"He got killed in the war, Paw."

"War killed lots of good men."

"We better eat, Paw."

"Yeah, you got guards out every night, ain't you?"

"I sure do."

"Good. Good."

Susie nodded from behind him to indicate that his concerns were satisfied, and everyone ate in silence, not daring to arouse his suspicions and start him over again. The young boys ran out to check on something. Reg and Ray headed for the bunkhouse. May had not returned from putting up the baby. Dale Allen excused himself and headed for the blacksmith shop to burn some midnight oil. Paw went off to bed and left Susie, the two Mexican girls working dishes, and Chet to drink his coffee.

"How's Mother?" he asked Susie.

"Wasting away. She won't eat. She doesn't care."

"I need to take those boys off of cattle herding for a day. Fix them lunch in the morning. They can go cut wood tomorrow."

"Think that'll help?"

"They won't mind herding cattle after a day of that." He chuckled.

"What do you know about Sammy?" Susie asked, sliding in opposite him.

"Nothing. He's a good man as a swing rider. Any reason?"

"He's polite around us. I just wondered."

"Ask Reg. They pal a lot. When is Louise coming home?"

"I suspect in a few weeks."

Chet looked at his coffee. "That won't be easy either."

"I bet you'll make it work."

"I'll have to. You girls getting along all right?"

"Sí, senor."

"The only ones that are, besides you and me," he said to his sister.

May came in the kitchen and smiled. "Is there any coffee left?"

"Sure," Susie said, and frowned at her. She wore a shawl and looked ready to go outside.

"I'm going to take some hot coffee and raisin pie out to him in the blacksmith shop," May announced.

Chet nodded his approval.

Susie hurried around to help her get it ready. On a wicker tray covered with a blue cloth, May left to build a relationship with her husband. God, Chet hoped it worked. He and Susie shared a nod at May's departure, and he went to shave with a kettle of hot water off the range.

Scraping his face with a straight-edged razor at the smoky mirror, he wondered how it would all work out. He needed to go to Mexico and see about the cattle they were holding for him down there. Leaving the ranch would not be best under the circumstances. Maybe by Christmas, things would settle down enough to let him make the trip.

Funny that Paw mentioned his brother at supper. He couldn't hardly believe that he really was dead. Mark Byrnes could have slipped through the cracks. But Chet had no way to know for sure. News of his death had come by word of mouth. It was too late in the war for anything official to come from the Confederacy. Still, in seven years, he should have shown up. He was dead, he had to be—why didn't Chet believe it? It was like some unseen hand kept poking him. Mark Byrnes is not dead.

Phillip and Josephine had been kidnapped before the war, and he had no doubt they'd lost their lives in the traumatic change from being little kids to Comanche slaves. Cagle was two years younger than Dale Allen. He'd been near twelve at his disappearance—he might have survived. Some boys taken at that age had showed up again. The Comanche considered them to be future warriors and later, when found, they were more Injun than white around Mason. Some even liked the wild Indian ways, being waited on by squaws, and returned to being Comanche. An old lady had cried herself to death because her only son, who the army bought back, would not stay and farm with his father.

Who wanted to be "John" and work like a slave when he could be Yellow Hair and live like a buck?

Chapter 22

Rain beat on the roof of the bunkhouse on Friday when he got up. The precipitation had set in for the day. After breakfast, the older boys went down to the barn to fool with the Barbarossa colt. Dale Allen and May went off to work in the blacksmith shop. Astria was tending the baby for her. The small boys were playing some card game they'd invented. Chet worked on the ranch books at the desk. With all the extended family and hired hands, it was hard to make the money last. But it had always been that way for him. Somehow, so far, he'd managed to keep them afloat.

The cattle they'd deliver in Kansas the next summer would make them a good profit and should end his money worries. He entered all the expenses, dipping the straight pen in the inkwell and using his best penmanship to write down each item in the ledger and the cost. Bookkeeping was not his favorite job, but he took a pride in it, and in earlier times, his concise way of recording things had convinced bankers to loan him all the money he needed. Bankers liked bookwork. While his education was hardly more than five grades due to the lack of teachers or money to pay them, he had learned from an old neighbor named Jarvis how to do bookkeeping and why. Jarvis was long gone, but his stern lessons had not been wasted on a young Chet.

In January, he'd need to go to Mexico and get the steers he had contracted for. That would require money he'd have to borrow in San Antonio. No problem. Fred Lewis at the Grand Bank of Texas would loan him that money. But he'd also need a list of all the supplies the drive would require. Hans Grosman would cover that at fifteen-percent interest, and if Chet was lucky, he'd only need that money for six months.

"You look deep in thought," Susie said, coming by the desk.

"Aw, sis, I'm a damn cowboy, not a chair jockey. Maybe I could teach you how to do this."

"Sure, now I have help, I'd love to do it."

"Well, it goes like this. You take all the receipts and enter them. See this one written on this scrap of butcher paper for the salt I got? Seven dollars. You write salt here, then the price."

"I could do that. When do I start?"

"Right now—" He turned an ear to the dogs barking. Someone was outside. He scraped the chair on the floor. "I better go see who it is."

A blast of cool air and dampness swept his face when he stepped out on the porch to better see the rider under a slicker. When the unknown person dismounted, he could see that under the wide-brim hat it was a woman—Kathren Hines.

"Get in here. What are you doing out in this kind of weather anyway, girl?" Then he wanted to bite his tongue for sounding so sharp.

On the porch, she took the sodden hat off and shook her head as if to free her shoulder-length locks. Her hair, exposed to the rain, was curly around her face, and she nodded. "Pretty dumb of me, but I needed to ask a favor of you."

"You two quit gawking at each other and come in this house out of that weather," Susie ordered.

Gawking? They were talking. He stepped aside, and Kathren hesitated.

"But I'm all wet." Kathren looked unable to consider it.

"It will dry," Susie said, and caught her sleeve. "You will catch a death of cold out there."

Inside, he helped her out of the slicker. Then Susie hustled her off to the fireplace to warm up.

"Why are you out today?" Susie asked.

"I need some help and didn't know who to turn to. Someone's been rustling my cattle."

Chet frowned at her as he joined the two of them standing before the hearth. "Any idea who?"

"I can guess, but I can't prove it. So far, they have taken maybe a dozen or more. At first, I thought they were straying, and I began making wide circles when more weren't around. You know, the ones that came to the windmill tank at the house on a regular basis."

"Get some chairs," Susie said to him. "I'll get us all some coffee and we can talk more about this."

He brought back two kitchen chairs and set them down. It still roiled his guts to look at Kathren. "Here, sit down, I'll go get another one."

"Chet." She stopped him, obviously because they were alone in the room. "I'm sorry. I know you have lots of problems of your own, but I didn't know who to trust any longer."

He agreed and excused himself to go after the third chair. Susie brought out the coffee and cups on a tray.

In the kitchen after the other chair, he heard Kathren ask Susie, "Where is everyone?"

"Some of them are out fussing with Chet's new stallion in the barn. Rock went back to sleep, he sleeps a lot, and Mother is bedridden these days."

"Sounds awfully quiet in here," Kathren said over the crackling of the fire.

"I guess we're a quiet bunch," Susie said.

"Now who do you think's behind the rustling?" he asked, turning the chair backward and straddling it to face Kathren.

How many times had he considered what it would be liked to have her for his wife? Her blues eyes sparkled. The firm chin line molded her handsome face, and her lower lip looked like half a rose petal. Wet tight curls framed it all and trailed off.

"I think that Mitch Reynolds is in on it."

He stopped. Would they murder her, too, if they knew she'd come to him for help? "You've seen him around your place?"

Susie frowned. "Oh, Kathren, those boys are killers."

Kathren nodded. "That's why I'm here. I've never been afraid before. Never thought I couldn't handle things. But after Marla's murder—I've lost my nerve."

"Where did you see him?"

"I was down on the Barren Flats yesterday searching for my lost cattle and looked back. I could see his hat in the cedars. I'd know it anywhere. It has a broad silk-bound brim.

Besides, he's riding a bay horse with lots of white on his face, too."

"Did he follow you?"

Kathren nodded. "I doubled back and watched him reading my tracks."

She closed her eyes and wrung her hands in her lap. "I never slept a wink last night."

"Where's your daughter?"

"At my parents' house. Oh, if she'd been there, I think I'd've climbed the walls."

"He came around last night?"

With a pained look on her face, she started to speak. "The wind and all—maybe it was nothing. The house was locked and barred. But I knew I couldn't stay there a moment longer. I had—no one else to turn to."

"Rain's lets up, I'll ride over and look around. Meanwhile, Susie can fix you some food and you're welcome to sleep some here if you can."

"You have enough trouble. You don't need mine."

"Like it or not, I think we have to do something. Rustlers and folks snooping around needs to be cleared out."

"Have some coffee first and get warmed up," Susie said to both of them.

He accepted the steaming cup. Where should he start? He'd need to come around in the back way and to surprise anyone lying in wait. Best get Sammy to go with him. Reg knew how to run things around the ranch better than the new man. Blowing the steam off his coffee, he nodded—that would be the plan.

"You stay here until we're satisfied that there is no one at your place," he said to Kathren.

"Will you go by my folks' and tell them part of the

story? Dad doesn't need to get all involved in this. His heart's been acting up—that was why I—came here. Tell Cady it will only be a day or so and I'll be home."

He agreed, and slipped on his own raincoat to go find Sammy. He located him and Reg in the barn driving the buckskin Barbarossa colt around with a light harness. After he explained what they needed to do, Sammy went to get his things. Reg tied the colt up and helped Chet catch the two horses out in the muddy lot. They both about fell down in the slop trying to rope mounts, but they finally got them and led them inside to saddle.

"She thinks it's Mitch?" Reg asked.

Chet nodded, then finished cinching up Dun and slapped down the stirrup. Bugger was stomping around inside a box stall. The horse's actions reminded Chet that he needed to finish him off and get him back to Neddy. One big powerful horse and an athlete as well—make a horse for a crusader in armor, but he wasn't a draft horse. Sammy broke into his thoughts.

"We need rifles?"

"Maybe a dozen before its over, but two would do."

"You want that Sharps?"

"Sure."

The rain was beginning to break up, and a colder north wind swept in on its heels. They packed their bedrolls in case. After a quick lunch, they stuffed jerky in their pockets and hit the muddy road. He left Susie to explain to Dale Allen their purpose. It looked like things between him and May were healing. Her helping him in the shop had drawn them closer—Chet hoped it worked. Louise would be back any time.

They short-loped their horses toward Maysville, and

took a cutoff short of town, so in two hours they worked
their way through the hills from the east down to Kathren's
place. The wet cedar bows Chet brushed his legs against
soaked into his bull-hide chaps. He'd shed his slicker and
wore his jumper. Across his lap, the Sharps rested.

"I can see the house." Sammy reined up his horse.

Chet nudged Dun over and got out his field glasses. He
scanned the pens and stopped. A blaze-faced bay horse
stood in the back corral. "She's got company."

"Who?"

Chet handed him the glasses. "Check in the back pen
when he lifts his head."

Sammy took them, peered across the way, and then let
the binoculars down. His eyes narrowed, he looked at Chet,
as serious as Chet had ever seen him. "Sum bitch, that's
Mitch Reynolds' horse all right. What's he doing here?"

"Good question. I aim to ask him the same."

"Where's he at?"

"In the sheds or house. We better go in on foot."

Sammy agreed. "I can't believe this. What's he doing
here?"

"Scaring the crap out of Kathren Hines."

"Yeah. You've sure got some nice enemies. Real nice."

"Cowardly bastards," Chet said, and tossed his head
for Sammy to go left while he'd go right. Both were armed
with their rifles. Chet put a cartridge in the chamber of the
.50-caliber. The cartridges were individually wrapped in
waxed canvas to keep them dry. He hoped the ammo would
work when he needed it. The day had warmed some, but
the north wind still carried a chill.

Moving through the live oak and cedars to work downhill, he paused and nodded with approval at Sammy when

he waved to him before he went behind the pen containing the horse. No sign of Mitch. Chet stopped at the edge of the cover and watched Kathren's hens scratching around the small coop between him and the house. Where was Mitch at?

Obviously, so far Sammy had not found him in the sheds. Chet saw Sammy for an instant duck before he went into the last shed, a large hay shed to Chet's left. Shortly, he reappeared with a head shake—nothing. Chet made a sign for him to stay over there. He'd take on the house. The Sharps leaned against the henhouse wall, he walked softly toward the back door across the open yard. His fist wrapped around the Colt's redwood grips.

Then he spotted the corpse. Kathren's wet collie lying dead beside the back steps. A wave of anger swept over him. His breath shortened and his fingers squeezed the .44 so hard, his fingers ached. His first step on the bottom landing sounded gritty. He tried to make his foot fall quieter on the next one. It groaned slightly. His left hand twisted the knob, and the door opened with hardly a breath.

There was barely enough light in the kitchen, but he eased the door shut behind him, and that cut off the sound of the wind and any more air rushing inside. All the time, he tried to hear anything, like a sole on the floors or a creak of a floorboard. Then it came to him—someone was snoring. Had he caught the fugitive asleep?

Slowly and still cautious, he moved into the living room where Kathren's double bed was near the fireplace. There, curled up on top of the sheets in a fetal ball, was the nearly six-foot fully dressed form of Mitch Reynolds—snoring away.

His six-gun holster hung on the bedpost. After sizing up

the situation, Chet nodded to himself. He slipped over and stuck the muzzle of his cocked gun hard to the back of Mitch's head.

"I ought to kill you here and now."

"Huh? Don't kill me!"

"Don't move. I ain't made up my mind yet if I will or not. What are you doing here?"

"Ah—ah—no one was home. Shit-fire, get that gun off my head."

"You were going to kill and rape her, weren't you?" He had Mitch's face buried in the mattress under the hard-pressed muzzle.

"No—no—I swear to God—"

"God won't have you. Admit it right now. You were going to rape and kill her."

"All right—all right—what'cha going to do with me?"

"Take you to Mason and let you hang for killing Marla Porter. Now, where did you sell the cattle you rustled from Kathren?"

"I never—"

"Gawdamn you—" When Sammy broke in the front door, Chet whirled to see the shocked look on his face as Chet held the gun on Mitch.

"You all right?" Then Sammy motioned at the prisoner.

"I caught him sleeping." Chet turned back to Mitch. "Now, who bought those cattle you stole?"

"I ain't telling—"

Chet reared back and smashed Mitch's collarbone with the six-gun. The .44 went off in the bedding. The room boiled in gun smoke. Mitch was screaming for his life. With a hold on his shirt collar, Chet dragged him out of bed crying and squalling like a baby through the fog of gun smoke onto the porch, and stomped on his back with a boot to make him lie flat facedown.

"How's your hearing now?"

"I never stole no—"

Chet drove a boot toe hard into his ribs. "Pretty soon, you aren't going to need to hear me."

"Aw," Mitch groaned. "Drake—Dover Drake."

"How many?" Drake was a butcher down in the brush. Chet knew how to find him.

"A dozen maybe—"

Chet stomped him on the shoulder blade with his boot heel. "How many?"

"Sixteen."

"What did he pay you?'

"Five—I mean four bucks a head."

"Cheap enough price to get hung for." He shook his head in grim disgust "Where's Kenny at now?"

"New Mexico—I think."

"Where?"

"New—" A hard jab in his back with Chet's boot heel cut him off.

"I said where's he at?"

"I swear to Gawd he's in New Mexico."

"Get his horse," Chet said to Sammy.

"You hanging me?" Mitch asked.

"No, you ain't getting off that easy. I want you to have a trial for murder of a woman." *Of the woman I loved*.

Hours later, he and Sammy, with their slump-shouldered prisoner, rode up to Sheriff Trent's clapboard-sided home in Mason. In the twilight, Chet dismounted heavily and let his sea legs get under him by clinging to the saddle horn.

Trent came to the lighted doorway. "That you, Byrnes?"

"Yes, Sammy and I have Mitch Reynolds. Besides murdering Marla Porter, he's been rustling, and broke into Kathren Hines' house after terrorizing her."

The sheriff made a pained look. "You know that I've been trying hard to catch him and his brother."

"I know that, Sheriff. You've tried hard, but that bunch of his hid 'em out. Kathren came to my house this morning telling me he'd been rustling her stock and trailing her around. No doubt for the same reason he did it all to Marla—"

Gawdamn it, he was crying.

Chapter 23

The next morning, Sheriff Trent rode a few feet ahead of him on a good sorrel horse. A strong stink of pigs filled Chet's nose as they came out in the open and he could see the adobe jacales, the cross-bars that Drake butchered on, and the nearly naked brown children who blinked in disbelief at the sight of them. He could hear the sound of hogs fighting coming from where they were kept in a large pole pen to the right.

Unshaven and putting up an overall suspender, Dover Drake came outside and wiped his whiskered mouth on the back of his hand. Then he spit in the dust.

"Dover Drake?"

"You must be the sheriff."

"I am. My name's Trent. This is Mr. Byrnes."

"I knowed him." Drake folded his arms over his chest.

Trent rested his hand on the saddle horn. "A friend of yours, Mitch Reynolds, said he sold you rustled cattle."

"Friend—why, that son of a bitch ain't no friend of mine. I don't buy no rustled cattle. No sirree. All the cattle I buy have the owner's brand on them. I know Texas law. If this so-called friend sold me cattle, they must have had his brand on them."

"We want to see your hides."

"I ain't got many. I sold some to a hide dealer came through here a while ago."

"That's fine. I can check his hides later." Trent nodded like that satisfied him, and he dismounted. "I want to see the hides you have."

Drake looked at the dirt and stirred it some with his shoe. "That son of a bitch Reynolds sent you, huh?"

"He sent me."

"Well, the damn hides you want are in that building." He pointed at a nearby structure. "I should have known he hadn't bought those cattle like he told me he did. Worthless outfit."

The woman in the doorway, who looked quite pregnant, spoke to Drake in Spanish, and he said in her lingo, *"They are going to take me to jail."*

She dropped on her knees and began to pray and cross herself. Her wailing was soon joined by the children's caterwauling.

"I'll go find the hides," Chet said, anxious to escape the woman and her offsprings' emotional pleading.

Trent nodded, and put the handcuffs on Drake.

In the stinking dark shed, piled with hides, Chet went through the hides and picked out the ones with Kathren's 9Y brand on them. It became necessary to hold them up to the door's light to see the mark. The others he piled aside to find hers, and the stench assailed his nostrils and made his stomach upset. He was grateful for each time he got to step outside in the sunshine with a hide of hers and catch a breath of air. Soon, all sixteen were stacked on the ground and he blew his nose hard to try and clear the sourness out.

Meanwhile, Trent found a burro and slapped a packsaddle on him. They rolled up and lashed the stinking hides on the cross-buck tree for evidence. Then, with the handcuffed Drake riding another donkey, they headed out, leaving Drake's wife or mistress, whatever, still wailing and screaming Spanish cuss words after them.

"Tough job being a lawman," Chet said when they were no longer hearing her.

"At times, it's damn tough. But I didn't ask him to buy rustled cattle either."

Chet agreed. He could go back to the ranch and tell Kathren she could safely go home. The law had the rustlers and her antagonist as well. Mitch wouldn't bother her again. His brother Kenny, according to the information that he got out of Mitch, was in New Mexico.

He hoped he stayed there.

At the crossroads, Sheriff Trent stopped. He was headed for Mason. Chet shook his hand, thanked him, and then went west for home. It was near dark when he rode in and dismounted. He scrubbed his whiskered cheek. Would have been nice to have cleaned up first before she saw him. But he'd been in the saddle two days and there'd been no time for that.

Susie and Kathren appeared in the lighted doorway.

"Sammy told us you caught him. Get him delivered?" his sister asked.

"I'll put him up, Uncle Chester," Heck said, taking the reins.

He tousled the boy's hair and smiled. "Thanks. Yes, Mitch is in the Mason jail to await his trial for Marla's murder. Dover Drake's going to join him today for buying stolen beef. Oh," he said, clasping the porch post and looking up into Kathren's blue eyes. "Best I could learn, he stole sixteen head from you. That's how many hides Dover had with your brand on them."

She chewed on her lower lip. "I'm sorry I had to put you through all this."

"I reckon tomorrow I can take you home. It should be safe."

A look of being trapped spread over her face. "I can go—"

"I'm certain you can, but I'll take you home and be sure you and Cady are safe and sound."

Hell—she looked about to cry, and rushed over to hug him. How many times in his life had he dreamed about that happening? And he was as dirty as a pig. He closed his eyes and returned her embrace. Whew.

With Kathren under his arm, he went inside.

"Oh, Susie, the sheriff said to tell you hello. You must have impressed him in town." He could have sworn she blushed.

"That was nice."

The crew gathered in the dining room while he ate his meal and told them everything that Sammy hadn't. The food tasted good, and he couldn't recall eating much of anything since he'd left.

"Do you think they'll finally quit after all this?" Dale Allen asked, standing back and holding May's shoulder.

Chet looked hard at his brother. "No."

A hush fell over them.

"I know that's not great news. But Earl won't give up on his revenge until they throw him kicking in his grave. They have so much hate in them. Bringing in Mitch won't help either, but there's nothing else I could do." He held up his hand to stop Kathren's protest. "No need for you to get upset. I'm glad Mitch's in jail. Let the cards fall as they may."

The two men nodded in agreement.

"We think they've finally stopped driving cattle on us. So you did some good," Dale Allen said.

"Good. Maybe we can get caught up around here. Any word from Matt and J.D.?"

"No," Susie said.

He nodded to show that he'd heard her, and went back to eating his food. "They're big boys. They can find their way home."

"I hope they do soon."

"Matt's fussy about mules. I knew it would take some time for him to find good ones and then swap for them."

Kathren brought him some pecan pie on a plate. "We saved you a big piece."

He smiled at her. "That'll sure be a real treat."

Reg laughed. "Yeah, she threatened us on our lives if we ate it, too."

Kathren shook her head and held her chin high on her way after the coffeepot. "You can't do nothing around here that doesn't go unnoticed."

"Part of having a big family." Chet used his fork to cut a piece out of the pie. The first bite flooded his mouth with saliva. Not bad, not bad at all.

The next morning, frost covered everything. Chet had bathed and shaved the night before. He put on his newest pair of starched and ironed canvas pants and a white shirt, then brushed his suit coat, hoping it would warm up fast when the sun came up. Otherwise, he'd have to wear his waxed canvas drover's coat. The boys were busy hitching up the buggy team and saddling Kathren's horse to tie it on behind. He threw his bedroll in the buckboard on his way to breakfast. Might have to be certain that she'd be all right at her place.

"Well," Susie said, looking him over and acting impressed when he walked in the kitchen. "You sure look nice."

"Good," he said as Kathren came in the back door with some jars of fruit from the cellar.

"Good morning," she said. Her face lit up. He couldn't recall that ever happening before—her perking up at the sight of him. "Susie thought some peaches might taste good for breakfast."

"Great idea. We'll be ready to roll when breakfast is over. They have your buckboard hitched."

"I can ride home by myself." She set the jars down for him to unseal.

Straining on the rings, he undid them and she smiled. "Thanks," she said. "I'd forgotten men can do those things."

"We aren't all bad."

She stopped, bent over to get the jars, and looked him square in the eye. "I'm learning that, too."

If he'd ever felt that he had an inside track with her, at this moment his hopes surged. There might be a way for them to develop something more permanent from all this mess. Something he'd not even dreamed about while arresting Mitch or riding after the butcher Drake with Sheriff Trent.

The problem for him—how did he keep her feeling this

way? He better get off his high horse and get back down to earth. Anyone could have taken Mitch Reynolds—he'd been asleep. So what? Kathren was too big a prize for him to expect to hold on to. Better cushion himself for the fall. She'd go home and be safe and draw back in her shell. He'd be right back to having nothing again.

After the meal, he drove her to Maysville to pick up some supplies on the way. She wore a man's felt hat and a long black wool coat over her riding skirt and blouse. He knew that the two of them being together must have turned some heads as he helped her off the buckboard. Chet Byrnes and Kathren Hines, a recent widow, came to town together today would be on all the gossiping lips before dark—why, it might be on a page in the next day's edition of the *San Antonio Telegraph*.

"I won't be long," she promised.

"I'll go over to Casey's and talk to the loafers and check on you in thirty minutes."

She looked concerned. "I won't take that long."

"You can today."

"But—but you have things to do."

"Kathren, I'll get them all done by spring. Take your time."

"All right. I wanted to pick out some material."

He stepped on the rig and undid the reins. "Good. Thirty minutes."

He halted in front of the harness/saddle shop, tied up the team, and then walked through the batwing doors and inside Casey's Saloon. When he saw the big Irishman's face behind the bar, he knew something was wrong.

A masked man bearing a sawed-off shotgun reared up from under the counter and pointed it at Chet. His heart stopped. An ambush. Two men grabbed him by the arms and someone else drove an ax handle into his left kidney. A sharp pain from the blow blinded him. They were using him for a punching bag when the shotgun went off. Its percussion put out the lights and filled the barroom with acrid blue smoke. Chet was on his knees not feeling any shot in his body, but the battering blows with the ax handles changed to kicks. Then he collapsed face-first in the sawdust, too numb to know anything.

He awoke with his head in Kathren's lap and her brushing sawdust and dirt off his face.

"Who in the hell was in that welcoming party?" he managed to ask.

"They all wore masks," Casey said, squatted beside her. "Never said nothing. I think one of them was Shelby Reynolds. I busted that one had my shotgun over the head. You owe me three bucks for the whiskey bottle. It was near full. Then I wrestled the gun away from him and that's when it went off in the ceiling." Casey shrugged. "They ran out of here about then."

"Lie still," Kathren said to him. "Doc's coming."

"Let me sit up."

"Oh, all right. But you may jar something else loose."

"I'll be fine. Anyone else know who they were?"

"They all had masks."

"Recognize anything about them?"

The familiar faces around him came and went from his fuzzy vision as all shook their heads. He knew where the masked men came from—but they must have expected him to go to town. How? Lucky? Maybe, maybe not. Word had had a chance by then to get back to them about Mitch being in jail—why chance a daylight attack in a saloon? He put a hand on his side. They'd really worked him over.

"How long were they in here before I came in?"

Casey shook his head. "Minutes is all."

That meant they'd followed him and Kathren into town and knew he'd probably go to Casey's for a beer as he usually did. "Who's Shelby Reynolds?"

"Earl's younger brother from Fort Worth."

"He been around here long?"

Casey shook his head. "They said Earl sent him money to bring some shooters with him."

Chet dropped his head and rubbed the back of his neck. "I don't know what kind of shooters they are, but they ain't half bad at roughing a fella up."

Kathren made him look at her, and she used a white kerchief to brush more sawdust off his face near his tear ducts. "You sit still awhile. No telling what they've busted."

He forced a smile for her. "Did you get that material you wanted?"

"Yes, but—"

"I fed them chickens good before I left there, and turned the milk cow and her calf out together. But I bet they need some care. Help me up."

"Oh, Chester, you really should let the doctor look at you."

He made a face at her. "Help me up."

Shaking her head in disgust, she dropped down and gave him a hand. Pain wrenched though him. but he smiled when she had him on his feet. Forcing a grin for her, he caught the bar with his hand. "Go get your material. I'll drive over there."

For a moment, she hesitated. Then, with a peeved look, she turned on her heel and left him. He closed his eyes when she went out the batwing doors. "Casey, couple of you fellas get me on that seat."

"By damn, you're tough enough. Think you can stay on it?"

"Get me on it and—and then load her things in it over at the store 'cause I won't be able to get down and do that." He clenched his teeth and his breath caught.

"Here, drink this whiskey," Casey said, giving him a double shot.

He downed it. Then the big Irishman and a customer hauled him out and loaded him on the spring seat. Casey wouldn't let him drive, and stepped up to take charge. Chet was grateful. He knew, even with his elbows hugging his sides, he hurt and hurt bad.

"I had Carl stick two bottle of whiskey in your bedroll. You're damn sure going to need 'em," said Casey,

At the store, they loaded everything and Casey helped Kathren, who looked disapproving, onto the seat beside him.

"You sure you want to do this?" she asked Chet.

"Sure as I can be."

She dismissed him with a shake of her head and pulled down her felt hat brim. Then she took up the reins, clucked to the team, and they took off in a trot.

"I don't understand why you are doing this to yourself."

"I do—I never had a chance with you before—"

"A chance for what? What are you talking about?"

He looked out of his right eye at her, and the whole world weaved back and forth. "I'm talking about me and you—all these years—all this time—K-Kathren, I've really wanted you . . ."

"Oh, my God." Then she threw her right arm around him. The last thing he recalled was when he collapsed against her. His world went black.

Chapter 24

Chet couldn't be certain where he was for a day and a half. He spent most to the time in Kathren's bed. When he woke up in a groggy haze, he could hear Dale Allen's concerned-sounding voice talking to Kathren.

"Dale Allen's here," she told Chet.

"Casey sent word they'd worked you over," Dale Allen said, standing beside the bed. "Who done it?"

He tried to sit up, and that didn't work, so he eased back down. "Casey said it was Shelby Reynolds and some hard cases he bought back with him that Earl hired."

Dale Allen nodded with a grim set to his mouth. "For ten cents, I'd ride over there and blow them all to kingdom come."

"Aw, they need us—the family. We've got a trail drive to get on with. A ranch to run—why, I'll be up kicking in a few days." He hoped.

For the first time he could ever recall, he read in his brother's blue eyes the sincerity and concern that he shared with him about the whole ranch operation. He felt like for the first time in his life, Dale Allen realized the scope of their responsibility. The notion might make all Chet's suffering in the ordeal worthwhile. He'd gotten a partner at last.

"Thanksgiving is this Thursday," Dale Allen said. "You know Susie—"

Chet raised his gaze to Kathren. "Sis always makes a big deal about holidays."

"Well, you sure can't go."

"Would you drive me?"

It seemed to him it took the longest time for her to answer him. After more than hundred loud ticks of the grandfather clock on the mantle, he started to worry she might say no. Then, at last, she spoke to Dale Allen.

"If he don't pass out and fall off the wagon, we'll be there." From her tone, Chet knew she disapproved of the trip.

"Thanks. You want Doc to come look you over?" Dale Allen asked him.

"I'll heal. No, thanks."

"Casey sent you two more bottles of good whiskey and said to get well."

"Tell him thanks."

"I better get back if you don't need anything." With his fingertips on the brim, Dale Allen moved the hat in his hands around in a circle like a nervous tomcat.

"Don't need anything. Tell the crew I'll be there for Thanksgiving dinner."

"Or dead," she said under her breath.

"Hey, I can send the boys over with a bed in the big wagon to get him."

"No, Dale Allen, I'll get him there."

"Your daughter is invited." He looked around for her.

"She's still staying with my folks," Kathren explained.

"Oh, yes . . ."

Chet slipped off to sleep then. It was partially brought on by the whiskey she fed him and partially from what the hurting in his body demanded from him. When she woke him, he discovered she was sitting on the side of the bed armed with a spoon and a bowl.

"He gone?" Chet asked.

"A couple of hours ago. Time to eat if you're going to Thanksgiving dinner in a few days."

"You don't mind, do you?"

"What if I did?"

He blinked at her in disbelief. "You serious?"

"I'm always serious, Chester Byrnes."

"Why, I figured you'd be damn glad to be rid of a man you had to bathe, hold him up to relieve himself, and nursemaid all day."

Her head slowly nodded. "But I'll have to share you if I take you back."

"Hmm. You ain't giving up much. Why, I couldn't fight off a rooster attacking me."

She set the soup on the table, then turned back to bend over and push the stray hair back from his face, then bent over and kissed him. He closed his eyes to the tenderness of her mouth on his cracked lips.

Was he alive or dreaming that this happened? If it was a dream, for Gawd's sake, don't wake him.

She straightened up and gave her hair a toss back. "Now you must sit up some and eat. Let me help you."

With his arms tight to his sides to keep the pain under her tightly wrapped bandage around his ribs, she pulled him up and propped him with pillows. Then, with a small smile, she took up the bowl and spoon.

"I'd sure take some more dessert like that after supper," he said.

With a mischievous grin, she nodded. "Oh, there might be some left for you."

Two days passed, and he pushed himself to get up, first with her help. Then he began to get up on his own. He wanted to walk into that ranch house on Thursday. The effort wore him out, but he soon could circle the bed.

On Wednesday, she went for few hours to check on her daughter and parents. He was holding his breath when he looked out the window and saw some riders coming across the flats.

Damn, where was his gun? She had a rifle over the door, but he'd never reach that high over his head. Must be four or five of them—just right for the Reynolds bunch. At last, he discovered his holster set and slung it on the dry sink. That effort hurt his right side. He eased the Colt out and checked the cylinders—five shots. He'd make them count.

At the window again, he recognized the men coming. Then he collapsed against the wall. The cold swear dripped from under his armpits. They were his friends.

Wade Morgan, Jim Crammer, Elmer Stokes, Sy Calahan, and a cowboy he didn't know. He set the revolver on the dry sink and went to answer the door. Shaking his head over the impulse that had captured him, he unlatched the door.

"Get down and come on in," he said.

Sy Calahan, laughed, dismounting. "I told you that old coyote was all right. He's just up here keeping a fine lady company."

"That don't sound half nice," Elmer Stokes complained.

"It's the truth."

"Don't matter—she around?" Stokes whirled around to look for her.

"No."

"Still, it ain't nice to joke about delicate things like that."

Even Chet laughed, but he paid the price in hurt.

When they were all inside, Wade put some water in the coffeepot and swung it into the fireplace to boil. They all took seats and asked a million questions, as well as telling what they knew about the Reynolds hands.

"Two of 'em rannies vanished when they heard Sheriff Trent was coming down. So there's just Shelby and some piss cutter named Sharp left," Calahan said.

Chet sat in Kathren's rocker through it all, and fought drowsiness sipping on Wade's too thick coffee through the conversation about cattle, weather, and rain.

"I'm going home for Thanksgiving," he said.

"You up to it?" Jim Crammer asked.

"Kathren's going to drive," Chet said.

"Hellfire, Chet, why, I'd stay here till she threw me out." Calahan clapped his knees in a cloud of dust. His humor made them all laugh.

"Mr. Byrnes, I didn't want to bother you," Pinky, the drover who came with them, said, "but I came to see about work."

The handle didn't fit the tall lean man seated on the kitchen chair in the circle. Chet made him out as close to his age. His face was tanned to saddle-leather brown, and his bare snowy white forehead showed he wasn't without his hat much.

"You're no bother," said Chet. "You've been to Kansas, I take it?"

"Yes, three times. Last time up, I was second in command,

and Casey Thornton broke his leg when we were unsticking the chuck wagon north of the Red River crossing, so I was ramrod the rest of the way."

Chet knew Casey and had heard about his wreck going north. "My brother Dale Allen is taking the herd north this year. I want you to talk to him. Come out to the ranch for dinner tomorrow. Susie and the girls will have plenty to eat. I'm sure he can use an experienced hand."

"Thanks. I'll be there."

Jim Crammer stood up and finished his coffee before he spoke. "We're sorry we weren't in town when those buzzards struck you, or it might have been different."

"Jim, thanks, and thanks to all of you for coming to see me. But it might have been the best thing that it happened like it did. I took a beating—but no one got killed. Too many been killed around here even if they have been Reynolds men and their kin."

When Kathren returned, he awoke sitting in her chair. "Who came? I saw the tracks," she said.

"Oh, the fellas."

She bent over and kissed him with her arms holding a poke. Natural as the sun coming up. Man, he sure had gotten spoiled in the few days he'd been there.

"Mother sent some bread and sweets she made for you. Cady is having Thanksgiving with my brother Tad and his wife. Folks are going there, too."

"She miss not being home?"

"No. Mother dotes on her. She probably made the sweets. They have a time together."

"I hate to upset your holiday."

"You didn't—I want to tell you how worried I felt seeing all those tracks out there a few minutes ago." She was busy unloading what she'd brought in on the sink. "You get your gun out?"

"Yes, I didn't know who was coming."

"I felt the same way at first seeing the sign of their hoof-prints. Then I said no, Chet's there and he handled it," she said, hanging the holster set back on the peg.

"Chet couldn't get the rifle down." He chuckled, wanting to get up and swing her around, and knowing damn good and well in his shape that he couldn't do it.

"I never thought about that. Next time, it will be where you can get it."

"If I was well, you know what I'd do?"

"No."

"I'd polka you around this house."

"Why?"

"'Cause I feel like it."

"You're serious, aren't you?"

He leaned around to see her putting things up. "I'm as serious as I can be."

She tilted her head to the side and nodded. "No one has ever done that to me."

"Well, girl, I get better, I'll do it till your feet hurt."

She looked thoughtfully at him and then grinned. "I'll look forward to that. How do you polka without music?"

"I can't sing, but I can hum."

"You know, Chet." She stopped, put both hands flat on the dry sink, and looked hard at him. "I spent over ten years married to a man who never laughed. He told me on our wedding night that laughing and giggling was kid stuff and he wouldn't put up with it. So I never laughed or hardly even smiled around him the entire time. . . ."

Holy cow, what a poor way for her to have lived.

Chapter 25

With her driving in her best Sunday dress, the ride to the ranch wore him out. But once there, he waved away all the offers of help to get down as everyone came out in the midday sun to welcome them. Kathren had made three pecan pies, and the boys each carried one of them inside. Sammy took care of the team. Chet made it inside to a kitchen chair and sat down.

"Chester, you better tell these dumb boys if they don't start standing guard at night, them red niggers are sure going to sneak in here some night and murder us all in our beds."

"I will, Paw. I'll handle it."

"By Gawd, you better. I couldn't get nothing out of 'em."

"Where you going, Paw?"

"To bed. I'm tired. It must be late."

"Good night." Chet shook his head after the tottering old man went down the hall. Satisfied he was out of hearing, he shook his head at Dale Allen, who stood very close to May back from the traffic. "Next time simply tell him the guard list goes like this. He won't check on it. Hell, he's gone to bed here at dinnertime."

Dale Allen agreed. *Imagine that.*

"You want to say grace?" Susie asked him behind her hand.

"Sure. Something wrong?"

She looked around and then leaned over and whispered. "I have invited Robert to come eat with us since he has no family around here."

"Robert who?" he asked softly.

She looked put out at him. "Robert Trent."

"Oh, Bob—"

That must have made her madder, for she hustled off ordering her help around. Something she seldom did. Probably she didn't want everyone to know about the situation in case he didn't show up. Chet raised his glance to the embossed tin ceiling squares for help.

The sheriff arrived, and Susie introduced him around to everyone. He looked all slicked up, and so did Pinky, who followed him in by a few minutes. Chet introduced him and told Dale Allen that Pinky wished to talk to him after the meal about going on the drive. Dale Allen looked relieved and nodded his approval.

Dogs barking and mules honking—the long-lost Matt and J.D. arrived with long ears in tow. Everyone rushed outside to look at their purchases, and the desperate Susie began wringing her hands, saying to Chet that her big meal was ready.

He hobbled out on the porch and called things to order. "Dinner is ready. You two strangers wash up. Everyone else get inside and we can look at mules later. Come on, they've worked hard on fixing this meal."

"Nice of you to do that," Kathren said under her breath, skirt in hand, going by him.

He nodded and herded the crew back to the table. He could see Matt had done a great job. They were stout good-looking mules.

J.D. shook his head, going past. "Helluva a long trip."

"I want to hear all about it after dinner."

Matt came stiff-legged along after him and shook his head. "I about had to go to Fort Smith to find 'em."

"I can see that you did well."

The man beamed. "We tried. Home cooking. Smells great." And he went by.

When everyone was inside, Chet said a short grace, and they all began to fill their plates from the numerous bowls, and Susie passed the turkey platter around to help them. When she got to Chet, he whispered to her, "We can pass it. Go sit with your guest."

Susie about blushed. "I will. Have some."

"You know, you can be bossy," Kathren said, handing the gravy bowl to him.

"Never knew that. Something needed done. I'm simply hurrying them up."

Kathen laughed. He realized that he'd never heard her laugh in years. Not since their school and country dance days. She tried to smother it with a napkin, but that only made it worse. Then he began to chuckle at her attempt to cut it off, and the whole table laughed, it became so contagious. At last, she managed, "I'm sorry. I guess I hadn't laughed in a long time and it had to come out."

She dabbed her wet eyes with the napkin and looked about to sob.

"Now don't go to crying 'cause we all can't cry," he said, feeling pinned down by the fact that he couldn't hug her. He put down his fork, reached over, and squeezed her hand under the table. She in turn tightened her hand in his and nodded. "I'll be fine."

"Good. Now, J.D., when you get enough of this good food in you, tell us all about the mule deal."

"Well, we went to San Antonio and there weren't any mules worth a—none we wanted to buy. Then we went to Austin and the mules for sale there were worse. Fort Worth and Dallas—big places. Why, I seen more dang things than you could—well, ever believe. They said we needed to go to Fort Smith, Arkansas. I recalled Grandpa Rock and them come from up there."

He took a drink of water from the goblet and swallowed hard. "We never got there. Matt and I found these mules we brought home in Texarkana. I was sure dreading going much farther. All farming country and pine thickets out there in east Texas. Folks living in log shacks farming forty acres. I never knowed it before, but we live pretty good here compared to that kind of life."

"Thanks, J.D., and you, too, Matt," Chet said. "Those mules are sure necessary for the farming we must do here and hauling the chuck wagon. Susie, let's get out some wine and give everyone a small glass and we'll do some toasting to the good things around us. Sure we have problems with some other folks, but like J.D. just said, we do have a good life here on the bar-C."

Susie and the girls soon had the glasses out and the wine poured. Chet rose with a wince and held his glass up. "I propose a toast to Dale Allen, who's been running the ranch so well with me laid up, and our trail boss for next year. Dale, stand up."

May, about to bust the buttons off her Sunday dress, made him stand and raise his glass. He looked awkward, but nodded and they toasted him. Then Chet proposed a toast to Susie and the two girls for their wonderful Thanksgiving dinner. Reg proposed a toast to Matt and J.D. for buying the mules.

Then Susie rose with the last red wine in her glass and wet her lips. "We all know what Chet does for us, but I am very grateful for the wonderful job that Kathren has done taking care of him to get him back here today."

Chairs scraped on the floor. Everyone stood and they raised their glasses. "To Chet and Kathren."

Damn, he hoped he didn't cry—*again*.

After the meal, he parleyed with the men in the living room. "December, we need to check fences around the oat patches twice a week. We have to be sure we aren't feeding everyone's cattle on our grass. Sometime after Christmas, some of us'll go to Mexico and get our cattle I have bought down here. February, we trail-brand all the cattle we're taking. I don't want the ones we are taking along on our grass. So they'll come in here about the first of March, and on the fifteenth, Dale Allen and crew can head 'em north.

"Dale Allen, we can get the Mexicans up here to cut firewood. You and the boys are too busy working the range to mess with it. I want plenty of firewood at the house, so when you head north, these gals have a supply. I'll be back in a week or so and pitch in. Keep your eyes out. Two of those fellas who beat me up have left the country before Bob arrested them according to my reports. Shelby, Earl's brother, and a fella named Sharp are still around, or were earlier.

"Remember always go in pairs and don't take chances or fight with them if you don't have to. Any questions?"

"We can handle it," Dale Allen said, and they all agreed. Maybe he could get completely well in a few weeks, but the healing ribs and his sore muscles told him he'd sure overdone it that day. This setup with Kathren was a dream come true for him, and better than any tonic a doctor could give him in a bottle.

Susie put on a coat and took Trent on a tour of the ranch headquarters. Chet was glad to see the excitement in her eyes and the flush on her face. Trent looked focused on her, too. They went out the front door, and Kathren joined him beside the chair in the living room.

"It's a long ride home." She looked apprehensive about the matter.

He nodded. "I'm ready if you want to put up with me some more."

She glanced around to be certain they were alone so no one would hear her. "I didn't know how it looked to them. You and me?"

"I don't care—" Then something stabbed him in his left kidney, and he bolted up in the chair.

"You all right?"

"I will be—time for us to go to your place." He spoke to Reg as he came though the room. "Hitch the team, will you please?"

"Yes, sir."

She looked stern-faced at him. "You sure you can stand that ride?"

"Yes, ma'am."

"I just didn't want you falling off the wagon." Then she softly chuckled. "Sorry, I think I've found my laugh."

He leaned back and nodded in approval. "Finding that laugh is wonderful. Only way I'll ever get any rest is go with you. I'd have to do something if I stayed here."

"I understand. How was your mother?"

"Wanting to die."

She nodded tight-lipped.

"Help me up."

She shook her head in disapproval. "You're going to really be sore by the time we get back to my place."

On his feet with her help, he hobbled for the front door. If he ever caught that damn Shelby Reynolds, he'd peel his head open with an ax. The pain in his back, chest, and head made him dizzy when he stood on his feet.

Three hours later, she helped him down at her front yard gate. She'd been right—he felt real sore on his way to the porch—every step knifed him. He wanted to help her un-hitch. Instead, she herded him inside the house. In his chair with her gone to put the horses up, he toed off his boots and then limped over to the bed. He shed his britches and fell on the mattress. The house had grown cold, but he was too far gone to build a fire. His heavy eyelids closed and he slept.

"Wake up. Wake up. You're having a nightmare."

He opened his eyes and his shoulders shuddered. What was wrong? The warmth from the blazing fireplace swept his face as he managed to sit up and tried to clear his fuzzy brain.

"You were cussing and having a fit." She sat beside him on the bed in the housedress she'd worn to bed. The flat of her hand rubbed his shoulders, and he could have used hours of that treatment.

"I was trying to get my herd across the river. Someone kept driving them back at me."

"Who was it."

He shook his head. "I don't know, but I guess I lost my temper." He wet his lower lip and considered the dream—bad enough.

"I hope you never get that mad at me."

"Aw, Kathren, I won't. I promise."

She hugged him and kissed his cheek.

He laughed aloud. "If it don't sound too bad of me, I reckon I always wanted to share a bed with you. But I never put in—" Another sharp pain stiffened his spine. The sharpness halfway subsided, but it had caught his breath. "But I never figured I'd be so bad off I couldn't do anything about it."

They both laughed. It didn't hurt her like it did him.

"I guess we ain't getting our money's worth for all the gossip we must be getting." She wiggled around to pull her dress up some to be more comfortable.

He shook his head. "I'm sure getting mine."

He was. Whenever he got to feeling better, he planned to propose to her. Hell, all she could do was say no. She'd done that before, too.

Chapter 26

Two weeks before Christmas, he busied himself splitting stove wood. It wasn't like busting big blocks of firewood, but he had healed a lot and planned to go back to the ranch in the morning. Kathren brought him a cup of coffee from the kitchen, wearing the fluffy blue dress he liked. He sat down on the chopping block grateful for the reprieve.

"I guess Cady will be glad to be coming back home with you again?" He winked at her for the cup, and took the warm metal container in his hands. The daytime sun was heating up, but the air still held the coolness of night.

"She didn't sound that excited. She asked if you were going to stay with us. And when I told her you had to go home and work on your own ranch, she said, 'Ah, dang.'"

He nodded and blew on the coffee. It was hot.

"I think she thought you'd be a fixture here."

"What did you think about that idea?"

For a moment, she looked uncomfortable at answering his question. Then she nodded slowly. "I have tried to put it all in place. You and I. Was I so starved for the comfort of man, any man, or were you this tall handsome man that rode in my life like a fairy tale?"

"What did you decide?"

She raised up and blue eye gaze met his. "You let me laugh. I never thought I'd ever laugh again. I thought I'd lost all the humor in my life forever."

"Is that good?" He sipped some of the coffee.

"Of course."

"I've got cattle to drive up from Mexico. A cattle drive to get ready for. I'll be busy till spring—"

She stepped in and hugged his arm. "You will always have cattle to drive, Chester Byrnes. You will always be busy. That's how God made you. These days you've been here, I've seen how you tick better than I ever have in my life. Things like your zeal that I thought were flaws are really strong points because you above all are loyal."

"Now you've said all that, can you and Cady come to the ranch for Christmas?"

"No. We need to be at my parents' house for that. You need to be at your place. But the day after Christmas—you'll be much better by then—"

He waited.

A look of impatience spread over her face. "I don't have to spell out what I'm offering you, do I?"

"You and me? Here?"

"Yes."

"Count me in."

He set the cup down and held her. He still hurt, but the sharpness of his body's aches and pains had dulled a lot—in fact, he felt so good, he forgot all about them for a moment.

Close to her ear, he whispered, "I'll be here."

"Good. Make sure you're in one piece then, too."

He squeezed her to him and they both laughed.

* * *

The dogs greeted him when he drove the buckboard into the ranch compound. Still stiff, he eased off the spring seat in the warmth of the bright sun. Susie soon joined him at the corral gate, where he unhitched the team.

"Don't lift that harness," she ordered. "Put it down, those boys can do that later."

"I can't leave everything to them."

"Yes, you can. Tell me about Kathren."

"She and her nine-year-old are fine."

"That's not what I wanted to know."

He smiled at her. "We're kinda letting it ferment. No rush. We never argued much and we laughed a lot. You'd never believe, but Luther told her on their wedding night that laughing was for kids, not for grown-ups."

"Really?"

"Yes. At Thanksgiving, she laughed in our house for the first time in a decade. What's happening here?"

"Dale Allen is finally taking charge. He and the boys are really getting things done. You need to brag on them."

"I will. Where's Matt?" He searched around for a sight of him.

"Busy building me new cabinets in the pantry. You know those rough-cut boards that have been in there forever? Well, I'm getting smooth ones. No more slivers. He's really a good carpenter."

"Sounds like you have things going well."

"Uncle Chet's back," Ray announced as he and his younger brother Ty climbed up the far side of the corral like two squirrels. Then they looked for the horses at the other end, and made a fast descent and rushed over to scale that side.

"We sure missed you."

"I missed you boys." He patted them on their backs. "It's good to be home. What's been happening?"

"No much. We found a burro to ride for a few days, but Dad said cowboys rode horses and made us turn him loose. That old burro just came here," Ray said. "Probably some Mexican couldn't feed him, huh?"

"I bet. So what's he doing to replace it?"

Ray looked up at him with a frown. "Replace what?"

"Your burro."

"He wasn't ours," Ty said crestfallen. "He belonged to some damned old Messican."

"Ssh. Susie's here," Ray said.

"I never heard that," she said.

"Good thing," Ray said.

"Dad called him that."

"We ain't supposed to cuss."

Ty agreed with a nod.

By damn, he'd find them a pony in short order if Dale Allen couldn't. Best to buy just one and make them share it. If they had two, they might ride off to Mexico or someplace like the big boys.

"You three wash up. We'll have lunch shortly."

"We'll do that, Susie. You boys hungry."

"Yes, sir."

"Good, we're going to cure that in a few minutes." He turned to Susie in the doorway. "What about Louise?"

"She's not coming home until after Christmas. Wants to spend this holiday with her parents."

"That's fine."

"I thought so, too. What're your plans?"

"Oh, I'm going over the day after Christmas to see Kathren and we're going to celebrate then."

She nodded in approval. "Robert may be here for Christmas dinner. Depends how busy he is at his job, I guess."

"Good."

The next morning at breakfast, he explained to them about the steers he had contracted for in Mexico. He wanted to go get them the end of January. Then they'd only be on the ranch six weeks before the drive north, and not eat up all the grass that he might need later.

"Reynolds men have stopped driving cattle on us." Dale Allen said.

Reg waved his fork down the table to get their attention. "I heard they've been real busy trying to trap all their fattening pigs that got loose."

It was good for a round of table laughter.

"I'll check the oat fields and, Reg, you and the rest can check cattle today. I'm sending Dale Allen off to buy a pony."

His brother blinked at him.

"Ray and Ty need a horse if they're ever going to be cowboys."

May smiled, pleased, and whispered something privately to her husband. He nodded. "We can do that."

The two younger boys kept their heads down, busy eating, but they were like racers at the starting line, ready to run. Coffee mug in his hands, Chet wondered what Kathren was doing. Probably saddling up by this time to check on her cattle, making sure they stayed on her range.

She'd done that religiously while he was there—returning about noon to do her house chores unless she had a problem out there. That must have been her job when Hines was alive, too. He spent lots of time away. No one ever knew where he went when he was gone, but there'd always been plenty of speculation.

The fence looked in good shape as he circled the fields, and the oats were coming along. He could see the tracks where the deer were jumping the boundaries made of tight wire and upright cedar stays closely woven in them. An expensive enclosure, but it was the only fencing available besides wooden rails. A few blacksmith shops made wire with barbs or rowels on it, but his fencing was better than that— besides, that barbed stuff would sure scar up a horse or colt if they got in it. He didn't need anything that encouraged screwworm flies either.

It was past noon when he stopped to eat the cinnamon rolls that Susie had sent along. He was on a small bluff over a wide creek bottom planted with oats. A large eight-point buck crossed the open field below, then tested the air in search of some doe he'd missed breeding earlier in the season. The stag paused at the edge of the patch to rake a few small cedars with his antlers to mark his territory. Flat needles flew in the air. Then he raised his head and curled back his lips to strain his nose and tried again to locate her. That fat buck would make good eating, but Chet didn't have the strength to butcher him or even load him over the saddle. He'd get him another day. The cinnamon rolls drew the saliva into his mouth. While he ate them, he noticed some carrion birds in the sky.

Several buzzards circled in the west, and he decided to go check on what they were doing. The dun cat-hopping uphill and skidding on his heels down the steep slopes jarred him some. But soon, he could see the buzzards' interest was in a dead cow critter, probably, from the smaller horns, a young cow or heifer.

But what he saw and did not like was the fact that she'd been *slow-elked*. A term to indicate that they'd only taken the hindquarters and loin and wasted the rest. She should have been suckling a milk-fat calf, but he couldn't see any sign of one. If it was around there, it would be bawling its head off for her. They must have rustled it as well.

Dismounting, he squatted down in some discomfort and studied the horse tracks. The copper smell of death assailed his nostrils. Three ponies had been there. He'd bet they'd used the unshod one for packing. Some runover boot heel and sole prints were indistinguishable.

He picked up two spent .45 casings from in the grass. No doubt they'd shot her at close range between the eyes. The other bullet was for her calf. The rustlers left headed west. If he didn't ache all over so bad, he'd've tracked them. He still had lots of mending to do. With the loss of the cow noted in his logbook, he and Dun headed for the house.

Ty and Ray were riding double on a fat Welsh pony in the corral when he dismounted. They didn't even see or hear Chet ride in. Beside the corral, hugging his wife May, Dale Allen beamed at his sons. He nodded at Chet. "I found one."

"Looks good to me."

"He acts like he likes the boys, too," May said, looking excited, and Chet agreed.

"What did you find?" Dale Allen asked.

"Fences look in great shape. I rode them out. Someone

slow-elked a cow up above the pea patch in a canyon, and I guess they got her calf as well."

"How long ago?" Dale Allen looked upset.

"A day or two ago. Some tracks, but they were cold."

"Learn anything else?"

"They used a .45. Two casings." He leaned his back against the corral to find a comfortable place for his back, and braced his boots out in front of himself. There wasn't any place he could escape the aching.

"You're hurting?" Dale Allen asked.

"No worse than I've been."

"Sorry you had to take that beating for all of us."

Chet clapped his brother on the shoulder. "I'll mend. I've got some whiskey in those saddlebags. I think its time for me to have a drink. You want one?"

"Sure. You think they did it? I mean the cow killing?"

"Proving it might be tough. They left the hide."

Dale Allen got the bottle out and they both took a swig. His brother turned down any more, and led Dun off to put him up, talking softly to May as they went.

Still braced against the fence, Chet took another swallow of the smooth liquor and wiped his mouth on the back of his hand.

"Does that help?" Susie asked.

"No. But it makes so you don't care."

"You look tuckered out. Why don't you take a nap? I'll have the boys get you for supper."

"You know what?"

She shook her head.

"I let a fat eight-point buck go by this morning 'cause I couldn't load him on a damn horse by myself. And Dale Allen really wanted to ask me why I didn't follow those faint tracks—" He tried another shot of the whiskey. It was beginning to numb things. "'Cause I could barely get back on my horse."

"Good thing you didn't then."

He agreed, and took another one out of the neck of the bottle. Drunk, he wouldn't care how bad he hurt.

The next day, still sore from the day before, at Susie's insistence he tried to rest and stayed around the place. A jittery feeling of missing something made him restless, and he decided that he didn't have Kathren to talk to. Strange how their few weeks together had built a bond that drew on him that hard. It felt so natural for him to be around her. Her hand on his shoulder—her attention—small kisses—damn, he had it bad and two weeks left to go.

He cleaned firearms and when that was done, he went back in the kitchen and drank fresh coffee the girls made for him. Both of Susie's helpers acted happy about their jobs, and chattered in Spanish while he blew on the steam and tried to figure what he would do next. The books could wait—he couldn't sit still that long.

"There is a man at the front door for you," Astria said to him.

"Thanks." He rose and went through the living room. Hat in hand, Warren Hodges stood waiting inside the living room. A thin man in his forties who ranched south of Mayfield, he nodded, and his Adam's apple bobbed like he had trouble swallowing. He was wearing a heavy coat, and Chet told him to hang it up and come in and have a seat.

"Well, I heard about them beating you up in Casey's." He narrowed his blue eyes, taking a seat in the chair opposite

Chet. "I can't figure that bunch out. But I came over to tell you about my situation. Earl's brother and some tough gunny came by my place and told me I better not ship any cattle up north with you if I knew what was good for me. That made me mad, you know?"

"Would me, too. When did they do that?"

"Yesterday. They got me mad, you know? I grabbed my old shotgun by the door and told them to haul out or I'd perforate them with it."

"What happened then?"

"Shelby said I'd live to regret that, too—" Hodges shook his head and gritted his teeth. "Boy, oh, boy, I had a hard time not giving them both barrels. Ain't no one telling me what I can and can't do, you know?"

"I understand, Warren."

"I was a Ranger, you know?"

"Yes, I do."

"I ain't taking that crap. I need to sell cattle as bad as anyone, and they damn sure ain't telling me who I can send them with." His hands were close to shaking in his lap.

"Warren, we'll be glad to take your cattle to Kansas. Dale Allen's going to be the trail boss. He'll do a good job. Because of the problem, I need to stay here. I'm sorry I can't stop those galoots from threatening you. I'm trying to cool the whole thing down."

"I savvy all that. There's three of their boys rotting in jail now. You'd think they'd've learned, wouldn't you? You know, you just may have to kill the whole damn tribe of 'em to ever settle this."

"I hope not." Chet shook his head in disapproval

"Well, you can count on a hundred head from me."

Chet made it though the day—fidgeting. In the morning,

he'd have them saddle him a horse. Perhaps in the open air, he could look at things different and maybe get his mind straightened out. No telling—he sure missed Kathren.

After breakfast the next day, he rode up and looked over the remuda. The horses were wintering well, and checking the small bunches here and there, he saw no problems. Past mid-morning, a rider came on the fly, and he sent the bay horse called Shoat in that direction. Obviously, they wanted him back.

Reg slid his pony to a halt. "They shot and killed Warren Hodges this morning in Mayfield."

"Who shot him?" Was it over shipping cattle?

"Shelby and that Sharp fella. Warren shot Sharp. He ain't going to do nothing but push up bluebonnets. But Shelby got away."

"What else?"

"Dale Allen's gone into Mayfield to see what he could do for Warren's widow, Clara."

"Good." That would be a first. His brother was finally growing up. "We better head in and see what we can do."

"They said those two stormed out in the street and challenged Hodges when he rode in. There was lots of cussing went on and then the shooting began. Hodges shot Sharp twice in the chest and may have wounded Shelby."

"But he got away?"

"They said he did."

Maybe Hodges gut-shot him. Chet hoped so.

Chapter 27

His aches grew fainter. No more cow losses. J.D. took Susie in the buckboard to San Antonio for a few days on a holiday shopping spree. The boys were sorting the big steers out of the main herd and bunching them east of Yellow Hammer Creek.

Why were the days passing so slowly for him? Hodges's funeral proved to be a sad affair. Several of the older ex-Rangers came from all over for it. The name of Shelby Reynolds drew much of their ire. A reward of a hundred dollars for his arrest was put up afterward in Casey's Saloon. Dead or alive.

Chet promised Clara that when the time came to ship the cattle Warren had wanted to sell, he'd send a crew over to get them. The woman thanked him, looking red-eyed and very lost. She had no children. A niece was staying at the ranch to help her. Poor bucktoothed girl acted backward as a doe deer, but she took good care of Clara at the services. At least the widow had someone.

He wondered what Kathren was doing. She'd not come to the funeral. Probably never knew Warren, or didn't get the word. The real problem might be that others would cancel out on him about sending their cattle north because of all the talk that was what the shooting was about.

Sheriff Trent came by the ranch, and discovered Susie was gone to San Antonio. Chet decided that Bob looked let down by her absence, and invited him to stay for supper.

"I guess I better get back. I'd found there was a two-hundred-fifty dollar reward on that Sharp. I sent for it for Clara Hodges."

"Will they pay it?" Rewards were sometimes hard to collect.

"I'll get her the money."

"That's good. I'll tell Susie you were by. I know if she was here, she'd've been pleased you came by."

"Thanks," he said, looking a little uncomfortable at Chet's words. "I'm going to send a deputy down to Mayfield and station him there. He can't stop all this business, but it might help."

Chet agreed, and walked him out to his horse.

Trent gathered the reins, and then took hold of the saddle horn to mount his bay gelding. "I hope you don't mind me seeing her."

"Not at all."

"You know I'm older than she is."

"That's her decision."

"Good. I wanted to level with you."

"No problem. Come back any time, you're always welcome here."

Trent nodded and rode off.

He was serious about her. Chet watched him short-lope across the open country east of the house. What would Chet do without her? Lord only knows.

Dale Allen thought they'd have 550 three-year-old steers on the ranch to drive to Kansas. Chet's tally book showed a higher number if they hadn't strayed or died since he'd tallied them in. A five-percent loss wouldn't be unusual. Ten percent would be too high, but an actual count would be the real test. They'd know in February when they road-branded them.

Christmas Eve came and the ranch family gathered—all the Byrnes relatives and the crew including Sammy, Pinky, Matt, and the girls Astria and Maria. They sang some carols and Susie handed out the gifts. Rock and Theresa had already gone to bed, but Susie would have presents for them in the morning.

There were pullover shirts for all the men. Made of blue denim, they represented the handiwork of the ranch women. The crew looked shocked. They weren't ready either for their own pairs of red woolen long handles, which drew some red faces but plenty of appreciation. May was promised a new long woolen coat and two new dresses when Dale Allen got back from the drive in the fall and could take her to San Antonio. Then wool socks for the men, jack-knives for the three younger boys, and chaps. There were hunting knives for the older two. Some new bull-hide chaps and a Boss of the Plains gray Stetson hat for the trail boss, Dale Allen. A new pair of boots specially made to fit Chet by a man named Justin in Fort Worth.

New skirts and blouses for Astria and Maria. Their brown eyes about popped out when they opened the packages wrapped in plain brown paper and string. There were things for the baby, and a new windup alarm clock for the cook Matt. A gold pocket watch would not have made him happier. Oranges and hard candy. Susie opened her own present last. A blue Sunday dress made by a dressmaker in San Antonio. She held it up and whirled around.

Chet could see her dancing in it. He stood up and applauded her. The rest joined in.

"Don't ever send me up there again with her, Chet," J.D said, shaking his head.

"Why's that?"

"Man, I had more secrets to keep than I could think about since we got back."

"You did good, J.D.," she said.

"Thanks a lot. I can't recall any time in my life when I ever had a nicer Christmas," Pinky said, awed by all the things that were his. Wetting his sun-scarred lips and shaking his head, he looked close to tears.

The girls served hot cocoa and fruitcake. The evening came to a close and the celebrants went to the bunkhouse or their quarters.

Reg planned to ride over to Molly's folks' place for dinner the next day. Chet told him to be careful and not take the main way. The boy agreed and left the house.

Left alone at last, he and Susie sat in the living room and watched the logs in the fireplace blaze away. A knot or two exploded and the small burst fell down in the flames to be consumed.

"I have something for you," Susie said, and reached in her dress pocket and came out with a small box.

He frowned. "What is it?"

"Something you may need."

"I wanted to say buying them hands that underwear and socks about made them all cry."

"I'd seen their wash hanging out down there." She snickered. "They sure needed some. Go ahead, open it."

He agreed and pried the box apart, removing the lid. A small gold band ring rested in some cotton. "Who's is this?"

"It was Grandma Charlotte's."

"Reckon she'd approve of me giving it to Kathren?"

"I wouldn't know why not."

"I wished I'd've got her something—" It was too late for that—no way he'd find anything in time to go over there.

"You got her something."

He blinked in disbelief at his sister. "I did?"

"I'm pretty good on sizes and I had a divided canvas riding skirt, a fuffy blouse, and a waist jacket made for her in San Antonio."

He collapsed in the chair. "How will I ever repay you?"

"Just be yourself. We all count on you. This Reynolds business will surely go away."

"Can I be honest with you?"

"Sure."

He dropped his chin in defeat and shook his head. "I think in time we'll have to sell out and move to solve it."

"But our family built this ranch here—"

"Susie, if I could end it, I would tonight. But I'm afraid there ain't no end to it."

He rose and hugged her. "What did you get Bob?"

"I didn't want to get him too much, so I found a white shirt in San Antonio that will fit him. Sheriffs always need white shirts, I figure."

"I don't have to tell you he's got some age on you."

"I'm not afraid. And I'm not worried about being an old maid if he doesn't ask me. But he's the first man who ever stirred something inside me—you know what I mean?"

"I know what you mean." He held up the ring between

his thumb and index finger to admire it. "If I wasn't such a coward, I'd ask her tomorrow."

"I can't do it for you."

He closed his eyes and laid his cheek on top of her head. "How well I know."

Chapter 28

Early morning, he left with his gifts for Kathren tied on the horn and the ring box in a vest pocket. He wore his heavy coat; a shift to a north wind had blown in overnight. His Christmas underwear felt wonderful, and the new boots fit a little tight, but they'd stretch in time. Nothing could spoil this day for him. After ten days without her, he felt starved—but he sure didn't want to scare her.

He pulled down his hat brim and gave Dun his head. The big gelding could short-lope across Texas and not be winded. Taking shortcuts and the back way, in record time he reined Dun up and looked down on her place. He let the big horse catch his breath, then started off down the hillside.

She came out the back door and shaded her eyes with her hands to see who was coming. He could see her smiling a long ways from the house. Short-loping Dun, he rolled in beside her and dismounted on the fly. He swept her up in his arms and they kissed as hungry as he could ever remember.

"You didn't get me a present, did you?" Her gaze centered on the package tied ot the horn

"No," he said to see her reaction. "It's just a little thing."

"You did."

"Let me unsaddle Dun and we can go inside and you'll see it's nothing."

She threw her arms around his neck and kissed him with more abandon than the first time. His head spun while he was undoing the girth and stripping the saddle and pads off. With Dun in the corral, he kept the package away from her in a teasing way. Twisting and turning, they went to the house. Inside, he handed it to her and took off his coat.

"You shouldn't have gotten me anything." Unable to break the string, she used a butcher knife off the dry sink to make quick work of it. When she opened it, her blue eyes flew open. A small scream of excitement came from her mouth and she dropped on her butt atop the bed with the partially opened package in her lap.

"Oh, my God! You did—you did. Oh, Chester, it is gorgeous." She held the blouse up at arm's length. "How— how did you know my size?"

"You aren't supposed to ask those things. I just hope it fits."

"It will. It will. And a riding skirt. And a jacket. I never got a Christmas gift in my whole life this nice." She jumped up and began to undress.

He turned his back.

"How is everyone at the ranch?" she asked.

He could hear her rushing to get into the new outfit. "Fine. Susie really laid Christmas on them."

"Oh, my—" she said, and he turned around.

The lacy blouse fit her perfectly. It was dressy-looking with the riding skirt. He helped her into the jacket and tears began to run down her face. "I never got a present so nice in all my life."

She clung to him and they kissed. When their passion got beyond that stage, he tried to toe off his new tight boots. Didn't work. So after he'd hopped around on one foot to try to remove them, she shoved him on the bed with her hands on his chest and *debooted* him.

They were both laughing so hard, he had to wipe the tears off his face.

Late afternoon, he stood at the dry sink drinking water from a dipper. The cool room air swept the bare skin on his legs. He went over and added some more split wood to the dying fire in the hearth. Squatting on his bare feet, he watched the flames begin to consume the new fuel. Wrapped in a blanket, she came over and joined him.

"Merry Christmas, Chester Byrnes," she said in a smoky voice with her arm slung over his shoulder.

He nodded his head in approval. "Yes, this is."

This small house and Kathren sure made a helluva Garden of Eden.

Chapter 29

Did ja or didn't ja? That was the question Susie had to know when he got back to the ranch. He read it on her face, and she was about beside herself before they had a moment alone. Scratching his head, he shrugged. "Never had time."

"Oh, for heaven sakes, in two days. Do you mean you didn't have ten seconds to ask her?"

He shook his head and dropped his gaze so he didn't laugh. "We really didn't have any time for anything."

"Two whole days?"

"Someday you'll see."

"I think you were afraid to ask her."

"Maybe—I didn't want to ruin the neat time we had together."

"I saw that neat time written all over your face when you rode in."

"That obvious, huh?"

"Worse than obvious." She poured him some coffee, then sank on the chair across the table. "Do you think that you'll ask her?"

He shrugged. "In time, if she wants me to."

"She doesn't want to?"

"I never said that. We're kinda letting our relationship ferment like wine. And it keeps getting better."

"How did she like the outfit?"

"That was the frosting. She cried."

"Cried?"

"I guess Luther Hines never believed in Christmas either."

Susie shook her head. "He must have been strange."

"No, I think he must have been real self-centered. She did all the work on the ranch and he rode off most of the time. God knows where. I think she suspected where he went, but she never offered to tell me that part. When he was home, she said nothing could bother him."

"Where do you think he went?"

He didn't answer her at once. "I think he went far away and he robbed individuals on the road. Probably shot them and took their valuables. No witnesses. Highwayman, I guess you'd call him."

"Really."

"He had a small herd of cattle and yet he always rode good horses. They cost money. But the horses were all nondescript. No white markings. Other things about the way they lived told me he must have done something, for he had other sources of income. He was tough physically and cold-hearted as a north wind. There's some black chapter there that we may never know about."

"What are your plans now?"

"To get everything done for the drive. She knows I'll be busy. Maybe when that's over, we can talk more about our lives."

Susie shook her head. "What's on for today?"

"Get you some woodcutters to bring in wood. I'll ride down to San Lupe and see the man. He's sending me those families later to farm. Maybe they'll come up early and get you some more wood cut."

"Good."

He rode Strawberry, and the cool weather warmed as the sun rose. Dale Allen and his crew were skirting the south end, driving ranch stock back and strays off their land. At breakfast, his brother had told him that the problem of cattle being pushed on the ranch had eased up. Most that they turned back now were obvious strays.

Maybe the feud was dying. Shelby was still on the run. When Chet reached San Lupe, there were several heavily loaded carts with oxen hitched parked in the street. Don Miguel was overseeing things, and smiled when Chet rode up.

"Ah, they were just getting ready to go to your ranch," Miguel said.

Chet shook his and Pepe's hand. Pepe would be the *segundo* in charge of the men and had worked for Dale Allen for many seasons.

"We plant many acres this year?" Pepe asked.

"About like last year."

"Good. We can handle that."

"Dale Allen is taking the herd to Kansas, so I will be there this summer."

"No problem, *señor*."

"I didn't think so. The jacales are waiting. We must rebuild my sister's wood supply first when you all get up there. She likes for it to be dry before we uses it for cooking, so we need lots of it.

"I'll have frijoles, flour, cornmeal, and lard at the camp when you arrive."

Pepe smiled. "Good. By then we will be starved."

"I hope not."

Pepe dismissed his concern with a head shake and a mild smile. "It will be good to get back to work,"

"These are all good men with families," Don Miguel said as they went to the cantina for their usual drink and lunch.

"I guess it has been a tradition for years that the San Juan people spend the spring and summer and fall working at the ranch and then winter down here."

"Ah, *sí*. They raise gardens up there and bring home lots of food for the winter, too."

"Good. We'll hope it rains so we'll have crops to tend."

"Always they have a Mass and pray for a good season before they leave here. They know how important that is to their jobs."

Chet agreed. "I have had trouble with the Reynolds family all winter. Tell everyone to keep an eye out."

"We have heard about it. I will tell Pepe to be on the watch."

"If they threaten them, do as they say. I can straighten it out later. I want no one killed or hurt who works for me."

"I savvy. I'll tell them not to fight them."

"Good. I'll ride back and await their arrival."

"No worry, *mi amigo*. Your workers and their families are coming."

That resolved, Chet cut across country to Mayfield. He'd order those supplies he'd need for his farm hands so Grosman could have them freighted in if he didn't have them on hand.

At noontime, he stopped at Casey's Saloon and tied

Strawberry at the rack, The town looked quiet, and he went inside for a beer. Since he wouldn't get home for supper, he got something off the free lunch bar. A few loafers nodded, busy making sandwiches of German sausage and cheese at the counter.

"Hey, you all right, Chet? We ain't seen ya in a while."

"Last time I came in, they beat the hell out of me. I been staying away," he told the red-faced Casey.

"Aw, me lad, we'd never let that happen again."

Chet smiled. "I know that."

"Ain't been a one of them in town since," Casey said, drawing him a beer.

"Anyone heard from Shelby?" Chet twisted around and looked at the others.

"He took a big powder," one said.

"Good." Chet moved in and made his own sandwich with some mustard, ham, and cheese. On the side of his plate, he added cold potatoes mixed with sweet pickles. Back at the bar, he ate, sipped his beer, and listened to Casey.

"There's a new man bought the Whortons' ranch. He came in here from New Mexico. Said the Apaches were still too bad out there. He lost his horses twice to 'em. His name's Edgar Caufman."

"Sounds like Texas five years ago." The fresh rye bread fit the meat and cheese right for him.

Casey agreed. "Nice-acting fella anyway."

"We can use all of them we can get."

"That's for sure."

After his meal, Grosman told Chet that he could have the order on the dock any time he needed it.

"Day after tomorrow, I'll send the boys in after it," Chet said.

"That would be fine."

"You hear—" The storekeeper leaned over the counter to whisper. "They're trying them boys for her murder the last week of January. They call you to testify yet?"

"No, but they will, I'm sure." That notion did not set well. He had hoped to be down in Mexico bringing out their cattle at that time. Well, Dale Allen could go with the boys.

He swung by Kathren's place. It wasn't on the way home, but he felt drawn back to see her.

Her daughter Cady was feeding chickens when he rode up. She could smile as pretty as her mother.

"Where's the boss?" he asked, dropping out of the saddle.

"She's not back yet. Checking the cattle like she does all the time."

"You in charge of the chickens?"

"Oh, yes. They've started laying again, too. We've been getting one or two eggs a day."

"I guess they know spring's coming, too."

Cady was looking away when she asked him, "You going to marry my mother?"

"You know that you're the second person to ask me that in two days." He squatted down and watched her throw the grain out as the birds ran for their share.

She laughed. "Who else asked you?"

"It's got to be a secret."

"Oh, I'll keep a secret."

"My sister Susie."

"What did you tell her?"

"I guess we're thinking on it."

"Thinking hard about it?"

"I guess we are."

"Good. You keep thinking." She grinned at him with a mischievous look on her face.

He'd do that. At the sound of a horse coming off the hill, he rose and looked for her. She was coming in. Good, the sight of her warmed him.

"Hey, Mom, look who's here?"

"Well, stranger, you lost?"

"No, I was looking for work. Need a hand?"

Amused, she shook her head and flew off the horse. In seconds, she was in his arms and they were kissing like there was no else around. Her hard-breathing horse butted them to move until they broke up laughing.

"He really wants in the corral," Kathren said, and frowned at the gelding.

"We better put him in there." He took the reins and led the horse to the barn. Then he elbowed her aside and slipped off the saddle and pads.

"You're trying to spoil me," she said under her breath.

He searched for Cady and then smiled. "You need lots of spoiling."

"Well—you can see my girl is here."

"I like her. I'm not upset about that. I simply came to see you. Good reason?"

She pursed her lips and nodded. "We can't hardly—"

"Can't hardly what?" He gathered her in his arms and pulled her against him. "I have you. That's all I need. They're having the Reynolds boys' trials last week of the month, I learned today. I was supposed to go to Mexico then and get some cattle from down there."

"What'll you do?"

"Send my brother."

She nodded and snuggled in his arms. "I am very pleased you came by anyway."

"My Grandmother Cooney left me something I want to show you."

She slightly frowned at him when he dug out the small box and gave it to her, not letting her hardly get away enough from his hug to open it.

"Why—why—it's a ring?"

He nodded. Not hardly breathing. He couldn't swallow. Her ripe body was against his. Finally, he managed, "Susie asked me when I got home—did you ask her?"

"And?"

"I said no."

"And?"

"I got to thinking some maybe I should."

"Maybe?"

"Hell, Kathren, I'm having enough trouble doing this."

She pressed her fingers to the base of her nose to hold it back—but laughter broke out anyway. Then he began to laugh, too.

"What's so funny?" Cady asked, looking vexed at their hilarity.

"Chet's trying to ask me something?" She leaned out and handed the box to her daughter.

"Why it's a ring. Mother. It's a wedding ring!"

"I know, honey."

"Did you tell him yes?"

"He hasn't asked me."

"I know. He told me that."

"What did he tell you?"

"He hadn't asked you yet."

"Oh, Cady, you weren't suppose to ask him that."

"How was I going to find out? You won't say."

"Kathren Hines, will you marry me?"

"Tell him yes. Mom, hurry and tell him yes."

"Why?" she asked her daughter, winking at him.

"So the damn suspense'll be over."

"Cady Hines, don't you ever swear like that again."

"You know, I think Cady's right, Kathren. Will you?"

"Yes, Chester Byrnes. I'll marry you."

Cady went to shouting and circling around them like an Indian at a war dance. He felt ready to bust some buttons and with Kathren hugging him, they danced, too.

Chapter 30

Their mother died the next week. It was a cold blue day. Robert came down for the funeral services, and drove the buckboard with Susie dressed in black. Rock rode with them, though he was badly confused why he had to go instead of take a nap. May stayed home with the baby and the girls. The ranch hands under Matt guarded the place while everyone else went to the schoolhouse and cemetery.

Kathren and Cady joined him at the school. Their presence felt comforting in the cold building despite the wood stove being started too late to drive our the chill. For the first time, he felt a part of something besides the family. These two were about to become his own. What he'd grumbled about not having for years was coming to an end. He'd have a wife and a fine daughter as saucy as his wife-to-be.

"Theresa Myra Cooney Byrnes, born July 10th, 1812, in Shelbyville, Tennessee . . ." The preacher's words rang in his ears. His mother had only been sixteen years old when she'd had him. He'd never realized it before that moment. He knew then they lived in upper Arkansas when he was born on the fifteenth of November. Near a place called Carrolton.

It snowed that day. Grandpa Cooney told him about it when he was a boy. Said his mother wanted to call him Snow, but Rock said it was bad enough to be a stone. His son didn't need to be "white stuff."

He'd been named Chester after Chester Cooney, an ancestor who'd earned an officer's commission in the Revolutionary War. Sometime later, Major Chester Cooney fell overboard off a steamboat and drownd. No one said if he had been drunk or not.

Neighbors bore his mother's coffin up to the cemetery, and they all huddled under blankets or heavy coats at the grave site. He stood with Kathren and Cady, wishing the preacher's pleading call for souls to save could have been shortened.

He wanted to remember her when she was young, bright, and happy as well as when she sang all the time in the house. "Sweet Betsy from Pike . . ." He knew the words to all of them, including "Ole Dan Tucker" and also the "Blue Tail Fly." Before the Comanche raids and the loss of the three siblings—there were three living he knew about. Two others died at a young age. No wonder she lost her way in life. He remembered her shooting at those rabid screaming Indians out of a small hole in the sidewall of the ranch house and telling him as a small boy to keep his head down and to stay under the thick table.

After the last amen, he took his girls back to the schoolhouse, and the womenfolks got busy setting up the meal.

"When can you come see us?" Cady asked.

"Oh, Saturday."

"You can come see Mother. I won't be there. I'm going to Mason with Grandma to visit Grandma's sister."

"I'll miss you."

She wrinkled her nose at him. "I bet you two don't even know I'm gone that day."

"Cady," her mother insisted.

"It's the truth."

He had to agree, but he did it silently. Folks came by to tell him how they would miss his mother. They, too, must have remembered the younger, brighter woman in the box on the hill.

Cady was off talking to Heck when Kathren turned to him. "I'm sorry she thinks you are hers."

"I think she's very smart for her age."

"She is. If they can find a schoolteacher for a session, she'll finish the fifth grade."

"Don't worry about her and me. I love her and if you look in a mirror sometime, I think you will see yourself growing up. In fact, I recall going to school with a girl just like her."

She nudged him with an elbow. "Wait till I get you home."

"I can't hardly wait."

"You're not supposed to laugh at a funeral."

"She won't care. She might even have laughed with you years ago."

"I'll be good. If I can get my father to feed the chickens, I might come stay at my aunt's house in Mason while the trial is going on."

"I'd like that. Matt's not busy. He's our cook for the drive. He could come over and watch them."

"Really?"

"Let's plan on it."

"We can do that then." She agreed, looking pleased.

"I'm not rushing you, but they have a judge up there that marries people."

"Oh, I couldn't leave Cady out. She'd never forgive us."

"Just an idea."

"Keep thinking, cowboy. You aren't doing bad."

They parted outside after the meal until Saturday, and he went home with the rest of the family. Sheriff Trent told him the trial would start a week from Monday, and Chet agreed to be there to testify.

Thursday, he rode the field perimeter fences in a bitter cold wind that cut like a knife. His San Juan help was there and busy cutting firewood, though he doubted they were getting much done. A Mexican and cold weather did not agree.

It was a shot that came from nowhere. It ripped through some branches beside him. He booted his horse called Jim Bowie with both spurs, and in response the horse jumped out into space. The big black slid down a steep slope, landed in a bottom, and made a flat run for some cedars.

He slid him to a halt and jerked out the Sharps. One shot. Where had it came from? Two shots, you can locate the shooter. One shot when he wasn't counting on it had no source. If he didn't testify at their trial, they might get a jury to overlook the evidence—he wanted Marla's killers punished. Memories of her and their affair only made him heartsick.

Angry to the bone, he sent Bowie scrambling up the hillside, and topping a ridge, on the high point, caught a glimpse of a distant rider heading southwest. Was it Shelby? Could even be Earl.

He sent Bowie down that slope and hit the flat in a dead run. If the pony had the bottom he knew he had, they could overtake that rider and get him in range for the Sharps. With the reins, he crossed-whipped him from side to side. In a half mile, he could see the rider and his horse, obviously intent on finding someplace to hide. At that range, Chet would be lucky to shoot the horse—he whipped Bowie again and got another surge from him.

The gelding closed the gap, but it was still a long ways and he couldn't see enough to distinguish the rider, but the man was flailing his horse to get away. Chet put the stop on Bowie and swung down. The rear sight on the last notch, he zeroed in on the far-away horse, clicked the first trigger, then eased down on the second one.

The .50-caliber weapon kicked his shoulder like a big mule. The charge deafened his eardrums. The blast ran to the core and the smoke stank his eyes, but the glimpse he had of the rider and horse going ass over teakettle drew a smile. He didn't care which one it was—he'd taken out another back-shooter. Better go home and clean the Sharps.

Saturday, he rode over to Kathren's, and the two of them spent an easy afternoon before her fireplace making popcorn. Cady was *grandmothering* it for the day.

"You know, I'm not supposed to make you mad or get in a fuss with you," she said, looking back at him from where she squatted by the fireplace shaking the long-handled skillet with the cover.

"Who said?"

"My daughter. I think she's worried I'm going to run you off."

They both laughed. Cady didn't know there would be no running away on his part.

He rode home late Sunday afternoon, wearing his slicker in a drizzle. Moisture from gulf had blown in on a warming trend. Someday, having Kathren for his wife was going to be all right. He'd send Matt over to watch her place the next Sunday so she could drive up to Mason for the trial.

Plans can change. When he sat down with Dale Allen to discuss the trip to Mexico for the five hundred head, right off his brother said, "Matt wants to take a pack string rather than a chuck wagon to Mexico. That country is too rough the way we'll come back, and the river may be up."

When he'd gone down there before to get the cattle, he'd always bought the food for the crew from some small village venders. Dale Allen and Matt had other plans. He'd need to find someone to replace Matt. "Sure, you're the trail boss. You'll need five thousand dollars for the purchase. Don't take any scrubby ones. I mean, cut them out. Rodrigo is all right, but like all cattle traders he'll try you."

Dale Allen nodded. "Ten days if we get along good to get back?"

"I'd say so. Don't mess around below the border. Keep moving all you dare. There's enough outlaws down there to eat those cattle in one meal. All right, you're taking the hands with you, right?"

"I know that you have to go to Mason and testify. That'll leave the ranch unguarded."

"I'll ride up to Mason tomorrow and hire a couple of fellas that Bob Trent recommends to stay here while you're gone. What if I send Heck over to watch Kathren's place while she's up there with me?"

"He'd like that." Dale Allen shook his head. "Thinks he's grown up now."

"I have the money for the cattle in the safe. I'd not

carry it on me. Maybe hide it on the lead packhorses in a flour sack."

"Matt will know where to put it."

Chet agreed. His brother was taking a good lead in doing this job. It might work out well in the end. The next morning, Chet saddled and, after breakfast, rode for Mason. Matt took the buckboard and headed for Mayfield to get the last things he needed. They parted with a wave.

Chet found the sheriff in his office. Mid-morning sunshine streamed in the window, and Trent sat behind a pile of wanted posters and papers. They shook hands and exchanged pleasantries for the day, including telling Trent what Susie was doing when he left the ranch.

"I need two punchers that have some backbone. Any around here like that out of work?"

"I think we can find some for you." Trent rose and put on his hat. "Let's try the livery first."

A gravel-voiced man named McComb ran the stables and he knew "two good'uns," Rip Smears and Toby Hardin. "Them boys been trying to get on with an outfit for months."

"Where are they now?" Chet asked.

"Rip's doing day work and you can talk to Hardin down at Goldman's store. He's clerking. Rip'll be back this evening sometime. Good hand with a rope or horse."

"They tough enough if push comes to shove?" Chet asked.

McComb nodded. "They damn sure ain't no Momma's boys."

"I'll see Hardin. You tell Smears to load his things and come on down to the bar-C. It's west of Mayfield."

"Everyone knows where you live."

Chet nodded. That was no lie.

Hardin was hardly out of teens. When Chet talked to him in the store, he thought the young man was going to jump over the counter and go with him then and there. But Chet told him later in the week was fine and to give notice.

After lunch with Trent at a German restaurant, he headed for the ranch. Close to supper time, Heck met him at the corral. "Dad said I was going to watch Mrs. Hines' place while she was in Mason."

"You up to it?" Chet asked, stripping out the latigos and then hefting his saddle off the snip-faced sorrel.

"You bet. What all will I have to do?"

"Feed the chickens. Gather the eggs and milk the cow and be sure everything's all right."

"Oh."

"What were you expecting?"

"More like ride the boundaries and send her strays home."

"Maybe the next time."

"I'll do her a good job anyway."

"You'll be the man in charge. Cook your own meals and all."

"I can handle that if she's got eggs and beans."

"I'm sure she does."

Heck nodded. "Reckon she needs a hand to work full-time?"

"Not now anyway."

"When am I going over there?"

"Saturday."

"I reckon this outfit can do without me that long."

"I bet they have a hard time," Chet said, and looked up. A tall lean rider in a worn-out shirt and a frayed wool vest rode up. In the last of the sundown, he looked like he'd had seen some hard days. His pony was a stout mustang, powerful built, and his black mane flowing down on both sides of his ewe neck.

"Rip Smears, sir. McComb said you needed some help." Rip pulled off his glove and when they shook hands, Chet knew by his calloused palm this man would work.

"Chet Byrnes. I do if you understand we're involved in a feud. To make it short, you might be in the middle of a war."

Smears tucked his gloves in his gun belt and nodded. "As long as you don't want me to herd sheep, I'll be fine with what comes."

"No sheep. Let's go eat and meet the rest. We can put your horse up later."

"I guess that means I have the job?"

"Yes."

"You don't like how I'm doing, tell me 'cause I'm a big boy. I'd rather cowboy than eat almost. Last man I worked full-time for got up one morning and fired me 'cause I was making too much noise reshoeing his horses and woke him up."

"That ain't likely here."

"Good."

Hardin came Friday on a thin two-year-old colt that about fell over when he dismounted him. On first appraisal, Chet guessed the youth lacked many of the skills he got hiring Smears, but the eager boy acted enthused.

At supper, Matt offered more news. "I know it's sure going bother everyone here, but I learned in Mayfield today that Earl Reynolds had a bad horse wreck this past week. He shattered his right arm so bad that Doc says he'll never use it again. I guess we all ought to all cry about that."

The .50-caliber blasted again in Chet's brain. The acrid smoke burned his eyes and the glimpse of horse and rider going end over end replayed in his mind. *He'd got him.*

Chapter 31

Dale Allen and crew left for Mexico the next morning. Chet could hear the squeal of the oxcarts coming. They were delivering wood to stack on Susie's large pile. Out in front of the parade came Pepe, hiking under a dusty straw sombrero, wearing a long serape, and using a staff.

He used his stick to point to the carts stacked high with wood. "We have the *señorita*'s wood."

"You have done well."

"I left two men to make more cedar stakes for your fencing."

"You think of many things," Chet said to praise the man.

"Next week, two of the men will start plowing. The rest will make stakes if this is enough firewood."

"No one has bothered you?"

"No, *señor*."

"Good. I have new mules. The mule man is gone to Mexico for two weeks, but I am sure your men will know which ones to harness."

"Pedro knows mules."

"Good. I have to go to Mason and I'll be gone for a few days."

"No problema."

"Thanks, I know I can count on you. Give my sister the order for food you will need. She'll see you get it."

"Gracias, patrón."

He and Heck left for Kathren's at mid-morning. Heck had a bedroll tied on behind his saddle. Ray and Ty were on the pony to accompany them to the creek. Then they were to ride right back. Susie waved from the porch as they left out. The next generation of the Byrnes clan rode with Chet. He'd sure need to expand the ranch to ever make it work for all of them.

At the ford, he send the younger ones home and he and Heck went on to Kathren's outfit.

"This is Heck," he said when she came out on the porch. "Matt had to go to Mexico and cook for the crew. Heck'll be watching things. Brought his bedroll and all."

"Pleased to meet you. I think you've met my daughter Cady."

"Yes, ma'am."

"She's with her grandparents, but I am certain she'd be pleased you were going to look after our stock. She helps do that."

"Oh, I'll do my best."

"I'm sure you will."

She winked, pleased, at Chet. "Come in. Dinner is ready when you two wash up."

After dinner, Chet and Heck busted stove wood for her. She stacked it for them. The afternoon passed congenially. Supper over, Heck took his bedroll to the hay shed to sleep after saying good night to them. Left alone, Kathren took a place atop Chet's lap on a kitchen chair and they talked quietly.

"I see some of a boy I once knew in him. He has broad shoulders for a boy. I don't mean like physically, but I mean to take charge."

"He's the firstborn. You could expect that."

She pushed the hair back from Chet's forehead and looked hard at him. "How will this trial go?"

"I hope it resolves the matter."

"I'm not digging, but you had an interest in her?"

He nodded. "She was leaving him. I found the letter— bloodstained and walked on that night."

"Oh, Chet, I'm sorry."

After a deep breath, he nodded. "I never showed it to anyone but my sister. I didn't want to harm her reputation. But the hearing kind of took that away from me."

She hugged him and put her face on his shoulder. "I hope this trial solves some of that."

"I've tried to put it all behind me."

"I didn't mean to upset you, but I see it did. I wanted to tell you I'll set that wedding day soon. I hope I didn't sound like I was backing out when you offered to marry me in Mason."

"No, I want Cady strewing flowers down the aisle on that day."

"I'm sure she could do that. Let's go to bed. I want you to hold me tight all night. I feel like I need it."

So do I.

They took her buckboard to Mason on Sunday and tied his horse on back. The weather warmed up, and the bright sun danced atop the water in the creeks and tanks. On the seat beside him, she hugged his arm from time to time, making a connection that warmed his heart.

They ate dinner at the same German restaurant he'd

eaten at earlier in the week with Trent. Then he delivered her to her aunt's place.

"I can walk to the courthouse tomorrow."

He shook his head. "I'll be here in the morning to accompany you over there."

She shook her head as if awed by him, and threw her arm around him. "You never cease to amaze me, Chet Byrnes."

"Is that you out there, Kathren dear?" a short gray-haired woman asked from the porch.

"Yes, and I want you to meet my man." She turned back him. "Come meet Martha. She'll love you."

He called for Kathren in the morning, and they strode the three blocks to the courthouse. In the hallway, Trent tipped his hat at Kathren and then introduced them to Sam Kringle, the state's prosecutor.

"You know they hired Bryan Moore to defend them."

"I don't know him," Chet said.

"He's high-priced and down here from Fort Worth."

"With all these confessions?" Chet looked at both men for an answer.

"It's like starting over. He's going to try to discredit all that. I wanted to warn you before you get on the stand."

"And Chet," Trent said. "He'll try to get you mad so the jury will see that and it will make them think you did it."

"I understand."

"He's clever. Good day, ma'am." Kringle left them and moved off with Trent. They were talking to each other as they disappeared through the tall, hand-carved courtroom doors.

She gripped his arm. "Give them hell."

He nodded. "I will."

"I know you will."

The courtroom was crowded. A deputy showed them the row reserved for them that he was overseeing. Both defendants appeared hollow-eyed when they were brought in under heavy guard. Neither of them looked at the crowd. They sat at the long table like no one else was there

Everyone rose as the stern faced Judge Burton came in, rapped his gavel, and court began. The jurors to be seated were mostly German farmers. Twelve were selected by mid-morning. Moore's complaints and frequent, long-winded objections were short-lived—Burton told him that they were unnecessary. But the obvious intention of the lawyer in the tailored suit with the plastered-down light brown hair was to show off his legal knowledge to try and impress the jury. His clients, Scotty Campbell and Mitch Reynolds, pleaded not guilty. In the opening statement, Kringle called Marla's murder a heinous crime.

Moore objected.

Judge Burton asked what his objection was.

"There are many proper ladies in the audience that do not need to hear such allegation."

"Overruled." If Burton's eyes could have burned Moore down, they'd've done it then. "Anyone, man or woman in this courtroom that wishes to leave since the details of this case will be very graphic, please do so now."

No one left a seat. "Very well, Mr. Moore, be seated."

"Yes, Your Honor. I just wanted to be certain—"

"Very well. Proceed, Mr. Kringle."

Then came Moore's rebuttal. "I will introduce witnesses that will swear that neither Scotty nor Mitch were near this unfortunate woman's place on the date of the crime he is talking about . . ." By Moore's words, they simply had arrested the wrong men. Chet had to agree to himself that the man was smooth, and he acted with an authority about him that would make a person wonder why the defendants were even on trial.

Doc Henry took the stand first, describing the murder scene, Marla's body, and the knife wounds.

"In your observation, would you say that Marla Porter had been raped before her murder?"

"Yes, numerous times."

"I object, Your Honor. How could Dr. Henry know for a fact that she had been assaulted like that if he wasn't there?"

"Dr. Henry," the judge asked, "what evidence do you have to that?"

"The bedsheet that she wrote Kenny Reynolds' name on with her own blood had numerous amounts of dry semen on it. I also found and noted that she had large amounts inside of her."

"Thank you, Doctor."

Moore sat down.

The bloody sheet was brought in and the doctor testified that it was found under her body. That she wrote the letters of Kenny's name with her index finger in her own blood before she died.

The writing was shown to the jury.

When his time came to question the witness, Moore asked the doctor many questions, but Doc held up, and at last, before he let him go, Moore's final question was, "Doc, you've treated lots of these folks in the jury box. Have you ever treated either of these two boys seated over there?"

"I probably have."

"Have you ever known them to lie?"

"No." Doc shrugged as if waiting for the next question.

"That's all, Your Honor."

Chet was next and after being sworn in, he told how he discovered the front door left open and went inside to find her bloody body on the bed. Pained in his heart all over again, he finished answering Kringle's questions.

When it was Moore's turn, the lawyer strode over and stood so he was between Chet and the jury. "Tell me, Mr. Byrnes. Were you and Mrs Porter having an affair?"

He hoped that Kringle would object, but he didn't. "Yes."

"Were you frequenting her place when her husband was not there?"

"I object." Kringle rose.

"Mr. Moore, what is the purpose of your line of questioning of the witness?"

"Your Honor, Mr. Byrnes is a confessed adulterer by his own admission. He also shot the defendant Scotty Campbell in the leg for no more reason than he was peacefully riding across his ranch to go see a sick friend. And then left him for dead. Then he snuck up on poor Mitch Reynolds when he was asleep and for no reason at all beat him up with malice."

"Mr. Byrnes, did you shoot at Mr. Campbell for crossing your ranch?"

"Your Honor, this man shot at my ten-year-old nephew Heck Byrnes and me from ambush with a Sharps rifle. Yes, I shot him, and would have killed him for endangering my nephew's life."

"Proceed, Mr. Moore, but I warn you be more direct."

"I will, Your Honor."

When Moore asked him if he had killed her because she wanted to break up with him cold chills ran up his jaw. The man's intent was to put the blame on anyone but his clients.

"No, I did not kill Marla Porter, but those two over there did, with Mitch's brother Kenny helping them do it."

"You have no proof of that."

"None but their own confessions to me. Both of them said that they brutally raped and killed her."

"Your Honor, I object to the witness's remarks. I wish them stricken from the record."

"Mr. Moore, I think you brought that on yourself. Continue."

"No more questions, Your Honor."

"We shall adjourn for lunch."

Outside in the sunlight, he realized Kathren was holding his arm. "I thought you were going to explode on that stand."

"Yes, I got too mad."

"Do you miss her?"

He glanced over at her. Then he shook his head. "She's a memory is all. I gave her up the day they buried her. Somewhere it says life is for the living and we should go on."

"I wondered."

"Don't wonder anymore. I am over Marla and very much with you."

"Good," she said as he took her hand.

The trial ended by four o'clock, and the jury debated for forty-five minutes to return a verdict. Then foreman announced, "We the jury find the defendants Mitch Reynolds and Scotty Campbell guilty of the rape and murder of Marla Porter."

The silence was so deep, a creaking floorboard sounded like thunder.

"You can't kill my son!" An older woman with her hair in a tight bun ran up to the fence and a bailiff stopped her. "He didn't do it! I swear he didn't."

She collapsed in the man's arms, babbling about it was wrong.

Order restored, the judge pronounced the sentence for them: on February fifteenth to be hung by the neck until dead. Court was dismissed.

The woman's shrieking wails grew louder as she tried to reach out past the man restraining her from the defendants being led off by armed deputies.

Trent stopped Chet and Kathren in the hallway. "I'm sorry for what Moore tried to do to you on the stand, Chet, but justice has been served."

"No problem. But only two thirds of it was served today," Chet said.

"We'll get him too. Good day, Mrs. Hines." Trent tipped his hat. "Tell Susie hi for me."

Chet agreed.

"I guess we go home in the morning?" she asked.

"Yes, we do, and get on with our own lives."

A buggy pulled beside them, and with his head all bandaged and his right arm in a sling, Earl Reynolds stood up. His left hand was pointing and he was shaking his finger at Chet.

"Gawdamn you, Chet Byrnes, I'm going to get you and all your fucking clan before I'm done if those two boys of mine hang!"

"Get out of here, Reynolds, before I send you to hell."

"No, you listen, you son of a bitch—"

"Chet! Chet!" Kathren stood in his face, holding his arms. "He's not worth it. Hear me?"

Hear me?

Chapter 32

The crew returned from Mexico with the steers. They all looked tuckered out. Two of the cavy were limping when J.D. drove them in.

"What's wrong with them two?' Chet asked.

"Turned up limping is all I know."

"Have any trouble?" Chet asked Dale Allen when he dismounted.

Dale Allen turned to J.D. "Better cut those two horses out. Let Chet look at them. No, we only had two scrapes with outlaws and they rode off."

May ran out of the house, and he hugged and kissed her, then looked up at Louise. "I see you made it back."

She nodded, and turned on her heel and went back inside.

"We got along great," Dale Allen said, going off with his wife. "I'm ready for Kansas."

"Good," Chet said after him.

"He did fine," Matt said, working with Reg to untarp the packhorses. "You'd of been proud of him."

Better than that, he'd chosen his wife over Louise. Susie

came out next, drying her hands on a towel and looking things over.

"Everyone fit as a fiddle?" she asked.

"Ready to dance, too," Matt teased. "We're all anxious for some of your cooking."

With everything under control, Chet went to the corral and joined J.D., who had the two horses hitched to rails.

"They didn't have stones in their frogs. I checked that."

"It's more in his joint. See the swelling? Must have strained it. He don't get better, we won't take him to Kansas. We'll cull him back."

"I think Mustard here needs shoes."

"Won't hurt. Some horses need them. Others get by fine and never have to have them no more than we use them. Make sure he gets shod close to the time when you leave."

"I got a a few more need their hooves trimmed."

"We better work that out. I'm taking five of you to Kathrcn's to get her steers sorted out and then driven over here."

"What did they do about Scotty and Mitch?"

"Found them guilty."

J.D. nodded.

After supper, Chet told them about the trial. He left out the personal parts. He did mention Mrs. Campbell's plea for her boy and Earl's threat to him.

Things began to happen fast. Six of them rode to Kathren's the day after they arrived home. They brought a pack-horse loaded with food and Matt went along.

Chet took off his hat, standing in her yard, and scratched the side of his scalp as he talked to her. "I love your cooking, but you can't cook for these wolves and show us the cattle. Matt's handling that for you."

"You're excused this time. Matt, there's the house, have fun."

"I will, Kathren. I will."

She pulled on her riding gloves and went for her saddle horse. "Most of them are on the Walker Flats. I've been busy."

"You have been," Chet said, leading his horse beside her.

"How are things at the ranch?"

"Bustling with the drive coming up in less than two months."

"I know. I only get to see you on Saturday nights."

"I guess I better fix it up so you see me more often."

"You'll have more time when they get off to Kansas." Then she stepped in the saddle and pulled down the brim of her hat.

"I sure will," he said.

She winked at him and turned the powerful gelding around. "Let's go get those steers."

In three days, they gathered a hundred head of her biggest steers and cut them out. He planned to drive them to the ranch the next morning. They were alone, standing in the starlight, loosely holding each other, when he looked down at her.

"I guess there's been nothing in my life that I've looked forward to more than you and me being together all the time," he said.

"We'll do it. I promise you."

He hugged her to him. "I know, and we'll take picnics and have time just to be us."

"I'm writing all this down."

He looked to the heavens for help.

When her cattle were at last with the ranch's herd, he began assign the men each day to keep them bunched on that side of the creek. He wanted at least fifteen hundred, since it was Dale Allen's first time to ramrod. That many would suit a new man.

First week in February, they road-branded Warren Hodges's consignment with a single bar on the right side. After two days at gathering, they went to work. It was done using a squeeze chute. The boiling dust and stinking burnt hair scorched his nostrils, but by late afternoon, they had them marked. The next week they went to the Jenks ranch, rounded up the one hundred head, and put the brand on them.

It rained the day they brought them to the ranch

"Week from today is the day they hang 'em, right?" J.D. asked him, riding at his side.

"You been thinking about that?"

"Sort of. One day, you think you know someone like Scotty. The next day, they do something like kill Mrs. Porter."

"I think they drug him along. But he never stopped 'em. He was there the whole time."

"Hell, he shot at you and Heck." J.D. spurred his horse on, obviously upset by it all.

"What's eating him?" Reg asked, looking after his brother short-loping ahead off into the mist.

"This hanging business is on his mind."

"Hell's fire, it's got us all. The three of us, I mean?"

"I think you're right."

"Guess you'll go over and see her, huh?"

"I'd like to." Chet had had Kathren on his mind since

he felt the first swish of rain that morning. "You want to go see Molly?"

"It sure would beat lying around reading the same old *Gazette* in the bunkhouse."

"It damn sure would. I'll tell Matt what we're up to."

Reg gave him a salute. "See you at breakfast in the morning, Boss."

And he rode off.

"Reg, he's off to see his lady," Chet told Matt. "After we put these steers on the flats, I reckon you and the boys could drop by Mayfield and soak up a beer or two," He handed Matt a few dollars for the cause. "I'm going over to the 9Y and check on things. Don't get in any wars. I mean, no fighting with them."

"We'll keep a low profile."

"Good, see you in the morning."

Matt agreed with a smile, and everyone close spread the word. "Thanks," came back in a chorus.

An hour later, he stood on her stoop with rain running off his slicker and his hat ten pounds heavier. She looked hard at him. "I wasn't expecting you."

"I thought it would be a good day for a picnic."

She chuckled and pulled him inside. "Cady, we have company."

"Did he say picnic?"

"Yes. That's just his cowboy humor, my dear."

Her slender ten-year-old, Cady, looked him over as he slipped off the wet slicker. "I get it."

"Some of the best picnics of my life were on a blanket in front of a fireplace."

"Where was that?" Cady asked.

"Cady," her mother said, raising her voice. "He might not want to share that information."

He said privately to Cady, "She's worried it's about the other women in my life."

"Tell me."

"My Grandma Cooney—"

She gave him a small push with both hands. "More cowboy jokes, Mother," Cady said.

"See, you can't trust 'em. We'll make popcorn and sit on the floor in front of the hearth."

"Good, and he can tell stories."

"They probably won't be stories young girls should hear."

"Why not?"

"Because you have to do more growing up to hear them."

He shook his head. Two women picking on him might be more than he could handle.

"How is the cattle gathering going?" she asked, preparing things.

"Good. We've made good progress. My brother is taking a good hold of things. He'll get headed north by March fifteenth."

"How long does it take to get up there?" Cady joined them with her long-handed popper.

"Oh, six weeks across Texas, six more to Kansas, three more from there."

Cady took charge of making popcorn on her knees. Some thunder rolled across the land, and he shared a nod and wink with Kathren.

They discussed Susie, the ranch, and avoided the matter of the feud, which he was grateful for. Eating popcorn, and drinking sweet lemonade, they whiled away the afternoon, laughing and teasing.

"I'm sure glad you and Mom are getting married," Cady said, leaning back, her hands braced behind her. Lots of her mother's features made her an attractive young girl.

"Why's that, Cady?" he asked.

"'Cause I like doing this. Sitting around and all of us laughing and having a good time. We never do this much."

"Well, we'll have to do it more often."

"Good, I'll love it."

"The rain's let up some now. Maybe you should do the chores," Kathren said.

"Okay, but you just want him to yourself."

"Cady."

"Yes, Mother, I am going."

Cady was soon dressed in a slicker, and went off to feed the chickens and milk the cow. On her knees, Kathren crossed the blanket to kiss him. "I'm sorry about my daughter."

"Why, she's you all over."

"Good. You can stay tonight. She sleeps in the side room and if we don't—ah, make too much noise—" She tossed her hair back and looked him in the eye. "I guess she's going to have to get used to us being together anyway."

"You're calling the shots. I can ride back to the ranch."

She chewed on her lower lip, then acting if she was thinking he might leave, caught his arm. "No, I want you to stay here—with me."

Before sunup, he left her place and headed for home. When the sunlight came, the diamonds of water drops sparkled on everything. It would be a great morning ahead, and he short-loped for the house across the soggy ground.

The crew was saddled up and fixing to leave. Dale Allen told him they were going to be certain the steers were all east of the creek and staying there. A day of bunching them wouldn't hurt. At least his brother had good thoughts as the herd boss. He'd make it.

"I'll check on my farm crew up there and join you later," said Chet.

"No problem. Those two hands you hired to stay here are working out all right."

"Good." Chet rode up to the house. In the living room, he found his father in his chair napping.

"Morning, Dad."

"Hmm, helluva morning. I told your mother that ground's too wet to plow. How come they going to plow it like that?"

"Aw, they ain't plowing today."

"Huh? Why, don't they know a damn thing about farming."

"They aren't plowing today," he said louder.

"Huh? Who's plowing?"

"No one, Dad. No one."

Susie came to the doorway and waited for Chet to follow her back. "You can see. He's losing it bad."

"Yes, I see. But there isn't a thing we can do about it."

"He doesn't hurt anyone," she said, pouring him some coffee.

"How are you and—" He looked around. "Louise getting along?"

"No problem. Maria helps her clean her house and she acts more satisfied to be here."

"Good. Something's wrong. Shreveport and the South could not have changed her that much."

The hot cup in his hand, he looked up and smiled when May and the baby came in the kitchen. "Oh, you made it back?" May said.

"Yes, I sure did."

"Well?" May looked hard at him for an answer.

"Well, what?" he said back to her, taking the baby and hoisting it in the air

"You know what. Susie and I want to know when does the wedding takes place."

"April or May. She's talking late April."

"What can we plan on?"

"Oh, we'll simply get married by some judge and go on."

"Not on your life. She never had a real wedding with him. We're going to give her one," Susie said.

He held up his hands. "You tell her."

"We will." And they agreed in a defiant way that he wasn't about to argue with.

Chapter 33

He went to the public hanging. Not because he wanted to, but because he felt it important he show up there for Marla. Kathren went with him. They drove up to Mason the day before. Kathren stayed at her aunt's. He went by and picked her up at five in the morning with the buckboard. Although he had offered to let her sleep in, she calmly told him she would be there at his side.

So they stood back behind the near silent crowd of onlookers in the chill of the predawn, and he could see the two nooses hung from the scaffold in the lamplight. Trent had several guards armed with rifles standing by.

"They're bringin' 'em." A hush fell over the crowd. The ring of chains and leg irons was the only sound until a few birds began to wake up and chirp. Sunup was beginning to purple the eastern horizon. Both boys looked haggard in the yellow lamplight. To Chet, they looked too young to be up there.

From the scaffold, Trent read the judge's orders. The two were asked if they had any words. Both shook their heads. The minister prayed aloud for them. The chains were removed. Their legs and hands were bound behind them. Trent put the nooses on them, then the hoods, and a deadly silence prevailed. The snap of the trapdoors opening drew a breath-sucking noise from the assembled.

The two bodies swung like pendulums. Both of their necks were broken in the fall, and they'd never suffered. Neither of them had said a word of apology. But he had a flicker of bitter memory pass through his mind with a vivid vision of Marla's bloody corpse.

He helped Kathren onto the spring seat. He recognized one of the Campbells standing beside the scaffold with a wagon and coffins to take their bodies back. Reins in his hand, Chet clucked to the team. Time to get back. Anxious to leave the whole thing in Mason, he made them trot harder.

"Bad morning?" she asked.

He looked off at the early blooming peach trees in a small orchard beside the road, and then he nodded. "Reminders, I guess, of why I was there."

"I was going to ask you if late April was a good time."

He nodded and forced a smile. "You need to talk to my sister and sister-in-law. They want a big wedding. Dress and shindig at the ranch."

"Why?"

"They said you had a small wedding the first time. This one needs to be a big one."

She looked at the brim of her hat for help. "We're just getting married."

He laughed, and then he hugged her with his right arm. "You talk to them. I can't."

"What if we run off then?"

"Those two would cry. But the date suits me fine."

She gave him a stern look. "Good, I'll speak to them."

He nodded his approval and made the horses go faster.

The next morning, he rode back to the ranch. When he arrived, they were saddling up to go collect the cattle of Warren Hodges's widow. The new boys were going to work keeping the steers bunched in the bottoms. J.D. and Heck were doctoring and shoeing lame-footed horses. He spoke briefly with Dale Allen, and went inside to tell Susie the news about a wedding date in late April.

His sister did not take it lightly, and said she'd speak to Kathren, or maybe she said she'd convince Kathren. He never was certain. He left to check on his farmhands.

The plowing had commenced. Five mules up on the sulky plow and two teams of oxen, one each on the hand-held plows. Earlier, Dale Allen had sharpened all the plowshares, so they were flopping over the short grass and weeds. The rest of the help was checking the boundary fences, putting in new stakes where they were broken He'd try for a hundred of corn—that would be lots of corn to plant, cultivate, and gather.

That checkup on his farmers completed, he rode over to see about the Hodges roundup. Matt was cooking at a campfire east of the home place. Chet dropped off his horse, hitched him on a picket line, and walked up. A large hunch of beef on a spit over the crackly blaze smelled heavenly.

"How's it going over here?" Squatted at the fire ring, Chet used a handkerchief on the handle to pour himself a cup of coffee.

"Oh, all right. Pinky had a bad wreck this morning. His horse hit a hole, broke a leg, and had to destroyed. He'll be sore for a while."

"Where's he at?"

"Hell, riding one of Hodges's horses, and he damn near threw him when they caught him." Matt dropped to his butt on the ground, the stiff leg out in front. "Casey said to tell you to keep an eye out. They really want your hide bad."

"Tell them I'm around. Come get it."

"No, when we stopped for the beer the other day, he sounded sincere as hell."

"I figured after they got them two buried this week, they'd be boiling mad over again."

Matt agreed with a bob of his head. "How are you going to end it?"

"I guess kill the whole damn lot of 'em."

"Big order."

"Yeah. You know that you can cut a rattler's head off and him still bite you."

Chet sipped the coffee and thought about his options again concerning the Reynolds family. Nothing new. He also had Matt make him a list of the things he'd need for the chuck wagon.

He rode back home with the crew after supper. Reg and one of the hands were going to stay with them overnight. The trap fencing wasn't too well kept up. So they were going to take shifts riding around them at night to hold the cattle in. Matt stayed with his cooking gear and food for the next day's branding, and offered to take a shift if they got too tired.

It was long past sundown when the crew reached the ranch. Susie came out and looked relieved when he told her they'd all eaten.

"How's it going?"

"Too fast. They'll be heading north in no time. How did things go for you today?"

"Fine," she said as he herded her inside the house.

"How about Louise?"

"She's a different person since she returned. She's even civil to May."

"Good. I'm going into Mayfield tomorrow and cut a deal for the supplies with Mr. Grosman. Matt made me a list today. Grosman'll need to order part of it, I'd bet."

"Good idea. You going to be able to let them go without you?"

"Sure. Why?"

"You've been the one for so long. I just figured that you'd have to go along."

"Dale Allen—"

She put a fingertip to his lips. "He's fine. Doing more than he ever did. It just seems strange is all."

"It will have to be. Besides, I'm getting married."

"Yes, and I'm talking to her, too."

"Well, what about you and the sheriff?"

"I don't know. I think I flattered him by inviting him out here, but he doesn't act like a man anxious to take a wife."

"Disappointed?"

"If I don't please a man, I don't please a man. Better to know now than marrying one and discover it later."

"I guess you're right. I can't hardly wait. Her daughter, Cady, and I get on fine. I think she's as big a tomboy as her mother ever was."

"Where will you live?"

"Now we haven't ironed all that out. But we will."

"Good to have a plan before you agree to be her husband."

"You may be right, sis. I'll work on it some."

"I'm not trying to scare you out of it. Lord knows, I'd love you to have a wife."

"Then I'd be out of your hair, huh?"

"Not so! Not so!" He retreated out of the kitchen with her pounding on him lightly with her fists.

The next morning, he rode into Mayfield and stopped first for a ten-cent draft beer at Casey's to learn the latest gossip.

"Cassidy Boys were up here looking for cattle to take to Kansas."

"They get some?"

"Yeah. Campbells, Farleys, and Reynolds folks are sending some up the trail with 'em. All folks that I figured wouldn't go with you anyway. Though I never figured that Farley would fall in with 'em." Casey shook his head. "I always thought he had his head on square enough."

"Everyone has to choose sides in a deal like this for or against. I probably upset Jim Farley sometime about something."

Casey nodded. "Keep on your toes. They get drunk in here, they talk tough about what they're going to do you."

"They can come any time. Three of 'em's been hung, one shot, and the two's on the run from the law."

"Watch your backside. They won't challenge you. They'll shoot and run."

He thanked Casey for his concern, and then he walked across the street leading Soapy, a tall bay, to the hitch rack over there. Mr. Grosman greeted him when he came in under the bell over the door.

"I'll be right with you, Chester."

The gray-haired Jewish man always had a proper way when he talked to people. The ladies were all Miss or Mrs.

to him. Most men were Mister, but when he did use a first name, it was proper, too.

When he finished with the older lady, he smiled at Chet. "I guess you are ready to go north?"

Chet nodded and walked over. "Dale Allen's taking them up there this time. I have so much to do, I better stay here."

He agreed like a father. "So what can I do for you?"

"I want to finance the supplies I'll need."

"There is no problem there. I will give you the same terms as last time. That's fifteen-percent interest."

"I understand. Now here is my list. I brought this to you early so if you must order anything you'd have it."

"Very good."

"Since this problem continues, I won't write my name or the ranch brand on any of these items. They might damage them to get at me."

Grosman nodded slowly in agreement. "Such a shame. Such a shame that it goes on."

"I can't stop it. I try to avoid it."

"Oh, I understand. When will you need all this assembled here?"

"He's leaving for Abilene the middle of March."

"Good. I will have it all here a week before. How is your sister, Miss Byrnes?"

"Susie is fine. She sent her regards to you and the Mrs."

"She is such a wonderfully nice lady."

"I count on her a whole lot." The matter settled, he decided to swing by and see Kathren before he went home. He short-loped Soapy in the windy mid-morning sunshine. He discovered her herding a bunch of cows and calves eastward that had strayed to the western limits of her place.

Standing in the stirrups, she rode over with a smile. "What brings you out?"

He swung down and dropped the reins. She ran over and he hugged her. Then he swung her around in a circle and kissed her hard.

"Whew," she said, sweeping off her hat with her blue eyes twinkling. "You sure beat shifting cattle back."

"How's Cady?"

"Fine. I have her doing math since they won't have school this year up here."

They squatted down. "How come?" he asked.

"Can't find a teacher, they say." She slapped the reins on her chaps.

"I had to order the supplies that Matt will need on the drive today so Grosman has it all."

"Matt's a nice man. I sure enjoyed him when they were over here."

"Matt's a good man. They're hard to find. I'll help you drift the cattle back. I'm certain that you have work to do."

"I don't usually have company. Thanks."

Before they parted, he kissed her again. "Whew, it won't be long till mid-April, will it?"

"Not near fast enough."

"My thinking exactly." She went for her horse.

When the cattle were gathered and resettled, they rode back to her ranch together. Cady ran out of the house to greet him.

"I thought you were mad at us," Cady said after he dismounted and hugged her shoulders.

"No."

"Well, anyway, you came by."

"Cady, he has a ranch much larger than ours to run."

"I know, Mother. I just like for him to come by and see us." She held the reins while he undid the latigos. He tossed his kac on the corral and thanked her.

"Do any of those boys at your place dance?" she asked, walking beside him.

"Some. J.D. can dance. Why?"

"I've been learning how. Would you kinda mention it to him that I can dance?"

"Cady, if that boy wants to dance, he'll ask you."

"But Mom, how will he know I can dance if he doesn't have word about it?"

"Boys can tell who to ask."

"I'll handle it," he said in confidence to Cady.

The next morning after breakfast, he kissed Kathren hard in the cool windy predawn and felt pulled apart as he left her. In a short lope, he pushed Soapy for home. Arriving there at mid-morning, he dismounted at the house. Obviously, the hands were gone. He went in and checked with Susie.

"How did it go this morning?" he asked, putting his hat on a peg and removing his jumper.

"I didn't hear you come in," Susie said in the middle of making bread. "How's Kathren?"

"Those girls are fine. How's things here?"

"No problems. Dale Allen and crew left out to check on the cattle situation. He's concerned they may have started pushing cattle on us again. Reg saw some other brands on our land the other day when he went to see Molly."

"Good. How's the house?"

"Fine. Louise went to Mason for the day."

"By herself?"

"Yes, you know how she is. I wanted one of her boys to go along, but she waved that off."

"She going to spend the night?"

"Yes."

"I wish she'd've listened to you."

"You know how she is."

"Not your fault." He shook his head. Maybe the Reynolds clan had given up on their actions against him. The notion that Louise was alone, though, going over there, roiled his guts. He better go check on Pepe and his farmers and see how the corn planting was coming on. Always lots to do.

Chapter 34

The night before they left, he and Dale Allen went over the list of cattle. They had five hundred steers from the ranch, five hundred from Mexico, Hodges's one hundred, Morgan's two hundred, Jenks's one hundred, and Kathren's one hundred.

"That makes the count," Chet said.

"Fifteen hundred head."

"Yes, that's plenty. Enough that we can pay expenses off the five hundred if we can sell them all right and still make those folks some money," Chet said. "Get some sleep. You won't get much from here on."

Dale Allen would need all the sleep he could get.

On a cloudy morning in mid-March, Dale Allen and his crew started off for Kansas. Heck rode in the chuck wagon with Matt as the cook's helper. Whip Malloy was the horse wrangler. Sammy and Reg were the swing riders, and they guided the direction and the speed of the herd. They tried a big six-year-old black steer called Midnight as the bell leader. In a few hours they'd know about his leadership abilities. In no time they learned that the black steer was well chosen for the role of *His Majesty*.

Chet rode north with them the first day. The two younger boys rode double on their pony as far as the north end of the horse pasture. At mid-afternoon, the drive stopped at Cedar Creek, and the point riders threaded the cattle along the bank to drink and then let them graze the rest of the afternoon.

One busted cinch, and the unseated cowboy named Bailey had a headache after falling off his horse turning back an errant steer. The rest went smoothly. Chet played a quiet role, letting Dale Allen handle the operation.

"Good day," Chet said. "There's always some fighting the first few days of the cattle drive, even though they were thrown together a few weeks ago. Who's the boss is name of the game."

"And there's always some steers that are troublemakers," Dale Allen said.

"Eat them."

"You're serious, aren't you?"

"I've even shot them and left them for the buzzards. Troublemakers aren't worth two cents."

"I'll remember that."

"You have things in order. A schedule to ride herd tonight. Good luck."

"You leaving?"

"I figure you can handle it."

Dale Allen nodded. "I'll do my damnedest."

"That's all I can ask."

Chet rode back toward the ranch in the twilight, relying on Roan to get him there because with the cloud cover, it would be a dark night. Not taking the herd made him feel guilty, but it would be good for Dale Allen. His brother needed to take care of something—he'd do fine.

Past midnight, bone tired, he fell in his bunk, and slept hard until the morning bell rang. Bleary-eyed, he washed his face and headed for the main house.

"How was the herd and crew?" Susie asked at his entry.

"Ready to fight a bear. First day went well."

His ranch hands Rip and Toby, the shorter one, came in and smiled at the sight of him.

"Them boys get along okay yesterday?" Rip asked, straddling a chair to sit down.

"Doing good."

"Late yesterday, me and Toby patched a break in the lower oat field fence. There were twenty cows and calves in there that we drove out."

"Can't blame 'em. Those oats are doing good since the rain began. Keep an eye on those fields. We'll need that hay."

"Yes, sir."

May, looking a little red-eyed, and the baby came in to join them. She asked about her husband and Chet assured her he was fine.

"I'll sure miss him," she said, and forced a smile.

"He'll be back in late summer all tanned and relaxed."

"Yes, I imagine he will be."

Chet cradled a cup of steaming coffee in his hands. He regretted that he hadn't signed on more cattle to take north, but the fifteen hundred would be enough for Dale Allen's first trip. He better saddle up and go check on his corn-planting operation after breakfast.

* * *

He was close to the bottomland where he expected to find them planting when he heard what he thought was crows fighting. But when he rode over the ridge, he could see three riders herding his white-clothed farmhands with their hands high out of the field. What in the hell were they doing?

He slipped off Sam Bass, slid the Sharps and the cross sticks out of his scabbard. Those three had their nerve chousing his help. He set the sight and studied the thick-set one on horseback ordering them around in the circle. The first trigger set, he squeezed off a shot with the second one. The man, his arms outstretched, flew off his horse, and the other two, trying to hold their mounts, looked wide-eyed in his direction.

Chet deliberately reloaded and took aim, but they were already on the run, whipping and driving to race across the plowed ground. He put the rifle on safety, then stowed it, and rode up to the Mexican men.

"What were they doing?" he asked Pepe as he dismounted.

"*Señor,* they were driving us like cattle. Telling us we had to leave here. Threatening us with our lives."

Chet nodded and went over to the man lying facedown in the dirt. Fresh blood came from his vest where the bullet must have entered him.

"Who is he?" Pepe asked.

"Frank Dutton, he's Earl Reynolds brother-in-law."

"Why did he want us to leave?"

"So I couldn't get any corn planted."

"Who were the others?" Pepe asked as the tension on the men's faces around them began to relax.

"One I think was his son, Garland. The other fella I'm not sure."

"What will we do with him?"

"Sheriff Trent has a deputy in Mayfield. I'll take Dutton to him."

"Will they come back?"

"I don't think so." He raised his voice. "I don't think they'll be back. I'll keep an eye on you."

They began to talk among themselves and thanked him. He assured them they'd be safe and told them to go back to planting corn.

He rode into Mayfield with Dutton's corpse belly-down over his horse. His appearance with his burden in the village soon had several curious folks coming out to see what he would do next.

At Casey's, he dismounted, hitched the horses, and went inside.

"That deputy around?" he asked Casey.

"No. He went to see about a stolen horse."

"Where's Gunner?"

"What happened?" Casey asked, drawing him a beer.

"Dutton, his son, and another galoot were threatening my farming crew with pistols when I rode up. Telling them to leave or else. I took out Dutton and the other two fled."

"What's going on?" Gunner asked, coming in the saloon's doors.

Chet shook his head. He'd go through this story several times before the day was over.

It was near dark when he rode in. Skirt in her hands, Susie ran out. "You all right? Astria's friend Maria came and told us about all the trouble you had this morning at the fields and shooting a man."

"Frank Dutton, Earl's brother-in-law. Frank, Garland,

and some hand were herding the men out of the field at gunpoint."

"Is he dead?"

"Dead as a rock."

She shook her head in dismay. "I have supper in the oven."

"Good, I haven't eaten a thing since breakfast." He looked around. With Heck gone, he'd have to put up his own damn horse. It wouldn't hurt him.

Four weeks went by without another incident. Their wedding plans were in place for the following Saturday. Nothing had happened since the hearing about Frank Dutton's death when it was ruled a justifiable homicide. Kathren had agreed to a small ceremony at the ranch—Susie, Louise, and May planned to embellish it somehow.

Chet was in the blacksmith shop tacking shoes on Strawberry when Susie came screaming. "Oh, Chet, where are you? They've killed Dale Allen!"

Dale Allen? Killed? His heart stopped and he dropped the hoof he held in his lap.

Out of breath, she collapsed against a post in the building. "Heck's here. He's exhausted to death, rode day and night, he said, they attacked the crew." She swallowed hard. "Dale Allen is dead. Oh, my God—" She collapsed sobbing in his arms. "What will we do?"

"Where are they?"

"Across the Red River, he said."

"Those sonsabitches waited till they were out of Texas."

"What does that mean?"

"There's not much law up in the Nations."

"You better talk to Heck. What will we do?"

"I'll need to go up there and see what I can do about the cattle and the men."

"But your marriage—"

"Kathren will wait. She'll understand."

"Oh, Chet, why, oh, why have they done this?"

"Revenge. Cold-blooded revenge." And he'd answer them with more of their own poison.

After he talked to the worn-out youth and learned the killers had also taken the horses, he knew he had more problems. Roan was saddled and he rode fast for Kathren's. She needed to know what had happened and what he had to do.

At the sight and sound of him coming so hard, she rushed out. "What's wrong?"

He piled off the hard-breathing horse and ran up to hug her. "They've raided the cattle drive. They killed Dale Allen, shot Matt, killed Pinky and another cowboy, and took the horses."

"The Reynolds men?"

"Yes. Heck said Shelby, Earl, and Kenny were the leaders. I know we have plans, but I must go help those boys and get those cattle to Kansas."

"I know that. I'll still be here, Chester Byrnes. You take care and come back to me."

"I will. I promise."

He kissed her good-bye, then leaped on the roan and raced back for the ranch. With all that time during his ride, since he had Kathren taken care of, he began laying plans. Hire some more hands, find some horses and have them sent up there. He couldn't wait for them. Whoever was left with the herd would need him as soon as he could get there.

Heck rushed out of the house when he rode in. Sleep had helped the boy. He looked rested anyway.

"What do I need to do?" he asked.

"Pick us out three horses apiece, so we can ride them in relays—what's wrong?"

"I better let you choose your horses. You know them better than I do."

"I can do that."

"How is she?" Susie asked.

"She's fine. Understands. I need you to go find Jim Crammer. Have him buy me about thirty horses and find some good help to deliver those horses to me in the Nation."

"What are your plans?"

"That crew needs me. Heck and I are going to relay three horses apiece and get up there. I can hire some hands around Doan's store, and buy some horses up there, too."

"I'll go see Jim Crammer in the morning."

"Good."

"What will you need?"

"Jerky to chew on. We're going light."

She agreed.

"How's May?" he asked, realizing she had lost a husband.

Susie shook her head like she didn't want to explain the whole thing. "I sedated her. She's sleeping. What about his body?"

"Somehow I'll try to bring it back when I come home. I can't promise I can do it. I'll try to."

"Oh, Chet, I hate all this that's been piled on you."

"Susie, we'll survive it all." Then he hugged her tight with a knot in his throat he couldn't swallow.

Heck was saddling his choice of horses.

"How did it all happen?" Chet asked.

"We were in camp that night. Things had been going good. Dale Allen kept saying we'd have stampedes and for all of us to be ready—but—the cattle were all right for the most part. He did like you said. We ate the worst spooks in the herd before we crossed the Red River.

"I was in bed when hell broke loose. They rode in and went to shooting. They shot down Dad—I mean he didn't even have a gun. Matt got one of them with a shotgun, but they shot him several times. Sam emptied his pistol at them. Reg shot one of their horses and thinks he wounded Shelby, but we didn't know. They also killed Pinky and Arnold, that boy from Kerrville. It was bad, and then they ran off the horses. Them night herders somehow held the cattle. Sam left to track the horses. Reg sent me right away down here to get you."

Chet nodded. "I know it's been tough. You did a man's job."

"I owe a man for the horse I traded for mine for up on the Colorado River."

"We'll see he gets paid."

"That horse I had was so tuckered out he'd not've gone a step more."

"We'll pay him maybe on the way back."

"Good. You ain't riding that Bugger horse, are you?" Heck asked as Chet led Bugger out of the stall.

"Yeah, I think he's the toughest horse I've ever seen, and I may need one that stout before this is over."

He choose Dun and Roan besides. He'd like to have taken Strawberry, but the ride over to her place and back had taken some of the edge off him that he would need to make this relay ride work.

Susie came with jerky wrapped in butcher paper for each of them. "When do they need to cut the oats?"

"When the oats are in the milk stage."

"And they need to keep the grass and weeds out of the corn, right?"

"Pepe and those men are reliable farmers."

"I know but—"

"I agree, I wish I could leave someone who could oversee it all."

"Chet, we can handle it. Go on."

She tied a canvas ground cloth and blanket on the back of his saddle while sidestepping the dun's footwork—as if he sensed the excitement.

Heck took his roll, which she had for him, and did the same. Chet jammed the Sharps in his own scabbard and a .44/40 in Heck's.

"I need to get five hundred dollars out of the safe and put it in a money belt," Chet said.

She nodded. "I'll go do that while you finish here."

Each one had two saddled horses and a spare animal to ride later. When they rode to the house, Louise came out. She shielded her eyes against the sun.

"God be with you two." She shook her head in disbelief.

"He will be," Chet said and dismounted, handing Heck his reins and leads. He about bumped into Susie coming out the front door with the canvas belt in her hands. "It's all in there."

Unbuttoning his shirt, he threaded the belt on, and rebuttoned the shirt. "You all take care. I will be back."

He swung in the saddle—no time for more words.

They short-loped north. "Crowd that Bugger horse, he don't lead as well as I'd like."

When Heck moved in behind him, the big high-headed horse caught the stride, and from there on did good.

Miles passed under them, they changed horses, and then they rode on into the night. After midnight, he walked the horses for a mile or so, and then told Heck they could hobble them and sleep a few hours.

The next morning, he grained their mounts at a crossroads store. He and Heck had some fried eggs and cold biscuits that the man's wife fixed for them while the horses rested, and then they rode on.

By the third morning's light, with his eyes burned out like sand pits, Chet planned to be at Doan's store on the Red River. He beat his own time, and it was still nighttime as they galloped the last few miles across the rolling plains to the crossing. No lights on in the store when they came down the last slope, and the Red River shimmered before them in the moonlight.

"How far north is the herd?" Chet asked as they reined their hard-breathing horses down to a walk.

"Two days, maybe twenty miles. We used almost a day crossing, so we didn't make many miles the first day."

Chet understood. "If you want to stay here and sleep some today. I'll go on and find them."

"No, I want to be with you. I have a small pistol in my saddlebags that Reg found for me to take along for my own protection. But I ain't no shot with it. You don't mind, I'll ride on up there with you."

"Sure. I can imagine being upset as you were waking up to all that."

"Naw, that wasn't the worst part." He shook his head, looking sad. "Paw and I were finally talking—"

Even in the darkness, he could see the diamond tears on the boy's face. The whole thing stabbed him in his gut. It only made him more determined as he studied the outline of the last outpost in Texas—Doan's adobe store building— to find those killers and send them to hell.

Chapter 35

Corwin Doan was a thin young man who originally came from Ohio. He walked out on the porch and stretched and yawned big in the predawn. "You fellows are up early—oh, aren't you the boy came down the other day telling about the attack?"

"Yes, sir. There here's my Uncle Chet."

"Good day, sir. How may I help you?"

"I need some horses and drovers."

"Oh, that might be a big order. There could be some at Denison. I bet I can find you three or four hands. Horses would be high."

"How high?"

"Forty bucks piece."

"Get me twenty. I can pay you now or when I return from Kansas."

"I can wait for that money. How about the men?"

"Six if you can find them." Chet rose from the rocker. "I'm Chet Byrnes and we met last time. Well, the first time I met you was when you all had a tent here."

Doan nodded as if he recalled that time. "I remember those days, sir. We're a little better off today."

"Yes, you are. The boy and I are going on. I'll send someone back to get the men and the horses."

"No. I know I can find you some of those men you need, and I'll send them up there to you with the horses I can find."

"You have a deal. Take us across the river, please."

Doan blinked at him. "Why, you've been riding for days. I can tell. Won't you stay for some food?"

"I'd rather be with my outfit."

"I understand. Let me get my shoes on and I'll take you across. The boy isn't up yet."

"Thanks."

Doan reeled them toward the north shore. "That's a mighty big horse under your saddle. Biggest horse I think I've seen save for a Percheron or shire, but he's saddle stock?"

"He's a real saddle horse and a giant. Maybe over seventeen hands high. But he's fast and tough."

"Whew. You make a sight riding him."

"I knew I'd needed a tough horse for this job, and I have him on loan from a little gray-haired lady."

"Indeed. He's a woman's horse?"

"That's who he belongs to."

The barge landed. He shook Doan's hand and thanked him. "Tell them they're looking for the bar-C outfit."

"They'll catch up in the next few days."

"Thanks again. I'll square up on the way back. Let's go find 'em, Heck."

At sundown, they rode out of the trees, and Chet could see the cattle were spread over a great grassy flat. After a thanks to the powers that be above, he nodded to the weary boy. "Heck, you did good. We're there."

Reg in an apron came wading over in his chaps and wearing an apron. "Thank God."

"I already did that," Chet said, and dropped out of the saddle. "Sorry you boys have had such hell."

"Wasn't your fault." Reg dropped his head in defeat. "Sammy's coming in. He can tell you about the horses."

"Did he find them?"

"Yeah, but they're a pretty tough bunch that's got them, and they wouldn't give them back."

"Mr. Byrnes." Sam blinked in shock. "Am I glad to see you."

"Chet," he corrected him. "Now tell me about the horses. Who has them? How many are there?"

"Well. Those Reynolds riders must have hired them to help them make the raid. They got the horses as their pay, and they want fifty bucks a head to give them back. No way that me or the boys could take that bunch on. They're tough."

"How many of them?"

"Six or so."

Chet nodded. "How far away are they?"

"Ten-twelve miles."

"You know their layout?"

"Yes, sir."

"Let me sleep for a few hours and you, Reg, and I will head over there and get our damn horses back for starters. Reg, no cook, huh? Where's Matt?"

"He's over there. Ain't doing much good. But he's alive."

Chet nodded and went to the fly they had built over Matt. He ducked and took a look. Matt's pale white face scared him.

"You sure made it up here in a big hurry," Matt managed to say.

Chet nodded. "I want you taken to Denison so a doctor can look at you. As soon as Heck gets some sleep, I'm sending him after a buckboard."

"Aw, hell, let me die. You've got cattle to move."

"I ain't leaving here till we get that buckboard."

"Chuck can go get one. Heck's done in," Reg said. "I wanted to do that before. He won't let me."

"Send him. Here's some money. Tell them I'll pay the bill when we get back. Listen, Matt, I don't aim for you to die."

"May as well. With my stiff leg, I'm about as valuable as horse turds in the trail."

"You better get a hold of yourself. You've got lots to still do for this outfit."

"I should have shot that damn Earl. Him and his shattered arm hanging there on his horse and cussing you all. Maybe I'd've ended it all if I had."

Chet knelt down beside him. "Shelby was the one in charge?"

"Him and Kenny. I don't know who killed Pinky. There were others." Matt shook his head in surrender.

"Rest easy, pard. We'll find 'em and they'll pay for this."

"I hated it. Dale Allen was doing a great job. You'd've been proud and we were making good time."

Chet nodded. He hated it worse for Heck. *He and his father had been talking . . .*

When the buckboard was sent for and things were being taken care of, Chet refused the offer of food and curled up in his blanket. He'd told Sammy to be ready to ride at midnight after their horses. Get him up then regardless. Visions of the pale-faced Matt lying on the pallet kicked him in the gut—he fell hard asleep.

"Midnight, like you said," Reg said.

He looked up at the starlit faces of the three. "Cattle all right?"

"We've got enough night herders. It's horses that we're short."

"We'll take the horses that Heck and I brought."

"Yeah, we have them saddled."

"Good. I'll get awake here in a moment." He sat up and ground his sore eyes with his palms.

In a short while, he had some reheated coffee and felt enough awake to ride.

"Tell me what they have," he said to Sammy as the four of them walked to the picketed horses.

"A log saloon or store. And some cabins they must live in. A big fella named Wallace is in charge. He's the toughest one, Rudd Wallace. Bunch of breeds. One of them has a blind eye. He's mean-looking, played with a big bowie knife the whole time I talked to them, stabbing it in a table."

"Nice man. Where are the horses?"

"They pen them at night. Some Injun boys herd them in the daytime to graze."

"I figured if we took the horses, they'd come after us and might spook the cattle," Chet said. "So I want as many taken out as we can tonight. That means shoot first and ask questions later. It ain't easy to do that, but they would do that to you."

They nodded in agreement.

"I'll take the saloon. Each of you boys take a cabin. Try not to kill any woman or children, but when a man busts out stop him."

He looked for their hard nods as they rode four abreast. "J.D., you got any problems with that?"

"No, sir."

"Just remember, it's you or them. Be careful."

"What if they want to surrender?" Reg asked.

"Fine, but watch them with your pistol cocked."

"This Wallace is bigger than a bear," Sammy said.

A few hours later, they came down through the shadowy post oak, and Chet could hear the sleeping horses stomping and snoring in the large corral. On foot, they slipped around the pen, and each man took a cabin and he took the saloon building.

"Give me time to locate him," he said, and they parted. "Hold your places and be mindful; there could be more than one man in your cabin."

When he drew the drawstring up, the saloon board door opened with a creak on leather hinges. The room stank of home brew, bad whiskey, and some rank human musks. He left it open for the light. A loud snore like a bear gnawing on wood filled the night. Upstairs. That was the source of the noise. His first step on the stairs made the wood creak in protest, but the snore absorbed it.

Six-gun in his fist, he mounted them, and soon was in the attic. He located the large form under some blankets on the floor. It was the source of all the noise. Soft-footed as he could be, he soon squatted beside the sleeping man, grateful for the little light coming in the attic from the small window.

"Don't make a word." He jammed the pistol muzzle against the man's temple.

"Huh?"

"I'll send you to hell right now. Shut her up," he said,

noticing a woman lying beside him had awakened with a start.

"Be quiet, bitch!"

"You make one funny move and I kill you."

"I won't. Who are you?"

"The man who owns those horses out there."

Wallace laughed as Chet made him get facedown and tied his hands behind his back. "I'll find you and kill you," he threatened.

"You should have done that first, then stolen my horses. Woman, you go downstairs ahead of him. You try anything, I will shoot you, too."

She obeyed him, acting awed.

"Who are you anyway?" Wallace asked again, starting down the steps.

"I told you. And if you break for that open front door at the bottom of the steps, you're dead. Don't think about it."

"Think you got it all figured out, huh?"

"I've got you covered and you'll die first. Don't tempt me. There's a dozen of my men out there and they all have guns."

"You a marshal? One of Parker's men?"

"No. Now get on the porch. I'll tell you what to start hollering."

"Huh?"

"Tell them to come out. That we have you surrounded. Hands in the air or we'll kill them." He used his gun barrel to poke Wallace into action.

"Hey."

"Do it louder."

"Hey, throw down your guns. They got us, boys."

Chet fired his pistol into the porch roof. "Next time it'll punch your ear. Tell them louder."

"Surrender! The sumbitches got us!" Then a shot.

"You all right?" he asked, hoping for the answer.

"Yeah, but he ain't." It was Reg.

"Fine. Bring them all down here and set them on the ground." Chet turned to the saloon. "Woman. Bring two lamps out here."

"What next?" Wallace asked as Chet pushed him off the porch and made him sit on the ground in his one-piece underwear.

"We have a cure in Texas for horse thieves."

"We only found three of them," Reg said. "That other one's near dead."

"How many more were here, Sammy?"

"That's all except for the bowie knife Injun."

"He ain't the one Reg shot, is he?"

"No, this was a little fella."

"That was Portuguese," Wallace said in disgust, and laughed aloud. "You didn't catch Dogkiller asleep. I bet he's miles away from here by now."

"Reg, make the nooses. We've got cattle to move."

"Yes, sir."

"Any of the four of you want to pray, go ahead."

"You ain't got the nerve to hang all of us," Wallace said.

"Mister, we hang horse thieves all the time and don't lose no sleep over it. The bar-C bunch don't put up with rustlers," J.C. said.

"The law'll get you."

"I'll bet they turn their heads and say it's a shame them boys got hung up on a clothesline." Chet said, grateful it would soon be daylight. The nooses were soon tied, and he slung the first rope over a large oak limb. Then he marched Wallace over and placed the hemp around his neck on the left side of his face.

"Get on the chair."

"If I don't—"

"Then I'll gut-shoot you and leave you to die slow."

Wallace stood on the chair. Reg drew the rope tight and tied it off.

Only the birds chirped.

"You have anything to say?" Chet asked.

"No."

Chet kicked the chair out from under him. The rope creaked and the limb bent under Wallace's weight. His neck cracked like a dry stick and Wallace hung limp.

They hung the other four, including the wounded man, on various other branches until five corpses swung from the oak tree and swirled gently in the soft morning wind. Then the —*C* horses were collected from the pen under the shifty eyes of the Indian women and the small dark-eyed children hiding in their skirts. Maybe sixty head, Chet guessed, about two thirds of the bunch they took.

Mounted up, they drove the horses back to the herd. At camp, Chet went to check on Matt. The boy wasn't back with the buckboard yet.

"How many horses you get back?" Matt asked

"Two thirds of 'em."

"That's enough to get started."

"Yes, it is. But we're sending you to Denison to a doctor before we leave."

"Aw, hell, go on—"

"*I* do the going-on part. Where's the damn whiskey for this outfit?"

"In the chuck box marked salve."

"You want a drink?" Chet asked, starting for it.

"Yeah. I'd have one."

"I'll bring you one when we get through. Them boys can stand one. We've been kicking chairs."

"Huh?"

"Out from under horse rustlers."

Matt nodded. Chet went for the whiskey. Damn, this job got tougher.

Chapter 36

Chuck arrived with a buckboard and four hands that Doan sent and twenty-one more horses. Matt was carefully loaded in the rig.

"Now you be sure that he's going to be taken care of," Chet instructed the young man. "Here's forty dollars for the doc. Tell him I want the man alive, but if not, then have a Christian funeral and I'll settle with 'em when I come back. Then you take your time and catch us. We'll be headed north."

"Yes, sir, Mr. Byrnes."

"Chuck. You take good care of him."

"I will. sir."

His new hands were Cosmo, Dyke, Jim Bob, and Bugle. They looked like typical drovers, and each said how proud he was to be on the trail again.

Bugle said he could cook, so Chet agreed to try him. They were planning to move out in the morning. After breakfast, they headed them up and began the drive. That afternoon, some thundershowers passed overhead and the cattle, all spread out to graze, made it through them. Still, that was no guarantee that the next time they wouldn't jump up and stampede. The big steer's bell was tied off until morning, and Sammy bragged on him as a good leader.

Bugle wasn't Matt, but his food passed the boys' muster. Heck showed him some things Matt had done and he used 'em.

Days straggled on, and the afternoon storms became more frequent. Two weeks later and what Chet considered halfway across the Nation, the creeks began to take on rock bottoms and there was less scrambling to unstick the chuck wagon at each crossing.

A wide expanse of prairie with wildflowers and dry grass, mixed with new growth, began to take over the landscape. Purple, yellow, and orange were part of the petal colors. White blossoms on the wild plum thickets and the emerging elm trees all spelled spring, like the noisy meadowlarks and killdeer scurrying about the land.

A dark black bank began to gather in the northwest at mid-morning. It would be close to dark by Chet's calculations before it would strike, but it could sure have high wind, hail, and lightning in it. The herd grazed with only a head toss at a pesky fly or a bawl for a separated buddy.

"Don't unsaddle or pick you out a fresh horse," he told the lead riders. "Load your bedrolls in the wagon. We're eating supper early and moving cattle tonight. We've got miles of rolling country ahead. If that black steer can lead us and we miss a tornado, it will damn sure beat riding down a stampede."

He passed the word on to all the riders throughout the afternoon. This might be their greatest challenge yet. Bugle and Heck were ready. They were going to sit out the storm where they were at and catch up in the morning. Their mules were hobbled and everything was staked. Even the wagon was tied down to save it from blowing over.

Bugle looked grimly at Chet. "I had time, I'd dig us a cellar."

"Times like these, it would be nice to have one," Chet agreed.

The boys didn't joke at supper. Three changed horses because their horses were acting worn out, and then Whip Malloy, in charge of them, said he'd head north before the herd and keep east of them. Chet trusted him and agreed.

"Think it'll work?" Reg asked Chet where they were squatted on their boot heels drinking coffee.

"Ex-Texas Ranger Charlie Goodnight said last year in Abilene it was the best way. Get 'em on the move. It's hell on men and horses, but so is a stampede."

"That's good enough for me."

"Find old Blacky and soon as that wind starts blowing, you jerk that rag off his clapper and head 'em north."

"I'll tell Sammy."

"Good."

On board Roan, he waited. Though a storm might look like it was barreling down on a person all at once, it usually took a slower pace. That let the tension mount higher in the individual waiting with baited breath for its arrival. Then the first cooler drafts swept in and struck Chet.

"Head 'em up!" he shouted, and the clear ring of Blacky's thick silver bell rang across the land. Horned heads flew skyward, cattle got up and stretched, and then they began to bawl and horns knocked on each other. The wind grew faster, and in the distance thunder shook the air and ground. They were off and rolling.

Daylight soon began to darken, and the long trot of the

cattle began to stretch out as their hooves rumbled with the thunder and pea-size hail began to beat on both hides and men's hats. Blinding flashes and nearby explosions of air deafened him. Rain in sheets and torrents ran off Chet's hat and down his chin.

His shouts at the herd were soon absorbed by the louder roar of the wind and the bawling of the cattle. Day turned completely to night. Temperatures dropped like a rock, and being under the rubber slicker turned from clammy-sweaty to chilly and caused gooseflesh on his arms. Riding hard beside the cattle was going well despite the discomfort. Lightning danced on their horns. Four hours later, things grew calmer and they began to slow. The storm went east, and his swing riders began putting the herd in a circle.

In the predawn, the exhausted night herders rode around the herd. The rest collapsed on the ground where they could find a mound and not a puddle.

"All hands are accounted for," Reg reported as he swung down.

"Good. It worked—this time," Chet said.

"Worked damn good," Sammy bragged, and then he laughed. "Besides that, we're thirty miles closer to Kansas."

"You two ever hear where Earl, Shelby, and Kenny went after the raid?" Chet asked.

"No, but Earl was swearing at us that night. He said that we better not even consider going to Kansas because we'd never get there, they'd see to that."

"Big threat, but he took our horses or had them taken. You boys figure that he might be laying up there waiting for us?"

"So much has happened, I have no idea," Reg said. "Where would they be?"

"There's some saloons and whorehouses north of the

Arkansas River at a place in Kansas called Wichita. It ain't nothing but a sin hole and a place to get robbed. When we get closer, I may ride up and see if they're there."

"Hey, I might like that place." Sammy grinned big, and then he laughed.

"Hey, most of those women in those outpost brothels are so ugly a dog wouldn't love them."

"What about your wedding?" Reg asked.

"I put it off when we learned about the raid."

"Damn, that's a shame. I wondered what happened, but figured it wasn't none of my business or you'd've told us."

"No. She said she would be there when I got back."

"Nice lady. That the one you sung to?"

Chet chuckled. "Yeah. But that was years ago."

"I bet she ain't forgot it either."

"I never asked her." He wasn't going to either. "I had some more problems after you boys left. I shot Frank Dutton trying to run off our Mexican farm help."

"Huh, why them?"

"Anything, I guess, to cause us trouble. I doubt that Earl knew about it happening, him being up here waiting for you all."

"Who else was there when you shot Dutton?"

"Garland and, I guess, a hired hand. I never dreamed that they also planned to waylay you all once you got in the Nation."

"What are we going to have to do?" Reg asked.

"Maybe move somewhere else. I don't think as long as we live on Yellow Hammer Creek it will ever be the same again."

"Hey, we were there long before those Georgia crackers came to Texas."

"Won't stop them."

"When do you reckon the wagon will catch up? I'm hungry." Reg rubbed his belly.

"Malloy is bringing in the horses." Chet noticed them coming across the rise to the east.

"He's half horse himself," Reg said in disgust. "Should we go look for Heck and Bugle?"

"No. I hear 'em." The sound of Bugle's horn tooting came clear across the prairie, and the wagon was a dot heading toward them.

"Better build a fire or we won't eat till noon." Sammy shook his head in disgust and looked around. "Everyone up. We've go to find some wood or dry cow chips. Wagon's coming and if we ain't got a fire going, he'll never get anything cooked till noon."

"I'm going to ride ahead and see what I can find," said Chet. "We move in the morning if I'm here or not."

"Keep your head down," Reg said after him. "Come on fellas, you heard Sam, getting this fire going is serious. We can rest all day after we do that."

Rest all day. When had he had that chance? Not since courting Kathren anyway. How was she doing? He hoped they had left her alone. If anything happened to her—he'd kill every one of them.

Dale Allen, doing the best thing in his life, lying in a cold grave. No, they'd pay. He short-loped across the soggy prairie thinking about Kathren. Several miles from his camp, he spotted a turned-over wagon. It was a farm wagon fitted with bows and a new canvas top. He rode over to see if the owners needed any help.

The closer he drew, the louder the crying became.

When he rounded the wagon, a red-faced young woman screamed, "Savages!"

She clutched two small girls to her skirt. She couldn't be over sixteen years old, and her face and nose were red from crying.

"Ma'am, my name's Chet Byrnes." He slipped off his hat and nodded to her. "I guess the storm did this last night."

She bobbed her head woodenly and swallowed. "It kilt him, too."

He went over and lifted the blanket to see the man's face. Under the cover, he looked to be Chet's age or older.

"That your husband?"

She agreed.

"I didn't catch you name."

"Abby for Abigail."

"Yes, ma'am. And these pretty young ladies?"

"Tanya and Lana."

"I guess you were going somewhere?"

"New Mexico."

"I see. Where are your mules?" He searched around to look for them.

"No. They were horses and they ran away when the lightning struck Olaf."

"Which way did they go?"

She pointed west.

"I'll be back. Fix those girls some food and you eat, too."

"But I can't—"

"You have no choice, ma'am. You have to live for those two children."

Woodenly, she agreed.

He bolted into the saddle and rode west. A pair of rusty

red Belgiums raised their heads when he saw them and drew near. They were in full harness, he noted with grim approval. The horses and harness were there. All he had to do was up-right the wagon and get the woman on her way. Maybe back to Missouri where she and those girls belonged.

Back at the wagon, he learned she had boiled some corn mush and fed the girls. When she offered him some, he decided to eat his own jerky. Seated on the ground while she ate from her bowl, she appeared to be in a better mental condition than when he'd found her.

"We must unload the wagon and then turn it over to see if there is any damage to the running gear."

"I understand."

"Unloaded, I think those horses can turn it back up. If not, I'll go get some of my men and do it."

"You have men near here?"

"Cowboys, drovers with a herd of cattle."

"Oh."

"Now help me unload it."

They worked hard all afternoon, and had everything stacked up outside. Even the bows and canvas were taken off, and the sideboards. He hitched the horses to a doubletree attached to a chain tied on the far side of the wagon. Then, taking the reins, he clucked to the horses. They hit the collars and acted shocked. He spoke to them. They danced around.

"Get up!" he finally shouted with a hard clap of the reins on their butts, and the wagon tipped over on its wheels. He discovered himself skidding along on his boot heels to stop them. Eventually, they stopped.

He walked up and patted them so they would settle down. He turned, and the small woman was bringing the sideboards. The wagon still had to go back together. They recovered as much of the busted flour barrel as they could. That and the rest of her things were set back inside by sundown, when everyone collapsed on the ground. The bloody light flooded the plains and the ground around them.

"Do you have a wife, sir?"

"No, I have a fiancée at home."

"Oh, she is a very lucky woman. Not many men would stop and help a woman with two children."

"Why do you say that?"

"Three men rode by earlier today and wouldn't stop. They even laughed at my plight."

He looked hard at her. "Can you tell me about these men?"

"One of them had a bad arm. It just hung down and swung in the wind. I thought no one would ever come by and help me."

"Abby, was he round-faced and heavyset and wore a gray hat with silk around the brim?"

"Yes, you know him?"

"Abby, did they say where they were going?"

She shook her head. "I can't say what he said to that younger one."

"What did he tell him?"

"It was bad. I can't say those words."

He reached over and took hold of her upper arms. "God will forgive you, Abby. Tell me what he said. I must know."

"He said—Come on, Kenny, I'll—I'll get you a prettier whore than her to fu—in Washitaw." She buried her face in his vest. "I was so scared."

Inhaling deep, he hugged her tight. He could see Marla Porter's bloody body all over again. How close Abby had come to death she would never ever know.

Chapter 37

Nothing to make a cross out of. He promised Abby he'd do something later. When the burial was complete, to a crickets' chorus, he said a short prayer over Olaf's grave. Then she put the girls to bed under the wagon. Off in the starlit night, a coyote howled and another answered. She scurried back and sat close beside where he used a wheel for a backrest.

"I hate those wolves."

"They're only coyotes."

"Sound like wolves to me. Mr. Byrnes, would you hold me in your arms?"

"Sure, but—"

"Mr. Byrnes, I don't care about my reputation. I don't care about anything. I spent all of last night shaking in the rain, trembling and so afraid, just knowing I was going to die. I knew my husband was dead. He was never coming back and I would soon be dead, too. And my girls torn apart alive by wolves. Now that I am safe, just hold me tight all night, please?"

Her calloused small hands squeezed his face and she

kissed him. He felt himself caught in a web and pulled down by forces greater than he could resist.

Dawn came in a purple glow. She fried them mush for breakfast. There was no way he could let her go on by herself.

"I'm taking you with me to Abilene. You can help with the chuck wagon, and from there you can decide what you want to do. I'm sorry, Abby, I can't be a part of your life. But I can't let you and those little girls fall prey to the vultures on this prairie either."

She swallowed hard. "I didn't—"

His fingertips on her lips silenced her. "Nothing happened between you and me."

"But—"

He shook his head till she swallowed and agreed.

"We'll join the cattle drive today. I simply found you, buried your husband, and brought you with me. I have several nice young men who will be civil to you. I expect you to resist any advances. If you pick one, that could cause trouble."

"I understand." She bowed her head.

"Good, and when we get to Abilene, you can decide where you want to go, but that is near two months away. You are to help Bugle and Heck cook. I pay fifty a month for a cook."

"I shall be very grateful—"

"No, Abby, I don't expect a thing but what I asked."

"Yes, sir."

"Chet," he corrected her.

Up on the wagon seat ready to drive the team, he looked

off to the north. Those three Reynolds men were up there somewhere waiting for him, or at least his crew, to try to cross into Kansas. Ten days to two weeks away—maybe he needed to ride on ahead and settle with them.

Her hand on his arm, she said, "We're ready, Chet."

He nodded and clucked to the Belgiums. They stepped out in a jog that made the harness ring.

At mid-morning, J.D. rode up and swiped off his hat at the sight of her. "Chet, we were getting worried."

"This lady's husband was killed by lightning night before last. The wind turned over her wagon and we've been busy. You know where Bugle is taking the chuck wagon?"

"I do, sir."

"J.D., drive her and these fine girls up there and tell those two she is the third cook. Hobble her horses and see she is all right. Her name is Abby Petersen, and they are Tanya and Lana."

"Sure proud to meet you, ma'am. I'll tie ole Hoot on the tailgate."

Chet set the brake and tied off the reins. "That's my nephew. He's a polite boy."

"Yes. Thank you so much again," she said.

He short-loped back to the herd and told Reg who he'd helped and how the Reynolds riders were ahead somewhere waiting to intercept them. He waved to Sammy across on the far side of the point, and then rode back to see how the others were doing.

That afternoon while the cattle were grazing, he held a war council with Sammy and Reg. If those three were in Wichita, he needed to eliminate them before they hired some gunhands. Both boys were impressed with the small willowy girl-woman, and let him know that he could find gold in a junk pile.

"I couldn't leave her out there alone, even with her wagon up and her all right."

"You did the right thing. She's cute," Reg said, and then shook his head as if embarrassed at what he was thinking.

"Cute, hell—she's pretty as a picture."

"Boys, I need some help. We need to set this herd down for two days and ride up there and end this Reynolds business."

"How close are we?"

"Over a week, I'd bet," Sammy said.

"I thought two," Reg said.

"In five days, if I haven't found out, I'll ride up there and locate them."

"What will happen to Mrs. Petersen?" Sammy asked.

"Oh, I don't know. She said they came from Missouri and they were going to New Mexico."

"Was her husband crazy?" Sam asked.

"I don't know a thing about him. He looked a lot older than her. Maybe mid-thirties, but I never asked. Age of those little girls, I figured she must have gotten married at twelve. When we get to Kansas, maybe someone will drive her back to Missouri, or I don't know. One thing for certain, her and those girls would not have survived long in the Nation on their own."

"But those Reynolds men rode right by her wreck and never offered to help her?"

"Right. Earl promised Kenny a prettier whore than her in Wichita. She calls it *Washitaw*."

"They just didn't want to be bothered, did they?" Reg asked with a sour look written on his face

"Right. But Kenny may have been the main instigator in Marla Porter's death, and them riding on may have saved Abby's life."

The two agreed.

"Well, we'll all sure look out for her and them girls," Sammy said, and Reg agreed.

Along the way, signs with mileage had been set on posts, and most were fairly accurate. Chet found one with several markers the next day. Wichita thirty miles. Abilene one hundred and twenty-five miles. Hell, a long ways. There were some others that he disregarded. Two days, the herd would be there.

He rode back and found the remuda. With his head high, Bugger stood out. Chet rode in, roped him, and brought him out.

"You needing a powerful horse, Mr. Byrnes?" said one of the riders with the remuda.

"Chet. Yes, I'm going into Wichita and try to find the men that killed Dale Allen."

"My, my, sir, you be careful now. We all think a lot about you and sure won't want anything to happen to you, sir."

"I'll do that. Thanks."

"That sure is a big horse. My, my, he sure must be a handful to ride."

Finally in the saddle after three tries on the circling Bugger, Chet dismissed his concern and loped off.

He joined Reg at the point. "Sign says thirty miles to Wichita. Stop at midday, make your assignment, and you two ride up there and look for me. You won't miss Bugger."

"We'll be along."

"Don't rush. I'm going looking for 'em."

He short-loped the big horse until the cottonwoods

along the Arkansas showed up. Then he walked him to the ferry. A grizzly-faced old man came out of a shack made out of packing crates.

"Kin I help ya?" Then he spit sideways and the wind about took his crumpled cowboy hat, but his hand caught it.

"I'm looking for a man who can't use his right arm. Him and two others cross here lately?"

"Come over an hour ago."

"Going south?"

"I said so, didn't I?" He spat again. "Him, some boy, a bad-talking dude. I hate cussing. He needed his mouth scoured out."

"You have any idea where they went?"

"Went to Tom McCory's Ranch. Biggest mess of outlaws and no-accounts hang out there. I think them three's going to steal a cattle herd."

"Where's this ranch at?"

"You ever been to Preacher's Spring?"

"No, sir."

"Ride south till you come to the first main stream. There's a broken-down wagon on the right and that road goes to McCory's is right there. But I can tell you they're tough as steel wire, they are."

Chet tossed him a silver dollar. How much time did he have? "Two men riding bar-C horses come by here, tell them where I have gone."

With a smile on his whiskered face, he nodded. "Bless you, sir. I'll do that."

He never saw the boys on his ride back, and found all kinds of activity in his cow camp. Reg and Sam were still there. The good horses and the men Jim Crammer sent had finally had arrived. Four top hands shook his hand. But then he asked Reg who the two men in suits were who were talking to Mrs. Petersen at the chuck wagon.

"Deputy U.S. marshals from Fort Smith," he said in a lowered voice and with a fretting look on his face. "They're asking if we know anything about five horse thieves that were hung."

"What did you tell 'em?"

"It sure wasn't us."

"Good. I'll go to meet 'em."

"You find them Reynolds riders?"

"I think they're at some outlaw hangout west of here. These men might help us." He gave a head toss at the lawmen. "You mention Dale Allen's death?"

"No, sir."

"I will." He set out to speak to them.

"Good day, gentlemen. My foreman says that you're deputy U.S. marshals."

"We are. I'm Roscoe Berry and that's Jim Knight. We're up here investigating a five-man lynching in the Choctaw Reservation north of the Red River."

"I don't know anything about that. But the three men who killed my brother Dale Allen Byrnes are nearby. I'm Chester Byrnes of Mayfield, Texas. This is my herd."

They all shook hands.

"The ferryman told me the McCory Ranch was where those killers were going."

"You have witnesses to this murder?" Knight asked.

"Six men here will testify that Earl, Shelby, and Kenny Reynolds were all in on the raid that killed Dale Allen, Pinky, Arnold, plus shot up Matt our cook."

"This happened in the Indian Territory?"

"Yes. They're buried fifteen miles above Doan's store in the Indian Territory."

"You can expect trouble any time if you go into McCory's, you know that?" Knight asked.

"Myself and half a dozen of these men will back you," Chet said. The men all agreed listening close.

"In the morning then, we will ride in and ask for those killers," said Knight.

"What if they won't come out or ride off?" Chet asked.

"We will have the place surrounded. But Marshal Berry and I have to bring them in alive to collect our expenses and fees."

"Fine. I want justice for Dale Allen's death. Now, since we aren't going till in the morning, I need to see about things here." He walked over to Heck, Bugle, and Mrs. Petersen. "Can you feed all these people?"

She smiled. "We made plenty. We won't run out of anything."

The other two agreed.

"Good. Gents, let's eat, then we'll decide who goes with who. Marshals Berry and Knight, you are our guests. Then Virgil, Tad, Bill, and Larry, who just arrived, are next. Then the crew."

Abby brought him over a heaping plate of food and utensils. "Boss's supposed to eat first."

"Hey, I'm one of the boys here."

She looked kinda peeved at him. "No, you ain't. You're lots more than that, ain't he, fellas?"

"Damn right, ma'am."

"Then you sit on the ground and eat this food. This outfit needs you. One day here and I can tell that."

He obeyed her and, standing in line, they all snickered at her words.

The two marshals joined him. Knight led the conversation. "We are really here investigating the lynching of those five men down on the Choctaw Reservation."

"Oh?" Chet said between bites

"Yes, parties unknown hung a bootlegger named Wallace suspected of several crimes but uncharged. Four others with known criminal records and warrants out for them were all hung in nooses and a chair was kicked out from underneath each one of them."

"Sounds like the world won't miss 'em."

"Lynching is anarchy, sir. The Judge, Issac Parker, wants the law followed to the letter and all these lynching stopped."

"Can't help you there." He took another forkful of Abby's rich white gravy and mashed potatoes. She'd made it. Them two boys had never made anything that tasty in their lives. "But—" He used his fork to point. "These Reynolds men did murder my brother and two of my hands in that camp."

"Your men will have to come to testify in Fort Smith, you know that."

"I will pay their expenses out of my own pocket for them to go to the trial and to get back home."

"You're pretty serious about this."

Chet stopped eating. "They murdered my brother. He has a wife and daughter. That boy over there is his son. He has two more sons in Texas younger than that boy. They're all going to grow up without a father."

"I understand. But like Roscoe said, we make our living bringing in live prisoners to the court in Fort Smith."

"We won't kill 'em unless they won't give us another option."

"Good," Berry said.

"With this many men, we can surround the place and no one will escape," said Knight. "I am entitled to hire you men who go over there as posse men for one dollar a day and ten cents a mile. I shall count it as two days and have forms for you to file unless it lasts longer," Knight said.

Good, maybe they'd forget the lynching. Chet started to get up. Then Abby arrived with a piece of apple-raisin pie. "Dessert, sir."

"Abby, I don't mind being babied, but for gosh sakes, call me Chester."

"Yes, I will, Chester."

He was about to cut off a piece of the pie. Saliva was storming in his mouth in anticipation when one of the twins came by with a small kettle and refilled his coffeepot.

"Was your supper good?" she asked.

"Yes, it was."

"I liked it lots, much better than corn mush."

"I did, too."

"You never ate any mush. You ate jerky."

"Oh, that's right. But this was much better, I agree."

She nodded that he had things right and went on filling cups.

He better tell the truth or those girls would set him straight. In a few hours, he'd have all those Reynolds boys in the custody of the Hanging Judge's men. Sounded too good to be true.

Chapter 38

Eight men rode out of camp around the large batch of quiet cattle and past the night riders circling the herd. The man they passed the closest to was playing a mouth harp as he rode his horse at the perimeter of the herd. He waved under the starlight at them, and they rode on in a trot, Berry and Knight in the lead.

McCory's place was set in some timber. Knight sent Sammy and four men with instructions on how to ride around and come in from the back. He told them to use their rifles if needed and be sure not to shoot another posse member. Everyone else rested and waited to give them time to get in place.

Chet could hardly sit still. He was this close to ending a large part of his troubles and having Dale Allen's killer in jail awaiting trial. In the cool night air, he paced back and forth until Knight struck a match and checked his pocket watch.

"Mount up. They should be there by now."

When they reached sight of the dark buildings and corrals, Knight spread them out, saying the main house was where he expected most of them to be sleeping. Chet and

Virgil took the shed on the right. They found nothing but some dusty hay, and came out as the light of dawn began to appear.

Knight was in the open when he called out. "McCory, this is Deputy U.S. Marshal Jim Knight. Tell everyone in there with you to step outside hands high. I have a large posse surrounding your house and no one needs to die."

Someone must have tried the back door to escape. A warning shot made him swear.

"I've got my damn hands up and don't shoot."

Seconds ticked by. Chet and Virgil had their rifles aimed at the house. Chet's mouth was dry and he could have used some coffee. He'd have a hard time not to want to gun them down when they came outside. Justice would be served—he needed more patience.

"All right," a loud voice said. "I'm coming out. I ain't armed."

"Tell the rest to do the same."

"I ain't their boss."

"McCory, you better tell them or you're going to be in the cross fire."

"You heard him. He's got the guns. Don't be foolish."

They filed out. Finally, Kenny and Shelby came out.

"Earl can't raise his right arm," Shelby said, looking around for the posse as he stepped out of the building.

Knight shot a look at Chet, who nodded it was so. "Tell him to come on out, but don't make a false move," said Knight.

"He won't."

McCory and his three men were separated from the Reynolds men. The fourth member of McCory's gang was marched around front, while Sammy checked the building and herded two women and three small children outside.

"That's all and we could find," Reg said.

The prisoners were checked for weapons, producing knifes and small guns. Then Knight told them to sit on the ground. Chet and the others joined them in front of the house. He ignored the Reynolds men and the strong temptation to shoot them on the spot—*let the law take its course*.

Knight took out a small book and began to take down names. He wrote them with a small pencil. When he came to the Reynolds men, he spoke to them. "I am binding you three over to the grand jury in Fort Smith for the murder of Dale Allen Byrnes and two drovers named Pinky and Arnold."

"You ain't got any proof—" Shelby grumbled.

"Six eyewitnesses."

"A good lawyer will make a circus out of them."

"I can tell you don't know Judge Issac Parker, mister. He ain't known as the Hanging Judge for no good reason."

Berry came from around back with a copper tubing coil and a crock jug.

Then Knight turned to the others. "We need to take the rest of you to Fort Smith for making illegal whiskey. Marshal Berry has found your copper tubing and several jars of whiskey in the root cellar."

"Can't we post a bond and show up there later?" McCory asked.

"No. Judge said we were to bring you in 'cause you'd only make more whiskey while you were out on bond."

"Ah, shit."

"Byrnes, will you see about getting us some food? Sam, you and your boys saddle them some horses so we can take them out after we eat. I'll need to arrange for some transportation to get them to Fort Smith."

Chet told the two women and children to go inside. He and Virgil followed them into the sour-smelling house. Between the nicotine and the odor of old socks, Chet wasn't certain anything they cooked would be appetizing to him, but everyone needed to eat.

"What do you have for food?"

The two women, neither one of whom was attractive, shrugged, and turned up their grimy palms like they had little to cook. High cheekbones, dull eyes, and dressed in stained gowns. Their hair hung straight and uncombed.

"We got some oatmeal," the taller one said.

"Cook it—wait. Wash out that pot first."

She shrugged like it didn't matter, and went to the water bucket and dipped some water in it. After sloshing it around, she threw the water outside. He went over and looked at the pot.

"That's too nasty to cook anything in."

"You fix it then." She shoved the pot at him.

"You watch them, Virgil. I'll take this out to that well and clean it."

Sammy soon joined him. "What's wrong, Boss?"

"They wanted to cook oatmeal in this damn pot ain't been washed in years." He was on his hand and knees scouring it with sand.

"Can I do it?"

"No, go make some coffee if they have any."

"Sure thing."

"Get the cooking range going and boil some water for the dishes." He'd bet they hadn't been washed in years either.

The pot was finally thoroughly washed, and he rinsed it.

Then, with water drawn from the well, he filled it half full and carried it back. Sammy came out and got water for the coffeepot. "Fire's going. They've got some scorched beans I guess are coffee."

"Don't you touch a thing," Chet said to the two of the women standing back. "I'll heat some water and you two can wash and rinse the cups and dishes we're going to eat off of."

"Got trouble?" Knight asked, coming in the open door.

"No, I've got sloppy help. We'll have some oatmeal and coffee in a while."

"You don't know how lucky you are to have those three running your chuck wagon. Me and Roscoe have eaten some tough meals up here."

"You'd've had the shits in two miles of here eating from what they wanted to use for a kettle."

Knight laughed and then shook his head. "I hope you will bring those witnesses to Fort Smith."

"Let me get my cattle to Abilene and I'll be ready."

"A deposition from each of them when you get to Abilene and sent to the Judge's office in Fort Smith would help hold the prisoners."

"I'll do it first thing when we get there."

"Good. What will you do after that?"

"I hope to get married back home in Texas. I was supposed to do that weeks ago." He stirred the oats in the boiling water on the stove.

"Well, good luck."

"I'll need it."

After oatmeal and bitter coffee, the prisoners in irons were mounted up on a chain of horses, and they headed back for the herd. But before he left the yard, Chet got a cussing-out that would have made a sailor blush from the tall woman standing in the doorway.

He sat Bugger, shaking his head in disbelief at her anger. Then he stretched his stiff back and tossed his head at Virgil. He'd be glad when this drive was over. *Man, she was foul-mouthed.*

"You ain't heard the last of this," Earl said when he rode past him.

"Listen, Earl, when I hear them drop that trapdoor, I'll hear the last of you, and till then, you can sit in jail and rue the day that you shot my brother Dale Allen."

"I'd of got you, too, you sonofabitch."

Chet gritted his teeth, rode in close, and kicked Earl so hard in the leg that his horse shied. "Next time you call me that, I'll kill you."

At the herd, Berry gathered all the signed posse cards, promising the money would be there for them when they got to Fort Smith. The marshals then took their prisoners and rode on to find a wagon to haul them in.

Chet rested on his bedroll, looking at the azure sky and the red-tailed hawk circling on the updraft. Abby came by and joined him, seated on the ground and hugging her knees. Then she sprawled on her back to look at the sky.

"You reckon them three seen me?" she asked.

"Why?"

"I wanted them to know it was me turned 'em in. They'd've stopped and been civilized, they might not be going to the gallows today, huh?"

"I imagine you're right, Abby."

"Where you going to dump me off?" She rolled over on her stomach, propped herself up on her elbows, and stared off across the prairie. Intent on something, she went to chewing on a grass stem.

"I didn't plan to dump you anywhere. We're going to Abilene. If you want to go home from there, I'll send one of the crew to drive you there."

"I sure ain't going back home."

"Oh?"

"My pappy sold me to Olaf Petersen when I was twelve years old. For two mules and two crosscut saws. I sure ain't letting him sell me again."

"Sorry."

"He wasn't supposed to marry or even mess with me till I was sixteen." She laughed. "You seen how long that promise lasted—that's Lana and Tanya. They're three."

"So where would you like to go?"

"I never seed Texas."

He closed his eyes. "I've got two widows now down there now. My brother's and my uncle's."

"Maybe you need to start a home for them." She giggled.

"I have."

"Well, unless you dump me, I'm going back with your outfit."

"You can earn your way. Them boys love you cooking."

"Thanks. Sure am proud we've got that settled." She rose up, brushing the dry grass off her dress front. "I better clean up. Folks'll get the wrong idea. Me down here talking to you and getting grass all over me, huh?"

He shook his head. They probably would.

Chapter 39

Abilene, Queen of the Cow Towns, bustled when he rode up the street, and the tinny sound of pianos filtered out of the batwing doors. Doves in low-cut blouses hung out of open second-story windows and flirted with anyone who would pay them attention. Every once in a while, they struck a deal with a man and lured him up to their parlor. Chet ignored them.

The Cattleman's House was the largest saloon, and most of the buyers could be found in the there, either playing cards or simply resting their shoes on the brass rail and drinking whiskey. Something Chet never touched until the deal was done. When he pushed in the batwing doors, he was looking for Hiram Dugan, who'd stopped him two days before, saying he'd give ten cents a pound for his cattle.

"Hey, that you, Byrnes?" a familiar man asked folding up his hand of cards and getting up. He strode over. "Kelsey Pitts. I bought your cattle last year."

"I remember you. What're you paying this year?"

"Market's down bad. Best I could go is six cents this year."

"Shame. A man offered me ten on the road."

"That was a come-on." Pitts made a face to dismiss the claim. "No one's paying that much for them."

"Then he better tell me to my face. We're talking all steers, three or older. No cows or bulls in 'em. You know. You bought 'em last year."

"I might give seven, but I'd not make a dime at that price."

"No sense buying cattle that you can't make money on." Chet stood on his toes to try and locate Dugan. No sign of the man's bowler hat. "I'll see you, Kelso. You get interested my herd's south of town. Bar-C outfit."

"I know your outfit well. We've traded before. How many head?"

"Fourteen hundred and some."

"I'll see what I can do."

Chet nodded, and left the crowded place. He crossed the street to the Texas Star Saloon and had a draft beer for twenty cents. Boomtown prices. Everyone had money came there, or at least until the con men, crooked card sharks, and pickpockets got to them. Not to mention the ladies of the night who were as deft at getting in a man's wallet as the rest.

High-stakes poker games made more profit that cattle drives ever could. In years past, he'd seen cattleman lose all they got for a herd in a high-stakes game and go home broke.

"Well, if it ain't ole Chet hisself up here." Fancy Dan Downey hooked his elbows on the bar so he could face the crowd and let them see his rhinestone-studded cuffs and the heavy gold chain on his watch.

"I wouldn't be here this year, but those Reynolds boys shot my brother down on the Red River in a raid."

"They what?"

"You heard me. They killed Dale Allen, a cowboy named Pinky, and another called Arnold. May have killed my cook, too."

"What—what are you doing about it?"

"Nothing."

"Nothing?"

"No, the three of them, Earl, Shelby, and Kenny, are rotting in Judge Issac Parker's jail waiting to hang."

"Fort Smith, huh?"

"Yes, and I'll be there to see them swing."

"I would, too." He clamped Chet on the shoulder. "Sorry, I didn't know."

Chet downed the flat-tasting beer and went back to camp.

"Find your man?" Abby asked, bringing him coffee when he dismounted.

"No. But he'll be around. Several others will drive out and try to steal 'em."

She pursed her lips, looking serious. "If we're going to be here long, we'll sure need some supplies."

"Send Reg after them."

"Okay. Coffee, dried apples, raisins, sugar, canned milk—"

"Abby, I don't need to approve a list. Have them throw on a case or two of canned peaches and some tomatoes too. May as well celebrate while we're here."

She frowned at him, concerned. "I didn't want to break you."

"No problem. We made it here and we'll be going home

shortly. I ever get a price worth a hoot on these cattle, we'll head out of here in a hurry."

She smiled. "I'm ready."

"So am I, girl. So am I."

Ten days went by and no sign of the buyer. The best offer so far was eight cents a pound. Chet grew more antsy by the day. Drovers were selling for those prices, and more cattle herds arrived every day.

"Chet. Chet." Abby came running across the prairie holding up her skirt so a fair part of her shapely lower legs showed as she churned toward him. "I think he's coming. I recognized that gaited horse."

Chet dropped the hoof on Dun that he'd been shoeing, and looked hard at the rig coming in their direction. She might be right.

"Whoa. Hey, Dugan here. I've been out to Hayes a-looking for cattle. Sorry I wasn't here, but you still got them steers, all right?"

"Ten-cent-a-pound steers?"

"That's what I told ya, that's what I'm paying. I've got to get cars here on the siding, and then we can go to loading and paying. Them steers sure look a lot fuller on this good Kansas grass than they did the other day."

"They're good cattle."

"I agree, and the man getting them will be excited. Just what he needs."

"Send me word when you are getting the cars. We'll start bringing them in."

"Nice to do business with a real man." He doffed his hat to Abby and smiled big. "Nice to met you, too, me lady."

"The same, sir."

"I'll have word on my cars in twenty-four hours."

"That'll be fine."

Dugan drove off.

"Guess that'll show then other scallywags that you ain't to be messed with," Abby said.

He leaned into his tender back and closed his eyes. "I'll be sure of that when they're in the cars and I have the money in my hands."

"I can loosen that back fur ya."

"Oh, how?"

"Get on your belly and I'll straddle your back and pound it with the sides of my fists."

"Sounds kinda wild."

"Aw, it ain't. Get down there."

He did, and she was soon sitting on his butt beating him lightly with her fists. In a short while, his tight back muscles let go and he about fainted. It worked.

"See?" She leaned over and whispered in his ear. "See, I can do lots more than cook."

Facedown in the sweet-smelling grass, he nodded, feeling spent. "You done good."

Reg took her list, and came back in a few hours with two packhorses loaded down. She issued a can of tomatoes and one of peaches to each of the cowboys. They were like kids at Christmas, squatted or sitting cross-legged on the ground, laughing and carrying on. They all proposed to her. And they went on and on, saying she was why they got the special treats. Reg even bought the twins hard candy.

"Boys, for you who did not know, that buyer Dugan was here this morning and he's taking the steers at ten cents. We'll start loading in the next few days and then head for home. Get those steers in the cars, I can pay you here or pay you in Texas."

A hurrah went up, and some rebel yells, before they all turned to the cattle with worried looks—had they stampeded them? A few steers got up and stretched. The cowboys all shook their heads that they were lucky that time.

Bunch by bunch, they drove them into the pens and weighed them. The steers weighed on average eight-fifty. Dugan acted pleased as they filed in the pens to be loaded on the scales, with more coming behind them.

The stockyard clerk was working to keep track. Dugan had Virgil checking on him, and Reg did the company counting.

It was dark when the last bunch rolled into the yards. The count they agreed on was 1,458 head. That meant they'd arrived with ninety-seven percent of the cattle they left Texas with, and that was a solid figure. Ninety percent was good for most outfits. And the total amount for them was seventy bucks short of $124,000 worth of beef.

Chet collapsed his butt against the side of the scale house. He could pay off all of their debts and have a good nest egg. His fees alone would pay for the drive, or most of it anyway. They'd finally be out of debt with money in the safe. And Dale Allen wasn't there to celebrate with him.

He walked out to where his drovers were squatted down along the outside fence of the stockyards. The small switch engine was moving cars as other outfits loaded.

"Boys, it's been a helluva deal. Couldn't have made it without a one of you. I'm paying a twenty-buck bonus tonight. We'll be going home after I settle with Dugan."

He went down the line paying in twenty-dollar gold pieces, and shook each man's hand. He motioned for Heck to come along with him, and they rode back.

"Had any supper?" she asked when the two rode in past sundown.

"No, ma'am," Heck said. "And we're starved plumb to death."

"The rest stayed in town?" she asked.

"It's their night to hoot at the moon," Chet said, stripping off his saddle and pads.

"Been strange around here, not having a critter to bawl except ole Blacky," she said, serving up bowls of stew. "Kinda of peaceful-like."

"It's a good thing, too," Heck said. "I don't miss 'em. Do you, Chet?"

He pressed his back to the side of the wagon. "Aw, you just start all over again."

"Well, eat your stew," she said. "And tell me how that works. The girls was mad at me tonight for putting them to bed when they couldn't talk to the cowboys."

They laughed about it to the tune of the crickets.

The next day, the hungover cowboys arrived in camp. Three of the boys drew their pay, going on with another herd to the Red Cloud Agency at Fort Robinson, Nebraska.

Rest of the crew slept all day, while Chet went to town and arranged to be paid the money. The currency was counted twice and he put it all in a new valise.

At the wagon, he and Abby hid the valise in the false bottom of a flour barrel and then scooped the flour back in the drum. She smiled at him when they finished, and wrinkled her small nose at him. "Fancy safe."

"It better make it home."

She put the lid on it. "It will."

He laughed at the flour all over his front, and he went swatting it away as he climbed out of the chuck wagon. "We head for Texas in the morning."

Three weeks later, after they crossed at Doan's, he paid Corwin Doan what he owed him and bought some supplies that Abby needed. Some of the riders collected their pay and thanked him, then headed for Denison. He also learned that Matt had recovered and gone on down to the ranch.

Chet swung by Fort Worth, found a dressmaker to fit Abby in a ruffled blue dress, bought his boys new pullover blue denim shirts, rusty brown canvas pants, and new suspenders. They all took baths and dressed up for the final ride home.

Even the twins got new outfits. The wagons rumbled south. The mules and draft horses were grained for the trip, as were the saddle horses—anxious to be going home, they pushed hard each day, rain or shine.

The Texas sun had some kind of hot power in July, and before long everyone was complaining about the heat. But when they started down into the hill country, and the live oak and cedar began to dot the country—he felt better. This was his land.

Second of August, they drove in. Their once-new clothes were a little dusty, but Chet was so glad to be home, nothing'd spoil it. Then he noticed Kathren on the porch and threw his hat in the air with a shout. "Girl, you are a sight for sore eyes."

He swung her around and when he stopped, Reg said, "This is Abby Petersen. That's Lana and Tanya. Lightning killed her man. She told Chet where the Reynolds boys were going."

"What about the Reynolds boys?" Kathren asked.

"Earl, Shelby, and Kenny. They're all in the Fort Smith jail awaiting trial for the murders. We have to go up there in October and testify. A lawyer took the hands' testimony in Kansas, and I have a telegram says that the trial is to be held October sixth."

"Will you go?" Kathren asked.

"Yes. I want to see justice served."

"I understand."

Susie took her new ward inside, and he could see a twin in each arm had her fascinated. Good. "How have things been for you?"

"Fine. My father is not well. I guess I'll need a day man. I can't run both places and them apart."

"What's wrong with him?"

"His heart. Doc says he has to rest a lot and take things easy. That would be like telling you that. He won't listen."

"What can I do?"

"Take me home." She lowered her voice. "And hold me tight all night long. I can't tell you how much I've missed you."

"Me, too."

"You better eat some supper. Susie will be upset with me taking you away when you first arrive home."

"She'll understand. I'll tell her I'm leaving—with you, of course."

"All right." She agreed, sounding small.

"One minute." He rushed into the house and pulled Susie aside. "I'm taking Kathren home. She has chores to do and her father and all. Abby can show you where the money is hid. Put it in the safe tonight."

"Of course. Have a nice reunion." With a quick a peck on her cheek, he waved to them and hurried outside. His horse was tied on the tailgate, and he stepped on the buckboard.

"Let's go home."

"Yes." She hugged his arm. "It's been a while."

"Too long. Far too long."

"How did the cattle do?"

"I'd say close to eight thousand dollars for your part."

"Oh, are you certain?" She looked wide-eyed in disbelief at him.

"Yes, there were ninety-seven percent of the cattle delivered, they averaged eight-fifty, and they brought ten cents a pound."

She slumped back on the seat. "Luther wanted to sell out because we owed half that much and couldn't seem to ever get it paid. I told him to give us another year—you know the rest. He walked out."

At last he knew her story. *Grim, and he never ever let her laugh.*

Chapter 40

Her father's health situation put their wedding plans on hold. She hired a cowboy to ride her father's lines. An older man named Shuck Means, he'd spent many years living by himself in line shacks and liked the work. In fact, he got embarrassed talking to her, she told Chet.

His oat hay in the stacks looked good, and the corn would make a fair enough crop. Chet bragged on the hardworking men and their accomplishments. The quiet Mexican people gathered in the small village and listened in awe to hear him tell about the trail drive. It was no time until he had to take the cowboys to Fort Smith for the trial.

They arrived in the river city two days before the trial, and he put their horses up in a livery that they recommended at the federal courthouse. He found a clean rooming house, and they stayed there. Taking a bath the night before, and putting on their pressed clothing the next day, they were ushered in to sit in the second row behind the grim-looking Reynolds boys, seated with their lawyer from Kansas City.

The prosecutor, Dalton Morgan, told Chet and his men

not to fear the big-town lawyer that the defendants had hired. They had a story, stick to it. Chet felt certain they'd make good witnesses. The trial lasted all day and into the night—the Kansas City lawyer tried everything. Tried to make the judge mad so he'd get a retrial. Nothing worked, and the dark eyes of Issac Parker could have melted steel when the attorney antagonized him.

Nine o'clock—the sun was setting across the Arkansas River. The courthouse was stuffy hot and the foreman of the jury, now back in their box, stood and said, "Your Honor, we find all three defendants guilty of murder in the first degree of Dale Allen Byrnes, Pinky Smith, and Roy Arnold."

"Approach the bench," Parker's clerk said, and the three did so.

"You have been found guilty of murder in this most heinous crime. Do you have anything to say for yourself?"

"Yes, Your Honor. My son there, Kenny, was only along with us. He don't deserve to die," Earl said.

Judge Parker spoke to Kenny. "Kenny Reynolds, is it true that you were also on the scene of the murder and rape of a rancher's wife in Texas?"

"I never—"

Parker waved him silent. "For this heinous crime and mass murder, I sentence you three to hang by the neck until dead on December second, the Year of Our Lord 1873. Court dismissed."

Chet slumped in the chair. *They would hang. Dale Allen, I have done all I can do.*

"Chet? Chet?"

He looked up, and a concerned Reg was talking to him. "It's time for us to go home."

"I'm not hungry. You boys go on. I'll just go back to the room."

"We did it, didn't we?"

"Yes, we've done all we can here." They'd already taken away the three condemned men. He dried his wet palms on his pants. The prosecutor was there to shake his hand and congratulate him for bringing the boys back to testify. *It clinched the case.*

Thunder rolled in, and some heavy showers came down. He was soaked to his skin in cold rain by the time he reached the boardinghouse. Why did he feel the worst was still ahead? He opened the front door and looked at the staircase in the dim lamplight.

The notion of the long ride home left him empty. Was he sliding off into what his father had? Losing his mind? Was he drunk and didn't know it?

There had to be an answer to this curse they lived under. There had to be place for his tribe—a place without enemies where they could ranch. In Texas, there would always be cousins, their pals. The list would never stop growing of folks that wanted them dead.

For that cult, he'd made martyrs out of them three— Earl, Shelby, and Kenny. He undressed and dried himself with a towel. No, he'd find a place. Another Eden for the Byrnes, and they'd all escape this feud and its treachery. He climbed under the sheet and thin blanket and shivered until he fell asleep.

Then he dreamed of a great valley with a river running through it. That would be his land when he found it. He'd know it when he got there. There the feud for him and all his family would finally be over.